Praise for The Ballad of Midnight and McRae

"I'd be shocked if Lederman's story isn't in your Top Five novels of the year. Yes, it's that good."
—James L. Rubart, best-selling author of Rooms *and* The Five Times I Met Myself

"Featuring star-crossed lovers, intense action, myth, and magic, *The Ballad of Midnight & McRae* enthralled me with vividly realized historical settings, clever, witty dialog, and cameos by underrepresented historical figures. It's the literary equivalent of *Lonesome Dove* meets *Oppenheimer* meets *Kodachrome*—with a dash of *Zen and the Art of Motorcycle Maintenance*. Highly recommended!"
—Ami McConnell, founder of WriterFest Nashville and former Editor-in-Chief of Howard Books/Simon & Schuster

"A powerful blend of love, social justice, and spirituality...*The Ballad of Midnight and McRae* is a tour-de-force that could change how people see the world by opening their eyes to magic, adventures, and inclusion— all while questioning what real religion is and defining love as the true engine of progress. If you are into LGBTQ+ literature, you will enjoy the story...also perfect for those who love historical fiction and enjoy Western fiction and stories packed with adventure and magic realism."
—The Inkish Review

"Crisp and exciting, full of life, striking detail, some historical figures, and urgent moral inquiry. [A] richly humane Western exploring love, justice, and

myth with moral urgency."
—A BookLife Reviews "Editor's Pick"

"A lyrical, thought-provoking, fantastic, and clear-eyed tale about the madness of war and violence. I loved it!"
—Michael Partridge, co-chair of the George MacDonald Society

"Lederman's rich cast of characters will pitch camp in your head and refuse to leave. Caleb McRae is a man who loves God, but he loves justice more. And that puts him in a terrible bind, because the man he loves makes a compelling case that Caleb's is an unjust god...a brilliant novel. I only wish I could have read it forty years ago."
— *R.S. Ingermanson, best-selling author of the* City of God *and* Crown of Thorns *series*

"*The Ballad of Midnight and McRae* is an expansive and soulful journey through the deserts of the American West, both literal and emotional. Reading this book was like sitting around a campfire with an old storyteller who knew just when to drop his voice, when to make you laugh, and when to break your heart. Jess Lederman writes with a fierce tenderness, blending lyrical prose with grit and grace. The writing burns—sometimes with beauty, sometimes with the pain of recognition. I loved that the novel doesn't hand you clean answers—it wrestles with God, with sin, with longing, and never lets go. But this isn't just a heady book full of big questions—it's also wildly entertaining. Lederman throws curveballs and magic into the dust of the Old West, and it all works...[This] is a tale for the seeker, the wanderer, the broken-hearted believer, and the stubborn skeptic. It's for anyone who's ever chased something they didn't fully understand and found themselves in the process. I'd recommend it to lovers of literary fiction, fans of Cormac McCarthy or Marilynne Robinson, and anyone who believes that stories still have the power to save."
—Thomas Anderson, Editor In Chief, Literary Titan

PRAISE FOR THE BALLAD OF MIDNIGHT AND MCRAE

"[A] beguiling five-decade-long queer love story about two men committed to their own versions of righteousness and salvation—and, especially, to one another, through both heartbreak and reconciliation...poignant, intriguing, and soulful..."
—Kirkus Reviews

"A compelling historical epic...thought-provoking and uplifting."
—Blue Ink Review

"A historical love story takes on mythic significance in the moving novel *The Ballad of Midnight and McRae.*"
—Foreword Clarion Reviews

"This is a remarkable book. In a polarized world, where there are fewer and fewer safe spaces for conversation between those who disagree, between those who inhabit different world views, Jess Lederman invites us into a story where just such conversations can and do happen, where opposites meet and find new understandings and so much to share. In the story of Midnight and McRae we are enabled to hear the long conversation between Pagan and Christian, and within Christianity between Protestant and Catholic, and on a personal level between father and son, between lover and beloved, and deep within ourselves, the conversation between the person we are pretending to be and the person we really are. And all these vital conversations are enfolded in and arise from a compelling story set on the frontiers, the badlands, and the formative days of America itself, the place where so many of these conversations need to take place."
—Malcolm Guite, English poet and Anglican priest, and author of Sounding the Seasons: Seventy Sonnets for the Christian Year

"...a complex, well-written, immersive, thought-provoking read."
—Priscilla Bettis, The Well-Read Fish

"Loved it! This is a book as wide and deep as the western landscape in which it's set, full of imagination, bound together with love and faith...There's mythical creatues, mysticism, war, loss, and fights against bad guys too! A great read."
—Rachel Deeming, Reedsy Discovery

Some of the many reader reviews on Goodreads and Amazon:

"Historical fiction is difficult to get right because fact and fiction are opposites but must appear side by side in this genre. Jess Lederman understands that and really manages to meld the two together. The story pulls you in effortlessly. Great character development plus excellent dialogue made this a fast read."

"Profoundly moving, meticulously researched, poetic, passionate, stirring, this was a terrific story that's wonderfully told! Jess Lederman skillfully evokes the landscape and times, squarely placing the reader right along with the characters. I was completely enchanted and couldn't put it down."

"An extraordinary novel in its plot, creation of memorable characters, and grasp of U.S. Southwest history. Lederman gives us stunning action and dialogue, cinematic landscapes, and a love story for all to embrace."

"What an adventure, first with the fathers then the son and daughter. It all tied together perfectly, and I was enthralled start to finish. I'll seek out other novels by Mr. Lederman."

The Ballad of Midnight and McRae

Jess Lederman

Published by Azure Star, LLC
For information about rights or permissions, contact jess@jesslederman.com

ISBN: 978-0-9986030-8-7
Cover design by Alexander Von Ness, nessgraphica.com

For the lost and lonely,
the spat and shat upon,
the outcasts and misfits of this world.

“The course of true love never did run smooth.”
— from *A Midsummer Night's Dream,* by William Shakespeare

"The fire of God, which is his essential being, his love, is a fire unlike its earthly symbol in this, that it is only at a distance it burns—that the farther from him, it burns the worse...”
— from *Unspoken Sermons,* by George MacDonald

“Then I was standing on the highest mountain of them all, and round about beneath me was the whole hoop of the world. And while I stood there I saw more than I can tell and I understood more than I saw; for I was seeing in a sacred manner the shapes of all things in the spirit, and the shape of all shapes as they must live together like one being. And I saw that the sacred hoop of my people was one of many hoops that made one circle, wide as daylight and as starlight, and in the center grew one mighty flowering tree to shelter all the children of one mother and one father. And I saw that it is was holy.”
— from *Black Elk Speaks: Being the Life Story of Holy Man of the Oglala Sioux,* by John G Neihardt

Part One

Lie Down in Fire

Chapter One

Into the Desert

My father was one of the last great lawmen of the Wild West.

His name was Caleb McRae. He was born in 1876, a fair-haired child with eyes the clear cold blue of a mountain lake. The son of a Broad Street banker, he grew up in Greenwich, Connecticut on a sprawling estate, yet cared nothing for money or the shiny things it can buy.

Justice was his only passion.

He thrilled to read of Revelation's hundred-pound hailstones raining down on sinners and devoured dime novels that told tales of the Texas Rangers. In his imagination it was he who collared John Wesley Hardin, the murderous outlaw, and Sam Bass, robber of coaches and trains.

As a young boy he learned to ride. He bought a six shooter when he turned thirteen and taught himself to blast tin cans off fence posts at fifty paces. He chopped cords of wood to build the muscles in his arms, and by fifteen was broad-shouldered and an inch over six feet tall. At seventeen he left his family's Presbyterian church and became a Baptist, blithely ignoring his father's stern warnings not to evangelize on the streets of downtown Greenwich.

One secret tormented him: he had no desire for girls and found his gaze lingering on other boys. Might he, of all people, be a *pansy,* a *fairy,* an affront to the Living God? No, impossible, the Lord must be testing his righteousness. All right, then; Caleb would not let Him down. And so, in a solitary ceremony late one midsummer's eve, he knelt before a cross he'd fashioned from old railroad ties and vowed to renounce his sinful thoughts and wayward dreams.

In his eighteenth year he set out for the Lone Star State, delighted that his parents had cut him off without a dime. How much easier it would be to enter the Kingdom of Heaven!

He made his way to Austin, convinced the Rangers to let him sign on, and two years later was sent to the brawling boomtown of El Paso. The railroad had brought prosperity, and with it came gunfighters, gamblers, con artists, and thieves. Few lawmen lasted long.

For my father, it was perfect.

I keep a newspaper clipping on my writing desk, a black-and-white photograph that appeared in the *El Paso Herald* in December of 1898. Though its ostensible subject is a certain Mayor Magoffin, my father's hulking image dominates the frame. He's the only clean-shaven man in the picture, and his hair, while not long, is a leonine mass of what must have been golden curls. There's a broad-brimmed Stetson in his left hand and a Winchester rifle in his right. He's wearing an oilskin duster and has an air of regal authority that belies his twenty-two years.

Caleb McRae was fierce and fair and never backed down, and in a few short years led the taming of El Paso. By the turn of the century, his life had become routine. He put away garden-variety bad guys, became the youngest Elder of the First Baptist Church, and prayed for the chance to do something great for the glory of God.

In the spring of 1900, rumors spread of an outlaw who'd been plundering the Arizona and New Mexico Territories, rustling horses and cattle on both sides of the Rio Grande. His name was Henry Midnight, and his legend grew with each passing month. He was lean and lithe and wore his raven hair long like the Indians. He dressed in black and rode a pitch-dark Arabian stallion, the two mere phantoms of the night, invisible to lawmen's eyes. Rumor had it he'd killed a man in Arizona and escaped from jail only hours before he was to be hanged; he'd become a jewel thief, snatching an emerald necklace from the night table of the mayor's wife while she and her husband blissfully snored. The Tejanos, who'd gotten the short end since the Anglos came to El Paso, sung his praises. And if the

Jesuits were especially generous in their provisions for the poor, it was thanks to the Midnight bandito donating the proceeds from his latest haul.

These stories, however fantastic, intrigued my father, the last most of all. What if the man were not entirely in thrall to Satan, what if there were hope for his soul? Caleb McRae of the Texas Rangers made two vows: he'd deliver Henry Midnight to justice and bring him to the Lord.

My father pinned a map of the El Paso Valley on his kitchen wall, marked the date and location of each of Midnight's crimes, and by the summer of '01 a pattern began to emerge. He devised a theory to predict where the rustler would strike next and for weeks led stakeouts, all to no avail. And then, on a moonless August night, as he peered out from a hill overlooking the back section of the Double-Bar Ranch, three figures on horseback appeared.

The capture would have been fast and smooth if his men had followed the plan he'd so carefully devised, but one of his deputies broke from cover too soon and their advantage was lost.

Midnight and his men fled, each in a different direction. My father had no doubt which was Henry, for the rumor that he rode a black Arabian proved to be true. The outlaw had a good half mile on him and was heading southeast, into the Chihuahuan desert. What had happened to the others, my father had no idea; the chase had come down to just the two of them.

Hours went by, and a hint of dawn appeared on the eastern horizon. Where was Midnight leading him, and how long would this go on?

No matter.

He had his Winchester and his Colt 45, some hard biscuits and dried beef and a gallon canteen. Boaz, his Appaloosa, could keep up with anything on four legs. If he had to chase Midnight to the gates of hell, Caleb McRae would get his man.

He spurred his beast on.

Chapter Two

On the Cusp of the Fifth World

In 1953, after returning from the war in Korea, I found myself in Barstow, California and ducked into a roadhouse to find some respite from the heat and quench my thirst. An old-timer with a guitar was providing entertainment, and I heard him sing half a dozen verses of the tale of Captain McRae's pursuit of Henry Midnight. By then the story had merged into myth, with the bandito leading the Ranger across the West Texas badlands in vast concentric circles, spiraling toward a fateful conclusion, an epic chase that lasted for months, or years, or perhaps was still going on.

What really happened?

Is it truth you want, or mere facts?

Regardless, here is the tale as it plays in my mind.

They raced over the salt flats in the cool of the morning, then through pale green fields of bristlegrass and on into the high desert, thick with agave and Spanish dagger. My father stopped at a stream to rest his steed, let him drink, and refilled his canteen. Though he lost sight of his quarry for a time, he soon picked up the trail.

The outlaw kept a fast pace through the heat of the day, and by sunset they'd covered over forty miles.

My father held up well enough on the second day, but that night, his third without sleep, he began to wonder if his mind was playing tricks on him. Sometime in the small hours two javelinas snuffled up out of a desert wash and began to engage in a spirited debate over whether the Ranger ought to bear left or right. Kangaroo rats joined in the discussion, their huge eyes luminous under the crescent moon. In the end he decided the arguments for left were more convincing, and by daybreak Henry Midnight was back in view.

On the afternoon of the third day the heavens unleashed a fierce summer storm that sent flash floods coursing through the arroyos. My father whispered comforting words in Boaz's ear, murmured prayers to the Father of Lights. Though he was soaked through, the dampness and danger revived him and sharpened his senses. He breathed in the sweet musky smell of the chaparral and knew in the depths of his being that the moment of triumph was at hand.

That night the Milky Way was like a river overflowing its banks, the sky a riot of stars.

At dawn he came upon the outlaw kneeling by the side of his Arabian stallion, deep in grief. Henry Midnight had ridden his beloved horse to death. There was no fight left in him.

My father offered his condolences and then, as he cuffed him, asked "Do you know the Lord, Christ Jesus?"

"Please, sir," said Midnight, who startled Caleb by speaking with a British accent. "We've a hundred miles of desert to traverse and but one horse. Take me to the gallows if you will, but spare me your sermons."

There was no way Boaz could bear the weight of both men, which made their journey back a daunting prospect indeed. My father decided to bide his time. It was better to demonstrate Christian charity than discuss it, so he shared his water and biscuits and dried beef with the rustler. Sometimes he had Midnight walk and at other times he led and let his captive ride.

The two men exchanged a few words, then a few words more, and soon were in full-fledged conversation. Henry was twenty-seven, my father twenty-five, and they turned out to have much in common, to their mutual surprise. Both had been entranced by tales of the Wild West from their earliest years and had chosen roads in life that left their parents reeling. Midnight had grown up in England, his father a Peer of the Realm. He'd attended lectures in ethnology at Oxford before coming to the States to study the aboriginal Americans and learn their ways. For five years he'd lived with Hopi and Apache tribes. It was among the latter that he'd gone native and discovered a knack for the sort of guerilla tactics at which the Apache excelled.

The outlaw claimed he, too, had a passion for justice; the white man had stolen the land and livelihood from the Indians and Mexicans, while he only rustled from rich ranchers who could well afford to lose a small portion of their herds. Did Caleb doubt him? He had but to ask Father de Souza, who would confirm his donations to the Jesuits.

Around noon they stopped to rest in some welcoming shade. My father hobbled his horse and then bound his captive's legs and tied him to a mesquite tree, which Midnight said he understood completely, discretion being the greater part of valor.

Thereupon Caleb McRae lay down and fell into a deep sleep, untroubled by dreams.

When he awoke it was dark and a thin slice of moon had climbed nearly to the zenith. The ropes and handcuffs that had secured the rustler were gathered up neatly nearby. The revolver my father had taken from him and put on his own belt was missing. He shook the sleep from his head.

Where was Midnight?

Gradually he registered the scent of broiling meat. Henry had built a fire, killed and skinned a jackrabbit, and was tending it on a spit.

"Hope you don't mind, McRae," he said. "I was awfully hungry. I prefer my rabbit rather well done. And you?"

My father nodded.

"Right then. Come here, you can make yourself useful."

He'd collected the fruit from a stand of prickly pear cactus and showed my father how to carefully peel their skins to remove the spines and reveal the ripe red figs within.

As Midnight pointed out, there were no grains or vegetables, nor even a simple table wine, but all things considered they enjoyed a fine repast.

The men traveled from sunset to sunrise and slept through the heat of the day. Whether or not he believed every word of the outlaw's story, my father no longer bothered to secure him, reckoning Midnight could escape from anything he might devise.

He had not, however, abandoned his intention to evangelize. Had Henry been brought up in the Church of England? Well, yes, in the sense that his parents had dragged him along to All Hallows by the Tower on Sunday mornings for a number of years. But it had come to naught.

After some negotiation, they reached an agreement: Henry would listen attentively to my father's recounting of the Good News, and for every Gospel story, he'd tell the Ranger one of the sacred Hopi myths—an exceptional honor, if truth be told, the Hopi having no interest in proselytizing.

It was a fine night for discourse, with a breeze from the west cooling the sweat on their brows. The sun had set and the men were both walking, leading the Appaloosa by the side of an arroyo in the gathering darkness.

"In the beginning was the Word," said my father, "and the Word was with God, and the Word was God." He continued reciting the preamble to John's Gospel from memory. Surely those verses, so full of grace and truth, would touch the outlaw's heart!

Henry responded with the story of the dawn of space and time, when Tawa, spirit of the sun, formed the First World, home to creatures much like mites and ticks who lived miserable lives in dark, dank caves.

After hearing the first of John's Seven Signs, the turning of water into wine, Henry explained that Tawa, dissatisfied with what he had ushered into being, called forth Spider Grandmother to lead the little insects on an arduous journey to the Second World, where they transformed into wolves and bears.

Another world followed, and my father found it of some interest that Tawa, seeing evil abounding, destroyed his Third World in a great flood, though not before Spider Grandmother had fashioned boats made of hollow reeds for the handful who were not entirely corrupt. Later on, after hearing some of the highlights from Revelation, Henry revealed that we are denizens of the Fourth World, living on the cusp of the Fifth, the World That Is to Come. What life will be like for the Righteous Ones allowed entrance, one could only imagine!

"So, do you believe?" the outlaw asked.

My father stared back at him, incredulous.

"Well, it was a long shot," said Henry Midnight. "One can only plant the seed, it's up to Tawa whether or not it takes root. Or to Spider Grandmother, I'm not entirely sure."

A few moments passed before my father deigned to respond.

"Amuse yourself all you like," he said, "but give yourself up to Christ or to the furnace of horror men call hell."

"I've given myself up to you, is that not enough? And just what is it *you've* surrendered? Not your pride, I take it."

"Only my own will for His."

"Oh, come on. Did you ever feel more alive than chasing after me? Is this not your passion? Will you not claim it for your own?"

To these questions my father made no reply.

After they'd walked another few miles, Midnight tapped him on the shoulder and pointed toward a constellation blazing in the northern sky. The Perseids were just beginning to streak through the heavens, and for a while the two men paused to gaze up and marvel at the shooting stars.

They found shelter the next morning in a shallow cave, and that evening my father awoke to find Henry Midnight already up and about.

"Perhaps you were only trying to get my goat last night," he said to the outlaw. "But you got me thinking."

"Ah. That's not a crime, I hope. And your thoughts?"

"I believe I'm doing what the Lord's made me fit to do. You're right, though; I love the chase, love it with everything in me, and if He asked me to give up the Ranger's life one day, that'd be a bitter pill. I'd be doing His will, but my heart wouldn't be in it. So you see, I don't pretend to righteousness, Midnight; I'm as much a sinner as the next man."

"Seeing there's not another in sight, the next man's me—and as to sin, it's a fair bet I've got you beat. My thievery aside, I've never been one to resist the temptations of the flesh."

His devilish grin was not without charm.

"Whether doled out by the teaspoon or barrel-load, sin's sin," said my father. "We're done for without God's grace."

Not far from them, a golden eagle swooped down into the agave, snaring a black-tailed rabbit.

"Silver-tongued as I am," said Henry Midnight, "I doubt I could talk that bird into sharing its dinner. Tried to find us something earlier and came up empty-handed. I was out there a ways and all at once heard the hiss of a rattlesnake, but it was only a burrowing owl, fixing me with its stern-eyed stare. Lives like a prairie dog, strange creature. Bad omen, seeing that owl, I had no desire to make him into a meal. And earlier I dreamed of the red fox the Apache say stole fire from the sun. That's a worse omen yet."

"You believe in that nonsense?" asked my father. He walked over to Boaz and began picking pebbles out of his hooves.

"I've a love for the mysterious and fantastic," replied Midnight. "Your Bible's replete with the wildest imaginings, and those are the bits I like the most. As to omens, Captain, do with them what you will. You're the leader of this caravan, I'm merely your humble prisoner."

"Well let's move out," said Caleb. "You ride, I'll walk for the first few hours. With a fast pace we'll be in El Paso the day after tomorrow."

"A delightful thought," said Henry, scratching the beard that was darkening his face. "I've heard they allow a man to dine well before he's led to the gallows."

You may well be wondering why Henry hadn't killed his captor and escaped the first time he slipped his bonds. That's the question my father had been mulling over, and here's what he'd come up with: That the outlaw didn't have it in him to kill a man. That the hunted dream of giving up like an exhausted man yearns for the sweet release of sleep.

I believe something else was at work.

The intensity of my father's gaze, the massiveness of the man, the kingliness of him, the sense that if he was not pure, purity was his desire—I think all these things fascinated Henry Midnight. Attracted him, delighted him. Perhaps he even found the Ranger's pomposity endearing.

And surely there would always be another chance to get away.

Chapter Three

The Cougar Queen

Henry and Caleb spent much of the night's journey trading stories of their first days in the West. At times my father wondered if it was appropriate to be enjoying the desperado's company quite so much.

It's only that I want to win the man to Christ, he thought.

Who was Henry Midnight, really, my father mused, a misguided soul ripe for conversion, or a con man, playing him for a fool?

"I've half a mind to believe you donate the proceeds of your thieving," he said, mounting the Appaloosa as the outlaw began to walk in front. "But you set yourself above the law! Others *earn* the money they give away."

"And bully for them," said Midnight. "I've not the patience. You talked the other day of *justice.* What do you mean by the word?"

"Giving a man what he deserves," my father replied.

"Well then, does the Indian, the Tejano, the Black man deserve dry dust for his dinner? The landowner to fatten himself at the expense of the poor? Tell me, McRae, what *does* a man deserve?"

"We're all of us sinners who deserve the flames of hell," said my father. "But those who put their faith in the Lord are saved by grace, thanks be to God."

"You've side-stepped the question," said Midnight, looking back with a wry smile. "However, I'm intrigued. If there came a day when all bowed down to your Christ, then in his kingdom justice would be quite beside the point, wouldn't it. There'd be none at all. Only grace."

My father was contemplating his response when disaster struck.

They were traversing a ridgeline, preparing to descend a hundred feet to the desert floor, when the ground beneath Boaz gave way. Horse and rider tumbled halfway down the hillside, and before they'd slid to a stop my father knew El Paso had become a distant dream. He'd heard the Appaloosa's left foreleg snap, felt his own left knee wrenched hard enough to cause him to cry out in pain.

"Caleb!" called Midnight, and scrambled down after them.

My father stroked Boaz' neck and withers and talked to him softly. Then he rose to a sitting position and ended the steed's suffering with a single bullet.

Midnight surveyed the damage and used his shirt to wrap my father's knee.

"Put your arm around my shoulders," he said, squatting down on Caleb's left.

"I'm too big for you to drag thirty miles," my father said through gritted teeth. His leg was in agony, there was no way it could support his weight.

"Have you never studied the principles of mechanics?" asked the outlaw. "This is more a matter of brains than brawn. Take Archimedes—with a long enough lever he could've moved the world. Now up we go."

My father doubted he had mastered any arcane secrets of leverage, however. The man was simply stronger than he looked.

"An Apache shaman once led me on a spiritual journey," Midnight said some hours later. He'd been keeping up a one-sided conversation to distract both of them from the pain of the long, slow desert trek. "After much chewing of peyote, he left me alone to seek out my guardian spirit. Which I'd high hopes would be a wolf or eagle or bull. For four days and nights I fasted in a sacred place before the spirit made itself known. And do you know what it was?"

"Not a clue." It was only force of will that kept my father from groaning with every step they took. "A jackass, perhaps?"

"Ha! Clever, that. No, a dung beetle. And that's fortunate for you, Caleb, because the little buggers can carry a thousand times their own weight."

The men took shelter by a large yucca tree, bone tired and beset by a gnawing hunger. My father became feverish as the sun rose and the shade dwindled to a few square feet. Henry soaked his bandanna in water and was daubing my father's face when there came a cry that chilled them as though a mist had suddenly obscured the midday sun.

It was the sound of a woman in the throes of an inconsolable sorrow.

The cry came again, this time closer, and the outlaw raised his revolver.

"Don't—" my father began to say. Henry put a finger to his lips.

"A cougar," he whispered, and cocked the hammer.

A thin breeze brought the smell of it to their nostrils.

The next sound they heard caused my father to reach up and guide Henry's gun-hand down. He didn't resist.

It was a soft, gentle purring. From out of the mesquite shrubland came the cougar queen, her eyes like polished citrine and onyx, her teats swollen with milk. She lay down, encircled them with her body and nuzzled them close. Henry licked a few drops, then he and my father sucked hungrily till their bellies were full and they'd drifted into a deep and blissful sleep.

"Were you dreaming?" I asked my father after hearing the story over breakfast when I was perhaps ten years old.

"Nonsense!" he replied, his voice edged with anger. "It was all as real as this table before us." He gave it such a terrible thump with his great right hand that crockery went flying.

Fearful as I was, my curiosity gave me the courage to press on.

"What did Henry have to say about what happened?"

"The glory of God's mercy left even him speechless. You listen to me, boy: with the Almighty all things are possible. You'll recall how the ravens provided food for Elijah as he hid from Ahab in the desert by brook Cherith."

The legend of Romulus and Remus seemed more to the point, but I kept that thought to myself.

I'm old now, however—for I write these words in my ninety-fourth year—and have seen too much that is astonishing, inexplicable, and desperately beautiful to doubt my father's tale.

Chapter Four

Darkness and Light

The men awoke refreshed, Caleb's fever having broken as they slept, and found they could hobble at a reasonable pace. During the course of the night their conversation came back round to their fathers.

"Rotters, the both of them," said Henry Midnight. "Self-important, lucre-loving louts."

"Watch your tongue," Caleb cautioned.

"An anatomical impossibility. But it's not all bad, being the offspring of a patriarch manqué. There are sons who set their sights on emulating their papas, surpassing their achievements, and a fine lot they are, I'm sure. The likes of us, though, who seek fulfillment as our fathers' antipodes—our motivation, fueled by a loathing for what we might otherwise become, is surely greater, our passion to succeed the more intense."

My father laughed despite himself, and then his face darkened.

"I don't know," he said. "I've prayed for the strength to love my father."

He regretted the words as soon as they'd been uttered, being in no mood for one of the outlaw's blithe replies. But Henry lapsed into a contemplative silence.

"I expect *you'd* make a good papa, Caleb," he said after a while. "I'm not cut out for it, myself."

It was not a subject my father was eager to pursue.

The two limped on through a moonlit field of saltbrush and sage and had likely covered twelve miles by the time the eastern sky grew light.

When they stopped to rest, a few faint clouds dotted the far horizon. These moved in steadily and grew black and heavy and yet there was no rain. My father and Henry slept fitfully and awoke to a grim gray world. No twilight followed sunset, only sudden nightfall. They moved slowly through the darkness. Jagged flashes tore through the heavens, and still not a drop fell to earth.

The wind gusted hot and dry and brought no relief.

They had just reached the beginning of the grasslands when my father pointed toward a host of glowing orbs coming toward them from the west, the likes of which he'd never seen.

"More of your evil omens, Henry?"

The outlaw looked for a long moment and spat into the dirt before he answered.

"No harbingers, those. That's death itself riding the wind."

It was ball lightning, globes of fire moving like luminous tumbleweeds through the storm-haunted night.

Ahead of the men half a mile the bristlegrass began burning. A detachment of the ghostly spheres passed them by and alighted in the mesquite scrub a hundred yards to their rear, setting it ablaze.

The wind was in their faces and the grassfire raged toward them, a wall of flame.

"You might have a chance, running through the fire behind us," said my father. "I'll see if I can't burrow down into the earth. If it's my time, so be it."

"Nonsense," said Henry Midnight. "We'd both of us end up as flambé. Now follow my lead, we've little time."

He rummaged for his tinderbox, took out a striker, charcloth, and flint, and set the bristlegrass just behind them on fire.

"What in God's holy name—" exclaimed my father.

"We'll wait as long as we can," said Henry, "then lie down midway into the burn. The flames won't touch us, and there'll be air to breathe close to the ground."

"You've done this before?" my father asked as the outlaw pulled him to his feet.

"There's a first time for everything, old boy. An Apache blood brother of mine heard of this business from a Lakota woman who swore it saved her cousin's life."

The maelstrom roared closer, its heat already scorching their flesh.

"NOW!" cried Midnight.

He marched them forward and they lay down amid the smoldering ashes.

In the moments before the conflagration came upon them, my father imagined he could hear a chorus of voices within its hiss and crackle and roar. *Behold the sinner's fate,* they sang. *An eternity of anguish in the flames that burn but do not consume!*

It's too late now for Henry, he thought. *I missed my chance to bring the man to Christ. What a failure I am! I've not loved the Lord my God with all my heart. And even now, entangled by the cords of death, I have not prayed...*

Then the fire reached them and passed around the burned-out grass, and though the very air seemed to boil above them, when they rose minutes later they were singed but not burned.

After the men made their way clear of the smoke and the broad swath of badlands charred by the fire, my father sank to his knees.

"You have delivered my soul from death," he quoted from the Psalms. *"Indeed, my feet from stumbling, so that I may walk before You in the light of the living.* I thank you, Father, and lift up Henry Midnight, the instrument of your mercy, that you might enter into his heart and so save his soul from perdition. In your son's blessed name I pray, Amen."

"His *instrument?*" asked the outlaw, seemingly in outrage. "That's how you see me, is it?"

"I tell you, Henry, as I kneel here in this dirt, there's no higher honor. Surely you can understand that."

"I most surely cannot. When the Hopi shaman created a great earth oven at Mishongnovi, and its fires spread and could not be controlled, it was Spider Grandmother he called on, and do you know what she did? She hiked up her dress and spread her legs and pissed on it. And that was that. But your Ancient of Days couldn't be bothered to roll over in his great heavenly bed and let out a trickle to save us."

My father stared at him in amazement.

"What if I don't *want* him in my heart?" Midnight continued. "What about that, Caleb? Do I have any say in the matter?"

"I've wondered," my father said softly. "The Free Will Baptists make a decent argument. But now I'm thinking it would be best if it wasn't up to you at all."

Henry spun on his heel and walked off in disgust.

He returned an hour later with leaves he'd gathered from the greasewood chapparal. These he boiled to create a healing salve for their faces and hands, which were as red as the flowers on a Christmas cactus from their time in the hot ashes.

The men's energy revived after feasting on the prickly pear from a nearby grove, and they decided to press on in the few remaining hours of darkness.

"I'm grateful to you, Henry," said my father at long last.

"Yes, well, that was rather a close shave," said Midnight. "Something you'll tell your grandchildren about, I reckon."

Toward daybreak the north wind cooled the desert air, and the clouds finally gave forth a gentle rain.

The men awoke to find the skies had cleared, and by the time they set off the heavens were aswarm with stars.

"I doubt we're more than ten or fifteen miles from El Paso," said my father. "Even with this bum leg of mine, we should make it by morning."

The outlaw curled his lip and sniffed the air. "I can smell the hoosegow from here."

For a moment my father could not remember the theory he'd concocted to explain why Henry hadn't long since escaped, and in the next moment he wished Henry had vanished into the desert the first time he'd slipped his bonds.

Then he put those thoughts out of his mind. He had the man's revolver in his belt and no need to sleep before they reached El Paso.

His duty was clear.

It was a slow, laborious limp through the grasslands, and Henry was rarely silent for long.

"What a mystery up there," he murmured, gazing up at the firmament as they paused to catch their breath. "What a vastness. Tell me, can you find the Seven Sisters?"

"Of course," my father replied, lying on his back and taking in the great dome above them. "The Pleiades. I can navigate by the stars as well as any man."

"The Hopi call that patch of brightness the hole in the sky. They say it's from there we entered the fourth world, this world, and became what we are today. I never tire of their legends, Caleb. Tawa transforming us from bugs to beasts to men! Rather puts me in mind of that Darwin chap whose theory's got everyone in such a lather."

"The one who claims we're the offspring of apes?" asked my father. "My sense of dignity cries out against such a notion. But formed from the dust of the earth, then given the breath of life by God Almighty—there's both humility and grandeur in *that.*"

The outlaw smiled.

"I'm not entirely sold on Mr. Darwin's theory myself. Though it strikes me that our lives are a process of becoming; we none of us end up where we began. Might that not be true for the race of men as well? It intrigues me, imagining what's to come."

A nighthawk glided silently above the bristlegrass, searching for insects in the moonlight. Some moments passed before my father made his reply.

"You wonder what future awaits? The New Jerusalem, city of the Living God. Eternal bliss for those who belong to Christ."

"Ah, you've traded the vinegar of hellfire for more honeyed words. I wonder, though, just how blissful your New Jerusalem would be, for all its streets of gold and gates of pearl. A place of eternal light! It sounds oppressive, really, the never-ending glare of it. Speak true—would you not miss the darkness?"

My father ran his hands through his hair and laughed at his own frustration. "You've read John's Revelation, then?"

"Oh, I relish your Bible's stories, Caleb, it's the sales pitch I don't care for. For my money there's not much difference between a minister preaching and a mountebank hawking miracle cures. Salvation or snake oil liniment, take your pick. But when the medicine wagon comes to town, I'm more at home with the side-show freaks."

"You mistake the urgency of a true physician for the flimflam of a scoundrel," said my father. "There *are* maladies that lead to death. And remedies that restore to health. Now help me up, we've miles yet to travel."

He put his arm around Midnight's shoulders and together they rose to their feet.

"The truth reveals itself," Henry muttered. "It need not be sold."

They plodded on into the night, Orion and the Great Bear marking their way.

"You know, Henry," said my father. "You could always just close your eyes."

"Hmm?" The outlaw looked at him quizzically.

"If it was darkness that you longed for in the world to come."

"Ah. Very thoughtful, Caleb, I'll keep that in mind."

Coyotes yipped and howled far off in the desert's hidden places.

A feeling of vertigo came over my father. He was intensely aware of Henry's strong right arm supporting him, the sinewy muscles in the man's neck and shoulders, the comfort of his presence. Aware that at times he was not eager for their journey to come to an end.

He blinked away gnats the nighthawk had missed.

There were flashes of brightness whenever he closed his eyes.

Chapter Five

A Sinful Man

The moon sank behind the Franklin Mountains as the men limped and hobbled and stumbled through the predawn twilight hours.

"When my Boaz went down," said my father, "we were talking of justice. I said it's giving a man what he deserves. Do you think otherwise?"

"I say it's a man getting what he *needs,*" replied the outlaw. "A chance to make a living by the sweat of his brow. A decent place to call his own. His daily bread."

"Oh? A man can work from dawn to dusk, eat his fill, fall asleep on a goose-down mattress and yet have *nothing* of what he needs most of all."

"Ah, the missionary's siren song. What hell have they not unleashed upon the earth in providing for the heathen's needs! Do you know what the name 'Hopi' means? The peaceful ones. They were like lambs to the slaughter when the Spanish came with their guns and their God."

"I'm well aware that Christians sin," responded my father. "Neither are the red men innocents. Your Apache brothers are hardly lovers of peace."

"It's true their blood runs hot. Apache is *our* name for them, I'll have you know. They call themselves the Dine'e—the people. The human beings. Apache means *the enemy.*" Henry forced a grim smile. "Which according to your King should keep them safe from His followers. So tell me, Caleb, *do* you love your enemies?"

"That's cheap, Henry. I've never claimed to be a saint."

"Yes, we're both of us sinners, and I'm glad for it." He ran his left hand over the week's worth of beard that covered his face. "Let's not quarrel."

The two walked in silence for a while. The breeze brought forth a sweetness from the grass, and the air around them was suffused with a soft light heralding the break of day.

"Tell me," said Henry, casting a sidelong look at his companion, "have you ever been in love? Enemies aside, of course."

My father laughed dismissively and shook his head.

"Oh come now, is there no girl you steal glances at in the next pew on Sunday mornings? Me, I take my pleasure where I find it, but you've the makings of a fine family man."

"I've had no time for romance, chasing after you and your ilk."

"Have I ilk?" asked the outlaw. "I rather consider myself *sui generis*. But if I'd known my doings were keeping you from conjugal bliss, perhaps I'd have found—"

He stopped short, narrowed his eyes, and peered into the distance.

"—more honest work."

The jocularity was gone from his voice.

Wavering on the horizon like a hazy mirage was the town of El Paso.

They made their way across the salt flats and came at least to the main road. Perhaps a mile or so to the east a wagon or carriage was approaching, heading toward town. My father separated himself from the outlaw and limped a few feet away.

"Damn you, Henry Midnight," he said, his voice hoarse with emotion. "It's a hanging crime you're wanted for. You could have made a break for it that first night after you freed yourself with your wizardry. You could have been long gone. Damn you for thinking yourself above the law. Damn you even for your kindness."

"Do what you think just, Caleb. I've been wondering what you would decide."

On Henry's lips was the hint of a smile.

My father's left leg buckled, and he sank to his knees. When Henry reached for him, he waived the outlaw off.

"What I think *just?* What you or I *deserve,* what we *need*—that's for the Lord to decide." His great right fist pounded the hardpacked earth and the energy seemed to drain out of his body. "I am a sinful man."

"My friend," said Henry, and he knelt down. "I'm sorry."

My father looked to the east. Whoever was approaching was only a quarter mile away.

"Stay quiet," he said. "I'll do the talking." He took Henry's revolver from his belt and handed it to him. "Now help me up."

Once the outlaw lifted him to his feet, my father stood tall and waved his Stetson.

"Whoa!" called out an old-timer driving three pairs of oxen. A flatbed freight wagon carrying a load of sawn lumber pulled up alongside the two men.

"Sir! I'm Captain McRae of the Texas Rangers. My friend and I would appreciate if we could ride with you into town."

The bullwhacker looked them over and raised his eyebrows. Their clothes were ragged and filthy and singed by fire, their beards encrusted with sand.

"Y'all look like Bowie and Crockett after Santa Anna stormed the Alamo. McRae, are you?" He spat out a stream of tobacco juice. "Well, you're big enough to be him, I reckon. You boys stink worse than goats, but if you sit far 'nuff downwind I won't mind overmuch."

Henry helped my father into the back of the wagon and climbed in after him. The driver shouted a few questions that received monosyllabic answers, then lapsed into silence. The oxen plodded and bellowed, and the first slanting rays of sunlight painted the salt flats in shades of gold.

"Go your way," my father whispered as they reached the outskirts of town. "Only stay clear of the Trans-Pecos. For if I come after you a second time, it won't end well for you, Henry, I promise you that."

The outlaw searched my father's eyes.

"If there's a god in the high heavens," said Henry Midnight, "may he keep you from harm."

He kissed my father on the lips, jumped from the wagon, and ran, swift and lithe and graceful, till he vanished from view.

Chapter Six

Praying for the Dead

"How could you justify letting Henry go when you'd sworn to uphold the law?" I asked my father after a dinnertime recitation of the tale. It was a cold November day in 1941, only a few weeks before Pearl Harbor. I was nearly fourteen and looking to pick a fight, though in truth I was glad he'd set the outlaw free.

Henry's parting kiss had been conveniently left out of the story.

He scowled at me. "The man was an unregenerate sinner, if they'd hanged him he'd have been lost for all eternity. No, Matthew, I'd high hopes Henry would yet surrender to Christ."

"Then you should never have collared *any* criminals guilty of capital crimes, only pickpockets and jaywalkers and litterbugs. I mean, is there anyone you *don't* have hope for? You always say with God all things are possible."

His eyes narrowed ominously. "Are you mocking me, boy?"

"No sir. I've asked a fair question."

Since becoming a preacher not long after I was born, Caleb had grown the sort of beard Abe Lincoln favored—though his was as white as his leonine locks—and begun carrying a large, rough-hewn walking stick, giving him the appearance of an Old Testament prophet. He rose and reached for it and I flinched, sure he was about to vent his anger, but my father only leaned against his staff and regarded me with a mournful expression.

"How little you know of life. Some decisions feel like a weight you must lift that will tear the very sinews from your bones. You pray for guidance and yet see no clear answer, only sin on every side. If ever you're faced with such a dilemma, may it be God's will you'll choose for the best."

"Did *you?* Was letting him go the right choice?"

"Yes," he said. "Of that I've no doubt."

"Why?" He had answered me gently, a rare mercy, yet still I pressed on. "Because he was such a great friend? You've told me more about him than about my mother, your own wife, but where was Henry Midnight when she died and left you with an infant son? You don't know, do you, or I'd have heard about it at least a thousand times." A cold current of fear ran through me, but I was in too deep, there was no backing down. "And I thought you told me he never came to Christ. Of what use was it then, to let him go free?"

Our eyes locked. My father's face was a pale mask, impenetrable.

"What *use* was it?" His eyes burned into mine and I dropped my gaze.

"Get down on your knees," he said.

I knelt.

"Pray with me that Henry is yet among the living." He knelt down beside me. "Pray that the Lord in His mercy will enter into his heart. I've read you the parable of the importunate neighbor, the one who came at midnight asking for bread, and for his persistence was granted what he sought. Those who ask, receive, praise God. We'll pray here until the stroke of twelve."

The kitchen clock showed a quarter to eight.

I mumbled words that echoed my father's, but inside, in my own secret heart, I prayed for my mother. He'd told me praying for the dead was foolishness, which only made it all the sweeter. Not that I had any strong belief in a God who might hear my prayers. But if there *were* any such God as he worshipped—one who cast hundred-pound hailstones at those destined for perdition—I'd be ready for him. With some help from my seventh-grade science teacher, I'd calculated the diameter of the icy projectiles at about eighteen inches, not quite so intimidating as I'd at first imagined. I was agile and fleet of foot, a jitterbugging fool at school dances on Saturday nights. I'd dodge whatever came my way.

As my knees ached and my boredom and anger grew with every passing hour, I imagined Henry Midnight an outlaw still, holding out to the end and never surrendering to Christ.

Chapter Seven

The Flying Machine

Nothing was quite the same for my father after he returned to El Paso, having failed in his quest to capture the Midnight Bandito. He worked harder than ever, pursued outlaws with a cold fury and filled the city's jails, but found no satisfaction. Never one to socialize, he became yet more of a loner, a taciturn, grim-faced keeper of the peace.

And yet he was living in an age of miracles, a time when the amazing was becoming commonplace.

"Bank-robbing, rustling, them's crimes of the past," said his lieutenant, Jude Bryce, one fine, bright morning in January of 1902. They were outside the Sheldon Hotel, watching the mayor board the city's new electric streetcar on its maiden voyage to Juarez. "Electricity's worth more than cattle or gold, only a matter of time till someone figures out how to steal it."

My father grunted and narrowed his eyes. Electricity, indeed. Incandescent lights were being installed everywhere; was Henry even now mourning the darkness?

A gramophone began playing in the hotel lobby.

"Just down around the corner of the street I reside, there lives the cutest little girl I have ever spied..."

"Now *that's* what you need, cap'n," said Bryce, who considered himself quite the lady's man. "A sweet Rosie O'Grady to call your own. There's a passel of pretty gals in this town, if you haven't noticed."

"Tell you what, Jude," my father replied. "I'm going to pay a call on those Garner boys got chased this way from Chaparral. You stay here and keep a sharp eye out for any electricity thieves."

"Whoa, what'd I say?" asked the lieutenant, but my father had already turned his back and walked away.

Caleb McRae's reputation grew until only the most ignorant of outlaws ventured anywhere near El Paso. Which only burnished the legend of The One Who Got Away. Sometimes lawmen arrived from Lubbock or Amarillo or further east, bringing news of Henry Midnight's latest coup. A trunkful of gold coins, snatched in broad daylight! Over a hundred head of cattle, vanished without a trace!

There were no mentions of electrical thefts.

When the newspapers came in from Galveston, San Antonio, and Dallas, he bought them all and took the afternoon to scan every page. He took down his old map of the valley from the kitchen wall and put up a new one of Texas. Any time he read or heard of Henry's exploits, he'd draw circles and arrows and scrawl notes off to the side.

To what end he couldn't say.

On a brisk December afternoon in 1903, my father had just sat down with the Dallas paper when a front-page headline caught his eye.

FLYING MACHINE SOARS THREE MILES!

A grainy picture showed a winged contraption much like a glider, some ten feet off the ground. He scanned the article quickly, poured himself a cup of coffee, and read it again.

Evidently two brothers had stolen the secrets of birds and been born aloft on the winds of Kill Devil Hills. Years of work in secret, then a moment of reckoning on the sandy coast of North Carolina.

Self-propelled. No balloons attached. Fifty-nine seconds in the air on their third try.

He leaned back and closed his eyes. Sometimes in his dreams my father came untethered from the earth and learned to catch currents of air rushing through an azure sky. He roamed the heavens like a golden eagle, looked down from a vast height and saw himself on Boaz, chasing Henry Midnight across the salt flats and into the desert waste. Saw them hobbling together for a hundred miles, watched from afar as they lay down in burning embers. He'd wake oppressed by loss and longing, get out of bed and kneel in prayer. *Have mercy on me, O Lord, for I am beset by an unholy fire.*

Enough of such thoughts! He poured himself another cup and read the article one more time. The airship was like a box kite with propellers and a gasoline engine. Those Wright brothers were clever, but they had nothing on Henry Midnight! An airship might be perfect for getaways. He could be soaring over the swamplands to a hideout in East Texas right now.

Do what you think just, the outlaw had said, looking at my father with his beguiling, inscrutable smile. *I've been wondering what you would decide.*

Chapter Eight

The Gold Watch-Fob

One day in the spring of 1904, Major James L. Garrison, commanding officer of the Texas Rangers, surprised my father by showing up at his desk without warning.

"There someplace we can talk in private?" he asked.

"It's just you and me," replied my father. "Bryce won't be in till afternoon."

The Major set down a satchel, leaned against the wall and eyeballed him for a bit. It was his first time in El Paso in quite a while; he'd rarely made the arduous journey from Austin once it became clear Caleb McRae had things under control.

My father returned the stare, poker-faced. He noticed his boss had gotten soft since the last visit. The man's belly was straining the buttons of his vest.

"Your lieutenant, he tough enough to be made captain?" Garrison asked.

"Yes," my father replied. He was curious, but had learned the power of silence.

"I'm of the same opinion. Had dinner last night with him and that pretty little thing he's fixing to marry."

This was news. He hadn't known of Garrison's arrival, nor that Jude Bryce was engaged.

"I like the way he thinks," the major continued. "Got his mind on the future. Mentioned we might need motorcars to keep up with criminal elements. Told me Henry Ford drove one nearly a hundred miles an hour a few months back."

"That was on a frozen lake," said my father, whose newspaper habit was helping him keep abreast of the latest developments in transportation technology. "We don't see many of them in these parts. My Achilles could run circles around any motorcar out here in the badlands."

Achilles was a hot-blooded beast, a dark bay Thoroughbred who stood every inch of seventeen hands.

"Maybe so, McRae, but times are changing." Garrison sat down heavily on a wooden chair across from my father's desk, rummaged through his satchel, and brought out a yellow orb about six inches in diameter. "Ever seen one of these?" He tossed it to him.

"Can't say I have." My father spun it on the tip of his prodigious index finger and threw it back. "A mite soft for ordnance."

"Grows wild in the West Indies, used to be known as the forbidden fruit. Started growing 'em in South Texas not long ago, in the Rio Grande Valley. *Grapefruit.*" The major took out a Barlow knife from his vest pocket, peeled the fruit, and handed over a slice.

My father set it on his desk and looked at Garrison with raised brows. "Not that I don't appreciate getting schooled in agriculture, but the Garner boys broke out of jail night before last. They're bad news, those two, had my hands full putting them away a couple years ago. Sheriff took off with a posse, came back empty handed. I was planning on heading out and rounding them up."

"I don't give a rat's ass about them Garner boys, McRae. Let Bryce handle 'em. You just sit back and listen up." Garrison snapped his knife shut. "I'm damn good at what I do, but I have this job because I know everyone worth knowing in this state. One of them's Harlon Gale of the Texas Agricultural Consortium. Ain't no one smarter or got more steel in his spine than that man. We fought side by side in the Fourth Texas Infantry, back in the War between the States. He and I were only sixteen, but eager for battle, so they handed us rifles and marched us north. Joined up with General Lee at Sharpsburg, he'd send us in when he needed men who'd storm the ramparts of hell. Think you've been through some tough ones, McRae? We were outnumbered two to one and fought McClelland to a draw on Union soil. September 17th 1862, that was the day eight thousand died. It's still with me, the stench of blood and gunpowder and rotting flesh."

He stood up, walked over to the window and looked out at the passersby. "I'd have gone to my Maker with the rest of 'em if not for Harlon Gale. He's a force of nature, a man you don't want comin' after you, as more than a few Yankees found out." Garrison turned back toward my father. "Gale says citrus is the future of the Valley in South Texas. There's already a couple dozen pump houses been built along the Rio Grande to irrigate farmland, and dozens more planned. The railroad connecting Brownsville and St. Louis opens up come July and they'll run a line clear through to Starr County. Harlon figures they'll be shipping to New York, Chicago, all them northern markets that need oranges and grapefruit and the like. So here's the deal, Captain: I'm putting you in charge of South Texas. You're moving to Harlingen, a little town they used to call Six-Shooter Junction. Ain't much there right now other than a Ranger station, but it's growing fast. Money's coming into the Valley, and trouble's sure to follow. Need a hard man like you to keep the peace."

My father's eyes narrowed to a squint. *Maybe Bryce could add grapefruit rustling to his list of crimes of the future.*

"Doesn't add up," he told the major. "Maybe you'll have a few more bank heists to clean up after and some con men and hustlers to round up. You don't need me for that."

"You're right, I don't. That's penny-ante stuff."

"So just what kind of trouble are you worried about?"

Garrison removed an impressively large Perfecto from his vest pocket and took his time lighting it before deigning to answer.

"Civil unrest, McRae." He blew a smoke ring and watched it drift.

"I see," said my father, but something else was on his mind. *Stay clear of the Trans-Pecos,* he'd told Henry Midnight. All those notes he'd been scrawling on the map on his kitchen wall, the forbidden desires he tried to chase from his mind. What might not happen if he left El Paso?

"Started with the poll tax that was passed in '02," the major continued. "You hear much grumbling about that out here?"

"Some, from the Tejanos. Can't say I blame them. A poor man shouldn't have to part with a week's wages to cast his vote."

"Yeah?" Garrison curled his lip. "There's more coons and greasers than hard-working white men in this state, you want them calling the shots?"

My father had long since become inured to the parlance of small-minded bigots, but that morning he heard the words as Henry would have heard them.

A fuse lit at the base of his spine.

"They're citizens, Major, same as you and me."

"They sure as hell ain't the same as *me,* McRae. Figured after ten years south of the Mason-Dixon line you'd have your head on straight. But that's all right, I can put up with that Northern nonsense long as you keep putting men behind bars." Garrison flashed my father a humorless grin and tapped some ashes onto the floor. "Or six feet under."

Take it easy. My father tried to keep the flame from moving any higher up the fuse than the small of his back. *Garrison's no worse than most.* "So, trouble began with the poll tax. How about you tell me where grapefruit figure in."

"Valley land used to go for twenty-five cents an acre before word got out about the train into Brownsville. Sells for north of ten dollars these days, and Harlon's thinking twenty-five, maybe thirty by next year. Those Mexicans of ours been raising cattle in the Valley. Lost a good portion of their herds during the drought years and went into debt to the bankers. Well, now their property taxes are up forty-fold, heading toward a hundred-fold. So they got land and no way to keep it. Banks are foreclosing like nobody's business."

"And then selling to the Agricultural Consortium," said my father.

"You got that right." Garrison blew out a cloud of smoke that for a moment obscured him from view. "They're proud sons of bitches, those greasers, and hot headed to boot. This ain't sitting well with 'em, and it's only going to get worse. Last time we tangled over land was in '77. The El Paso Salt War. You can't have lived here without hearing of it."

My father nodded. Everyone knew of that bloody rebellion, but there was something else struggling to come to the surface of his consciousness, some other piece of the puzzle...

"Only time an entire company of Rangers surrendered," the major continued. "Twenty men! It's stuck in my craw all these years and I'll damn well make sure it don't happen again."

Salt.

The dream that had haunted my father's sleep early that morning broke loose from somewhere in the vaults of his mind.

He was having breakfast at the Guadalupe Café on Mills Avenue and finding his fried eggs and potatoes depressingly bland. There was no salt at his table, just a bowl of tabasco peppers sure to wreak havoc on his digestion. And not a waitress to be seen.

Next to him sat a Mestiza wearing a fringed shawl dyed emerald and sapphire blue. How strange—a woman dining out alone in El Paso! On her face were deep lines of sadness, but she turned to my father and smiled.

"You'll need this," she said, and handed him her salt-shaker. "Such a common thing, yes? And yet so precious."

"Thank you, Abuelita." My father could not look away from her eyes, dark as black onyx yet warm as a summer night. He felt as though he were looking through them to a depthless sky filled with stars...stars like grains of salt...

No longer was he Caleb McRae, but a Tejano whose family had for generations made the trek to the salt beds of the El Paso Valley. Some they'd use in their everyday lives, some in the silver mines, and the rest they'd barter along El Camino Real all the way north to Santa Fe. It was no one's and it was everyone's, and it had always been that way.

And then in 1866, done with slaughtering each other in the great Civil War, the Anglos allowed their people to file for mineral rights. No longer did the salt belong to all!

"What madness is this?" my father cried. "Will they next lay claim to the air we breathe, the water that slakes our thirst?"

He would pick up his rifle and make a stand in the name of all that is decent and right...

"McRae!" Garrison thundered. "You got something else you'd rather be doing?"

"No sir." My father blinked and took a moment to get the Major back in focus. "Just taking a moment to cogitate on the matter."

"Cogitate on this, Captain: I want you with me when I head out, day after tomorrow. Need you to beef up the South Texas battalion, bring on some men who shoot straight and ride hard. Men who'd rather die than turn tail and run." He took a last long puff and stubbed out his cigar. "But what's in it for you, right? Now we get to the good part. You're making what, a hundred a month? I'm popping that to one twenty-five. And there'll be a twenty-dollar gold piece any time you have to use deadly force dealing with them deadbeat ranchers. A danger bonus, if you will. Might just add up to a fair sum."

My father had walked away from a trust fund that would have paid him over five grand a year. It was funny enough to laugh at, if you were in a laughing mood. He stared at Garrison, his face a mask, the fuse burning just inches below his neck.

"Single guy like you travels light," said the major. "Anything more than your rifle and bedroll we can have sent on." He took out a new Perfecto and prepared to light up. "So, what do you say?"

Something shiny caught my father's eye; Garrison's gold cigar-cutter watch-fob, dangling from his vest pocket. That was new.

"Let me ask you something, boss. Are the Rangers funding that bonus, or Harlon Gale?"

Garrison raised his eyebrows but stayed silent.

"The banks aren't auctioning off those foreclosed ranches, are they," my father continued. "Just letting them go to the Consortium for the tax arrears." He could see the major's face growing red with anger, and for the first time that morning allowed himself a smile. "But the best part is, your pal Harlon's cutting you in on the deal."

"You yellow-dog Yankee bastard!" The major was on his feet, his hands balled into fists, a vein pulsing on his neck. "By God, you'll take back those words."

Ignition.

My father rose to his full height; Garrison was not a short man, but my father was a good three inches taller and his shoulders were broader than the Rio Grande.

Henry wouldn't waste his spit on this man.

It was as though a blast of wind had extinguished the blaze of anger in his mind. The adrenaline that had been pumping through his body abated. He took off his badge and set it next to the slice of grapefruit on his desk.

"Bryce will make a fine captain," he said, and walked away.

"Go on, leave with your tail between your legs. People been telling me what a queer bird you are, I just chose not to believe 'em. Well, you're finished, you can rot out here on the edge of nowhere or crawl back up north, makes no difference to me."

My father left the building and crossed El Paso Street, heading to his small apartment.

What was this unfamiliar feeling?

Ah: lightness. Peace.

He hesitated for a moment at the intersection of Wyoming and Mesa. Might the Houston and Dallas papers be in yet? No, too early.

For the first time since he was a child, my father was unsure what to do next.

Chapter Nine

A Texas Cowboy

Through an abstruse method of triangulation—a mystical mathematics—my father had determined Henry's location, and Achilles was bearing him swifter than eagles to the outlaw's lair. He dismounted at the mouth of a cave blocked by an enormous stone, managed to roll it aside, and entered the darkness within.

Where was Midnight?

Ahead he could make out a glimmer of light. My father wended his way forward, avoiding razor-sharp stalactites that hung from the cavern roof. He could hear the beating wings of vampire bats and smell their acrid odor.

Ah, there, at last! A man crouched before a fire, his back to my father, roasting a rabbit on a spit.

"Henry?"

The figure rose and turned.

My father gasped and fell to his knees.

A man robed in white, wounds in His hands, regarded him, a fierce anger burning in his eyes

"Repent! *You have set yourself on the path to perdition. The pit awaits. You will not always have this chance*—Repent!"

"Forgive me," my father whispered, touching his forehead to the cold stone floor, but the Lord was not so easily appeased. It seemed he was pounding his fist, or perhaps a staff, against the cavern wall...

Loud knocking on his front door woke my father from his dream.

He pulled the covers over his head. Two weeks had passed since he'd quit the Rangers. For the first few days he'd spent much of his time at the First Baptist Church, but his conscience troubled him; as the pastor droned on during Sunday service, or his fellow elders indulged in interminable prayers, his thoughts would drift back to the long, desperate trek through the desert with Henry by his side.

No one in El Paso seemed overly eager for his company once my father was no longer Captain Caleb McRae.

Indeed, who *was* he now?

"Go away!" he called out.

His tormentor knocked louder.

He climbed out of bed uttering rarely used oaths, put on a robe, picked up his Colt 45, and flung the door open. "You're disturbing the peace." He brandished his weapon. "*My* peace. Be off with you."

A slightly built, middle-aged man was looking up at him with raised eyebrows. My father hadn't bathed or shaved for some days, and his blond curls were in wild disarray. He realized with a sinking feeling that the sun was already approaching the zenith. How could he have slept till noon? And his caller looked oddly familiar, he'd seen him somewhere before. Yes, a picture in a book, but which he wasn't sure...

"Captain McRae," said the man. "Sorry if I've shown up at a bad time, but it's my one chance to see you." He gently pushed the barrel of my father's gun away from his face and smiled. "Now that feels a mite more hospitable. It's an honor to make your acquaintance. The name's Charlie Siringo."

My father stepped back, dumbstruck. "Sir, I read *A Texas Cowboy* when I was ten years old, and if I read it once I read it fifty times. That story of you going after Billy the Kid, well, that's pretty much why I'm here today." He opened the door wide. "Come in, please."

"That's right kind of you, Captain." Siringo followed him in and looked around. The windows were closed and the shades were drawn. Dishes were piled up in the sink. It was dismally dark and the air was stale.

"I'm no captain," said my father. "I resigned my commission."

"Yes, the news reached me," said Siringo. "That's pretty much why *I'm* here."

"Oh? Go on, have a seat." My father pointed to the kitchen table. "I'll boil us some coffee."

"Tell you what, Caleb. Why don't you go freshen up, pull on some trousers, and let me do the coffee-making."

Independent-minded as he was, my father knew when it was time to follow orders.

He came back ten minutes later to find Siringo had done a decent job of cleaning up the kitchen. Sunlight beamed through the open windows, and the aroma of strong coffee and sizzling bacon filled the air.

It was good to feel hungry again.

"Hope you don't mind my cooking up the sowbelly," said Siringo. "I'm a fair degree famished myself."

The two men polished off the bacon in short order and my father filled two mugs with steaming coffee.

"I heard enough to know you're a hell of a Ranger," said the detective. "Mind telling me why you quit?"

My father ran his index finger around the rim of his mug. "My boss and I just didn't see eye to eye, that's all. I loved the work."

"Okay. I'm going to take a wild guess you don't have anything else lined up just yet."

"You'd be right about that."

Siringo settled back in his chair and studied his host for a long moment. "There any phrenologists in this town?"

"You mean the docs that try to make sense of the shape of your skull? None that have hung out a shingle."

"Pity. Well, let me tell you a story. When I was not much older than you, I thought I was done with the cowpuncher's life, tried to settle down and run a business. Came home every night to my wife and little girl. But men like us, there's fire in our blood, isn't there."

My father's face reddened, though Siringo showed no sign of noticing.

"So," the detective continued, "back in '84 I was living in Caldwell, Kansas. One day my little lady and I see a handbill announcing a 'world-famous phrenologist' was going to be lecturing that evening at the Leland Hotel. Imagine that! I had not the slightest notion what he'd be talking about, but seeing as the circus wasn't in town, off we went. Lecturer turned out to be an elderly blind man, his eyes nothing but white. That old gent laid his hands on my head and claimed I was cut out to be a detective. Laughed it off at the time, but two years later I joined the Pinkerton Detective Agency. That was eighteen years ago, and I've loved most every minute since."

"I doubt you're shilling for a noggin noodler," said my father. "So I take it you're giving me some career advice, Mr. Siringo."

"Oh, more than that. If I recommend you, you're good as hired. And call me Charlie." He stared wistfully at his empty plate. "Got any bread or biscuits to sop up that bacon grease?"

"Just some hardtack, I think."

"Well that's better than using our fingers." Siringo stood up and walked over to the map on the kitchen wall while my father searched through his pantry. "Sorry, but I'm a professional snoop. You mind?"

My father looked over. "No secrets there."

"Judging from the crimes you've noted, looks like you're tracking the Midnight Bandito. Heard about you going after him a few years back."

"If I ever meet anyone who *hasn't* heard, I'd like to shake his hand."

Siringo laughed. "They get away sometimes, Caleb, you do the best you can and move on. I'm just surprised Midnight's stayed in Texas this long, hasn't lit out for the territories or the northwest." He turned from the map and looked at my father. "It's almost like he wants to get caught."

My father shrugged. "He's not my concern anymore."

"Yeah?" The detective looked at him dubiously. "There's an entry here marked day before last. Look, we got a lot in common, you and me. I *live* for putting bad guys behind bars, just ask my ex-wife. I've chased outlaws in Mexico City, nabbed gold thieves in Juneau, Alaska. Pinkertons put me on the Union Pacific train robbery in '99, only just wrapped it up."

"Heard Butch Cassidy was behind that one." My father brought over the hard tack and the men dug in.

"Yes, Mr. Robert LeRoy Parker, the most daring desperado of our time, though your man Midnight might give him a run for his money, I suppose. Butch's Wild Bunch made off with fifty grand and killed two sheriffs who were on their trail. I posed as an outlaw myself, became the gang's best buddy, learned all their secrets. Rode with them from the New Mexico Territory to their mountain hideout in Hole-in-the-Wall Wyoming, and I can tell you there's some godforsaken desert in between. Now most of that Wild Bunch is either locked up or dead. Except for Cassidy and the Sundance Kid, they lit out for South America in '01, and good riddance."

The two men shared stories for the next few hours and continued their conversation over dinner at the Guadeloupe Café.

"So here's how it is," said Siringo as the meal drew to a close. "Even loners like us can't do it all by ourselves. Tom Horn was a great help to me on the Union Pacific case, he was another fellow who went his own way, like you and me. Only trouble with Horn, he was always too quick to pull the trigger, got himself hanged in Cheyenne last November. So the Pinkertons are short on men who think like I do, men I can trust. You join up, Caleb, we'd work together more than a few times, I can tell you that."

My father looked down at the remains of his steak and potatoes and thought for a bit.

"Sounds like I could expect to travel quite a fair amount if I did sign on," he said. "I mean, outside of Texas."

He could hardly believe how pitiful his voice sounded.

"Well, sure. We go where we're needed. Where we're sent."

"Of course." My father lifted his head to meet the detective's intense gaze. "I can't tell you what an honor this is, Charlie, you wanting to work with me. But I'm going to have to sleep on it."

Siringo studied my father for a moment, then leaned back in his chair and smiled.

"You ain't ready, I can see that plain as day. Look, they ever ask me to chase down Mr. Midnight, I'll get in touch, see if we can't at least team up on that one. But I need to head out before the sun sets. Going east this time—West Virginia. Folks been murdering each other over there like there's no tomorrow. Which, come to think on it, there *won't* be for a good number of them. So I'll just pay the bill and saddle up."

My father started to protest and Siringo waved him off.

"This one's on the Pinkertons." He took a firm grasp of the check and reached for his billfold. "Can't remember when I last had to use my own money for a meal."

Outside the café, the men shook hands and went their separate ways.

Meeting his childhood hero had lifted my father's spirits considerably, but now he trudged along, eyes downcast, a black mood settling deep into his soul. The thought of returning to his apartment oppressed him. He wandered down empty streets to the edge of town, lingering near the Mission Nuestra Señora de Guadalupe as its bells chimed the hour.

What Hamlet-like indecision was this—too fearful of his own desires to seek out Henry Midnight, yet unwilling to repent? He could hear his younger self screaming at him in fury. What wouldn't he have given for a chance to work with Charlie Siringo? He could only imagine what the eighteen-year-old Caleb would do if set loose on this miserable incarnation of his own self, ten years later!

The butt-end of a rifle stock smashed into the side of my father's head, sending him reeling. A second blow knocked him to the ground.

He looked up through a film of blood into the smirking face of Lucius Garner.

"Hey, Beau," said the elder of the Garner brothers as he stripped the lawman of his weapons. "Break in those new shit-kicking boots of yours, why don't ya."

"Never *could* do your own thinking, Beau," said my father.

A steel-tipped toe caught him hard in the solar plexus and he vomited his lunch and dinner.

"That's for two years in the lock-up," said Lucius. "And we're just getting started."

"Sumbitch puked on my new boots," said Beau. "Now that makes me mad."

"If I pound his skull in with the Winchester, how long 'fore I break through to his brains? I'm thinking five or ten good whacks, tops."

"Only one way to find out." Beau reached for the rifle. "Lemme have a crack at it."

It was then my father heard the sound of a man chanting, saw blurrily through his one good eye the approach of a darkly hooded Jesuit from the nearby Mission, his robe fastened by a cord around his prodigious waist. *Just what I need,* he thought. *Not the cavalry but a fat monk.*

"*Fratres, agnoscámus peccátanostra!*" pronounced the newcomer.

"Get lost padre," said Lucius. "I'd already've blown your head off, if it weren't bad luck to kill a priest."

"My child," said the monk, who spoke with a thick accent my father could not quite place. "Perhaps you do not understand. I have come to take your confessions."

The brothers laughed heartily at that one.

He's not Mexican, thought my father. *Maybe Spanish.*

"But this is no laughing matter." The monk moved to within a few yards of the outlaws. "Before I can administer the sacrament of extreme unction, you must be in a state of grace. For this, heartfelt confession is required."

"Back off, padre, *now.*"

"Are you choosing to die in your sin?" asked the Jesuit, incredulous. "The consequences are rather severe."

"What the hell—" Lucius' eyes narrowed and he began to swing the Winchester around, but the monk was too quick for him, his robe flashed open and he began blasting away, a Remington revolver in each hand.

Beau fell on top of my father and rolled off, his face frozen in an idiot's grin. Lucius, stretched out nearby, appeared to have four nostrils and three eyes.

"It was wise counsel our Lord gave His disciples, to carry a sword." The monk holstered his revolvers. "And two suffice, indeed." He made the sign of the cross over each of the brothers, murmured a few words in Latin, then kneeled by my father's side, stanched the bleeding, and wiped his face with the edge of his robe.

"You will not look quite so handsome for a while," he said, "but I do not think you are too badly hurt. Sister Angelica is a mistress of the medical arts, and can tend to your wounds in the Mission. Let us rest here for a bit, then I will help you to your feet and we will manage together the few steps across the street."

My father gaped up in bewilderment. It seemed he'd lived through something similar a thousand years ago, in another life. Hard to focus, though, with a dozen demons pounding on anvils inside his brain.

"These robes can be exceedingly useful at times," said my father's rescuer. He threw back his cowl, revealing a pudgy face, fine head of fiery red hair, and a full beard. "Allow me to introduce myself, Captain McRae. I am Father Baltasar Benedito de Souza, at your service!"

Chapter Ten

Unstoppable Force, Immovable Object

"There's something I've never understood," I said to my father, breaking the sullen silence that had prevailed during our dinner. "If de Souza was right there in El Paso, why hadn't you ever gone to see him to find out whether Midnight had told you the truth? You didn't want to know, did you."

It was April of 1945. We were living in Los Angeles, where my father pastored a Free Will Baptist church. I'd just turned seventeen and was angry that he'd refused to give me the parental consent required to enlist in the army. Any subject would do for a fight.

"You're not as clever as you think you are," he replied. "Henry knew the priest would vouch for him, either way. You've not yet learned to think before you speak."

It was not until years later that I learned the true nature of my father's feelings for the outlaw; in my youth, he had only ever told me they were good friends and business partners of a sort. I never imagined he saw Henry as a temptation to be avoided, a test of his faith. De Souza was the gateway to something he desired but could not imagine ever having, a priest who lurked on the periphery of the Outer Darkness.

"You talk all the time of justice," I said, determined to find some new angle to argue. "Was de Souza acting justly when he gunned down the Garners?"

"It's all too easy to second-guess a man's decisions, though I'll tell you this: de Souza had the drop on them, and still emptied both revolvers into those men. Siringo would have taken them alive."

"Really? You told me those two were cold-blooded killers. Letting them live would have meant risking both your lives."

"There are worse things than death, Matthew. We die well if we die doing what we think is right."

"Yes, but what's right? That Bible—" I pointed to the King James he'd been reading from during our meal—"is all over the place, bloodthirsty one minute, peace-loving the next. Does a Christian turn the other cheek if it means leaving others defenseless? How far do you take it, dad? Should we stand by like sheep and let the Japs take over? You really think it's wrong for us to fight?"

"You've heard my sermons," he said softly. "Shedding blood is not the Way of the Lord."

"Maybe that's why fewer and fewer folks are showing up on Sunday mornings."

"I follow my conscience, boy, no matter the cost."

"Yeah, well Conchies are cowards, and they talk just like you. Hiding behind their Bibles to avoid the draft. I just don't want the war to end before I turn eighteen."

"How have we come to this?" my father asked, more to himself than to me. He leaned back in his chair, a deep sadness in his eyes. "It doesn't seem so long ago when you'd crawl into my bed, frightened from some childish dream, and I'd hold you and whisper stories into your ear until you fell asleep."

I had no such sentimental memories. His words only stoked my anger, and I rose to my feet.

"I'm not a child any longer, who believes whatever nonsense you spout. The same God you claim frowns on killing is only too ready to consign non-believers to eternal torment. Well, even the Garner boys would have finished you off at some point. I'd sooner worship *them!*"

That did it. My father pushed back his chair and stood, his face red with rage.

"I'll not have blasphemy in my house!" he roared.

"Just give me that consent and I'll be out of your life. Tonight. Right now."

"I will not."

He was both unstoppable force and immovable object, buffeting my past and standing in the way of my future.

I turned and walked away, thinking, even if he gives me a licking, it will only sting for a while.

One more year and I'll be free.

Chapter Eleven

A Man of Flesh and Blood

Sister Angelica stitched the deep gash in my father's left temple, applied a poultice made from the pulp of a prickly-pear cactus, and kept him awake for several hours for fear that he might lapse into a coma. This last task she accomplished by leading him and Fr. de Souza in the singing of hymns, accompanied with considerable gusto on the accordion. When the priest led him at last to a small chamber and helped him into bed, he slept well into the afternoon of the following day.

My father woke to see the icons on the wall opposite his bed come gradually into focus. Stern-faced saints and a doe-eyed Mary, gilded in gold leaf and set aglow by the sunlight slanting through a grated window.

Where was he? The events of the previous day came back to him in bits and pieces. Charlie's sad smile when they shook hands and parted ways. Lucius Garner's malicious grin. He reached his hand up to touch the poultice. Ah, yes. The nun's tender mercies. Her music was another matter.

After a while my father sat up, swung his legs around, and set his feet on the floor. A little shaky but not too bad, all things considered. De Souza had taken no chances with the Garners, he'd blasted them six times each. *Father* de Souza, he reminded himself.

He studied the Virgin Mary, who was gazing sorrowfully on the infant Jesus. She'd been so young when Gabriel appeared with his terrible and wonderful news. *I am a servant of the Lord,* she'd said. Imagine, the fate of all creation resting on the narrow shoulders of a teenage girl. And then Simeon's grim prophecy, *A sword shall pierce through thy own soul also.* Even his words could not have prepared her for what was to come.

The gravity of parenthood made his head spin even more than it already was. Would *he* ever be a father? It seemed a far-fetched notion. Henry had thought he'd make a good one, though. Surely he'd do a better job than his own parents.

Strange thoughts! He concentrated on clearing his mind and stood up, steadying himself with one hand against the cold stone wall.

He had made his way about halfway down the long corridor outside his little cell when Fr. de Souza caught up with him.

It didn't take much convincing for my father to accept the priest's invitation to rest and recuperate at the Mission. Returning to his dreary apartment held no appeal. He sent word to the stables to make sure Achilles would be well taken care of and resolved to spend his time seeking direction from the Lord.

Fr. de Souza invited him to five o'clock mass before dinner. *Really isn't half bad,* he thought, *the way these Papists go about their business.* The daily masses and hourly prayers, the comforting darkness of the chapel. He especially liked the Benediction on Sunday morning, listening to hymns and Psalms, smelling the incense that billowed from the thurible being swung by an elderly priest. Frankincense and myrrh, Fr. de Souza told him. The sweetness of the Lord, the bitterness of death.

My father was intrigued by the gold- and silver-plated sunburst, bejeweled and topped by a cross, that Fr. Alejo raised toward the end of the Benediction. The *monstrance,* such an odd word for something so beautiful.

"It holds the consecrated host," Fr. de Souza said softly. "Christ himself is here, blessing us."

Hoc est enim corpus meum. The bread and the wine, what far-fetched fantasy to think of them as the real body and blood of the Lord of the universe! Roman nonsense, but still, there was something about the ceremony that stirred him, the mystery of it, as the priest held up the host and the Brothers chanted the *Tantum Ergo* in their black, hooded robes.

"I lived for a time in the city of Bogota, in South America," Fr. de Souza told him over dinner that evening. "The San Ignacio Church there possesses a most remarkable monstrance that took three goldsmiths seven years to sculpt, after which they encrusted it with emeralds. So many, in fact, that it became known as *La Lechuga.* The lettuce." He laughed, finished off his second glass of wine, and smacked his lips. "A clever ploy by my Jesuit forbears to hide gems from the Spanish Crown during the Kingdom of the New Granada." He dropped his voice to a conspiratorial whisper. "I tell you this because our mutual friend and I were inspired to adopt a similar strategy."

It was the first time Fr. de Souza had made even an oblique reference to Henry Midnight. My father said nothing, but remembered the rubies in the Mission's monstrance and thought back through the crimes he'd been tracking. He'd always been dubious of the jewel thefts attributed to Henry and considered them merely an embellishment of the outlaw's legend.

"Of course we'll sell them, eventually, and give the proceeds to the poor," the priest added, motioning for one of the Fathers to pass the wine decanter. "It's all just a matter of timing."

After Fr. de Souza took his leave, explaining he'd be gone for several days, my father began spending time in the Mission library, looking for something to occupy his mind.

"What do you know of our founder, St. Ignatius?" asked Fr. Alejo, coming upon my father leafing through the pages of a book.

"Not a thing."

"Ah, you might enjoy his story. Inigo Lopez de Loyola was quite a cowboy himself in his younger days. A swordsman who fought duels at the slightest provocation! And who could never resist a pretty girl."

"I would like to hear more," said my father, "though it would be a waste of time trying to convert me to Roman ways. I stand before my Savior needing no intercessor, responsible for my own decisions. I could never take orders from the Pope."

"Nor pray to the saints or the Blessed Virgin, I imagine." The old priest sat down next to him. "So let us simply talk as brothers in Christ. You speak as many do in this country, with a great reverence for individual freedom. You're familiar with St. Paul's Epistle to the Romans, yes? Do you recall how he introduced himself?"

My father thought for only a moment. "As a servant of Christ."

"Yes, and the sort of servant he meant we would today call a slave. There's a divine paradox there, don't you think? For never was there a freer soul than St. Paul, even when bound in chains. His freedom came from being a slave of Christ."

"Christ's slave, not the Pope's."

"In that we're quite in agreement," said Fr. Alejo. "Let me ask you, my friend: what do you mean when you speak of freedom?"

"Simply the absence of constraints on what a man can do."

The priest smiled. "A most American answer. You measure your freedom by the extent to which others limit your actions. St. Ignatius looked *inside* and sought freedom from impulses and obsessions and desires born of egoism, ambition, and pride. From everything except the will of God."

My father heard footsteps echoing down stone hallways and the faint sound of an organ playing a hymn he could not quite recall. Looking inside himself was the last thing he wanted to do. Damnation almost seemed a tolerable alternative.

"Forgive me if this offends you," said Fr. Alejo, "but you strike me as a man who is not comfortable in his own skin. You are at a crossroads, unless I am very much mistaken. I have been through much in my long life, more than you might imagine. If you ever care to unburden yourself, mine is a willing ear."

My father looked down at the floor. "Thank you, that's very kind, but there is really nothing I have to say." The wound in his temple throbbed, and for a moment he wished the pain were yet *more* intense.

"Will you accompany me to the chapel for five o'clock mass?"

My father nodded his assent.

"I offer you this most Ignatian advice," said the priest as they walked together through a cobblestone courtyard. "Make no decision under the influence of an inordinate attachment. And in your bleakest moments, remember that God may be found in all things. I will pray for you, Captain McRae."

The sun's last rays set the chapel's rose window on fire, Christ at the center in crimson and cobalt blue, judging all creation.

An inordinate attachment. Well, wasn't that exactly what he'd been praying to be freed from? Surely he'd be judged by his actions, not the emotions, however potent, that roiled his thoughts and plagued his dreams.

The organ poured forth music filled with longing, the incense drugged my father with its sweetness. High above sat Christ the judge on his heavenly throne; but there He was also, behind the altar, on a life-size crucifix affixed to the wall. Jesus, man of flesh and blood, all but naked, hanging there in agony, pierced and broken.

Sharing in my father's pain.

Later on he knelt in prayer on the stone floor by the side of his bed and stayed there until it was time for morning mass.

Two days later Father Alejo handed him a Western Union telegram.

MIDNIGHT CAPTURED IN AUSTIN.

EXECUTION IMMINENT. OUR GUEST MUST MAKE HASTE.

DE SOUZA

A remarkable sense of calm came over my father. *When the time comes for decision, it's not so very hard. Whatever the High Council of Heaven may make of it, there is no other thing I can do.*

He bid farewell to the priests and to Sister Angelica, returned home for his bedroll and Winchester, and within the hour Achilles was bearing him east.

Part Two

Enter the Avengers

Chapter Twelve

Chasing Butterflies

"Well if it ain't Caleb McRae," said Tom Tetley, captain of the Ranger squadron that covered the Texas Hill Country. He was standing in the entryway of the Austin County Jail, a red-brick, fortress-like structure whose fourth-floor tower served as a gallows. "Here to find out how I caught the bandito? Sure as hell didn't have to chase him to hell and back, return empty-handed with my clothes in shreds and my ass on fire."

"Where you keeping him, Tom?"

"Aw, you sore? Real shame Garrison had to give you the boot. If you're hard up for cash, we got stalls need mucking, just say the word."

"I'm going to ask you one more time, politely," my father said softly, and there was something in his voice that gave the captain pause.

"Hey, just having fun. What the hell you want to see Midnight for, anyway? We need to keep him alive for another three days, then he'll swing."

My father stared at him, dead-eyed.

"Two flights up, far end on the right. I'll give you ten minutes."

My father swept past him.

"Know how I got him, McRae?" Tetley called after him. "Outsmarted the bastard. He fell right—"

The rest of the captains's words were lost in the clatter of my father's boots up the stone jailhouse steps.

"Been a while, Sean." He exchanged salutes with the guard on duty on the third floor, a man he remembered from his first years with the Rangers. "I'm going to have a few words with your notorious prisoner."

"Good to see you, Captain." Nobody ever forgot Caleb McRae. "But we're under orders not to open his cell door."

"That's all right, I won't be long."

All he could think of, approaching the outlaw's cell, was how loudly his heart was beating in his chest.

Henry, seated on the floor of the bare cell in shackles, regarded him with a wry smile. He was pale, and thinner than my father remembered, his raven hair yet longer, cascading over his shoulders.

"What are you doing here?" my father asked gruffly.

"Waiting for you."

My father eyed his chains. "Are those bonds so much stronger than the ones you slipped three years ago?"

Henry laughed. "I could be a free man in fifteen minutes if there were anywhere I cared to go."

"Then what—"

"Oh, hush, I'll explain in a moment." Henry rose with some difficulty and approached the barred door. "I was thinking of our conversation concerning this New Jerusalem you rave about. You told me if I missed the darkness whilst in that fair city, I could just close my eyes. And if I did, Caleb, might I not then sleep, and if so, perchance, find myself beset by dreams?"

"I suppose. What of it?"

"Come now, your dreams cannot be so different from mine. Even in the New Heavens and New Earth, even in the Hopi's Fifth World, the specters of past sins, our moments of cowardice and treachery and greed, might still haunt our sleep."

The redness of Henry's lips, accentuated by the ghostly whiteness of his skin, unsettled my father. He looked down and considered his response.

"You're thinking of it the wrong way," he said, returning the outlaw's gaze at last. "It's not our bad dreams that most oppress us, but the ones in which our deepest desires are satisfied. Our imagined happiness vanishes like morning mist when we arise. What emptiness follows! But imagine, Henry, waking to a world infinitely better than the best of your dreams."

"Ah." A smile spread across Midnight's face. "You never cease to surprise me, Caleb. I've missed you."

Their faces were separated only by the thickness of the iron bars.

"And I've missed you."

My father felt again the strange vertigo he'd experienced with Henry in the desert. *Nothing's as it should be; it's as though I were looking up into the night sky and seeing the dark side of the moon.*

He took a step back. "Tetley's real proud of himself for having snared you."

Anything to change the subject. Moments of cowardice, indeed.

Henry smiled. "The man thought I'd be tempted by a travelling exhibit of Spanish doubloons, the whole thing couldn't have been more transparent. But here's the funny part, Caleb. Before I let him catch me, I stole the coins, every one, and replaced them with the cleverest counterfeits you've ever seen."

"I imagine de Souza is off to find a buyer south of the border," said my father. "Perhaps he'll trade them for rubies, and Fr. Alejo can fit a few more in the monstrance. But be serious while we still have time, and tell me what devilishness you're up to."

"On the contrary, I've set myself on a path most angelic."

He reached awkwardly into his pocket, withdrew a scrap torn from the local paper, and pressed it into my father's hand.

GOVERNOR'S DAUGHTER AT DEATH'S DOOR

17-Year-Old Presented Only Last Month at Austin Debutante Ball

The article included a grainy photograph of a well-dressed young woman with elaborately coiffed hair.

"A mysterious fever," Henry continued, "and the poor girl's in pain with every breath. The local physicians are useless, and even the specialist brought in from St. Louis is stumped. Eminent man, too, with spectacles and a long gray beard. So here's my plan: I'm going to cure her in return for a full pardon. What do you think?"

"What makes you imagine the governor will let you anywhere near his daughter?"

"My Jesuit friends and I were rather substantial contributors to his campaign. We greased the wheels with both candidates, if truth be told—Governor Lanham's a loathsome swine, really, but one does what one must when the people's welfare is at stake."

"There's still the small matter of actually healing the girl."

"Fear not, Caleb; I learned at the feet of a wonderfully wise Hopi medicine man. Even as we speak, Fr. de Souza is chasing after Monarch butterflies. He's likely found the little creatures on some canyon bottom, lighting on the orange blossoms of the butterfly weed. Its roots cure all manner of lung ailments. Flatulence as well, you might note. And the good Father is not without some arcane knowledge of the healing arts himself. Has he told you of his time in Bogota?"

"Only in passing."

"A tree grows in the Andes mountains, the *cinchona*. The priests who accompanied the conquistadors were for the most part a pestilence on the face of the earth, but I'll say this to their credit, they discovered the cinchona's miraculous curative properties. The peelings taken from its trunk are known as *Jesuit bark*, and they extinguish the most hellish of fevers. When Louis the Fourteenth's son was in the throes of malaria delirium, it was that very bark which cured him."

My father heard boots on the staircase but kept his eyes on Henry. It was a small miracle they'd had any privacy at all.

"I'm among the few who know the formula that saved the Dauphin," Henry continued, talking as though they had all the time in the world. "Seven grams of rose leaves, two ounces of lemon juice, and a strong decoction of the peelings, served in wine. Which variety is unclear, but given the tender age of the patient, I'm thinking a pale rosé."

"McRae!" Tetley called out in the most stentorian voice he could muster. "Time's up."

"Go," whispered the erstwhile outlaw. "Stay at the Mission Santa María, Fr. de Souza will find you when he returns."

It was only years later, when my father saw Harry Houdini perform one of his legendary feats of escape wizardry, that he understood why Henry Midnight had allowed himself to be captured. It was showmanship, pure and simple. No longer content with engineering a jailbreak by conventional means, he'd found a way to transcend every escape he'd made before.

That day in Austin, my father understood that Henry needed to be loosed from more than shackles and iron bars. The lawless life he'd been leading had boxed him in, and only grace could set him free.

Chapter Thirteen

Freedom

Two days after my father's arrival in Austin, the governor condescended to allow Henry's friends to wait in one of the parlors of his great mansion while the prisoner attended to his daughter. They'd been supplied with tea and lemon cookies and a tray of petit fours in white icing which Fr. de Souza gobbled with considerable gusto.

"My God, man, but you've an appetite!" Dr. Schotz, the eminent physician from St. Louis, looked at the priest with undisguised contempt.

Fr. de Souza seemed oblivious to the doctor's remark, but my father bristled. "Watch your tongue, sir, when you address a man of the cloth."

"Man of the cloth, indeed! You're charlatans, both of you, associating with that long-haired desperado. If you'd any decency at all, you'd let the poor girl die in peace."

"Oh? Then what are *you* still doing here, sawbones?"

"Impostors and frauds!" Schotz seized the last of the petit fours and stormed out.

My father shook his head. "He may have a point, Baltasar. What are we counting on, do you think—our prayers, your Jesuit bark, or the Hopi's Butterfly Weed?"

"A most mysterious alchemy of the three," the priest replied. "I'm not concerned; our friend is a man possessed by the Holy Spirit."

"I'd like to think so. And yet, despite your witness and mine, Henry's yet to come to Christ."

"It's more a matter of whether Christ has come to him, is it not?"

"Isn't that yet more damning?" asked my father. "To refuse to answer when the Son of God is knocking at his door?"

"The Lord is perhaps more patient than you, my friend." De Souza dipped a lemon cookie in his tea and took a contemplative nibble. "But I question your assumption. Why are you so sure Henry has *not* answered the Lord's call?"

"Do you mean to tell me he now believes?"

"Not as you do, to be sure. But in the thrust of Jesus' teachings, in the gloriously impossible demands of the Sermon on the Mount, yes, Henry Midnight believes with all his heart. He may not recognize the source of his belief; he surely fails each day to live up to what he believes, as do we all; but he believes."

My father regarded him dubiously. "We can agree he believes in justice, in helping the hungry and helpless and oppressed—but if that suffices, does salvation come by works, not faith?"

"Oh, *that* tiresome canard." Fr. de Souza slurped some tea. "Who knows how God calls a man, and what He calls him to do? Abraham showed his faith through *action*—by following El Shaddai into the great unknown. Many set their ample bottoms in church pews on Sunday mornings and pride themselves on their faith in God, yet never *live* that faith. What our Savior will say to them on the Day of Judgment, I shudder to think; but if Henry met his maker this very afternoon, I do not doubt the Lord would greet him as his good and faithful servant. And then I suspect even Señor Midnight would bend the knee."

To this my father made no answer.

Henry was escorted to the parlor by deputies after he'd ministered to Annabelle Lanham for nearly four hours. Dark circles shadowed his eyes and his shirt was stained with sweat. When the guards took their stations outside the parlor door, he collapsed on the couch.

"You might avail yourself of these cucumber sandwiches," said de Souza. "I can attest they've been freshly made."

"How's the girl?" asked my father.

Henry shrugged. "I've done all I can. Now we wait."

"It is in the hands of God," said the priest. "Let us bow our heads in prayer."

My father stole a glance at Henry, who had shut his eyes and was murmuring softly—but was he praying to the true God of heaven, or to Tawa, or Spider Grandmother, or some nebulous Great Spirit?

Such thoughts distracted him from the yet more perplexing matter of what life might be like if Henry's wild plan for pardon succeeded. If they were both free men.

And yet, am *I free?* my father wondered. Father Alejo knew better.

And if not, whose prisoner was he?

A considerable commotion broke out somewhere in the mansion, with shouts and screams and a great stomping of boots on marble floors.

The door swung open and a large gentleman burst in, his face streaked with tears, while Tom Tetley stood just outside, scowling.

"Her fever has broken!" announced the governor, his voice hoarse with emotion. "My Annabelle sat up and kissed me and asked if we might set a date for a cotillion ball. So we did!" He laughed with joy. "Y'all are invited, even the Pope's man here, so make sure and leave your calling cards." He knelt in front of Henry, who alone had stayed seated, and handed him a document marked by the Great Seal of the State of Texas. "Henry Midnight, you are hereby granted a full and unconditional pardon."

Henry nodded and smiled softly in thanks.

"You steer clear of trouble now, son. We ain't doing this a second time, you hear?"

"Count on it, gov'nor," Henry replied, putting on a thick Cockney accent. "It's the strait gate for me."

"Well I'm glad to hear that, Midnight, I truly am. Now if you'll excuse me, I've much to do, Mrs. Lanham is a bit overwrought."

The governor left, followed by a flurry of servants and aides.

Tetley watched them go, then turned back to his former prisoner with a sneer. "You don't fool me for one damn moment."

Henry blew him a kiss.

The captain flew at him, but my father's massive frame blocked the doorway.

"It's over, Tom."

"This ain't over, not by a long shot," the captain snarled. "Not for Garrison, and not for me." He stood there another moment, glowering, then walked away.

My father closed the door. "Congratulations, Henry." He put out his hand.

Midnight, ignoring the great proffered paw, stood and wrapped my father in a bear hug.

My father patted him awkwardly on the shoulder and looked at Fr. de Souza for help.

"Surely a celebration is in order!" proclaimed the priest.

"Indeed." Henry disentangled himself. "Let's see if Josiah Johnson's place lives up to his boasts. It's quite popular, though. How would you feel, Caleb, being seen there with me?"

"A former lawman and a former outlaw, together, is that what you mean?"

Henry just smiled.

"Well, then," said my father. "Let's head over to Johnson's and dine."

"Splendid," said Fr. de Souza, and he slid the remaining cucumber sandwiches into his cassock pockets.

Chapter Fourteen

Portrait of Prometheus

Josiah Johnson's Roadhouse and Inn was a rowdy establishment that smelled of beer, sweat, sawdust, and well-done slabs of prime beef. Its eponymous owner, my father discovered, was a small man who seemed to consist mostly of an astonishingly large and unruly beard.

"Josiah here made quite a name for himself fighting the Comanche in the Red River War," said Henry. "Then he soured on the American side, befriended Chief Quanah Parker, learned their language, and lived with them for a time. Your old gang had more than a little to do with his conversion," Henry added, addressing my father, who looked inquiringly at their host.

"I wasn't sorry to hear you left that legion of locusts," said Josiah. "Quanah's mother was a white woman who'd been kidnapped by Comanche when she was a child. The Rangers nabbed her during a raid, back when Quanah was a child, brought her back to her white family. She was thirty-three years old by then. Starved herself to death when they wouldn't let her return to her people. And that's just one story. Only thing crueler than *killing* an Indian is—"

"You're a damn cheatin' scoundrel!"

The shout came from halfway across the room, where a poker game was in progress.

A weather-beaten old-timer in overalls was raking in a large pile of greenbacks. The loser, a younger man, slid back his chair, stood, and reached for his revolver. Josiah pulled a sawed-off shotgun from under his duster and was at their table a moment later.

The room fell silent.

"Don't move, don't even *breathe,* Sam Yokum." Josiah pressed the double barrels to the base of Yokum's skull. "Sweetpea here don't need to cheat to take your money, you just never could play this game. Here's the way it is: I'm going to take your pistol—" he reached for it gingerly and slipped it into his pocket—"and you're going home to mama. I might possibly give it back in the morning. Now *git.*"

Josiah watched Yokum slink away.

"Ladies and gents!" he announced, walking back to my father's table. "We have here with us my good friend, the once notorious outlaw, Henry Midnight, who this very day was pardoned by the governor of our great state." He put a meaty claw on Henry's shoulder. "You haven't done nothing—what the hell's the word—*untoward* since then, have you, Henry?"

"No sir. I'm a new man, as honest as the day is long."

"Well there you have it! Your wallets are safe enough, boys, but I'll caution you to keep a close watch on your wives."

There was a ripple of laughter. Some mock threats were called out to Henry, a new hand was dealt at the poker table, and the muffled roar of conversation once more filled the room.

"There's a blind fellow plays the guitar and sings here on Saturday nights," said Josiah. "Wrote a song couple years back called 'The Ballad of Midnight and McRae.' Way he sang it, a man would think Caleb here was chasing you yet." He clapped Henry on the shoulder and then winked at my father. "If you ever do snare him, Captain, better keep a tight grip. He's a slippery sumbitch."

He laughed and walked off to banter at another table.

My father's face tensed. He was about to mutter something to Henry when a wiry man with an impressively large nose addressed Fr. de Souza.

"Excuse me, good Father, but you wear the black robes of the Society of Jesus, yes?"

"I do indeed." The priest peered up at him and smiled. "It seems the wings of the morning have carried us both far from home, my friend. From your accent, I take you for a man from the Basque country. I, Father Baltasar de Souza, am Portuguese, myself."

"Yes, I'm a proud Basque, like your St. Ignatius, blessed be his name. Until my twenty-third year I lived in San Sebastian, not ten kilometers from Loyola. Allow me to introduce myself, I am Abarran Zabala. My Christian name is Basque for *Abraham*. My little family—" he gestured toward what seemed at least a dozen men, women, and children spread out over the next two tables—"is not yet so numerous as the stars in the heavens or the grains of sand on the shore, but my Arrosa and I, we are working on it."

A formidable red-headed woman, who'd just quieted the two youngest and most rambunctious of the Zabala clan merely by raising one eyebrow, turned toward my father's table.

"Eh, big talker, you will be lucky if I do not make you sleep on the floor tonight."

Abarran laughed, kissed his wife, and turned back to the priest.

"Pull up a chair and drink with us, sir," said Henry, "if you can spare the time before your next act of procreation. I am the 'once notorious' Henry Midnight, and this gentleman beside me is my nemesis—and dear friend!—Caleb McRae."

"Barkeep!" called out Fr. de Souza. "Another bottle of red!"

Much shaking of hands and drinking of toasts ensued.

"You're a long ways from home," said Josiah. "What drew you Zabalas to Texas?"

"Ha! That is, as they say, a long story."

"Make it a good one," said Henry, "and we'll keep your glass filled."

"Very well, we Basques are anything but shy. My tale begins in 1876, the year of disaster, when the forces of Alfonso the Twelfth overran our sovereign state. My brother Ganiz had a young child, and I was betrothed; we resolved to flee rather than be conscripted into the Spanish army and sent off to die in their infernal wars. But where to go, what to do? We drank and sang and cried to heaven! What then should come but a letter from our uncle Gorka, who had emigrated to Argentina many years before, then sought his fortune in California panning for gold. If he didn't find riches, still, he made enough to buy a herd of sheep from a rancher's widow in Elko, Nevada. A thousand ewes and lambs, a few proud rams, and a border collie named Sirius." He crossed himself at the mention of the dog's name. "Dear Sirius, without whom he surely would have failed. Such an animal!

When he passed on, Gorka built him a tomb worthy of the pharaohs of Egypt. We joined my uncle twenty-seven years ago, and Ganiz and I, we have shepherded in the Ruby Mountains ever since." The Basque turned to Fr. de Souza. "I ask you, Father, is there a nobler profession than shepherd?"

"None, to be sure," said the priest, and he refilled all four glasses.

"My uncle joined his faithful Sirius not long ago," Abarran continued, "and my brother and I have decided to raise cattle along with sheep. We've saved our profits these many years, and will make our purchase tomorrow, then send the beeves on by rail. My brother stayed behind in Nevada, and I brought my family that they might at last see something of the world." He took a long draught of wine and leaned back in his chair. "So—such is my story!"

"And a fine one it is," said Henry. "Who are you buying from, if I might ask?"

"Mr. Carter James of the Bar Lazy J."

"He's a fair man, people tell me; I never rustled any of his herd. Your family raised livestock in the old country, I take it?"

"Ha! My brother Ganiz was a stone mason. I was a carpenter."

"It appears you are living the *imitatio Dei,* "said Fr. de Souza. "I am impressed!"

Glasses were raised and much wine gulped down in Abarran's honor.

"Thank you, you are too kind. *Livestock!* As a boy, I never imagined such a life, yet here I am, and glad of it. In olden times, you know, we Basques could hardly be bothered with cows and sheep—nothing less than *whales* could excite us! O, my friends, no people have ever hunted the leviathan like the Basques. Our parish records show a Zabala, some sixteen generations removed, who spent his days in a stone watchtower overlooking the harbor, and beyond that, the Bay of Biscay, which is as fierce and beautiful as my own Arrosa. Upon sighting the spout of a whale, he'd set fire to a bale of hay, then run to ring the church bells, and the hunt would be on. Can you imagine the battle, my friends, the hurling of harpoons, the glory of the kill? Once the great beast had been dragged to shore all the town would join in slicing it open, stripping away the blubber, and rendering it into oil." He put his arm around Fr. de Souza's shoulders. "Throughout Europe, Father, in the blackest nights of the Dark Ages, Basque whale oil lit the monastery lamps."

"The better that my monkish forbears could illuminate their manuscripts," remarked the priest.

"Alas, we were too skilled at our craft," said Abarran, staring sadly at the dregs in his wine glass. "Whales had become a rare sight in the Bay long before I was born."

Henry turned to Josiah. "If we're trading stories, you ought to tell of taking Roosevelt to hunt javelinas in Corpus Christi, or helping him train Rough Riders in San Anton—"

He broke off as a young girl approached Abarran, clutching a notepad to her breast.

"Excuse me, poppa. Might I ask your friend to remove his hat?" She was pointing to my father, who judged her to be about fifteen years old.

"Eh, Joska, away with your rude interruptions!"

"Oh come now," said Henry, snatching off my father's Stetson. "Making a sketch, are you? Let's have a look."

"But I've only just—"

"The gentleman granted your request," Abarran said sternly, "have the courtesy to grant his."

Joska sighed, then held up the unfinished charcoal portrait.

"You flatter me, child," said my father, then turned to the Basque. "Your daughter has great talent!"

Abarran beamed. "She drives me to distraction, but no father could be prouder. Come here, girl, and give your poppa a kiss."

"My word!" said Henry. "If only she could have drawn my wanted posters all these years. You'll be a dead ringer for Apollo, Caleb, when she gets done adding your golden curls."

"Oh no, sir," said Joska. "You've named the wrong Greek god. See Mr. McRae's eyes?" She pursed her lips and thought for a moment. "He's more like Prometheus, bound in chains and pecked at by an eagle. Shall I draw *you* as Heracles, come to free him? Though of course I'd have to take some liberties with your physique."

Henry was, for once, at a loss for words.

"There is no book in the Elko library my Joska has not read!" Abarran crowed. "At school the teachers ask *her* questions. What am I to do with this girl?"

The evening passed in convivial conversation. When they finished dinner, Josiah rejoined them, bringing a complimentary bottle of mezcal he'd brought back personally from Oaxaca.

"And God made agave," said Fr. de Souza. "And it was good."

"*AITA!*"

A young man came running up to Abarran, white-faced and breathless.

"Zori," said his father. "Calm yourself. What is the matter?"

"Mother asked me to go up for her shawl. At the top of the stairs I saw a man leaving our room, and when I went in—our money—it was gone!"

Abarran stood and gaped at his son.

"This cannot be! You are sure, Zorion? You looked well?"

Arrosa turned to confront her husband. "*Tentel hutsa zara gero!* You left our fortune—and your brother's!—in our room?"

"I meant—I had intended—"

"*Txoriburu!* Of all the Zabalas since the dawn of time, none have been more dim-witted than you. And now your children and I will pay the price!"

"Excuse me, please," said Josiah. "Zorion, this man you saw, was he a swarthy fellow, bald and thin as a blade?"

"Yes, much like that."

"Carlos Moreno," said the proprietor. "He and his gang have been plaguing Austin for months." He stood up and looked at my father. "If we can't catch his trail, I've some notion of where they're likely holed up."

"We'll follow your lead." My father rose and donned his Stetson.

"Baltasar," said Henry, "are you in?"

The priest was already checking his Remingtons to make sure they were fully loaded. "Surely you do not need to ask."

"Do not fear, Mrs. Zabala," said my father. "Nor you, Abarran. We will recover your money, every cent. Justice will be done before the break of dawn."

"I will accompany you as well," said the Basque.

"That would not be wise," said Fr. de Souza as he reholstered his weapons. "Look after your family, my friend. And rest assured, against the four of us, the devil himself would not stand a chance."

The antique clock above Josiah Johnson's great oaken bar had only just struck the midnight hour when the quartet returned. No especially violent altercations appeared to have taken place in the proprietor's absence, and a piano player was thumping out a rendition of "Meet Me in St. Louis, Louis" on an ancient upright, much to the delight of the late-night crowd.

Abarran, oblivious to the revelry, was snoring loudly in his chair. Zorion sat beside him, staring at the floor, a picture of misery.

My father tossed a large sack on the table, heavy with gold double eagles, where it landed with a satisfying thud. Abarran's eyes shot open and Zorion jumped to his feet.

"Count your money," said Josiah, "and we'll secure it in my safe."

"Praise be to God!" The Basque fell to his knees. "I am forever in your debt. You have restored my honor—truly you are the Lord's own avengers!"

"We are, aren't we," said Henry. "I rather fancy being called an avenger. How entirely original!"

"When Caleb delivered the scoundrel to the city jail, hog-tied," said Fr. de Souza, "it was a thing of beauty."

Abarran poured some of the coins out onto the table. "You must accept these as the merest token of my gratitude!"

"Keep your money," said my father. "This is what we do. We set things right."

Chapter Fifteen

Under a Cheshire Moon

Henry, my father, and Fr. de Souza returned to the Mission Santa Maria and lingered in the courtyard, savoring their triumphs.

"Our adventures have inspired my next homily," said the priest. "I shall preach on our Lord reading the words of Isaiah, proclaiming deliverance to the captives and Good News to the poor!"

"And healing to the broken-hearted," Henry interjected. "Let's not forget that."

"For a non-believer," said my father, "you know a passel of Scripture."

Henry shrugged. "I never forget a catchy line."

Fr. de Souza yawned and rubbed his eyes. "Soon the cock will crow, my friends. I bid you goodnight. You'll find your quarters are on either side of mine."

"I'll not go to bed until after morning mass," said my father as the stout-hearted priest took his leave.

"Good," said Henry. "Let's stay outside and enjoy the cool of the night."

They sat down on a stone bench near a burbling fountain. My father breathed in the sweet scent of the wisteria covering a nearby wall, leaned back, and gazed at the stars blazing overhead in the velvet darkness. The great hunter, Orion, stalked the southern skies, endlessly pursuing the Seven Sisters.

What was it Josiah Johnson had told Henry about the "Ballad of Midnight and McRae"?

A man would think Caleb was chasing you yet.

"Henry," said my father. "Josiah warned the men to keep a close watch on their wives—how much of that was jest, how much truth?"

Henry laughed, and then, seeing my father waiting earnestly for an answer, his grin faded.

"Ah, Caleb," he said. "We can forswear our sins, and still they dog us. Please, put those words out of your mind."

"All right. I'm not even sure why I asked."

"Aren't you?"

My father stayed silent.

A few awkward moments passed before Henry spoke again.

"You told Abarran we set things right. I wonder, if there *is* a Supreme Being—Tawa or Brahman or your own Ancient of Days—whether he'd give me a chance to go back and do things over. To make them right."

"You mean actually send you back in time?"

"If I prayed hard enough. You know, on my knees and all that. I'd give anything for it."

A myriad of responses ran through my father's mind. Christ had made atonement for the sins of the world; only in Him would Henry ever find peace. Perhaps the Lord was even now using Henry's sins to bring others to salvation! And anyway, wasn't his friend's anguish simply the just consequence of his misdeeds?

He began to speak and then stopped himself, sure all of that would only come out as so much self-righteous prattle.

"How do you know your wish hasn't already been granted?" he asked, surprising himself with the question.

Henry raised his eyebrows. "Whatever do you mean?"

"Well—" A breeze rustled the leaves of the courtyard's lone live oak. My father found himself looking forward to hearing his own explanation, and took a deep breath. "Surely you wouldn't be sent back with all your present knowledge—that would make things too easy. No, all you'd return with is exactly what you have now—a deep desire to do the right thing. To have another chance."

"You're saying this is the past we're in, you and I?"

My father shrugged. "Stranger miracles have transpired. Therefore keep this always in mind: each time you're faced with a decision, it may be the opportunity to avoid the temptation to which you once succumbed. In so doing, you will have set things right."

"Ah!" Henry looked away for a few moments, then turned back and smiled. "I'm not sure a weight's been taken off or added—if I make the wrong decisions, I'll have doubly sinned! Nonetheless, I'm intrigued."

A silence followed, broken only by the cry of a coyote somewhere far beyond the mission walls.

"Henry," my father said softly. "What is it you want to do over?"

"Oh, leave it be. Anyway, according to you it hasn't happened yet, has it?"

"True enough." My father smiled ruefully. "And never shall."

Henry moved closer and rested his head against my father's shoulder. "Let's stay together, Caleb," he whispered. "Always and forever."

Every muscle in my father's body tensed. *Who is Caleb McRae?* he wondered. *I don't know myself at all. A man not comfortable in his own skin, Fr. Alejo had said. And yet, how* could *I be, until I receive my redeemed body, pure and undefiled? Tell me Lord, what you would have me do.*

No answer. Well of course not; anything else would make things too easy.

All my father could feel was the gentle pressure of Henry's head on his shoulder, all he could hear was the blood pounding through his veins.

The slender crescent of a Cheshire moon rose above the mission wall.

Is there something to smile about here?

Overhead, the heavens declared the glory of God. The Milky Way glimmered and glowed, comets raced through the empty vastness, worlds blinked in and out of existence, and amid them all Orion persisted in his hopeless pursuit.

After a while my father put his great right arm around Henry and felt the tension in his body gradually melt away.

They remained there together until the first hints of dawn graced the eastern horizon and the stars began fading from view.

Chapter Sixteen

Cast Him into the Darkness

Word spread quickly of what the "Avengers" had done for Abarran Zabala. A steady stream of petitioners were arriving at Josiah Johnson's seeking redress the law would not provide: poor folk who'd been swindled out of what little they had, wives and children of Black men and Tejanos who'd been lynched or gunned down, battered women.

Fr. de Souza had priestly duties to attend to, and Josiah a roadhouse to run, so the work of setting wrongs right fell mostly on my father and Henry. They laid traps for deceivers, hunted down murderers, exacted restitution where there was any to be found. Together they were close to perfection, like dancing partners who had long ago learned each other's moves, needing no words between them, only a gesture or glance.

Yet sometimes all their skill was not enough.

"Perhaps my father was right," Henry remarked after a week spent in futile efforts to restore land stolen from its rightful owners. "He wanted me to study the law, but the very thought bored me to tears. Face it, we're worthless without a barrister on our team."

Though Josiah approached every attorney he knew in Austin, it was well known that Midnight and McRae were in the crosshairs of the Texas Rangers, and none were willing.

Then there was the matter of my father's temper, an anger that at times rose up from deep inside him and could scarcely be controlled. That fall, he and Henry descended on Miles O'Shaughnessy, who'd acquired some choice grave plots in Freedmen's Cemetery and sold each dozens of times over.

"I've two hundred and sixty dollars in receipts you'll make good on," said my father. "In cash. Today."

"It's most regrettable," said O'Shaughnessy, "but I've a penchant for the gambling tables and lost every cent."

"You're a lousy liar," said Henry. "I sincerely advise you to rethink your answer. My friend here is not in the best of moods."

"What's this, the Sassenach are after me, even here?"

My father lifted the miscreant off the floor with one hand and held him at eye level. "I'm giving you a chance to redeem yourself. To save your own soul."

"Well now, sir, I was baptized as a babe, make my way to church of a Sunday, confess my sins, say my Our Fathers and Hail Marys as I'm told. So I'm as saved as the next man, for all that I give in to the odd temptation now and again. But then, don't we all?" My father's eyes narrowed, but O'Shaughnessy was too swept up in his own blarney to take heed. "Listen, my man, I'll find a fine plot to make good on each and every one I sold your friends. And for you, sir! I've just the place in mind, fit for the kingly likes of you. I'll throw in a marble headstone for good measure. Sure but the wife and young ones would be proud to come there and mourn you."

"It's your own grave you'll be needing." My father slammed O'Shaughnessy against the wall with a startling fierceness, then did it again twice more before letting him drop.

The Irishman spit out teeth and blood and my father reached down, intent on inflicting more pain.

"Tell me where you keep your stash, Miles." Henry wrapped his arms around his partner and pulled him back. "*Now.*"

O'Shaughnessy tried to sit up, then sank back down with a groan. "All right, enough. There's a loose floorboard in the hallway closet. Just take the stinking spondulix and go."

"Caleb," said Henry, breaking a long silence on the ride back to Josiah Johnson's. "What would you have done if I hadn't stopped you?"

"What does it matter?" asked my father. "Don't tell me you're feeling sorry for that slumguzzling swine."

"Come on, he's a worm like all the others, only more so. And yet he was able to light your fuse."

"I'll dole out a little justice when I feel like it, Henry. Don't lecture me."

"Ah, I see. You're the Lord's own avenger, how foolish of me to forget," Henry said angrily, and he spurred his horse on ahead.

While Josiah counted out cash for each of the folks O'Shaughnessy had swindled, their avengers were at a back table in the shadows, drinking whiskey, and it was only after he'd downed a few shots that my father finally spoke.

"What does it mean when a man keeps so much of his life a secret? Is that not proof of its shamefulness?"

"Not a bit," replied his partner. "It proves only the small mindedness of the crowd."

"The *crowd?* Most of the civilized world would call us deviants. Debauched."

"Laws might be passed by a show of hands, but not right and wrong. I've gone my own way since becoming a man, Caleb. The prophets in your Good Book were lonely men."

"Please, of all things to bring up, don't talk to me of Scrip—"

"Sirs!" interrupted a man who came rushing to their table. "There's a poor soul outside calling for you. Hurry, I am afraid he has not long to live."

They found a man sprawled on the wooden sidewalk, his clothes blood-stained and torn, murmuring prayers in Spanish.

"Señor?" My father knelt down beside him while Henry ran to get a doctor.

"*Eres un vengador?*" The man's voice was barely a whisper. *Are you an avenger?*

"Yes," my father replied in Spanish. "Tell me what happened."

"They are murdering the patriarchs."

"Who?"

The prostrate man struggled to speak. "*Agua, por favor.*"

"Fetch some water!" my father shouted.

A bystander offered his canteen.

A shot rang out, sending the canteen flying. A second shot silenced the wounded man's lips forever, splattering my father with gore.

"Don't move, McRae." Tom Tetley's Winchester was still smoking as he and Major Garrison crossed the street. "Put your hands behind your back. You're under arrest."

"What for, you murdering bastard?"

"Oh, we'll think of something," said Garrison.

"Looked to me like he was aiding and abetting a dangerous outlaw just now," said Tetley.

"It surely did," said the Major. "Good thing we got here in the nick of time."

Josiah came out from the roadhouse holding his shotgun. "What the hell you think you're doing, Jim Garrison?" A dozen or so black men and women, some bearing arms, closed ranks alongside him.

"Always knew you were an Injun lover, Johnson, but niggers, that's a new one. Small wonder I never cared for your whiskey."

"Josiah—all of you—put down your weapons!" called out my father. "Thank you. But go home. And trust me—this too will be set right."

Tetley cuffed my father and led him away.

When Henry returned with the local sawbones just a short time later, the crowd had dispersed and the dead man's body was being carted off to a pauper's grave.

Estan asesinando a los patriarcas.

The phrase echoed through my father's mind as he paced the concrete floor of a dank, windowless cell, in utter darkness.

They are murdering the patriarchs.

Three strides from the metal door to the back wall, four from side to side. He ran his hands over the smooth stone walls. What wizardry would Henry employ to escape? He'd not a clue.

The sudden glare of an incandescent lantern signaled the arrival of his silent jailer, who left some bread and water and emptied the chamber pot. The only way to mark the passage of time was by his growing hunger and the steadily increasing stink of his cell.

Murdering the patriarchs...

Garrison and Tetley had worked my father over pretty well before throwing him into solitary. He tried to concentrate on the dead man's last words, but his head throbbed and his whole body ached and he kept losing focus.

He started to pray, then broke off. What was the point? *Thou shalt not lie with mankind, as with womankind: it is abomination.* An impossible gulf yawned between him and heaven.

Bind him hand and foot, and take him away, and cast him into the Outer Darkness; there shall be weeping and gnashing of teeth.

And yet that need never be. He had but to repent.

No. My father pounded his fist against the stone wall. *I will not. I cannot.*

He slid to the floor, exhausted. *Have mercy on me, Lord. You made me what I am, You knit me in my mother's womb. I need you like I need air to breathe. But I need Henry, too.*

Justice had always been his passion. But what did the word even mean? Giving a man the punishment or reward he deserves, or, as Henry argued, giving him what he needs?

There seemed no way to reconcile the two when it came to justice for Caleb McRae.

Chapter Seventeen

Dreams, Fables, and Myths

If the flood waters kept rising, the woman in the fringed shawl would surely drown.

"Come quickly!" my father called out, hoping his friends could hear him over the howling wind. He waded in and motioned for them to follow.

To his horror, one by one, Henry, Father de Souza, and Josiah were swept away by the storm.

Still, he made his way toward the woman, the water soon up to his knees, then his waist, then his chest.

"Captain McRae," she said, and he realized with a start he could barely keep his head above water. "Take my hand."

She reached out and pulled him alongside her, onto dry land.

My father gaped up at the Mestiza.

"It's blowing quite a gale, eh, Señor? But then, such are the perils of life on the Rio Grande."

The door to my father's cell opened, awakening him from his dream. He was instantly alert, his whole body tense, though this time there were no shouts or kicks, no lantern's sudden glare.

"Caleb," whispered a familiar voice. "It's me."

"Henry." My father reached out into the darkness.

The two men found each other and embraced.

"My God, but you stink to high heaven. Come on, we'll put a good forty miles between us and Austin and then get you a bath."

My father stepped back. "Henry, you haven't thought this through."

"The hell I haven't. You and me, together, in this one life we have, that's what counts."

"No. We've work to do, and not as outlaws."

"You can't do it from this cell, Caleb, nor if they find an excuse to hang you."

"You've got to trust me." My father grasped Henry's shoulders with both hands. "I'll leave here my own way. Take care, Henry, and give my best to the others. Now quickly, before you're discovered—*go*!" He pushed Henry out and quietly closed the cell door.

My father was engulfed by a deep sense of loneliness. What madness was this, not leaving when he had the chance? No, the dream had spoken: he was being called to the Rio Grande Valley. To the lair of Harlon Gale, who was surely behind the murders the doomed Tejano had spoken of. This was no time to be on the run; he would face Gale as a free man.

For the first time in a long while he dropped to his knees and prayed as fervently as when his faith was young. Maybe, just maybe, the Lord had not abandoned him.

A sharp kick in the ribs woke my father a week later and he winced in the lantern's blinding light.

"There's only one reason your head's still attached to your body, McRae," said Garrison. "*Politics.* You and your pals are popular right now, the newspaper boys have made y'all into dime-novel heroes. It's all horseshit, but the Governor don't need any bad publicity, so today's you're lucky day, I'm turning you loose. But mark my words, the public's fickle as a two-bit whore. You're still in Texas when they turn on you, all bets are off. I were you, I'd make tracks for the Territories, or out California way." He paused to deliver another kick. "You hear me, you sumbitch?"

My father rose to his feet.

"If I'm free to go, then step aside."

Garrison sneered and turned away.

My father brushed past him and found his way up the stairs that led from the subterranean cell block, blinking as he adjusted his eyes to the light. He hitched a ride on a hay wagon and was dropped off not far from the small cabin he and Henry had been sharing for the past several months.

His partner was in the front yard, chopping wood. "Am I dreaming?" He stared at my father, incredulous.

"O ye of little faith!" My father laughed. "If any faith at all. There are other ways than yours, you know. I've much to tell you, Henry, after I scrub myself clean."

"Wait, I've a better idea. You've been living like a blind mole these past two weeks—I'll gather up some bread and cheese, we'll saddle our steeds and ride to the falls near Williamson Creek. Achilles will hardly mind your stench. Then we'll burn your clothes and bathe and you'll tell me all."

They rode along trails through forests dense with sycamores and Spanish oak. When was the last time my father had ridden purely for the pleasure of it? He couldn't remember. White-tailed deer nibbled on skunkbush, jackrabbits darted from thickets of Texas persimmon and Mexican plum. Every sensation seemed exquisite, every sound: leaves rustling in the wind, their horses' hooves pounding the loamy soil, the plaintive cooing of a mourning dove. My father was filled with thankfulness for the gift of freedom, of abundant life.

How many are your works, Lord! In wisdom you made them all...

At the falls they stripped and dove into the foaming waters, swam and dove again and cavorted like carefree youth. *If I never have another day,* he thought, climbing back onto dry land and stretching out in the warm October sun, *this will have been enough.*

"He sounds a right bastard, this Harlon Gale," said Henry, after my father told him what he'd learned from Garrison months before. "So I'm all for heading south. He's got the Anglo moneymen behind him and the Rangers in his pocket, though, which makes him rather more formidable than O'Shaughnessy and his ilk. Any notion of how we take him on?"

"No more than I had for getting out of that cell."

"Right, then. Well, things were entirely too easy, we need a challenge to keep us sharp. You pray to Jehovah and I'll see whether Spider Grandmother can't lend us a hand." Henry propped himself up on his elbows. "It must have been a kick in the guts, realizing Garrison and his crew were quite such a filthy lot. But you know, it's not exactly news. The Rangers have always been a force for darkness."

My father winced.

"Oh come now, Caleb. That poor soul who told you the patriarchs are being murdered wasn't the first Tejano the Rangers laid in the grave, and he won't be the last. They've always an excuse to kill a man whose skin is red or black or brown."

My father was silent for a while. During ten years with the Texas Rangers, he'd looked the other way until the truth bared its teeth like a rabid dog and cornered him and the ugliness was all he could see.

"To live the stories I'd read as a boy—I could imagine no better life. It all sounds like foolishness now. No. Worse than that."

"We're weavers of fables, spinners of fantastic tales," said Henry, "Hopi and Anglo alike. Don't be cross with me, Caleb, but you're making the same mistake with the god you worship. Far better to admit him a myth than bow down to a deity who commands the slaughter of his enemies and drowns the world in a fit of pique."

"You're talking nonsense now." My father felt his temperature rise. "Set aside whatever Scripture you don't understand. Without a good and holy God, without a guarantee there'll be justice in the end, life's a cruel, sad joke. I know in my bones that can't be true."

"Do you really? I think you strive so hard for justice because, deep down, you know there's only your own striving to set things right."

"You're wrong, Henry. We have the very idea of justice because we're made in the image of God, of Him who is Justice itself."

"Oh come on, we can't even agree on what the word means."

"Look, I don't pretend to have your intellect—I'm like a blind man trying to describe the sun, and perhaps all I can say is how good the warmth feels on my face. If you can add something to that, in your own blindness, all the better."

"A Platonist, are you?" Henry laughed and rested his head against my father's chest. "I rather like your turn of phrase, Caleb, and can add nothing to it whatsoever. Let's not argue anymore."

"And for that matter," said my father, deciding to press his advantage, "there're myths you've told about yourself and swallowed whole. You played at Robin Hood, judging which man deserved his cattle or his jewels. What arrogant pride!"

"Ah!" Henry looked up at my father imploringly. "Guilty, guilty as charged. I surrender, Captain McRae, and throw myself upon your mercy."

How dark were Henry's eyes, how long his lashes!

My father gazed back at him in stern silence, then allowed himself the ghost of a smile and enfolded his lover in his arms.

Chapter Eighteen

One Who Hides in the Shadows

My father, Henry, and Fr. de Souza decided to set off for the Rio Grande Valley that weekend. Josiah promised to follow as soon as he could. The 1904 election was only weeks away and, with the Democratic candidate scheduled to campaign in Austin, he was expecting the roadhouse to be filled with large and boisterous crowds.

Shortly before their scheduled departure, a thin man in a worn poncho showed up at the Avengers' table and introduced himself as Raoul Vasquez.

"I'm sorry," said my father, "but we can't take on anything new."

"Hmm, Señor, yes, I understand." Vasquez smiled, showing a gold tooth that glinted when he spoke. "And yet, there is nothing new under the sun, am I right?"

"Since you speak with the wisdom of Solomon," said Henry, "we'll at least hear you out."

"This you will not regret, Señor. Hmm, yes, indeed you will not."

My father motioned for him to have a seat.

"That fellow the Rangers shot down like a dog," said Vasquez, "his name was José Luis Sánchez." He paused, licked his lips, and looked at his hosts expectantly.

"All right," said Henry. "Keep talking."

"A man talks best if relieved of his thirst. Bring me some rum and you'll hear what I've got to say."

When my father nodded, Josiah arranged for a bottle and glass to be brought to the table.

"You wish to avenge the death of José Luis? The man who pulled the trigger, he is nothing. But I, Raoul Vasquez, know the name of him who orders the taking of life." He picked up the bottle and took a long swig of rum.

"I already know his name," said my father. "Let's find out if you do."

"Hmm, yes, I am not surprised, Señor, you are no fool. I speak of him who serves the powers of darkness, Harlon Gale."

"What do you mean by that?" asked Fr. de Souza. "Speak plainly."

"He is a very bad hombre, Padre." Vasquez downed more rum, then wiped his mouth with the back of his hand and muttered, "If he is an hombre at all."

"Do not play games," said the priest. "Tell us what you know."

"The Knights of the White Camelia ride again. They do the killing for Señor Gale."

"It's been over thirty years since I last heard of the Knights," said Josiah. "Confederate veterans, mostly, who terrorized colored folk after the war."

"Now Gale pays them to kill Tejanos," said Vasquez. "They strike like cowards, like jackals." He spat on the floor. "Should their intended victims fight back, it only gives the Rangers an excuse to hunt them down. Such was the fate of José Luis."

"There is more you know of Harlon Gale," said Fr. de Souza. "Speak."

"I have heard rumors, stories told late at night when men have had too much to drink." Vasquez stared at the priest through narrowed eyes. "They say he sold his soul to become a *nagual*. They say in that way he joins in the killing himself."

"The nagual's a shape-shifter in Mexican folklore," said Henry. "They can turn themselves into all manner of terrible beasts—creatures with a wolf's head and a lizard's tail, that sort of thing. Every culture I studied has one of those. Interesting thing about the nagual, though, legend has it there's good ones as well as bad."

"Pagan nonsense." My father moved the bottle out of the Tejano's reach. "You've given us precious little to go on. Why did you come here? Who sent you?"

"Sent me? Raoul Vasquez takes orders from no man." He eyed the rum mournfully, then looked around the table and lowered his voice to a whisper. "Of Harlon Gale, *el ángel de la muerte*, I can tell you no more. But this much I will say: there is one who stands against him. One who hides in the shadows and reveals himself to precious few." He showed them a sly grin and fell silent.

"Out with it, then." Henry eyed him with contempt. "Who is this man?"

"He interests you, hmm? Yes, indeed, as well he should. But it will take more than mere rum for me to speak his name."

My father showed him a five-dollar gold eagle. "You'll need to earn this. Speak."

"I will give you everything you need to find him. Only it will not come quite so cheap."

"I'd sooner wring your neck than pay you more. I'll find the man myself, or he'll find me."

Vasquez scowled. "Bah! The rum too, then!"

My father pushed the bottle toward him and tossed him the coin.

The Tejano bit down on the gold piece, looked at it, then slipped it into his pocket and withdrew a pencil stub and a scrap of paper. He scrawled a name and address, then slid it across the table.

Elijah Jones

9 Calle de las Sombras, Brownsville

Vasquez stood up and raised the bottle in the manner of a man making a toast. "It has been a pleasure, *mis amigos.* I wish you luck, and will tell you one thing more, free of charge: He is a dark man himself, this Señor Jones, yes, dark indeed. And yet, they say the enemy of your enemy is your friend, do they not?"

He laughed and, clutching the rum bottle close, walked swiftly out into the night.

Part Three

Night of the Nagual

Chapter Nineteen

Wings

"Name your poison!" said the man who'd just come up to the Avengers' table at a roadhouse near Corpus Christi, six days south of Austin. "Name's Eustace Jenks, and I'm buyin' drinks for every sumbitch in this room." His face was flushed and he swayed a bit as he stood before them.

"That's generous of you," my father started to say, "but—"

"We've a fondness for sampling the local mezcal," Henry interjected. "Much obliged, Mr. Jenks. What's the occasion?"

Jenks called out to the bartender, then turned back to their table. "Sold my ranch for a wad of cash thick enough to choke a longhorn steer. The missus and me, we're on our way to San Antone. First thing, I'm gon' get us a ten-dollar hotel room, have them bring us breakfast in bed—hell, maybe lunch too. But the second thing, now that's what's got me fired up."

"Dinner?" asked Henry.

"Ha! No, son, I'm buyin' me a horseless carriage. An auto-mo-bile, the biggest, fastest, shiniest one they got."

"And where will you go in this splendid carriage of yours?" asked Fr. de Souza.

"Hell, I'll just circle Alamo Plaza tootin' my horn till I'm too dizzy to –" Jenks broke off and stared at de Souza as though seeing him for the first time. "Well, damned if you ain't a preacher! Someone dyin', or gettin' hitched?"

"Ain't much difference 'tween the two, y'ask me," an old-timer at the next table chimed in.

The erstwhile rancher guffawed, then caught himself and frowned. "Sorry, Padre, it's a fine thing, holy matrimony. Not a jokin' matter, no sir." He turned to my father and Henry. "Am I right, boys? You two married?"

"We would be," said Henry, "but it's against the law, sadly enough."

"Ha!" Jenks grinned and slapped Henry on the back. "I like a man with a sense of humor. So where you fellas headin', anyhow?"

"Brownsville," said my father. "You've come from the Valley, I take it. How's the road the rest of the way?"

"Good enough. Y'all can make it in four days if your horses are well rested. But I got to tell you, son, ain't no paradise down there, no matter what you might'a read in some newspaper ad up north. I'd turn right around, 'less you got an appetite for cactus apples and javelin hog. Not to mention a river goes on a rampage ever' once in a while and floods the whole damn county stirrup deep."

"You made out well enough," my father replied. "Some northerner buy your ranch?"

"Hell no. Ever'one here knows you deal with Harlon Gale."

"You don't say," said Henry. "And what sort is he, this Gale fellow?"

"A real gentleman," said Jenks. "He's a reg'lar Civil War hero, though he wasn't but a kid back then. Shoulders even broader'n yours." He nodded toward my father. "They say he charged them Yankees single-handed when they was mowin' down our boys with a Gatling gun. Hell of it is, the man's blind now, makes his way around with a cane, led by a little child. Damn shame. But Mr. Gale ain't bitter, no sir, there's not a mean bone in his body."

"Here you go, boys." A serving girl placed an unmarked bottle and four shot glasses on their table.

"Y'all are in for a treat." Jenks began pouring shots. "This here's the local *mezcal de pechuga*. They take your everyday mezcal and distill it one mo' time with peaches and pecans. Hang a raw turkey over the still, too—just for the hell of it, I s'pose."

"Saúde," said Fr. de Souza, and the men downed their first drink.

Henry refilled the four shot glasses. "The Apache told me lightning struck an agave plant in the days of their ancestors, freeing the magical spirit, mezcal. I'll hazard a guess that was about the same time the Greeks were worshipping Agave, goddess of desire. Do you see the connection?"

"Hmm?" Jenks stared at the Englishman in befuddlement.

"Surely the goddess herself released that fateful bolt," Henry continued. "For, after all, love can strike like lightning."

"Indeed." Father de Souza reached for a bowl of pork rinds, twin pistols clearly visible under his open robe. "Love both earthly and divine."

"Ain't never seen a Padre packing Remingtons before." Jenks turned to my father and lowered his voice. "Them's two odd ducks you're travellin' with, son."

"Are they?" my father replied, deadpan. "I hadn't noticed."

The Avengers set out early the next morning.

"The dreariness of this landscape!" exclaimed Henry. "Have you ever seen such obstinate flatness? I ask you, could man ever have conceived of the divine in such a place?"

"Of course," responded Fr. de Souza. "Perhaps in just such a place most of all."

"Oh, come now. The Hebrews tramped endlessly through the desert, yes, but only when they cowered beneath Mt. Sinai did they hear Jehovah's voice in the rolling thunder. And your Moses ascended some promontory or other to gain a glimpse of the Promised Land."

"Mt. Nebo," said the priest.

"There you are. But this! It's hopelessly horizontal."

"For once, your imagination fails you. God's glory is always close at hand. Though we cannot see the Gulf of Mexico, we sense it is near. I imagine the Spirit of Yahweh brooding over its depths, filling it with the magnificence of life."

"Do you, now." Henry sighed.

"A Psalm comes to mind." Fr. de Souza paused. "Perhaps Caleb knows it."

My father hesitated for only a moment. "*They that go down to the sea in ships, that do business in great waters; These see the works of the Lord, and his wonders in the deep.*" He brought Achilles to a halt, then turned him toward the east. "I haven't seen 'great waters' since I was a child. It can't be more than twenty miles or so to the coast. Come, it will be good for us. Are you with me?"

"What's this?" exclaimed Henry. "Caleb McRae, dallying? Can it be true? Has the salt smell of the sea seduced you? How delightful!"

"Lead on," said Fr. de Souza, "and we will follow."

They rode through the marshy countryside, past stands of live oaks that loomed through the mist, huge, ancient, and gnarled. Some miles later my father halted by the edge of a swamp and gazed in fascination at a thicket of black mangroves, studying the bizarre geometry of their tangled roots.

Henry rode up beside him. "Curiouser and curiouser. Tell me what you see."

"They're like something out of the spirit world. Fantastic creatures, frozen in motion."

"Yes! I'm quite sure they'll advance another step or two if we turn away, only to stand still as statues the moment we look back." He turned to Fr. de Souza. "And you, man of the cloth, what thoughts go through your mind?"

"These trees have a strange beauty, do they not? And yet mangroves have always made me uneasy. They remind me that all creation fell with man, and the prince of the power of the air rules this world."

My father nodded. "I feel his presence with every mile we come closer to Mr. Gale. 'Gentleman' though he may be. But enough; we'll enjoy ourselves this day. Let's press on."

They passed through the darkness of the mangrove swamp and soon came in sight of the dunes. The men rode through salt grass and sea oats and over violet flowers that grew on vines snaking through the sand. At the crest of the dunes my father stopped and surveyed the scene: a long sweep of beach, the calm, veridian waters of Corpus Christi Bay, an island in the distance. Beyond that lay the Gulf. There was not another soul in sight.

Fr. de Souza announced that he and the horses would rest in the shade of some nearby oaks and "have their noon repast."

My father and Henry made their way to the water, shed their clothes and swam, then ran for miles on the hard-packed sand.

"For all my whining," said Henry, as they lay together on the beach, "it's glorious, this creation your Yahweh spoke into being. This fourth world. It's good, all of it, and you and I, we're a part of that goodness. No one can tell me this is wrong. Don't you know that? Don't you feel it in your bones?"

Yes, it's wonderful, my father wanted to say, *this great expanse of sea and sky and sand, the coolness of the breeze, the warmth of your body next to mine. I've prayed to*

God to bless this love I have for you, Henry Midnight, I've begged him, against all reason.

But he struggled against the bonds of his silence.

"Talk to me, Caleb," Henry continued. "Won't you give voice to whatever's in your heart?"

"What do you want me to say?" exclaimed my father at last. "You know what troubles me."

"Ah, the deity who looms, ever looking over your shoulder," said Henry, his eyes flashing. "Must I crawl on my belly before your Ancient of Days and beg his favor? Point me in the right direction and I'll do it, but I fear it would be to no avail." He stood up and flung a smooth stone as far as he could out into the water. "The Europeans came and pronounced the red man's ways barbaric after slaughtering them and despoiling their land. But among the Indians, men like you and I are accepted, even venerated. For we are *Those with Two Spirits*, male and female, and thereby doubly blessed."

"Is that what we are?" my father asked angrily. "*Blessed?* I'd say mocked, despised, wished dead."

"Listen to me, Caleb." Henry knelt down in the sand in front of my father. "For untold years the Hopis have lived in a place called Black Mesa. Legend has it that's where they settled after Spider Grandmother led them through the *sipaapuni*—the door in the sky—into this, the Fourth World. Why *there,* one might wonder, for the mesa's a vast expanse of barren rock most find a desolate and lonely land. And yet it's beautiful, with long sweeps of sandstone in pink and salmon and gold. It's a hard life the Hopis live, but a rich one, and they'd breathe their last before they'd ever leave. Well that's the way I feel about us, Caleb. Difficult as our lives may be, I wouldn't trade this time we have together for anything in the world."

My father listened to the waves breaking gently on the shore, to the cries of gulls suspended overhead, watched the rise and fall of his lover's chest.

"One night last winter," he said at last, "I dreamed of searching for you with a flying machine."

"How extraordinary. I was in the Panhandle back then, making the odd foray into Amarillo, and one day the wind blew a scrap of newspaper into my hand. It described the Wright Brothers soaring over the dunes of Kill Devil Hills. Couldn't stop thinking about it for the longest time."

"Nor I," said my father. "But I haven't told you the best part of the dream. I'd had to build the plane—no easy task!—and then spent weeks learning to fly. But when I took to the skies, what did I see above me but you, cavorting with eagles and hawks. Only you needed no mechanical contraption, no flying machine, for it seemed you'd sprouted wings. Though now I think you've had them all along."

"Ah." Henry smiled. "We'll fly together one day, Caleb. I'm sure of it."

"We'd better rejoin Baltasar," said my father, and the two men rose to start the long walk back.

They'd walked in silence for a hundred paces when my father stopped and turned to his partner. "You have my heart, Henry," he said. "God help me but it's true."

Chapter Twenty

Elijah's Militia

The Avengers had spent a fruitless morning in Brownsville trying to find someone who could direct them to Calle de las Sombras, when they came across a beggar with two stumps for legs.

"Bless me, Padre." The man was seated on the side of a dusty street, an upturned sombrero in front of him displaying a solitary dime. "Bless me, *por favor!*"

Father de Souza dismounted and placed his hand on the crippled man's shoulder. "The Lord bless and keep you, *mi amigo*. May He grant you His mercy."

My father appeared beside him and pressed a silver dollar into the man's hand. "We are searching for Calle de las Sombras, señor. Do you know the way?"

The beggar's eyes widened. "Go elsewhere, I implore you. It is a most dangerous place you seek."

"We have no choice," said the priest.

"God be with you, then. Continue to the train tracks, then go left for perhaps a mile until you come to the charred remains of an old church. You will find your street there, in *el barrio de los cuchillos.*"

"I couldn't quite hear the man," Henry said as they rode on. "What was that last bit he told you?"

"It seems," said my father, "we are bound for the neighborhood of knives."

The streets grew seedier and more desolate as the trio followed the rail line east to the edge of town.

They paused to gaze on the remains of the burned-out church, its name still visible above a gaping entryway: *Nuestra Señora de Lourdes.* Behind the crumbling stone façade was a field of weeds.

"It would appear there were no miracles to spare," said Henry.

Fr. de Souza made the sign of the cross and they turned left onto a street of small shops and tumbledown homes. Figures peered at them furtively, cloaked in shadows. From somewhere far off came the sounds of drunken singing and the cries of a forlorn child.

9 Calle de las Sombras was a dismal-looking saloon marked by a crudely painted sign.

El Atrapa Ratas

"The rat trap," muttered Henry. "One wonders if we're the rodents in question."

My father shrugged. "That's as may be. After ten days of travelling, I'm eager for action." He dismounted, tied Achilles to a hitching rail, and turned to his companions with the rare trace of a smile. "Let's go inquire after Elijah Jones. I'll buy the first round."

"For some reason," said Fr. de Souza, "I'm no longer quite so thirsty."

Inside the swinging doors the saloon was even darker than it had appeared. Four young women broke off their conversation and their faces lit up in smiles.

"Music, Mariana!" one called out, and one of them sat down at a dusty upright and began plunking out a lively tune.

There were no other patrons to be seen.

"I'm jealous of the tall one's curls," said another of the women as the Avengers made their way to the bar. "And the dark one—*qué guapo!*"

"Mmm. But *his* hair, it is longer than mine!"

"Three shots of mezcal," said my father.

The barkeep, who had a shaved head and wore a single gold earring, looked at him dubiously. "Whiskey, gin, or beer."

"Me, I like a man with some meat on his bones." One of the saloon girls sidled up to Fr. de Souza. "Eh, Gordo?"

"As for the girls," the barkeep added, "they drink champagne."

He's a she, my father realized, noticing the swelling breasts beneath her striped vest.

"Of course they do," said Henry. "In copious quantities, I imag—"

My father elbowed him into silence. "Actually," he said in a hushed voice, "we're here to see Mr. Jones."

"Never heard of the man."

My father found her ability to maintain a steely stare without blinking remarkable.

"Very well." He took out a folded note he'd prepared for just such an eventuality, along with a dollar coin, and pushed them toward her. "We'll leave, then. But if the gentlemen happens by, perhaps you could give him this."

She took the note, ripped it into shreds, and tossed them toward the ceiling.

As the men's eyes followed the fluttering shreds, three of the women they'd taken for painted ladies came up behind them with startling swiftness and held jackknives to their throats.

The barkeep held an eighteen-inch Arkansas toothpick in each hand.

"Move a finger," said the woman who was behind my father, "and we'll stick you like the pigs you are."

"Who *are* you?" demanded the barkeep.

"Relax, Marguerite," said a woman who seemed to have appeared out of nowhere at the rear wall of the saloon. "He's Caleb McRae. Formerly of the Texas Rangers."

The barkeep raised her eyebrows at that.

"Put away your knives, *mis queridas,*" the woman went on. "These men are not our enemies."

"Lucky for them," said the barkeep. She twirled both of her blades in the air, caught them and stowed them back below the counter.

Freed from the threat of imminent decapitation, my father turned to regard the newcomer, a slender older woman with reddish-bronze skin and a calm, regal bearing.

"I seem to be at a disadvantage," he said. "You are—?"

"Sofia Osorio Jones," she responded. "My apologies, gentlemen. These ladies take no chances with strangers. No harm was done, I take it?"

"Only to our pride," said my father.

"Then they did you a favor. Now come, I will take you to my husband." She turned and began walking toward the back of the saloon.

"Charmed, I'm sure," said Henry. He put his arm around Fr. de Souza's shoulders as they followed Sofia. "*Gordo* was unkind," he whispered, *sotto voce*. "You're not a pound more than plump."

Sofia pushed on a section of shelving affixed to the rear wall, which swung open to reveal a hidden hallway.

"Was it you who sent José-Luis to find us?" asked my father.

"You talked to him?"

"We were only able to exchange a few words before the Rangers shot him dead."

"A good man, though he was trying to bring you here for the wrong reason. More guns are not the answer to our problems."

Sofia knocked on an oaken door, then opened it and motioned for the Avengers to follow her into a room with shuttered windows, lit by a single oil lamp. "Elijah," she said. "McRae and the others are here at last."

A frail-looking Black man, his beard white with age, was seated at a desk covered with papers and books.

This was not how my father had imagined the leader of the resistance to Harlon Gale.

"Thank you, Sofia," said Elijah Jones. "Mr. McRae, Mr. Midnight—and El Padre Pistolero, for good measure! I know of your exploits in Austin. You've arrived not a moment too soon."

"I need to warn you," said my father, as he and the others seated themselves in front of Elijah's desk. "José-Luis died before he could tell us your name. We learned of you from a man calling himself Raoul Vasquez. You're taking great precautions, holed up here like this, yet Vasquez sold us your whereabouts for five dollars and a bottle of rum."

"Did he? Then he's eight dollars to the good and in no risk of running out of strong drink. Though my three bones are only due and payable upon your arrival." Elijah got up, poured ice water from a pitcher into glasses and offered them to Sofia and the three men. "Raoul's a snake, but he's the one man I could count on to get to you unscathed. I trust him because he hates Harlon Gale more than he loves liquor and money."

"I know the taxes are driving ranchers to desperation," said my father, "and Vasquez told us about the Knights of the White Camelia, but not much else. Fill us in."

"The Tejano ranchers are proud men, and Gale doesn't have the patience to wait for them to default on their loans. When a family manages to scrape together enough money to stay current, he kills the patriarchs and slaughters their sons. These so-called Knights who do his bidding have tasted blood and want more now that they know the law will look the other way. Gale pays them to spread terror, gouge out eyes, hack off limbs, nail the mutilated bodies to fence posts and set their heads on spikes. They captured two men of our little militia and put their dead bodies on display. The other men deserted in short order. Our women, though, are made of sterner stuff, they've taught the enemy to fear their blades. We're badly outnumbered, all the same."

"So where do *you* figure in, Elijah?" asked my father. "You don't have the look of a rancher."

"No, I'm just a man like you, with a thirst for justice."

"Fighting's one thing," said Henry. "But these foreclosures have to be fought in the courts as well. Is there a lawyer in these parts with the courage to stand up to Harlon Gale?"

"You're looking at him," said Elijah Jones.

"Really," said my father. "I knew there were Negro attorneys up north, just never expected to meet one here."

"The gunman John Wesley Hardin and I were admitted to the Texas bar the same year, I'll let you decide whose admission is the more astounding. There's a handful of lawyers of my race in the Republic, though not another within three hundred miles. I'm hanging on here by my fingernails."

"Well, you've outlasted Hardin by a fair margin. He was shot dead in a saloon in El Paso just before I got there in '96. What I'm wondering, though, is how Valley folk take to a colored man in court."

"That's where a priest could be of great help." Elijah turned to Fr. de Souza. "The presiding judge in Cameron County is the Honorable Aidan O'Connor, a man who never misses a Sunday mass. I might just have a chance with you by my side."

"I am your man," said Fr. de Souza. "The Portuguese and the Irish have long been close. Let me know the church he attends, perhaps I can gain his confidence there."

The men talked strategy, my father and Henry agreeing to join forces with the women to take on the Knights of the White Camelia. Fr. de Souza would join them whenever Elijah was not in court.

"I'm all in favor of your helping us with O'Connor, Padre," said Sofia, who'd been quiet up to that point. "I am curious, though, how you reconcile your Remingtons with your calling."

"My order is both passionate about justice and eminently practical. I do what I must."

"The first Christians needed no weapons to defeat the Roman Empire, a mightier foe even than Harlon Gale."

"One adopts different tactics at different times," said the priest. "The Lord Himself commanded his disciples to carry a sword."

"We either *fight* for justice," said Henry, "or let evil rule."

"There's a third way," said Sofia. "But you either see it or you don't."

My father groaned inwardly. He'd met such women before; they formed Associations for Peace and Tranquility, held tea parties where they'd bemoan the violence of men. But he knew his Bible, and it was as bloody a book as any he'd read.

"We ought to stable our horses," he said. "And figure out where we'll stay tonight."

"Our stables are nearby," said Elijah. "Marguerite can show you. As to shelter, the deserters left us with empty bunkhouse beds."

"Will you join us for dinner this evening, gentlemen?" asked Sofia. "You'll find the ladies and I more pleasant company than when you first—"

She broke off as a young woman appeared in the doorway, her clothes muddy, her face grim.

"Elijah, I've urgent news." The newcomer looked uncertainly at the Avengers.

"Speak freely, Valentina," said Elijah. "These men are friends."

"It's Raoul. I found his body just north of town. He'd been torn to pieces by a wild beast."

"Could it have been the Knights?" asked Elijah.

"No. I know what I saw."

"I've heard there are Mexican grays in these parts," said my father.

"No lobo is big enough to leave that creature's tracks."

"A single beast," said Henry. "Are you sure?"

She nodded, her face a warrior's mask in the glimmering lamplight.

"The nagual," said Sofia.

"Yes," said Valentina. "He hunts alone."

Chapter Twenty-One

Knife Games

That evening the Avengers and their hosts feasted on roasted pinion nuts, mesquite beans, and venison. The lemon scent of cinchweed and the sweetness of juniper ash perfumed the air.

"My compliments," said Henry. "I've not dined this well since my days on Black Mesa."

"We've something in common then," said Sofia. "My maternal grandmother was Hopi, my grandfather a Spanish soldier of fortune."

She and Henry traded stories while my father listened, annoyed and fascinated by Sofia in equal measure. "Were you raised to believe in the legend of the nagual?" he asked during a pause in the conversation. "Of men who can turn themselves into beasts?"

"My *so'o*—my granny—taught me there's more under the heavens than is seen with mortal eyes. You learned that from Scripture, yes? *We strive not with flesh and blood, but with principalities and powers and rulers of the darkness.* There are times, Caleb, when that spirit world reveals itself—and then we see demons."

"Harlon Gale, you mean."

"So it would seem."

"Earlier you cautioned us against combat," said my father. "Yet the Apostle's words you recited allude to righteous warfare."

"Do they? Paul wrote of striving, not violence."

"Enough," said Elijah, who spoke with the strength of a much younger man. "This is no longer a matter for debate. The enemy leaves us no choice. We'll fight Gale and his minions with pistols and knives, with our bare hands if need be."

"Yes," said Valentina, who until then had been silent. "By God, they'll taste my blade." She turned toward my father. "As will the Rangers, if they come against us."

Their eyes locked.

"You fear my loyalties are divided?" asked my father.

"I *fear* nothing," she replied.

"I trust these men," Elijah said sharply. "My faith in them must suffice."

"No, I understand her concern." My father stood and rolled up one sleeve, baring a powerful forearm. "Unsheathe your knife, Valentina, and we'll swear a blood oath to fight to the death against those who oppose us, whether Ranger or nagual or Knight."

She stared at him intently for a few moments and the fire faded from her eyes. "Save your blood, Caleb. You may well need every drop."

"Indeed, *mi cariño*," said Marguerite, whose shaved head was now covered by a black bandanna worn pirate style. "I fear for our new comrades-in-arms. Did you know they were captured without a struggle, and by mere women?"

"What a disgrace," said Mariana, whose knife had been at Henry's throat a few hours before. "Do you suppose they can even hold their liquor?"

"I have my doubts." The barkeep turned to the Avengers. "This afternoon you asked for mezcal. My uncle distills the nectar of the Tepeztate agave, we keep some of what he brews below the counter downstairs. But perhaps it is too strong for you boys. They grow on the sides of sheer cliffs, those agaves—just the thought of harvesting them would shrivel your *cojones*."

"I hear many words," said my father, "but I see neither bottle nor glasses."

The first bottle of Tepeztate did not last long.

"So how do you girls amuse yourselves?" asked Henry, as new shots were being poured. "*El Atrapa,* fine establishment that it is, seems to be in a rather dreary part of town."

"Our lives are simple," said Valentina. "We fight, we drink, and we play with knives."

"Also we deal Faro," said Marguerite. "Only you'd be wise to pass, our tables are gaffed."

"Also we make love," added Mariana. "But you boys are not really our style."

"Well then," said Henry. "What sort of knife games do you play?"

"I will tell you our favorite," said Marguerite. "It serves to pass the time. Two players compete. The first throws so her blade sticks into the floor, and the second must exactly match the manner of her toss. The roles are then reversed. The contest goes on until only one of the players has failed to match."

"Why that's mumbly-peg!" said Henry. "A child's game."

"Ah, you will perhaps make short work of us, then."

"Also," said Mariana, "both players down a shot of Tepeztate between each round."

My father noted the plank floors were pitted with holes.

"So, we shall play, yes?" said Marguerite. "Valentina will defend our honor."

"We shall," Henry replied. "And Caleb will throw for the sons of Adam."

Though my father put up a valiant effort, a few rounds after the third bottle had been retrieved he failed to match Valentina's toss.

"Never fear, gentlemen," said Fr. de Souza. "My years in South America were not entirely misspent." He stepped forward, drew from his robes a dagger with an elaborately carved handle, and flourished it with bravado. "Women—behold my blade!"

There was much raising of eyebrows, and even Teresa and Francisca, the most reticent of the distaff militia, whistled in appreciation.

"Years ago," declaimed the priest, "my Jesuit forbears in Paraguay not only preached the Gospel but fought to save their parishioners from the slave hunters of São Paulo. The Father Superior himself led the attack which routed the slavers, who fled into dark forests where cannibals feasted on their flesh. *This*—" he sent the dagger twirling into the air and caught it—"is the very blade he carried." He bowed deeply. "You may go first, señorita, I shall match you throw for throw."

Valentina toyed with him for the first three rounds.

"You've some skill, Padre," she said as the Tepeztate made its way around the room, "but it is time to bring this to an end." She arched backwards until her body described a perfect half-circle before executing her next toss.

"Alas for the honor of my sex," said Fr. de Souza, his shoulders slumping in defeat, "I no longer have the limberness of youth."

"Step back, Baltasar," said Henry, "and hand me that fine weapon of yours. Such circus tricks hardly impress a man who's held his own alongside Apache braves."

No one was quite sure just how many rounds the contest lasted, but when the last drops were drained from the fourth and final bottle, all were content to declare it a draw.

A pounding on the bunkhouse door awakened the Avengers early the following morning. My father answered, gun drawn, to find Elijah with his warriors in tow.

"Gabriela has been standing guard since dinner," said the attorney. He turned toward one of the women. "Tell Caleb what you saw."

"Something swift and fierce moved as a shadow in the night, a deepening of the darkness. It froze my blood as few things ever have."

"The worst of it is, Sofia's out there, somewhere," said Elijah. "It's not unusual for her to rise early and walk for hours. When Gabriela woke me, she was gone."

"Baltasar, stay close by Elijah," said my father. "Henry, let's you and I head out."

The priest already had his Remingtons holstered under his robe. Henry was kneeling on the floor, clad in his underwear, dunking his head in a tub of cold water.

"Each of you had better come with one of us," said Valentina, "seeing as you don't know the lay of the land. We're on the edge of the city, close by the river. It's treacherous out there."

It was agreed that my father and Valentina would search to the north, Henry and Marguerite to the south, the others in pairs to the east and west.

"There're still hours until dawn," Marguerite squinted at the sky, frowning. "And the moon has long since set."

"Also," said Mariana, "there's fog rolling in off the Rio Grande."

"Have no worries," said Henry, as he buckled his pants. "That's just the way we like it."

"We will find your wife, Elijah," said my father. "And if there's a nagual at large, we'll put an end to the beast."

With that they joined the women and ventured out into the mist-shrouded blackness of the night.

Chapter Twenty-Two

Hide and Seek

My father and Valentina set out on foot, since their horses would likely be spooked by the fog. They decided against carrying a lantern, which would only reveal them to whatever Malevolence might be stalking the neighborhood of knives.

"Do you never carry a pistol?" he asked her, noting the belt she wore, upon which dangled numerous sheaths.

"I carry what I need. The Wise Ones say the nagual can only be slain by a silver dagger thrust through its heart. We each bear at least one such blade."

"To each his own," murmured my father, glad to feel the heft of his Winchester rifle.

"Stay close by me," said Valentina as they entered onto Calle de los Sombras. "People here do not take kindly to strangers."

"Don't worry, if any sporting women accost me, this time they'll not gain the upper hand."

"I'm serious. We've trouble enough without you getting into more."

"We need to work together, Valentina. If you've an issue with me, lay it out now."

"Understand one thing and we'll get along well enough." She turned to look my father in the eye. "I take orders from no man."

"Have you heard any issuing from my lips? And never mind I'm a man, I've ten years of action under my belt. You're too young to think you've nothing to learn."

"I'm twenty, and I've fought for far longer than you. It's been one unending battle since I left my mother's womb."

"We've a job to do," said my father. "Let's just agree we'll do it side by side."

From Valentina's silence he inferred this was an acceptable compromise.

They continued on, alert to every sound but able to see no farther than the length of an outstretched arm. Every so often his companion threw back her head and let loose a series of wolf-like yips and howls, a code that would alert Sofia of danger. They could make out faint calls from the others, letting them know they too were still searching.

It occurred to my father that a wolf might seem an appealing appetizer to a hungry nagual, and if so, all the better. He was eager for a fight.

After a while they passed beyond the city limits and into rougher terrain.

"I say we keep going," said Valentina. "Sofia often wanders out here, she loves the wild."

"I'm all for it," said my father, and they pressed on into the night.

"Olly olly oxen free!" came the cry of a child.

"That's my nephew!" said Valentina. "*Hector!* It's Tina. Come toward my voice."

"Tia Tina! Emi and I are playing hide-and-seek, but she is being very naughty."

A moment later a boy of six or seven emerged from the mist. He smiled at his auntie, then gawked in amazement at her hulking companion.

"You and your little sister need to go home, *now,*" said Valentina. "Your mamá would whip you if she knew you were out at this hour. What were you thinking?"

"Emi got up to pee and woke me because she saw a big kitty. Then it became all foggy, and that makes the very best hide-and-seek!"

"*Emilia!*" shouted Valentina. "Come here!"

"I've been calling to her, Tia. She doesn't answer. Such a naughty girl."

My father crouched down to the lad's eye level. "What did you mean, Hector, about a big kitty?"

"I didn't see it. Emi says kitty's the hugest ever and so lovely. But I think it's only make-believe."

My father and Valentina looked at each other.

"Perhaps she's already gone home," he suggested. "And if not, her father can join us. We could use another pair of eyes."

"There's only their mother, and she'd be useless at a time like this. Emi might have fallen asleep—we'll first look carefully here."

"All right. Let's find your sister, Hector," said my father, and he sent up a prayer that the girl was safe and the fog might lift soon.

Emi, Hector informed them, liked hiding in hollow logs, burrowing into the ground and covering herself with leaves, and climbing small trees.

That doesn't much narrow things down, thought my father. She could be anywhere, invisible in the murk. "Valentina," he said, "surely our calls would have awakened the girl by now."

"You don't know small children. We'll head toward their home as we search. Hector, can you show me the way the two of you came?"

"Yes, Tia. It's over here." The boy took a few steps, furrowed his brow, then turned in the opposite direction. "Or maybe there, I'm not sure." His eyes filled with tears.

"Be strong, little one. All will be well." Valentina turned to my father. "Let's backtrack. I'll find my brother's place once I get my bearings."

They hadn't gone far when my father's ears pricked up at the sound of a familiar howling in the distance. "Any news?"

"No, it seems we're out of earshot. That's the real thing."

"Hector!" came the cry of a young girl.

"Emi!" Hector ran toward the sound of his sister's voice and vanished into the fog, followed closely by Valentina.

Just as my father started after them, a shimmering in the darkness stopped him cold.

He raised the Winchester to his shoulder.

Had his senses deceived him?

No, he could feel a presence hidden in the gloom.

"Caleb, where are you?" called Valentina.

"Stay back," he said in a voice of calm command. *Just this one time, obey.*

He slowed his breathing, filtered out the children's shouts, strained to see and hear.

Something's out there...

The fog began to lift.

My father crouched down to make himself less of a target and saw that he was perched on the very edge of an arroyo whose sheer walls plunged a good thirty feet to the dry riverbed below.

As he started to move, the ground beneath him gave way.

No! Grab on...

He clutched at the earth, but found nothing to hold onto, he was falling, and then a hand reached out, grasped his arm, and pulled him far enough that he could scramble up the rest of the way.

"You really ought to watch where you're going."

He found himself looking into Sofia's eyes.

What just happened is impossible.

"Thank you, Sofia! But my God—I'm more than twice your weight, yet you were able to lift me rather than be pulled over the edge yourself."

"Strength comes as the need arises, praise the Lord. Or do you think those muscles of yours will always suffice, without His help?"

"No, of course not. I only draw my next breath because He wills it."

He'd leave it there for now.

My father got to his feet and scanned the surroundings. The fog was high enough that he could see a fair distance in the pale, thin predawn light. He stood in a field of buffalo grass, not far from a lone honey mesquite, its top branches still obscured by the mist.

There were no threats in sight.

"Sofia!" Valentina approached them, Hector and Emi's hands clutched tightly in hers.

"I'm sorry," said Sofia, her words sounding more polite than heartfelt. "I meant to be back long ago. Elijah must be beside himself. But you should not have put yourselves at risk. Valentina, you know the night holds no terrors for me."

"Perhaps it should. The nagual may be stalking us," said Valentina, and she related what Gabriela had seen.

"She's mistaken," said Sofia. "Gabriela saw only a wild dog who roams the barrio, sniffing out scraps and bones."

Valentina's eyes widened. "How can you be so sure? I assure you, *I* was not mistaken about seeing Raoul's remains amid the nagual's tracks."

"How far from here was that?" my father asked her.

"Not three miles."

"Yes," said Sofia. "That was the demon's doing. But he's gone and will not strike again this day. *I know.*"

"Ah." The young warrior glanced at my father. "She has the sixth sense."

He raised his eyebrows. "Oh? Just what exactly does that mean?"

"Visions come to me," said Sofia. "Of things that are and that will be. My grandmother had this power as well. But it's not mine to command, it comes when it will."

"A gift of the Spirit, then," said my father.

He struggled, though, to make sense of all that had transpired.

"Emi," he said, as they hurried the children home, "the big kitty you saw—can you tell us what it looked like?"

His question was answered only by giggles.

"Did it scare you, chiquita?" asked Valentina.

"No, you silly! Kitty was beautiful, like you."

Valentina decided to stay for a while with her sister-in-law, who alternated between hugging her little ones and berating them, all amid a deluge of tears. So my father and Sofia set out by themselves for The Rat Trap, while above them a last few whisps of fog drifted in an indigo sky.

"Do you think the girl saw the nagual?" asked my father. *Do I actually believe in the creature?* he wondered. It seems he did.

"No," was all she deigned to reply.

"All right. It could have been a mountain lion, I suppose. Or anything at all, transformed by a child's fancy. Let's put that aside. Earlier you talked of trusting in the Almighty, who gave you the strength to break my fall. But there's such a thing as putting the Lord your God to the test. Venturing so close to where Vasquez was murdered, and in the dark of night..."

Something fell into place in my father's mind. "You went out hoping to find the nagual, didn't you. To find Harlon Gale."

A heartbeat passed before she spoke.

"I thought it more likely that he would find me."

"And then what? Were you hoping to *reason* with him?

To this she made no reply.

"Or perhaps you were counting on an army of angels to appear. But then again, you don't believe in violence."

Sofia gave my father a sad smile. "I'm sure you believe in the Bible's miracles, Caleb. And in all its wildest wonders. The Red Sea parting for God's people, only to close over the heads of their pursuers. Pillars of cloud and fire guiding them for forty years. It's only the command to love our enemies that you find too fantastic."

He shook his head. There were always those who took the notion that God is love to the point of absurdity. Argument was pointless. "I shouldn't mock you. You've courage, Sofia, I'll grant you that."

"You grant me too much," she replied, then stopped and threw back the hood of her cloak. "We've still an hour's walk ahead of us, I'd best let the others know I'm safe."

She cupped her hands to her mouth and let loose the high, clear call of a wolf.

It was answered by a distant chorus of yips and howls.

Our side this time, thought my father. Most likely, anyway; damned if he'd ask Sofia. He made a mental note to learn the women's wolven code and found himself wondering if Henry already had it down pat.

The thought of his lover lifted his spirits. He felt a keen longing to be with him and talk through this strange adventure, someplace they could be alone, in each other's arms.

Together they'd unravel all mysteries.

They were crossing a last stretch of field before the edge of town, the world still and silent but for the piping of a wood thrush in a bald cypress nearby, when my father was startled by a sudden feeling of—what? He searched for the right word.

Ah. Lightness.

Joy.

If only he could borrow Sofia's sixth sense! Not to hunt the nagual, not just then. Rather, he'd join his mind with Henry's so they could have this moment together: the rich smell of the earth, the coolness of the morning air just before sunrise, and there, on the eastern horizon, those few stray clouds set aglow, some a luminous gold, others stained the color of...

Blood.

My father's feeling of elation vanished like mist. All nature declared the glory of God, but there was nothing *natural* about Caleb McRae—he was an affront, a creature vile in the eyes of his Creator, his thoughts and actions flouting the mandates of Divine Law. The Lord had given up His very life for him—could *he* not give up Henry Midnight?

No. He could not.

Nor could he imagine living his life separated from God.

He plodded on by Sofia's side, eyes downcast, sick at heart.

Chapter Twenty-Three

The Man on the Other Side of the River

When my father and Sofia returned, they found Elijah, Marguerite, Henry, and Fr. de Souza gathered in the kitchen.

"I don't need to apologize to *you,* do I, dear one?" said Sofia. She wrapped her arms around her husband and kissed him softly on his forehead and on his cheeks and then lingeringly on his mouth.

"No," Elijah said when she leaned her head against his chest. "No, of course not."

"I'm tired to death, *mi amor,* and must sleep. Will you come?"

"I'll join you soon enough," he said, and watched her as she left the room.

"I'm pretty sure she only married you for money," said Henry, deadpan. He looked from the attorney over to my father, the light in his eyes expressing both delight and desire.

A torrent of conflicting emotions passed through my father in the next few seconds: shame at his constant vacillations, his failure to give as wholeheartedly and completely as Henry gave to him; guilt that he was betraying his God; anger that the Lord would have fashioned him this way in his mother's womb.

Gratefulness for finding love.

Elijah smiled wanly in response to Henry's jest. "Y'all have to be hungry. I'll tell you what—" He ladled batter into an iron skillet on the top of the wood cook stove. "You fill us in on what happened out there, Caleb, and I'll make more flapjacks. They're decent enough, as Baltasar can attest."

"He speaks the truth," said Fr. de Souza. "And if one applies sufficient quantities of bacon grease and molasses, one hardly mourns the absence of butter and maple syrup."

"That's a fair deal," said my father, and he leaned his Winchester against the wall, sat down next to Henry, and told the story of all that had transpired since they'd left.

"Val should have come back with you," said Marguerite when he fell silent. "I love her like a sister, but more and more she goes off on her own." She turned to Elijah. "As does Sofia. For all that she has the power of *el sexto sentido*, still, the danger is too great."

"They are who they are, Marguerite," replied the old man. "I could sooner command the wind to cease blowing than rein in those women."

"There's a third who goes out alone," said Henry. "Gale himself, if he and the nagual are indeed one. It's both his strength and his weakness."

"Yes." Fr. de Souza pushed back from the table and began cleaning his revolvers. "Though it's a weakness that will not much matter unless our skill at the hunt can equal his."

"One thing I'm sure of," said Elijah. "He knows you're here. His murder of Raoul was a message: *Behold the fate of all who oppose me.* He wants you to feel fear."

"If so, he is a fool," said Marguerite. "Let him come soon! Our knives thirst for his blood."

"Don't hold your breath," said my father. "He's not coming for us where we're strongest, nor should we waste our time hunting him. We hashed out a plan yesterday, and we'll stick to it. Are we together on this?"

"We are," said Elijah, and the women nodded their assent. "What concerns me is how we bring matters with the Knights to a head. When we crush them, the nagual will be all Gale has left. Then, Marguerite, your silver blade will be put to the test. But we have only been able to engage them a handful of times." He turned to the three Avengers. "You must find a way to make this happen faster."

"What we're doing now," said Henry, "is much like what Caleb did when he was chasing me: anticipating where the enemy might strike next and lying in wait. It's long and slow and dreary, but there's no other option."

"What of your wife's powers?" asked my father. "Have they not been of any use?"

"Not often enough. They're not hers to control."

"There may be another way," said Marguerite. "My cousin Louis is as white as the clouds on an April afternoon. There is no reason the Knights would know him, he lives more than a day's ride to the north. I've thought of asking Louis to come here, seek them out, and join them. He is only sixteen, but smart and strong and brave."

Elijah frowned. "The danger would be great. His parents would allow this?"

"I believe so. Their hearts are with us."

"I see. Well, I fought at his age, too. Write to him and his parents and be straightforward about the risk. If he agrees, we'll provide him with detailed advice and determine some method by which to communicate. Much as I'd like for us to meet with him, for his sake we can't chance it. Do you agree, Caleb?"

"Having an informant would be invaluable," said my father. "But there's more than bodily danger involved, Marguerite. To gain the Knights' confidence your cousin may have to go against everything decent and right. I'm loath to put Louis in that position without talking to him face to face."

"I want him to meet you," said Marguerite. "There will be a way."

"If Harlon Gale knows we're here," said Fr. de Souza, as the three men walked back to the bunkhouse, "the Rangers do as well."

"Yes," said my father. "It won't be long before they make their presence known."

"Ah, Caleb," said Henry, and he put his arm around his lover's shoulders. "A fine fix you've gotten us into this time! If we manage to survive the Knights and the Rangers and the beastly nagual, we'll likely all three of us end up as wanted men. But then, I rather enjoyed life on the run. And there's always Mexico."

"Or farther south," said Fr. de Souza. "Bogota was really rather delightful, once my nose stopped bleeding from the altitude."

My father's laugh died quickly. "You're right that when the smoke clears, there's a good chance we'll have capital murder hanging over our heads. Still, what we're doing is righteous, and I would not choose to run. Henry, you're the worker of magic, and Baltasar the crafter of prayers. We'll get through this, together, somehow."

"Take note, Friar Tuck," said Henry, "he's put it on us."

"I shall light the appropriate candles," said Fr. de Souza. "And trust in the Father of Lights. The knife-wielder spoke true; there *will* be a way. His way, and His alone."

Even Henry bowed his head at that, and softly echoed my father's *Amen*.

"I wish you'd been there with me when the fog began to lift off the Rio Grande," said Henry when he and my father were alone. "Tendrils of mist were rising from the water, as though the river were reaching up like a lover to touch the sky. The ghostliness of it! I saw lights moving perhaps a hundred yards away, on the Mexican side. Someone walking with a lantern, most likely. So close to me, and yet he might as well have been in another world." He paused, smiled, ran one finger along the line of my father's jaw. "Being with you feels that way to me, more often than I care to admit."

"I wish I'd been there." How pitiful his words sounded! My father's face burned with shame. But what could he say? That everything he'd seen and felt and wanted to share with Henry was trapped inside, that the beauty of those moments just before sunrise had been ruined by the confusion of thoughts that ran in an endless loop through his mind?

What a fool he'd sound.

It ought to be simple to tell God's will from his own, right from wrong, but these notions now seemed as tangled together as the roots of a mangrove tree.

"I thought of you as well," said my father, and he grasped Henry in his great arms, determined to show him in the only way he could the fierceness of his love and longing and the depth of his desire.

"Caleb," said Henry. "Come on, wake up."

They'd fallen asleep, entwined.

"Hmm?" My father opened one eye halfway.

"I know it bothers you, hiding ourselves away from the world, but we're in a place where that's hardly necessary. I mean, look about you! This might as well be the isle of Lesbos. Who's going to judge you here? Other than the All-Seeing Eye, of course, incessantly waving his rule book in your face and threatening to rap your knuckles like some cantankerous old nun. Baltasar has never said a word against us. Are you more priestly than he?"

"Staying holed up in The Rat Trap, is *that* what you're proposing? You wouldn't call that hiding ourselves away from the world?"

"I could be happy with you anywhere, Caleb. Even here."

"And I with you. But I feel called to more than this. There's something that lies ahead—something I can do for the glory of God. I don't expect you to understand."

"I thought you'd vowed to capture *me* for his glory. And here I am."

"I also vowed to make you a believer."

"Make me a *believer*? I'm far more of a believer than you! I believe in much that's in that Bible of yours—as I believe in the prayers of the penniless and the dreams of the dispossessed and in the tales of the native peoples who are one with this land." He raised himself up on his elbows, eyes flashing. "Is it really so fantastic to imagine that the Creator of the Heavens and Earth might have spoken through a Spider Grandmother as through the Hebrew prophets, as through a Micah, who went about naked, howling like a jackal and moaning like an owl?"

The two men rolled apart.

"I'm sorry," said my father, at last, and he moved close and put his head on his lover's chest.

"That's all right," said Henry. "I suppose this is a sort of penance I'm doing for past sins. Putting up with you, I mean."

"It must be difficult."

"Terribly."

They lay together for a long while, Henry running his hands through the golden ringlets of my father's hair, before falling at last into a deep and dreamless sleep.

Chapter Twenty-Four

Two Paths to Freedom

My father and Henry headed over to The Rat Trap the next morning, while children in tattered clothing ran down Calle de los Sombras, trailing clouds of dust. A mangy dog eyed the men warily before retreating into the shadows.

The bar was closed, its windows shuttered, so they let themselves in with a key and made their way upstairs to find Fr. de Souza and Elijah in the kitchen.

"Seeing as the mistress of the house is still sleeping," said the priest, who was tossing whatever scraps of meat he could find into a frying pan, "we are proving the resourcefulness of our sex by improvising a mid-morning meal."

"Marguerite and the others, they never cook?" asked my father.

"Oh, they do," said Elijah, "but with the women it's all turnips and berries and beans." He handed them mugs of sludgy coffee. "I'm grateful for the company of carnivores."

"My God, man!" said Henry, squinting warily into his mug. "I begin to understand why your skin is quite so black."

"I like a strong cup of joe myself," said my father, and he took a heroic slurp. "But I've a bone to pick with you, Elijah. We can't afford to have secrets from each other. Why didn't you tell us from the start about Sofia's gift?"

"Gift? She'd call it a curse. These visions drain her vital forces, she'll sleep straight through until tomorrow. The sixth sense was hers to reveal when you'd have ears to hear. Would you have believed in her psychic powers at first, any more than you believed in the nagual?"

"Perhaps not," my father conceded, and he wondered, *Why* do *I believe? I've seen no proof of man-beasts or the second sight. It's just that the world has suddenly become as strange as Scripture, and I'm feeling my way, deciding what to take on faith...*

"My wife is a mystery," Elijah said softly, gazing at the steam rising up from his coffee. "One I'm still puzzling over after nearly fifty years of marriage. Did Sofia tell you it was her idea to seek your help?"

"No. On the contrary, it's clear enough she thinks justice can never be accomplished by force."

"And yet you're here because of her. She knew of you from her mother, who still lives in El Paso. I'm not sure what to think of the matter—though I suppose in Sofia's blood is both the Spaniard's lust for battle and the Hopi's love of peace—a love, she claims, that is no different from that of Jesus."

"Her thinking is too simple." Fr. de Souza began doling out portions from a platter of charred meat. "Our Lord was both Lion and Lamb."

"*Abuelo!* What terrible smells are these? Burnt offerings to the Deity?"

A slender, dark-haired girl my father judged to be about fifteen came rushing into the kitchen.

"Go easy, Elliana," said Elijah. "These are our guests, the mighty Avengers. Gentlemen, meet Valentina's sister."

"Avengers? How wonderful and terrible! Do you have names?"

She soon knew them as Caleb, Henry, and Padre Baltasar, and shook each of their hands with a firm, strong grip.

"*Abuelo?*" Henry looked at Elijah with raised eyebrows.

"We have no children, Sofia and I," said the old man. "And so the girls—"

"Women," Elliana interjected.

"—the young women, they are like daughters and granddaughters to us."

"You won't mete out much vengeance with only *that* in your bellies!" Elliana scowled at the platter of blackened meat. She rummaged through the handful of items on the pantry shelves before finding the remains of a bag of flour and a can of baking soda. "Ah! Step aside, *por favor*, Padre Baltasar, there's just enough here for me to bake half a loaf."

"Bless you, child," said the priest. "That would be a fine way to mop up the last of the bacon grease."

"The Tejano ranchers are fortunate you married Sofia," said Henry. "You've taken up their cause, while your own people groan under no small oppression. Does that trouble you?"

"'My own people?'" Elijah frowned and sat up straighter in his chair. "Do you imagine there's a tribe to whom I owe allegiance? *Any man's death diminishes me,* Henry Midnight, *for I am involved in mankind*. You can hear the bell tolling, can't you? I believe that's why you're here."

"Are you not being harsh with our guest, *Abuelo*?" Elliana called out as she worked the dough.

Elijah was silent for a moment and then laughed. "I am, dear one. It was not such a bad question. I *am,* after all, a member of a tribe, or at least was born into one, and a man's origins mark him for life. Quite literally, in my case. Look closely." He pointed to a faded network of scars on both sides of his eyes and mouth. "I was born in Ghana, gentlemen, among the Balumae people. My mother had lost her first two babes, so I was marked by the *Wanzan*—he who is born with a blade in his hand!—to make me ugly to the gods of the other world. He seems to have done his job well. And perhaps I shall end this long life the way it began—amid the flashing of knives."

"Nonsense!" exclaimed Elliana. "My sister's blade could defeat death itself."

"That I believe," said my father. "And we've a considerable incentive to keep you among the living. You're the only attorney in the Republic of Texas who's willing to work with us."

"Ah! I shall double my rates forthwith."

"You came here as a slave, then," said Father de Souza. "From the eloquence of your speech, I took you for one born and bred in the northern states. I'd be most interested in hearing your tale."

"Would you, now. Hmm. What do you think, Elliana?"

"I think I'll simply fry the dough and feed you men all the quicker. But *si, Abuelo, absolutamente*. That would be the very best way to answer Henry's question."

"Fair enough, child." Elijah poured himself another cup of sludge and turned to the three Avengers. "So, then: in 1830, when I was six years old, my poppa and momma and I were captured by raiders and sold to the Dutch, who marched us more than a hundred miles to a slave castle on the Atlantic coast. There I caught glimpse of the ocean, and it was terrifying and thrilling all at once, its smell and sound and magnificent vastness. Then for months there was nothing but dungeon darkness and the press and stink of human flesh. At last we were herded onto boats and set to sea chained in cargo holds, and there I came to know a yet deeper circle of hell. Momma did not survive the Middle Passage, but Poppa resolved to live, and the unextinguishable flame of his hatred for the slavers did more than even food and water to keep us both alive."

A rustling from behind my father; Gabriela and Marguerite came quietly into the room and listened as Elijah continued his story.

"Within a year we found ourselves in Georgia, clearing malaria-infested swamps and planting rice. It did not take Poppa long to learn we were close to a land which had been ruled by the Spaniards until only a few years before, a place of refuge for slaves with the will and wits to slip their bonds. Were they true, he asked the Gullah slaves alongside whom we worked, these stories of free men and women, their skin as black as ours, living in a land called Florida? Ah well, they told us, once it was, but Jackson, the White Warrior Chief, had led his soldiers across the border twelve winters before, and seized Florida, and killed many Africans, and now he is Great Father of all the whites. Were no more of our people free? Poppa asked. And an Old One told him, some say black men dwell there still, only now deep in the wild, and some say they are the slaves of red men who live there too. But *escape,* he said, that is a crazy dream. First there are the plantation guards, and their dogs, and then the soldiers at the border, and then all the perils of a wilderness filled with monstrous beasts, and no way of knowing where these free men might be, if they are even there at all.

"Better to die dreaming of freedom, Poppa told me that night, than living the life of a slave. He asked questions, watched, and schemed, and pushed me to work hard, harder even than the plantation bosses demanded of a full-grown man, so I would grow strong and yearn for freedom with all my heart. Poppa waited until I was twelve years old and could live on a few scraps of bread and scant sips of water and still work a twelve-hour day.

"Then we made our move.

"We were six weeks in the swamps and forests, evading soldiers and steering clear of alligators and panthers and boars, and nearly despairing of our quest, when we were awakened early one morning by a strange and terrible sight: a half dozen red men armed with rifles, their hair festooned with feathers. They wore buckskin leggings and long shirts of pale green calico cloth fastened around the waist with a crimson sash. Poppa and I had taken knives with us when we escaped the plantation, but they seemed pathetically useless. Were we again doomed to be enslaved?"

The sizzle and scent of frying dough filled the room, but no one—not even Fr. de Souza!—so much as licked their lips.

"'*Estelusti,*' said one of the men, and he pointed to the south. When we stared at him blankly, he laughed and said, *Negroes*. It was one of a few words of English we had in common. *Eat,* he said. *Follow*.

"They were Seminole Indians, and they gave us dried venison and cool fresh water and led us to a sight almost too fantastic to believe: a village filled with men and women and children black as the richest soil, as anthracite, obsidian, onyx—black as me!—and as beautiful as the night sky, with smiles gleaming like the Great River that spans the heavens and eyes shining like the stars of the Drinking Gourd.

"These were the Africans who had escaped the plantations, the Negro Seminoles, not slaves to the Indians, but vassals, free men who paid them annual tribute and were their equals in all other ways. Red man and Black lived side by side, and together they fought the soldiers Jackson sent into the Florida jungle, and together they pushed the enemy back.

"I lived in awe of the hero of our village, John Horse, of whom a thousand tales of bravery and cunning were told. The huts we lived in did not have walls, only tarps that could be let down when the heavens opened and poured down rain. One day when the great man was off doing battle, I ventured close to his dwelling place and a curious object caught my eye. It was a Bible, something I'd glimpsed on a few Sunday mornings at the plantation when the slaver's shaman, robed in black, held it up before us, declaring it had all the power and glory of the white man's god. Was it the secret to John Horse's might?

"I looked about; there was no one, so I opened the book and turned its pages. What magical symbols were these? And the illustrations inside! Two white folk standing in a jungle, naked and unarmed. Hah! Surely they would be devoured in short measure by wild beasts! A huge boat—bigger even than the slavers' vessel!—braved storm-tossed waters, a giraffe sticking its long neck out of one of the windows. What could any of this mean? I paged through eagerly, mystified by the symbols, entranced by the pictures, and lost track of time.

"All at once a shadow fell across me and a great hand grasped my shoulder. It was John Horse himself! My blood ran cold. 'Are you reading, little man?' he asked me. 'I do not know what 'reading' means,' I managed to stammer in reply. 'When a man can read,' he told me, 'it is as though a hundred voices were speaking through those pages, telling a thousand strange and wonderful tales.'

"'How can I learn to read?' I heard myself asking, hardly believing I had the courage to speak such words. He laughed and told me to come back in the morning, in the darkness before dawn, before even the women were up preparing for the day. 'Come back,' said John Horse, 'Come back and I will teach you how to read.'

"Ah, the tales I read within the pages of that Bible! They fascinated and appalled and thrilled me. Young boys defeating giants! Battles fought between armies while the sun and moon stood still! Stories of vengeance, of seduction, incest, and lust! All these lit a flame inside me that would grow into a blazing fire when I met one yet greater than John.

"But I am getting ahead of myself." Elijah paused and sipped his coffee and for a few moments the room was silent.

"'You should have an English name,' the great warrior told me. 'One chosen from this Bible.' My mother had named me *Yendau*, which means 'bought as a slave,' not because she had the gift of prophecy, but to signify I could not be taken back to the spirit world like my older brothers. So I thought, perhaps Joseph would be an appropriate name, seeing as he'd been sold into slavery, yet prevailed. But John Horse said no, and went with me to Poppa, and he said, 'From this day forth, your boy shall be known as Elijah, for one day he will call down fire from heaven to defeat our enemies!'

"By then I was fifteen and the time had come for me to fight alongside my father, and Poppa grinned, and I was filled with pride.

"The Great White Fathers—first Jackson, then Van Buren, then Tyler, may their names be forever cursed!—could not countenance free Negroes and Indians in Florida and had vowed to remove us from the land. On came their armies, and ah, my friends, we fought them well! How my heart soared when we stormed the sugar plantations of the Atlantic coast and laid them waste, and the men and women we freed rejoiced and joined our ranks!

"We slew many soldiers, yet for every one that fell, two came to take his place, and in the end all our fighting was in vain.

"Not long into my eighteenth year, John Horse and the other chiefs agreed to save the lives of our women and children and old ones by agreeing to peace on the white man's terms. The slavers wanted none of us back on their plantations, so we would surrender our arms and move to a far Western land—Indian Territory, in eastern Oklahoma—and there, within those confines, we'd be free. Few believed this, of course, for out of the white man's mouth came endless lies. And yet we clung to a sliver of hope.

"They took us by boat to New Orleans, and from there we journeyed three months, a seven-hundred-mile slog through Louisiana and Arkansas in the sweltering summer, one cart provided for every twenty of us, and no provisions. Many old ones and not a few babes died along the way and were buried in hasty graves. By the time we reached the Territory, Poppa's hair had turned white, deep lines furrowed his brow, and his eyes were sunk in shadows. He could not have been much past forty.

"Such was our passage along the Trail of Tears.

"It did not take long for our worst fears to be realized. We'd been put under the Creek Indians, who sought to enslave us, and at night we stood guard against white slavers who came to kidnap our women and children. Our anger and desperation grew until Poppa and I and a small army of others joined with John Horse and Wildcat, the Seminole chief, and decided to flee.

"There were two paths to freedom: the Underground Railroad ran north to the state of Illinois, but it had a southern terminus as well. Mexico had long since outlawed slavery, and for decades many had found salvation on the other side of the Rio Grande. Surviving our escape would be a long shot; either route ran through slave territory for over six hundred miles. And yet it wasn't a difficult decision; we'd had enough of the white man's rule. Mexico it would be.

"We left under cover of night, carrying weapons we'd stockpiled and some dried meat and canteens of water and little else. In our travels through Indian Territory, we met a troop of Kickapoo who were eager to join us and together we fought our way through Cherokee land. By then there were nearly two hundred of us, all told.

"We endured much hardship and travail in the Texas desert, and buried our dead along the way, and there were moments when some wondered, like the Hebrews in the wilderness, whether we'd been better off as slaves. An Indian agent had put a bounty on our heads, and the governor of Texas was demanding our capture. But Poppa and John Horse were fierce for freedom, and we pressed on, heading always to the southwest, skirting cities and towns, until late one night we came to the springs of Las Moras and pitched camp, knowing at last the Mexican border was near.

"The mourning doves had not yet begun to coo when one of our scouts returned and woke John Horse: someone had stumbled upon us and was heading to town with the news. Fast as we could we sped to the Rio Grande and set about fashioning rafts out of anything we could find. And then the storm descended, a detachment of Texas Rangers calling for our surrender, and when our first rafts began to cross the river, their guns began blazing.

"We answered them with our rifles, and three Rangers fell, and then I heard Poppa groan and saw his shirt and pants were soaked with blood. 'Elijah!' he called out. 'Go now—I can still shoot, I'll hold them off.' 'No!' I howled, for I could not imagine life without my father. 'You damn well listen to me, boy,' he said, his voice like cold steel. 'I'm gut-shot and speaking to you from the grave. You must go.' And then John Horse was dragging me away, we were on the last raft crossing the river, I could hear Poppa's rifle firing again and again and the soldiers returning fire, and finally only the faint sounds of the enemy's weapons but by then we were on Mexican soil and dawn was breaking and we were gone, we were home, we were free."

Chapter Twenty-Five

El Nacimiento

"I'm sorry for what you endured at the hands of the Rangers," said my father. "It shames me that I once thought nothing more glorious than to wear their badge."

"Ah well," said Elijah. "The path you chose was one that led you here today, as my comrade-in-arms. We must all of us find our way." He drained the dregs of the coffee, then rose and set a pot of water on the wood stove.

Elliana took that as her opening to serve up the fried dough slathered in bacon grease.

"Thank you, my dear," said Fr. de Souza. "I feel as famished as if I myself had just traversed the state of Texas and crossed the Rio Grande. But please, Elijah, do go on."

"Indeed," said Henry. "We've yet to meet Sofia and the man greater than John Horse."

"You drive an old man rather hard!" replied Elijah as he settled back into his chair. "When it boils, Elliana, don't skimp on the grounds, mind you."

"I wouldn't dare, *Abuelo*."

"All right, then. We had entered into the badlands of northern Mexico, in Coahuila, and though we'd left the Rangers behind, we'd no clear idea what lay in store. One thing we did know all too well: this was territory frequented by the Comanche, and they were no friends of ours.

"John Horse sent out scouts, and soon enough we made our way to the state capital, Piedras Negras, a name we took as an auspicious sign, for it means 'black stones.' There he and Chief Wildcat presented themselves to the Governor. A dozen of us were honored to join them, and that night we feasted on baked goat and yucca flowers and toasted each other with glasses of *sotol,* which, our hosts boasted, makes mezcal taste like the piss of a syphilitic mule. We carried on late into the night. How they laughed when I excused myself to vomit up my dinner and drink, and passed out on the Governor's lawn! When I awoke the sun was already above the horizon. I feared I'd disgraced myself, but John Horse only put his arm around my shoulders and smiled. The Mexicans had granted us a fair bit of land in exchange for a pledge to defend the border against raiders from the north, which meant the Kiowa and Apache and most of all, the dread Comanche.

"For years Indians had been storming across the border to steal horses, which they'd trade to the Anglos for guns. The Comanches were a special terror to the Mexicans; many hundreds would come at a time, and almost as much as they loved stealing horses, they loved to fight. But this was nothing new, fighting was all most of us had known since birth. So we rejoiced in our newfound freedom and gladly answered their call to arms.

"John Horse and Wildcat led us to the land we'd been granted, and I built a home and married a girl—"

"A young woman, *Abuelo,*" said Elliana.

"—a young woman I'd freed from a sugar plantation not long before the Trail of Tears. Ah, my friends, what bliss! We'd settled in a place called El Nacimiento—The Birthplace—and soon enough my Sara was with child. *El Nacimiento*—how perfect was that name! Surely this was a rebirth for Negro and Kickapoo and Seminole alike! And for me, a chance to raise a child in freedom, sure Poppa was looking down from the heavens, his face wreathed in smiles.

"But once again dark angels gathered round me, and the curse that had haunted my mother returned with a vengeance. My son did not live twenty-four hours, and Sara, who had lost much blood, followed him into the spirit world soon after.

"My heart grew cold. Had I so angered the Almighty, if indeed He existed, that he would rain down such misfortune? Was I the pawn of a wager He'd made with the devil?

"I covered myself in ashes, and only the fury of battle allowed me to forget my grief.

"To the north of us, on the far side of the Rio Grande, the slavers had never forgotten nor forgiven our escape. It especially enraged the Texans to have a contingent of escaped slaves living in glorious freedom so close to their land! One day, word came to John Horse that the Rangers had been given a special commission: cross the border, ride like very devils of destruction and lay waste to El Nacimiento, slay the men and leave them for the vultures, but bring back the women and children in chains.

"By that time he was known as El Capitán Juan Caballo, and his legend had spread throughout the land. He told me what he'd heard, told me I must ride into battle by his side. I was in the prime of my manhood, my thirty-first year. My blood ran hot at his words and I pounded my chest and for the first time in a long while I felt joy.

"Soon enough our scouts reported the Rangers were across the Rio Grande. Red man and Black gathered at opposite sides of a canyon not far from the settlement and waited for the enemy to arrive, waited for them to be directly between us, and then John Horse gave the signal and we descended upon the Rangers like furies, like the army of angels Elisha saw riding chariots of fire. I cut down two men with my rifle, then three more with my pistol at close range. The desert floor ran red with Ranger blood; only a handful escaped with their lives, never to trouble us again.

"And so I gained some measure of revenge."

Elijah turned toward Elliana with raised eyebrows, and she brought over the pot and filled each empty cup with sludge.

"And yet life seemed empty of purpose and meaning, and I awoke each day more discontented than the last. I no longer relished combat with the Comanche, nor any sport. *Pray*, the Man of Sorrows had commanded his disciples, but I was not even sure what to pray for, and when I did the heavens answered only with silence.

"Reading Bible tales was my one escape from dreariness, and I longed for more. The day came when I saddled my steed and rode into Piedras Negras, hoping to divert my gloomy thoughts and find some new books. I wandered down several streets and a broad boulevard and then, on a shadowed side street, came upon a bookstore, *La Librería de los Ángeles.* I walked the aisles, scanned the titles, and turned the pages of this or that volume until a young woman came up and told me they'd be closing soon, was there something she could help me find? I looked into her eyes for a half-dozen heartbeats and said 'I believe I've just found it, ma'am.' Her face reddened, but only slightly, and she held my gaze. I told her there wasn't a story in the Bible I hadn't read at least a dozen times, that I loved them dearly but was seeking something new. She sat me at a table, brought over *The Pilgrim's Progress* and Butler's *Lives of the Fathers,* and we took turns reading passages aloud.

"That evening we dined at a small café and told each other the stories of our lives. Her mother had married a Mexican soldier, just as her grannie had done years before, and the blackguard had deserted them when she was only a child. She was then seventeen, and had left home to search for her father, to hear from his own lips why he'd gone away. She'd found him, all right, there in a small cemetery in Piedras Negras, in an ill-tended grave. But after she'd resolved to leave for home and packed her belongings, a Help Wanted sign in a bookstore caught her eye.

"I hardly need tell you, my friends, that her name was Sofia. I returned to Nacimiento only long enough to explain I'd met the woman I would marry and collect my belongings, then found lodging in Piedras Negras. A few words from Captain Caballo sufficed for me to obtain an administrative post in the Governor's office. Fall changed to winter, winter to spring, and by summer we were man and wife and once again life was sweet.

"Sofia stayed on at *La Librería de los Ángeles* and took over when the proprietor retired. When there were no customers, she'd read to her heart's content. My duties were light enough that I was able to attend university. In the evening we'd prepare dinner, she and I, and not a few meals ended with a bottle of wine while we read to each other from the Song of Songs and then dallied together in love.

"And yet the demons of ill fortune were not done with me and those I love; three times Sofia was with child, and three little graves there are in a churchyard in Piedras Negras. Finally we gave up all thought of having children. It was in the depth of her sadness that my wife first began to wander alone, sometimes for days at a time.

"But ah, my friends, in the spring of 1865, the seventh year of our marriage, the War Between the States came to an end and hope reentered our lives. It was not long before the United States Army contacted John Horse to see if any of us might be interested in returning, for they well knew our success in battling the Comanche. And that is when Sofia and I hatched our plan. Slavery was no more, we had nothing to fear; I could serve with the Army for a brief while, then we could travel to the Commonwealth of Massachusetts, a place that seemed yet more fantastic than the most fabulous legends of Ultima Thule. There the Negro had all the rights of citizenship as the White; there we could cast our votes and choose our leaders; and there were universities which welcomed women with open arms.

"That night we drank wine again, and held each other, and whispered in each other's ears.

"'*Behold, thou art fair, my love;*' I said. '*thou hast doves' eyes.*'

"'*For, lo,*' returned Sofia, '*the winter is past, the rain is over and gone.*'

"Early the next year we crossed back over the Rio Grande, and I reported to Fort Duncan, where I was affirmed as a citizen of the United States of America and an Army Scout. Soon I was transferred to Fort Bliss—no stronghold was more aptly named!—where my wife and I spent the next two years. This was in a region you know well, Caleb, for not many years later it was renamed El Paso. While I was chasing after the Apache, Sofia came to love the Chihuahuan desert, which became her second home. Jaguars and bears and reptiles innumerable held no terror for her; like St. Francis, she conversed with the beasts. And there, in the stark, bleak daylight and the dark beauty of starlit nights, there she first felt the strange power that coursed through her veins, the power her grandmother had passed on.

"'We will never reach Massachusetts,' she told me when I returned from patrol, and then she put her arms around me and kissed me much as you saw this morning. 'But never fear. *All will be well, and all will be well.*' And she leaned her head against me. '*And all manner of thing shall be well.*'"

"When I left the Army, Sofia and I packed our clothes and our books and boarded a train bound for St. Louis. From there we travelled to Chicago and transferred to a line carrying us to New York. We were eager to experience the enlightened ways of the North and delighted in having left the Southern states behind.

Elijah laughed grimly. "How naïve we were! White and Black of course rode in separate cars. There were no luggage racks in the Negro compartment, but we piled our bags around us and managed as well as we could, and midway through the two-day journey, we walked to the observation car at the rear of the train, to stretch our legs, take in some fresh air, and gaze out at the Ohio countryside.

"It was not long before three white men approached us. 'Didn't know they let niggers and wetbacks here,' said one. 'Don't think they do,' said another. 'You hear that, boy?' said the third, addressing me. 'You n' your greaser whore might want to make yourself scarce. Or maybe we ought'a just help you disembark right now.'"

"A few seconds ticked past and endless rows of corn flashed by and I had just about decided on which of the men I'd take apart first, when I heard footsteps behind me and a voice like Gideon's trumpet declaimed, 'Shut your mouths, the three of you, *this moment* and leave. I shall not warn you again.'"

"I turned around.

"Standing there was a tall, broad-shouldered Negro dressed in a fine suit, a veritable lion of a man, with a great mane of black hair, the beard of an African king, a noble forehead, and a terrible fierceness in his eyes.

"'It stinks in here,' said one of ruffians. 'Let's vamoose, I can hardly stand the smell.' And they slunk away.

"'Thank you, sir,' said I, 'for saving me the trouble of dispatching those fools. I am Elijah Jones'—for that was the surname I had taken, for lack of one better—'and this is my wife, Sofia.'

"'Ah, wisdom itself,' said our intercessor, bending over to kiss her hand after shaking mine. 'Frederick Douglass, at your service.'

"Mr. Douglass accompanied us back to our seats, where we'd left a stack of books. 'Victor Hugo!' he remarked, picking up a translation of *Les Misérables* we'd been reading. 'He and I could be great friends, I'm sure. A champion for abolition and for universal suffrage. We have gained a degree of freedom, you and I' he said to me, 'but what are we without the right to choose our leaders?'

"'No better off than women, I suppose,' said Sofia. Mr. Douglass's eyes widened and then he smiled and sat down, and told of his life—he was, you know, an escaped slave like myself—and of his work. We conversed like old friends until we arrived at last at the Grand Central Station.

"'If you will forgive my presumption,' he said, 'I suggest you abandon your plans to travel to Massachusetts. Come with me to Rochester instead. I've need of a secretary, Elijah, and am offering you that position. As to your plans to attend university, Sofia, I've just the thing. Mr. Henry Wells, of Wells Fargo, has only just opened a college for women not seventy miles from my home.'

"In the same year that Sofia graduated from Wells College, we moved with Mr. Douglass to the nation's capital. It was thanks to him I earned a law degree at Howard University, thanks to him I learned the art of oratory and came to understand the workings of power in this country, when to compromise and when to stand firm no matter the cost. We were proud to follow in his shadow for fourteen years.

"By the 80s, Jim Crow laws were rampant in the Southern states, and Negroes had all but lost the right to vote. Much as I loathed the idea, Sofia and I felt called to return to the South, and so we met with Mr. Douglass. Years before he had quoted to us from the prophet Amos, *let justice run down as waters, and righteousness as a mighty stream.* He reminded us of those words, only this time he added, 'those same waters, that same mighty stream before which evil shall surely fall, may sweep us away as well. I do not know if we will meet again; but you both are always with me in my heart.' We embraced, and he gave us his blessing, and we parted ways.

"You have perhaps received more of an answer than you bargained for, Henry, my friend. I have fought for the Black man, and for those of Mexican blood—to whom I owe my very life!—and would fight for the White man as well, if need arose. Only my strength is not what it once was, and thank God for these young women—" he cast a meaningful glance at Elliana—"my dear *hijas y nietas.* And for the three of you, who are an answer to our—"

Elijah broke off as Sofia entered the room, her hair no longer braided but streaming over her shoulders, her face deathly pale.

"Your prayers, old man?" Her eyes were wide and wild. "Will you call down fire from heaven? And if you do, whom will it not burn?" Sofia looked about in anguish. "Gabriela, Marguerite, my poor doomed daughters! Ah, Padre! I see a field of bones bleached by the sun. And you, Henry Midnight, even you will be struck down."

She knelt in front of Elijah and spoke in a whisper.

"All your bold words, all your prayers—how can you hope to hear the Lord's answer? Have you forgotten He speaks in a still, small voice?" She put her head in Elijah's lap and closed her eyes. "There is only one way we shall be saved," she murmured. "Through the power of His love."

For a long while he gently stroked his wife's hair, then gathered her up in his arms, shook off my father and Henry's offer of help, and slowly, his arms and legs shaking with the effort, carried her away to bed.

Chapter Twenty-Six

Something for the Glory of God

Though the Avengers joined the women warriors on nightly stakeouts, hoping to catch the Knights of the White Camelia on one of their raids, the next few months brought them nothing but weary frustration. On one occasion they returned to El Atrapa only to hear word of a brazen assault carried out in broad daylight; the Knights had cut down a patriarch on his way home from church, and when his wife and sons attempted to fight back they were slaughtered as well.

Valentina had tacked up a large map of the Valley on the kitchen wall and marked the location of every Tejano ranch Gale was likely lusting after. My father and Henry studied them with her, searching for patterns in the Knights' forays and agreeing on the location and tactics for the next stakeout. The urgency of placing an informer in their ranks was growing; Marguerite had written to Louis' parents, but had not yet received a response.

The only accomplishment they could claim came from Fr. de Souza's efforts with Judge O'Connor. He'd followed Elijah's suggestion to meet the judge at the Church of the Holy Redeemer, where in the course of conversation His Honor revealed a passion for Palestrina's masses and motets, which he'd heard in Boston as a young man. "Ah, you share my taste in music," the priest had declared, for never a man wrote more mellifluous polyphony than the maestro of the Renaissance, Giovanni Pierluigi da Palestrina! Following the revelation of this remarkable coincidence, the two had bonded over steins of beer.

"There's only so much he's willing to do," Fr. de Souza told his partners when he finally felt the time was right to turn his conversation with the judge to legal matters. "It's clear enough he's loathe to incur the wrath of Harlon Gale. But he can stall here and there, and slow down the pace of foreclosures."

"Well done, Baltasar," said my father. "That will buy us some time."

The winter of 1905 was one of the coldest ever in the Rio Grande Valley, but at last the Avenger's luck began to thaw. While they were staking out one of the more modest ranches, a small detachment of Knights fell into their trap. My father, Valentina, the rancher's two sons, and two other of Elijah's militia had hidden themselves in a stand of trees inside the perimeter fence, while Henry and four of the women warriors were positioned on a small bluff some fifty yards away. The women, my father had been pleased to discover, carried Sharps rifles, much beloved by buffalo hunters for their accuracy at long range.

"When it comes to scum like these," Valentina had told him, "I'd rather not soil my blades."

The party of nine Knights came directly between them.

"Freeze, or you're dead men," called out my father.

"Drop your weapons," cried Marguerite. "Surrender and live or fight and die."

The Dread High Dragon of the Knights' detachment looked to his left and right. Bandoliers crisscrossed his white robe and a scabbard dangled from his left hip. He threw back his hood, sneered, and turned to his men.

"There's no going back boys! Better to take our chances fighting the hell-bitches and their lackeys than face the wrath of the Beast." He drew a pistol from his belt, turned his steed, and charged toward the trees, the rest of his men close behind.

Elijah's Militia victory that evening was terrible and swift.

The battle was followed by reports of yet more savage violence wreaked by the remaining Knights. So it was welcome news when Marguerite received a letter back from her aunt, apologizing for the long delay. She and her husband had talked the matter over for endless hours, lit candles to the Blessed Virgin, and prayed for wisdom. As for Louis, he was brave and true and eager for adventure. *You are fighting on the side of the angels,* wrote Ines. *We await your arrival.* Louis' father, who'd fought the Kiowa and Comanche at Antelope Hills, scrawled a note at the bottom, after his wife's signature: *The boy's got my blood in his veins, he'll do us proud. God speed.*

Marguerite hitched Bonita, her favorite mule, to a cart she'd loaded with a great mound of empty flour sacks and set off with a heavy shawl wrapped tightly around her and a scarf covering her bald pate, looking for all the world like a harmless old *abuelita*.

My father and Louis met at last in a shadowed corner of the stables while Henry and the others patrolled Calle de las Sombras. The young man was a study in incongruity: his rosy cheeks showed not a trace of whiskers, yet he stood a good six feet tall, a flaxen-haired youth with a manly, muscular frame. He had an open, straightforward countenance my father found impossible not to like from the moment the two first shook hands.

"Why are you doing this?" my father asked.

"My mom told me about what's happening to her people down here, Mr. McRae, and it makes my blood boil! I love my cousin, too—" he glanced over at Marguerite, who was removing her scarf, "— strange duck as she is. And I'm itching to do something for the glory of God."

Ah, that, thought my father. He'd consecrated his service in the Rangers to such glory! It hurt his heart to think on it. Surely this lad was on a better path.

"This mission you've volunteered for—it's riskier than going into battle, riskier than anything I ever did as a Ranger. You could find yourself a target of those who seek revenge on the Knights—the son of some patriarch they've slain—or of the Knights themselves, should they ever doubt your loyalty."

"I ain't afraid, sir. Not of death or anything else."

My father smiled. "I don't doubt you, Louis. But there's something more important than the risk to life and limb: what you might have to do to prove yourself to the Knights of the White Camelia, what hateful acts they might command once you've given your oath of allegiance. Have you given that any thought?"

"Some. I guess you mean they might ask me to kill."

"Yes. Or worse."

"Rita tells me if we can't stop the Knights, scores more could die. She said the tip-offs I could give will be just what we need to stop 'em dead in their tracks. So, I don't much like it, but if we got to sacrifice one to save many, then that's what we'd have to do."

"What *you'd* have to do." *He's not callous*, thought my father, *merely naïve*. "You ever kill a man, Louis? Some child's father, some man's brother, some woman's son? Look him in the eyes and then go ahead and end his life?"

"No, sir." He blushed and looked at my father with an expression of surprise. "Are you saying you wouldn't take on this mission, if you were me?"

"I'm saying we've got to plan and do it smart."

"That baby face of yours, Lou," said Marguerite. "It might be your saving grace. Might not his youth buy him some time, Caleb? He could present himself as an eager recruit, but one still not ready to do the Knight's darkest deeds."

My father considered this for a moment. "I reckon you might be able to balk the first time they asked you to perform an evil deed, Louis. But that won't work more than once, and might not work at all. I think the best plan is for you to show up with your right arm in a sling from a piece of bad luck you ran into on the way down."

"Perhaps he got into a fight," said Marguerite, "and the other hombre's six feet under."

"Good thought. Point is, you'd tell them while you're waiting for your arm to mend, you'll do whatever they ask of you, sweep the floors with your left hand, stoke the fires, cook their grub. There's a decent chance that would buy you some time before you'd be forced to join in their violence."

"Mightn't they just tell me to go and come back when I'm healed up?"

"I doubt it, though it's only a temporary setback if they do. They're going to like the looks of you, Louis. You're a bird in the hand. Your parents didn't want you to leave home, but here you are, and when your right arm's ready, they'll wonder how they ever did without you. So I'd wager you'll be a Knight soon enough. The question is whether this ploy would buy you *enough* time. Because we need you to wait, and only get word to us when a major raid is being planned—or under way, if you're unable to find out in advance."

"Why, Mr. McRae? Wouldn't you want to try and stop every raid I get word of?"

"No, there's too great a risk they'd catch on. Sending us a message will be fraught with danger, you'll do it only one time, when our enemy is lusting after one of the larger ranches and sending in most of their men. Then, when their forces are long gone and the battle likely already joined, you'll disappear, your mission done. And we'll get you safely home. But listen to me Louis, and mark my words: if ever you're asked to do something your conscience cannot bear, come back to us the first chance you get. There'll be no shame in that—only honor in having done the right thing."

The three talked tactics for a long while: how Louis would find the Knights, how he'd get word to them when the time was right, and then escape. The fallback plans for everything that might go wrong.

And then a knock came at the stables door.

My father frowned.

He drew his revolver, motioned for quiet, and stood against the frame to the right of the door.

"Who's there?"

"It's Elliana," came the whispered reply. "Please—I want to see Lou!"

This is foolishness, thought my father, *but better to have her inside than out.* He unlocked the door and Elliana swiftly slipped inside.

"*Caramba! Louie!* How tall you've grown!"

"Ellie?" Louis looked at her, astonished.

She ran and threw her arms around him.

He hugged her in return and then, reddening, held Elliana at arm's distance and gazed into her joyful face. "Seems like yesterday you weren't but Valentina's kid sister, and now—" He shook his head in wonder, then turned to the others. "She used to tag along with me when I did chores, back when Rita and I lived up their way. Haven't seen each other in years."

"Tell you what," said my father. "We'll take a break, let you two catch up for a bit. For Louis' sake, Elliana, you must keep his presence in Brownsville a secret—only your sister, Marguerite, Elijah, and Sofia know he's here. Any further contact between the two of you must wait until his work is done."

"*Si, si*, Caleb, I understand. He is very brave, no? *Dios mio,* Louie, you're as big as your papi!"

"I'm stepping out for a smoke," said Marguerite, taking a cheroot from her breast pocket.

My father walked over to Achilles' stall and began working a curry comb in gentle circles at the top of the horse's neck. *Sixteen years old.* At that age, he'd been shooting tin cans off the back-yard fence, chopping cords of wood, dreaming of Texas. So sure that God was only testing him, putting him through a trial. *Lord, I turn my eyes from other boys when the feelings come upon me. Tell me I'm not evil in your sight, Lord, that I'm not accursed for wanting unholy things.* Surely it mattered that he averted his eyes and uttered Psalms of repentance!

Surely the Lord would lift the curse, put an end to the desires that coursed through his blood, tell him he'd met the challenge, won the race, let him join the body of Christ without the guilt of pretending to be someone he's not.

That would only be just!

But here he was, thirteen years later, only more deeply enmeshed in sin.

A surge of self-loathing passed through my father, and then he put those thoughts aside. He had Louis to worry about, and something important that needed to be done.

"Go now, Elliana," he said, rejoining the two youths. "We've matters to conclude."

Marguerite, watching from the doorway, stubbed out her cheroot and ground it under her heel.

"I like your cousin's idea," he said when Elliana had left. "Showing up with a bad arm after a fight to the death gives you both credibility and a decent chance you won't have to commit violence, at least for a while. But simply showing up with your arm in a sling won't do. Your appearance has to match your tale."

"I understand, sir. I got to look like I was in a fight."

"Cuts and bruises," said Marguerite. "Yes, of course."

"There are ways to make bruises look worse than they really are," said my father. "We'll put a few where they'll be plainly visible on your face, but your right arm needs to look a deep black and blue if it's ever exposed."

"Yes, that is wise," said Marguerite. "And I'll give you the sort of cut you'd have on your left hand, defending yourself against a knife-wielding hombre."

"All right," said Louis. "Let's do what's got to be done."

"You've the heart of a lion," said Marguerite, and she kissed her cousin on his forehead and unsheathed her blade.

"He barely flinched," my father told Henry later that evening.

"Brave kid." Henry put his arms around him. "It's the right thing we're doing, Caleb, hard as it is."

"Yes. I know." My father embraced his lover, then backed away. "But being right isn't enough, this plan needs to *succeed*. I'm going to spend some time in prayer."

He walked over to a window at the far side of the bunkhouse and stayed on his knees until a pale moon rose hours later, casting night shadows on Calle de las Sombras.

Do what you want with me, Lord, prayed my father, *for I know well my iniquity; only safeguard the life of this courageous young man.*

And so let your glory shine.

Chapter Twenty-Seven

What Then of Hell?

Several days after Louis had left to join the Knights, my father and Henry were in the kitchen, making plans with Valentina, when Elliana walked in.

"I know you're going on stakeout tonight," said the young woman, "and you *must* let me come along. It's only fair! My bladework is almost as good as yours, sister, and far better than most."

"One day," said Valentina. "When you're older. But not now."

"*Que?* I am but a year younger than Louis!"

"No more from you, Eli, or I will send you back to mother."

Elliana grimaced and turned to my father. "Have you heard from Louis? When will he return? I think he will kill the nagual, single-handed, if he has the chance!"

"Patience," said my father, smiling. "I don't expect any messages for a while, it's for his own—"

The sound of someone bounding up the stairs was followed by Gabriela flinging open the kitchen door.

"There's a strange little man in the bar who claims to know you," she said to my father and Henry. "José Johnson he called himself. Marguerite and Mariana are holding him at knifepoint, just in case."

My father and Henry looked at each other.

"Josiah, at last!" said my father.

Henry burst into laughter. "I suspect the randy old bugger is not minding his imprisonment overmuch. But we'll rescue him nonetheless. Send him on up, Gabi, and thanks."

"Roosevelt never campaigned in Texas," said Josiah as he and the Avengers and their hosts had dinner that evening, "since this state's about as Democrat as it gets. But Missouri was a toss-up, so I made my way to St. Louis when I knew he'd be there, seeing as Teddy and I are old pals. Figured it might not be a bad idea to have the president on our side." He paused to admire Elliana, who was busying herself in the kitchen.

"And is he?" asked my father.

"Well, not exactly. When I told him how the Rangers were in league with the devil himself, he didn't take that real well. You know, a passel of those Rough Riders who charged up San Juan Hill with him had been Rangers. He looked at me kind of funny and said, 'I'm loathe to think evil of the Texas Rangers, never met a one who was less than a man's man, a straight-up fellow who'd make his mother proud.' 'With all due respect sir,' said I, 'even prime beef can go bad a' times.' 'No, Johnson,' said he, 'it'll take more than some friend of yours getting himself thrown in jail to turn me against those fine men. But I'll tell you what, next time I'm out West, we'll meet up with Jack Abernathy, you and I, and go hunting. And old Quanah Parker, too.' You might not've heard Teddy invited the chief to his inauguration. Imagine that!"

Josiah's broad smile faded as the others remained silent.

"Well I didn't hit pay dirt with the big man, boys, that's for damn sure, but I'm here with my shotgun and Peacemaker and a fair bit of ammunition, ready to fight."

"And we're glad of it," said Henry, and clapped him on the back.

"Abernathy," said my father, "isn't he the man who captures wolves bare-handed?"

"That's the one," said Josiah. "Makes a fair living at it, too."

"And just how does he pull off *that* trick?" asked Henry.

"Puts his fist in the beast's mouth so it can't close its jaws. Damnedest thing I ever seen."

"I don't suppose Mr. Abernathy would consider joining the Avengers?" said Fr. de Souza. "Membership in our circle being quite prestigious."

"Quanah, too, for that matter," said Henry. "Presidents are all talk, I'd rather have an old Comanche on my side."

"Not real likely," said Josiah. "This old innkeeper will have to do."

"I'm curious what you think of the president," Josiah remarked to Elijah late that evening. "Him being a trust-buster and no friend to the robber barons. Seems to stand up for the common man."

The Avengers had returned from a fruitless stake-out and were drinking a second round of Tepeztate with Elijah and Sofia.

"The common *white* man, you mean," said Elijah. "Now don't get me wrong, I'll take Roosevelt over any of his rivals. But he sees Negroes as an inferior species and Indians as savage brutes. Yes, he admires their warrior spirit," he added, seeing Josiah's eyebrows raise up, "but only as you might admire a pit bull's spunk."

"Abraham Lincoln thought the same way," said Sofia. "Such thinking is in the very air these people breathe. Better to look at what they *do*, whatever they might say."

"Mr. Roosevelt's helped white men, that's true enough. But look at what he's left undone. It's the small-minded thinking and prejudice 'in the air,' as my wife puts it, that makes justice such an elusive goal."

"We're here with you," said my father, "that justice may run down as waters. Harlon Gale and those who stand with him will pay a price."

My father was convinced that he, too, would pay a price, and this he found oddly comforting. No one should get away with sin scot-free. God could extract from him whatever justice demanded—only let him and Henry be together one more day!

"*Pay a price*," said Sofia. "What good will that do to those he's harmed?"

"None," said Henry. "We stand against Gale not because he must be punished, but to stop the *injustice* he's wreaking in this valley. Caleb believes justice is done when a man gets what he deserves—but I say, what he deserves is what he *needs*.

Imagine, Elijah, if there really had been forty acres and a mule for every freed slave. Now that would have been justice."

"Indeed," said Elijah, and he motioned for Fr. de Souza to refill his glass. "The African's dignity—his humanity—was stripped from him when he was stolen away to these shores. Those forty acres would have secured not only his livelihood, but the right to guide his own destiny—to vote!—for think how many the poll tax has disenfranchised!"

"I've no argument with you there," said my father, "though I wonder at the practicality of the notion. How many slaves did Lincoln free?"

"Some four million," Elijah replied.

My father downed the rest of his Tepeztate and poured himself some more. "Then you're talking of handing over 160 million acres—I reckon that's an area larger than the entire state of Texas! I'm not sure even Sherman could have pried away that much land from white hands."

Fr. de Souza shrugged. "The Kingdom of Heaven is the least practical notion of all. Most of what the Lord asks of us seems well nigh impossible, does it not?"

"Granted," said my father, and stared for a moment into his drink. "But I believe you've proved my point about justice. The very act of giving the Negro the land he deserved would have delivered the punishment the slaver warranted as well. To satisfy only half that equation would be to leave justice undone."

"If the evil-doer is punished," said Sofia, "yet the wrong he's done is not set right, then justice is incomplete. But if it were the other way 'round, Caleb—the right set wrong, yet the sinner left unpunished—precisely what part of justice is left lacking?"

My father rolled his eyes. "Shall there be no consequences for vile acts?"

"Sofia asks well," said Fr. de Souza. "Here is my answer: God's justice is left undone until the last trace of evil is cleansed from the last sinner's heart."

"Must that be accomplished only through punishment?" asked Henry.

"I see no reason why that should be the case," the priest replied. "Though all too often there's no repentance without pain."

My father drank down his third Tepeztate. "What do you think, Baltasar: will God make all men good? Will he transform every heart, even against a man's very will?"

"God will one day be *all in all*, and Creation yet more gloriously perfect than before. What shade of darkness could then remain in human hearts?"

"Men are what they are, if you ask me," said Josiah. "I've never seen a one transformed."

"Why, you, yourself!" said Henry. "From slayer of the Red man to his bosom friend."

The innkeeper poured himself all but the last of the bottle.

"Elliana!" called out Elijah. "Bring us another, if you please!"

"Right away, Abuelo!"

"You're a sharp one, Henry," said Josiah, "but in this matter quite wrong. As a young soldier, I thought of the Cherokee as little better than wild beasts. Yet I've never willingly done wrong, and when I found myself grievously mistaken, at once resigned my commission and became their friend. But the sinful man embraces his evil and asks only what's best for himself."

"Well might *all* men ask that," said Fr. de Souza. "And if the sinful man at last turns to God because it's best for himself—indeed, sees that God alone will give him what he needs, God alone be his bliss—will not the hosts of heaven cry out in joy? Will the man's conversion—his transformation—be any less real?"

"To answer such a weighty question," said Elijah, as he uncorked the bottle Elliana had just handed him, "will undoubtedly require a fourth round."

The conversation wound down as the black of the morning sky shifted by imperceptible degrees to a deep sapphire blue.

"Listen," said Elliana, who was sitting on the ledge of the kitchen window. "The Inca doves have begun to coo. Does it not sound like they are crying, *no-hope, no-hope*?"

"Perhaps I should preach to them," said Fr. de Souza. "Like St. Francis, to raise their spirits."

"Oh, do, Padre Baltasar! The sun is coming, little ones. Have faith!"

"I'm done, friends," said my father, pushing back his chair.

"*You* can't leave, Henry," said Elliana, "till you teach me one more of your tricks."

"Oh, very well," said Henry. "But I warn you, an escape artist never gives away *all* his secrets."

"Go to bed soon, *nieta*," said Elijah. "Your sister and her friends have more sense than the rest of us. Let us be strong for the morrow."

"Which is already upon us," said Sofia, stifling a yawn. "Ah, for the sweet justice of sleep!"

"It seems to me we will surely find our feathered friends in heaven," said Fr. de Souza, as he and my father walked back to the bunkhouse. "For how could anything so graceful and gentle and lovely be lacking from the world to come?"

"My thoughts are elsewhere, Baltasar. When I asked you whether God will make all men good, I heard you say He'd leave no trace of darkness in any human heart. Is that what you believe?"

"I do."

"All people, past and present, and those yet to come?"

"Just so. I believe the Lord will lead all men out of the Darkness, that all will one day turn to Him and willingly bend the knee. My Father Provincial would not approve, of course; I'm not the most orthodox of priests. But I'm hardly alone in my thinking; not a few of the Church Fathers thought the same."

"Surely, though, you can see the problem. If what you say is true, what then of Hell?"

"Indeed!" Fr. de Souza turned to him and smiled. "What then?"

Chapter Twenty-Eight

The Choice

Word spread throughout *el barrio de los cuchillos* of the victory the Avengers and Elijah's militia had achieved. Some of the men who'd deserted came back, shame-faced, sons of slain patriarchs eager for revenge, and sons of the living anxious to defend their land.

My father and Valentina met with each one.

"Join us and you'll follow her orders no less than mine," my father told them. "We've our way and our rules. Obey them or you'll not ride along."

Bolstered by the sons of the patriarchs, Elijah's militia split into two groups and began staking out more of the Valley. Soon the one led by Henry and Marguerite intercepted another small detachment of Knights; those who fought were cut down, though two flung down their weapons and fled.

And in the court of the Honorable Aidan O'Connor, the pace of foreclosures slowed just a bit more.

Louis had been gone just over a month when my father was awakened one night by a rapping on the bunkhouse door. Henry's side of the bed was empty, the sheets cold to the touch. He rose and looked about. There was no sign of the priest, either.

Whoever was at the door knocked again.

My father crouched down to peek out the window.

Where was Mariana, who should have been standing guard?

He moved to the door, silent as a shadow, Colt 45 in hand.

"I've a blind man, here, Mr. McRae," came the high, piping voice of a child. "He's no more danger to you than I am."

"I come under a flag of truce, Caleb McRae," came a deep guttural voice. "Let's see if we can come to an understanding, you and I."

For a moment my father felt cold as ice.

He slipped the deadbolt, then stepped off to the side, his revolver trained on the door.

"All right, Gale. Come in."

The door swung open.

My father lowered his gun.

A great hulking bear of a man stood in the entryway, taller than my father and broader across, with a silver beard and darkened glasses over his eyes. His hand rested on the shoulder of a diminutive figure sporting a pork pie hat and a pencil mustache.

The little man smirked. "May my master sit and rest his bones?"

My father motioned to a nearby table and chairs.

The dwarf helped Harlon Gale to a seat and then stood behind him.

My father sat down across from Gale.

"What understanding do you think we could possibly have?"

"Come now, Caleb. We're both men who want what we want." He took an enormous cigar from his vest pocket, snipped off the end with a double guillotine blade attached to a golden watch fob—Garrison's had been but a poor imitation!—and snapped his fingers.

His lackey brought a flame close to the tip. Gale slowly turned the cigar and let it warm for a bit, then took a deep puff. He sat back and exhaled, disappearing for a moment behind a fog of smoke.

"You've been a thorn in my flesh, sir, I'll grant you that. But St. Paul and I have different ways of dealing with such matters." He flashed a broad grin and puffed out another cloud, vanishing, thought my father, like some sort of monstrous Cheshire Cat. "*My* strength is made perfect in *your* weakness. I can crush you and your friends any time I choose."

"Oh? Then why this conversation?"

"I like to keep things neat, my friend, and you're setting them up to get very messy indeed. But I doubt you understand the weakness I'm referring to. Certainly not your well-muscled physique, nor your prowess with firearms. No—" Gale eased back in his chair, puffed deeply on his cigar and blew smoke rings up toward the ceiling. "I mean the fine filigree of cracks that have begun to run through your soul. The doubts you harbor about your own salvation."

He leaned forward and put his palms on the table.

Gale's hands, my father noticed, were exceptionally large, their backs covered with fine, dark hair.

"It's not *me* you have to worry about, is it, Caleb?" he whispered.

"Enough of your nonsense," said my father, though he wondered if Gale could hear the violent pounding of his heart. "What is this understanding you spoke of?"

"Find a reason for you and your friends to leave the Valley. I suggest you take Mr. Jones and his wife with you if you care to save their lives. That will be your part of the bargain. As to what's in it for you—" another miasma of smoke momentarily obscured him from view—"I propose to cure you of one of your two afflictions."

My father narrowed his eyes and Gale chuckled.

"I can strip you of your faith, or of your love for Henry Midnight—of your desire for God or your lust for men." The blind man paused to take another puff, then blew out one smoke ring, then another, and then a third. "After all, Caleb, you know the day will come when you'll have to choose. And without my help—well! What a terrible day that will be."

The dwarf leered at him.

My father tried to still his racing mind.

"Do you doubt I can deliver on my promise?" asked Gale. "Look."

He removed his glasses.

Where eyes should have been, there was only a gaping blackness. My father stared into what seemed cavernous depths, and the longer he looked, the more he could see something—a glimmer—no, more than that, a flickering of flames...

"*Harlon Gale!*" cried the voice of a woman.

My father turned, but there was no one to be seen.

"By all that is holy, I command you to depart!"

Sofia, he thought, and then Gale bellowed in rage as shards of light skewered the room and my father was awake in the predawn darkness, drenched in sweat, his raven-haired lover holding him and murmuring Caleb, it's okay, you were only having a dream.

Chapter Twenty-Nine

The Approaching Fire

"In all the months since we met, Baltasar," said my father, as the two strolled together along the banks of the Rio Grande, "you've never brought up—never once mentioned—Henry and me and whether—" He broke off, flustered, then tried again. "What I mean is, what you think—"

Fr. de Souza waited patiently before finishing my father's thought. "What I think about you and Henry being lovers? I'll gladly share my thoughts, Caleb. Only first tell me why you ask."

"*Why?* Are you serious? Only that Scripture condemns love between men in the harshest of terms, and with the most dread consequences. Must I cite chapter and verse?"

"Spare me, please. One can prove all manner of vile nonsense with the words of Scripture, when quoted devoid of the Spirit—a skill at which the Pharisees excelled. It has not been many years since the Holy Book was employed to justify the enslavement of human beings, as our friend Elijah knows only too well." Seeing a look of frustration pass across his friend's face, the priest added, "But go on, tell me the passages that trouble your soul."

"Where to begin?" My father picked up a rock, threw it as high and far as he could, and watched until it splashed down a few yards short of the far side. "I'll start with Sodom and Gomorrah, upon which God rained fire on account of their sin."

"Ah yes, those two jewels of the Middle East. And for what sins were they punished, Caleb? The prophet Ezekiel made the answer quite clear: for their pride and their greed, for failing to lift a finger to aid the poor. But do go on."

"Surely the Book of Leviticus speaks plainly enough. I have committed abomination in the eyes of God."

"Indeed—and likely in so many ways!" Fr. de Souza waved to men navigating a flatboat up the river, who laughingly requested a blessing he was happy to provide. "Has a morsel of pork ever passed your lips, or oysters, or clams? Have you abstained from wearing garments woven from linen and wool? Have you stood steadfast against the blind and the lame, the disfigured and, yes, even those with testicles grotesquely maimed, and barred them from approaching the altar of the Lord?"

"Are you not engaging in Pharisaical argument yourself?" asked my father. "Paul declared us delivered from the law—by which he surely meant the sort of rules you mention—but he, too, condemned men like me."

"Did he, now. I don't carry the Old Testament with me—my back's not that strong!—but the Gospels and Epistles are ever close to my heart." He withdrew his New Testament from a pocket beneath the folds of his robe.

"Look toward the end of the first chapter of his letter to the Romans, Baltasar. And the sixth of his first letter to the Corinthians. Those words chill my blood."

"Well let's just see." Fr. de Souza read several verses from the King James out loud, then gazed at my father for a moment in silence. "The Apostle is writing about men who worship idols rather than the Living God, and that is hardly your abiding sin. He writes of those who *burn in lust* for other men. If your desires were intemperate, I would caution you, my friend, whether their object were women or men. As to St. Paul's chastisement of the Corinthian church, he speaks of the 'effeminate'—will those be damned who walk with a mincing step?—and those who are 'abusers of themselves with men.' I know not the Apostle's precise meaning by this latter phrase, but it suggests something sordid and dark. Such is not the love I see between you and Henry."

"But what guides your thinking?" asked my father. "This is nothing you could have learned from your Jesuit elders, or from your teachers. What in the name of heaven gives you confidence that what you say is true?"

"Only heaven itself. It is the *Spirit* who guides us into all truth, who teaches us all things—this we know from the Lord." Fr. de Souza held up his New

Testament. "The Bible exists to lead us to Jesus, to reveal Him as the very image of His Father. It is Jesus who is the Truth, Caleb, and the Truth of Jesus is love."

"Ah, back to 'God is love.'" My father balled his fists in frustration. "It's true enough, I know, yet look how those words have led Sofia astray. Is everything then allowed? Have we nothing to fear from God?"

"On the contrary. Our God is both Father and Consuming Fire, and he will burn you, Caleb, oh yes, he will burn you. That you love a *man* is not the issue, it is the quality, the substance, the depth of your love. The Lord demands that you love well, love as He loved us, He who was led by love to obey His Father unto death, even death on a cross. Oh, my friend, He will set ablaze everything about your love that is willful and self-serving and weak. And even now the fire approaches."

The men walked in silence on the pathway that led back to the neighborhood of knives. What Father de Souza had just said, mused my father, went against centuries of Church teaching; it was what he longed to hear, but seemed too good to be true.

And yet, what if Baltasar was right?

Even now the fire approaches...

For a moment he was no longer in the Rio Grande Valley, but the Chihuahuan desert in the storm-haunted night, his arm around Henry's shoulders, ball lightening travelling toward them like luminous tumbleweeds, the bristlegrass burning in front and behind...

"Caleb! Father Baltasar!" Valentina rode up to them on her chestnut bay. "I've grim news. Mariana found Judge O'Connor's body, mauled almost beyond recognition. They're now saying he was killed by a pack of wolves, but of course there was only one set of tracks."

"*Ut ille in requiem pace,*" murmured the priest, his face deathly white.

"How could this have happened?" asked my father, stricken that he'd failed to protect a man who'd risked everything to aid their cause. "Why wasn't Mariana with him when the nagual attacked?"

"Her horse was spooked on the way over and threw her. That stubborn man chose not to wait before taking his morning walk." She spat on the ground. "To die from such a stupid mistake!" Valentina wheeled her horse around, then turned back to my father. "When you return, Caleb, Elijah and Sofia are anxious to talk with you. Alone."

"You had a dream last night," said Sofia, after my father was alone with them in Elijah's office. "One involving both Harlon Gale and me."

"How—" My father had not even told Henry. "How is it possible you know?"

"I have not been forthcoming with you, Caleb, and must rectify that, for matters are coming to a head. There are times when I pursue our adversary in the spirit world. In the early hours of this morning, I followed him into your dream."

"You're telling me that what I dreamt was somehow real?"

"The spirit realm is yet more real than the physical world. I sense Gale's power growing stronger; that I prevailed last night gives me little comfort. He was simply surprised."

Another piece of the puzzle came together in my father's mind.

"This wasn't the first time you've entered my dreams."

"You're right. I took the liberty twice before and can only tell you I was led by the Spirit, for I scarcely know what reason. It seems you've a role to play, though I struggle to understand it, for your way is not the way of our Lord."

"Though Sofia and I differ on the use of force," said Elijah, "and I am as much a stranger to the spirit realm as you, I trust her with my very life." He reached out and clasped my father's hand. "Do not be angry that we withheld this from you, Caleb. You would not have been ready before."

I'm not entirely sure I'm ready now, thought my father, but he nodded and squeezed the old man's hand.

"I've come to a decision," said Sofia. "This evening I will begin a deep meditation on the sixth chapter of the Apostle's letter to the Ephesians. At some point—I know not how long it may take—I will try to enter our adversary's dreams."

"And then? What do you imagine will transpire?"

"In truth, I've no idea."

"But surely you have a goal!"

"Only one: to do the will of God."

"It is fraught with danger, what Sofia is attempting," said Elijah, who looked as though he'd aged years since the previous day. "She can use your prayers."

"Of course," said my father. "I'll pray for you with all my heart and soul and mind and strength."

"There is one more thing you must know," said Sofia. "And that I must ask of you." She closed her eyes, as though gathering strength, then opened them and regarded my father with the regal calm of a warrior queen. "I'm quite sure there are times when I am possessed by the spirit of a beast. Whether it is a guardian spirit or some malevolent force, I cannot say; I sense it is something swift and fierce, though I wake from these possessions with no memory of what transpired. So, then, promise me this: if in the course of the battle that is to come, you discover I have become an instrument of evil—perhaps even the nagual—"

"Sofia!" her husband objected.

"Elijah, please. Should it be revealed that I am of the darkness, Caleb, do as the Lord commands you. If that means my destruction, you must not hesitate. His will be done."

Memories of the night when he and Valentina went searching for Sofia and the nagual came flooding back. He'd seen a shimmering in the darkness, felt a presence lurking in the fog-shrouded night. And then the ground gave way, he was falling, and Sofia had reached out and grabbed him and *pulled him up* and that simply wasn't possible, not for a slightly built woman of her age.

"I'll do what is right," he said at last. "Count on it, both of you."

"Come," said Sofia, and she grasped both men's hands. "Let's pray."

"Sounds like I got myself in deep this time, hitching my wagon with yours," said Josiah, after Caleb had related to the other Avengers all he'd heard. "But I'm glad for it, friends."

"If Sofia had been possessed by the darkness," mused Henry, "then she'd have let you fall that night. I don't believe it for a minute. Gale's evil is quite sufficient, thank you very much. And now that you tell us of his powers, I'm wishing we had more priests like Baltasar on our side."

"*Are* there more priests like you?" asked my father, only half in jest.

"Not a one," said Fr. de Souza. "But look, here is what we need—" He flourished his New Testament and flipped pages. "St. Paul's Epistle to the Ephesians, gentlemen, from the sixth chapter:

"*Put on the whole armor of God, that ye may be able to stand against the wiles of the devil.*

"For we wrestle not against flesh and blood, but against principalities, against powers, against the rulers of the darkness of this world..."

Chapter Thirty

Vamos!

"How is Sofia?" my father asked Elijah. "Any change?"

She had fallen into a deep sleep not long after the three had prayed together. Two days had passed, and she'd yet to awake.

"No, not a murmur. She's still breathing, praise God, but otherwise she's still as death."

Henry, Josiah, Fr. de Souza, and Elijah sat in somber silence, drinking strong coffee that the old man had busied himself making. My father stood off to the side, watching as Valentina drew lines and circles on the Valley map that hung on the kitchen wall.

"What do you think?" she asked him. "It's something different, for a change. We could try it tonight."

He walked over and traced what she'd drawn with his finger.

"It's a good plan," he said, and then walked away and poured himself a cup of sludge. "But I wonder if it's different enough."

"You have some other idea?"

"We've been focusing on the Knights, but they're the body of the beast. Sofia is going after its head. After Harlon Gale. I can't help but wonder if we should do the same."

Valentina thought this over. "Yours is a bold thought, Caleb. But Sofia pursues him in the spirit world, where she may well be the stronger. Wherever he might venture in his dreams, in this realm it has been months since he's left his stronghold, where he's protected both by his own guards and by the Rangers. And as the nagual he has been a phantom."

"All true, Valentina." Henry pushed back his chair and got up to join them. "And yet, for precisely that reason, we would have the advantage of surprise."

"Bold, yes, but that is not what troubles me," said Fr. de Souza. "We fight now in defense of the ranchers, against marauders who trespass on their land. What you are suggesting would leave us no defense in the eyes of the law. And what would you do, Caleb, should you be fortunate enough to penetrate to the heart of Gale's lair? Kill a blind man?"

"From what y'all have told me," said Josiah, "that wouldn't be a real hard decision. And seems to me, if we had the sumbitch in our sights, he'd turn himself into—"

The door to the kitchen swung open and Marguerite burst through with Elliana close on her heels.

"Rita!" cried Elliana. "You must tell me what he says!"

"Elli!" Valentina grabbed her sister by the arm. "Control yourself, this minute."

"A message has come from Louis," said Marguerite. "It's in our code, and signed with the letter Z, which signifies it is from him and not sent under duress. Allow me a moment."

The room went silent as Marguerite sat at the table and studied a small sheet of paper.

"Wednesday night the Knights move in force against the Gutiérrez ranch. The west gate, just after midnight."

"Javier Gutiérrez," said Elijah. "Patriarch of patriarchs. His ranch is one of the Valley's crown jewels."

"Five thousand acres, at least," said Valentina. "We've staked it out before. The west gate though—" She marked a spot on the map to the west of Brownsville, not far north of the Rio Grande. "That's unexpected."

"Yes," said my father. "They'll need to go clear around the perimeter to get there. But it's the most vulnerable entry point."

"There are deep arroyos on that side that run up from the river," said Valentina. "If we can rout them, it will not be terribly difficult to cut off their retreat."

"There is a bit more to the message," said Marguerite, and she turned to Elliana. "Tell Elli I am well and will see her soon.'"

"When? Will he be part of the battle? You must take me along!"

"No!" said Valentina. "That is out of the question. You'll stay here and help to look after Elijah and Sofia. *Entiendes?*"

Her sister nodded sullenly.

"We've only a day to get ready," said my father. "Let's get to work."

Early Wednesday afternoon, not long before the Avengers were due to set out with the others for the Gutiérrez ranch, my father was walking back to the bunkhouse after talking with Elijah when he heard the faint sound of footsteps from somewhere in the shadows.

"Do not move, señor, or you're a dead man."

Mariana held her blade to the throat of someone whose features he could not yet make out.

"Easy, darlin'," said the man. "Don't want to get bloodstains on my good white shirt. Just had it washed."

"Charlie!" cried my father. "It's all right, Mariana, he's a friend."

Charlie Siringo stepped out from the darkness and shook my father's hand.

"Sorry to barge in on you like this," said the Pinkerton detective. "But I'm here on business."

"Glad as I am to see you, you've chosen the worst possible time. I've urgent business to attend to right now. Can we—"

"I haven't come to see *you*, Caleb. I'm here for de Souza."

My father felt a tightening in his gut. "What's this about, Charlie?"

"Make things a whole lot simpler if you just take me to him. I'm sure he'd rather you hear the story in his own words."

Ominous images raced through my father's mind: Baltasar absconding with emeralds from La Lechuga at the church in Bogota, intent on using them to feed the poor; converting the Spanish doubloons Henry had stolen into rubies for the monstrance at Nuestra Señora de Guadalupe; and who knew how much more! Henry had his pardon, but what laws might his friend not have broken, even if in the best possible cause?

"All right," he said, helplessly, and led Siringo through the bunkhouse door.

Inside, the other Avengers were preparing weapons and ammunition.

"Henry, Baltasar, Josiah. This is Charles Siringo of the Pinkertons."

"Well hell in a handbasket!" exclaimed Josiah. "If it ain't the Texas Cowboy himself! How are you, Charlie boy?"

"Been a while, Jo," said Siringo, with a wan smile. "Reckon I'm doing okay."

The innkeeper's grin faded. "This don't sound like a friendly visit."

"Baltasar Benedeto de Souza?" said Siringo, looking directly at the priest.

"I am he."

"The name Andrés Felipe Ramírez ring a bell?"

Fr. de Souza blinked a few times, then set down the Remington he'd been loading.

"Yes, all too loudly."

"Seems his family in Santiago doesn't give up grudges any too easy. Had you convicted in absentia back in '84, only there wasn't much they could do about it once you'd moved up here. Bad news for you is, a couple years ago the feds signed an extradition treaty with Chile. Ramírez' family owns silver mines. They're paying whatever it takes to get you brought back."

"What happened, Baltasar?" asked Henry.

Fr. de Souza let his head sink down for a moment, rubbed his temples, then straightened up and addressed his three friends. "I spent a year in Santiago after leaving Bogota. This was in the early 80s, when I was twenty-three and quite the man about town. Andrés Felipe's fiancée became rather fond of me—I thought it all innocent flirtation and played along. Pure foolishness on my part, though I had no bad intentions. He saw it otherwise. One night he appeared before my table brandishing a pistol, declared I was a scoundrel, and told me to prepare to die. Andrés Felipe fired and missed. I carried a Brazilian Nagant at the time. My aim was true."

"That was self-defense, Charlie," said Josiah. "You can't send him down there to some kangaroo court, that'd be a death sentence sure as we're sitting here."

"Wheels are in motion, Jo," said Siringo. "This is bigger'n me."

"I know you by reputation to be a decent man," said Henry, "We all of us make choices, every day. You can choose to walk away."

"They're right," said my father. "This is one time when—"

"Stop!" exclaimed Fr. de Souza. "Mr. Siringo must do what he needs to do. In truth, I am not an innocent man. I could have prevented what happened that day in Santiago, and on a thousand days since. My friends, I know you love me, but you cannot save me from this. I will not run from the consequences of my actions, but praise God that he sent Christ Jesus into the world to be the savior of sinners like me. Sir, I ask only one thing."

"What's that, Padre?" Siringo said softly.

"It is with the greatest of urgency that my friends and I must venture out this evening on a mission to save lives. If in the morning I am still among the living, take me where you will, so help me God."

"Tell me what you're up to, Caleb," said Siringo, and he leaned back against the wall and lit up a cigar.

My father told the storied detective how the Avengers had come to El Atrapa, and what had transpired since, though he left out any mention of Sofia and the nagual. Then he finished speaking and sent up a silent prayer.

"It's not exactly news to me that Harlon Gale's a stone-cold bastard," said Siringo. "And the Knights have always been scum. But I didn't realize how bad things had gotten down here. I know you for an honest man, Caleb. You giving your word you'll deliver the padre to me tomorrow?"

"I am."

"Damn it, anyway." Siringo went over to the window and stubbed out his cigar. "Should have my head checked for agreeing to round up a priest."

"Caleb!" Valentina called from the courtyard. "*Vamos!*"

"We need to head out," said my father, and he motioned for the others to follow him to the stables.

"*Wait!*" called Siringo, just as they'd reached the bunkhouse door.

"We're out of time, Charlie," said my father.

"I know," said the detective, hurrying toward them. "I'm signing on for the dust-up this evening. Reckon you boys could use some help, seeing as ol' Josiah here don't shoot quite as straight as he used to."

"Now that's the Charlie I remember," said the innkeeper. "But you'll eat those words."

"You're Henry *Midnight*, if I'm not mistaken," said Siringo, extending the erstwhile outlaw his hand.

"Indeed. And the pleasure is all mine."

"I'll meet you boys in a minute, my horse is hitched up the street. And Caleb—congratulations."

My father looked at Siringo quizzically.

"Looks like you finally did get your man."

Chapter Thirty-One

Run Down as Waters

The Avengers rode with five women warriors and seven sons of the patriarchs, having sent Gabriela ahead earlier to let Javier Gutiérrez know of their plans. He had five strong sons and grandsons and ten guards who patrolled his ranch. Combined, they were more than enough, my father reasoned, even if Gale had marshalled all his Knights for this raid.

A storm moved in from the Gulf as they rode, and anvil-topped clouds towered above them, steel gray and tinged with green.

Long before they'd finished their four-hour journey, the wind picked up and the first drops began to fall.

"You must be Elijah's militia." The guard manning the east gate wiped the rain from his eyes. "*Gracias*. We are grateful that you've come."

"We're glad to be here," said my father. "Is Señor Gutiérrez at the main house?"

"No, señor. He and your señorita and the rest are at the west gate and ask that you join them. They have set up a tent to keep dry."

"You're here alone?" asked Henry.

"Si, señor."

"If you saw the enemy approaching," said my father, "how would you alert the others? Do you have a flare?"

"Yes, of course, señor. I will use one now to let them know you have arrived."

They rode on as the guard shot a bright green flare up into the storm-swept sky.

"It was pure foolishness to have only one man at this entrance," said Valentina. "I expected more of Javier."

"What time is it, Josiah?" asked my father.

The innkeeper consulted his pocket watch. "Not quite half past five."

"Gutiérrez is overanxious, and eager to play the general. Though I'll be glad for that tent, if they had the sense to place it out of sight."

"I'm sure Gabriela has done her best to advise him," said Valentina. "But a crusty old Tejano is not going to listen to a young woman, full of himself as he is."

"Be a good idea to send him home," said Siringo. "If it could be done."

The path that led across the ranch ran for over three miles from east to west. The storm grew fiercer as they made their way, and great cracks of lightning split the sky.

"*Caleb—wait!*" Valentina rode up close to my father, who held up his hand to bring the procession to a halt. "Something's been bothering me, and I only just now figured out what it is. Javier has a proper patriarch's beard, and the guards told me he mocks men who don't at least sport a handlebar mustache. Every one of them was bearded when I was here last. But that man at the east gate was clean-shaven."

My father let this sink in. "How far are we from the west gate?"

"I doubt even a quarter mile. The land there, it's like a shallow bowl, with hills on either side. The arroyo is just behind the southern hill. It's a perfect setting for an ambush."

By this time Marguerite, Siringo, and the three other Avengers had gathered round to find out what was up.

"We may be riding into a trap," my father told them. "Let's circle back toward—"

"*Santo dios!*" cried Marguerite, as sheet lightning lit up the sky, illuminating a ghastly scene: a figure on a wooden cross that had been placed at the top of the northern hill.

"*The bastards!*" said Henry as he peered through field glasses. "That's Louis they've got up there! He's still alive."

My father's guts churned as he searched for a strategy that might turn the tables on the enemy. "They're using him as bait."

Henry nodded. "They know we don't desert our own."

"And they're right," said Marguerite. "Valentina! We're going for him, *now!*"

"Wait!" Valentina reached for her friend, but Marguerite had already spurred her horse on. "*Síganme!*" Valentina called to the rest of the women warriors, and they were off.

No choice now, thought my father, and Achilles leapt forward at his command, with the rest of the men close behind. *Gale's played us for fools. No doubt Gabriela and the Gutiérrez clan and his guards were taken by surprise and mercilessly slain. And dear God, Louis...*

Then he banished such thoughts from his mind.

The women were heading straight for Louis; my father directed the sons of the patriarchs to support them, then broke off with the other Avengers, intent on getting to the other side of the north hill as quickly as possible to outflank the Knights.

But there was no way that was going to happen.

More than thirty Knights swarmed over the length of the hilltop, and a detachment of a dozen Rangers broke out over the crest of the southern hill.

And yet, they'd caught a break, my father realized, for the enemy had made its move too soon. The women took to their long guns against the Knights, the Sharps deadly accurate at long range, and he was squeezing off shots with his Winchester against the Rangers, and one, then two, then three fell.

But the numbers were still against them.

Marguerite charged toward the cross, a woman possessed, firing as she rode, then slashing with her knife at close range until she disappeared from view as a horde of Knights closed in.

Valentina and her sister warriors and the seven sons of the patriarchs were close behind and were soon joined by Siringo and Fr. de Souza.

My father, Henry, and Josiah turned south to face the remaining nine Rangers.

Henry took down three and Josiah and my father another two each and then the innkeeper cried out and slumped over, shot dead. All the while the wind howled and the rain beat down, the storm raging like a wild beast.

A bullet tore through my father's left shoulder and he gasped with pain, dropped the Winchester, and began firing with his Colt.

Even now the fire approaches.

A thudding sound; Henry had fallen to the ground and lay motionless, blood streaming from his head.

And you, Henry Midnight, even you will be struck down.

It's the end of the world, thought my father, *the end of hope.*

He rode to meet the last two Rangers, and then Achilles stumbled and fell.

My father scrambled to his feet, gained cover behind an outcropping of rock, caught his breathe, and reloaded with one hand.

Lightning ripped the sky, and thunder followed not a second after.

To the north he saw Siringo fall, a half-dozen Knights heading toward him, and then Fr. de Souza was in their midst, blasting away with both Remingtons. The enemy surrounded the priest and riddled him with bullets, only to be cut down in turn by the detective. Siringo scrambled out of sight, and there was only the downpour and darkness and gunfire and screams carried on the wind.

The Lord is my light and my salvation; whom shall I fear? The Lord is the strength of my life; of whom shall I be afraid?

Of no one, my father told himself. *Now make them pay.*

He peered out from the edge of the outcrop.

Tom Tetley was standing ten feet away.

Their eyes met.

The two men fired at the same time and my father fell backwards, his right hand shattered by the impact of the Ranger's bullet.

Tetley dropped, a gaping hole in the center of his forehead.

My father looked upward toward the raging heavens, the black clouds boiling, the rain falling in torrents.

Yea, though I walk through the valley of the shadow of death...

A jangling sound.

He turned his head, saw two boots with silver spurs.

"So long, McRae," said Maj. Garrison, his shotgun pointed down at my father's chest. "Your luck's finally run—"

The Major's eyes widened, blood trickled from his nose and mouth, and he pitched forward, one of Valentina's knives having severed his spine.

"I'll be back," called the warrior, and she sprinted away.

My father faded in and out of consciousness for a long while, images from the past few months cascading through his mind.

A shimmering in the darkness, a presence in the gloom.

Something's out there...

It was no longer raining. He blinked the drops from his eyes, tried to rouse himself. Overhead the clouds were ragged, broken, scudding across the face of a pale full moon. From somewhere in the distance came the sound of rushing water.

He sat up, suddenly panicked, and sucked in great gulps of air, oblivious to the pain in his shoulder and hand.

"Henry!"

The memory came back to him: Henry, fallen, bleeding on the ground.

I see a field of bones...

"Caleb!" Siringo came running. "That young man they had up on the cross, he's still alive, Valentina's tending to him right now. And every one of the whoreson bastards are slain. Lie back, I'll wrap your—"

"Have you seen Henry?"

"Took a bullet in his ribs, another that grazed his head and knocked him out cold. He's in pain, but he'll be okay. There's just the four of us left."

"Then help me up, I'm going—"

The roar of a wild beast rent the night and drowned out the rest of my father's words.

"What in the name of God—" exclaimed Siringo.

"The nagual," my father murmured. "Harlon Gale."

The creature was making its way along the crest of the northern hill, heading toward Valentina and Louis, who was stretched out on the ground. It was wolf-like, with monstrously massive jaws and eyes that glowed hellfire red. Reared up on its hind legs, the nagual stood well over seven feet tall.

"Should have warned me, McRae," said Siringo as he took aim with one of the women's buffalo rifles. "I would've brought a Gatling gun."

He and Valentina fired round after round, each hitting its mark.

The impact of the bullets only caused the beast to take a few steps back.

Valentina dropped her rifle and ran toward the nagual, moonlight glinting off the silver dagger in her right hand.

Within a few strides of the beast she let her blade fly, aiming at its heart.

The nagual knocked it aside with a swipe of its great right paw, each of its claws longer and sharper than the knife she'd just thrown. It turned its head, searching, until my father was certain it was looking straight at him, its mouth twisted in a rictus of hatred, and let loose a triumphant howl.

Siringo unsheathed his Bowie knife "She's not going to fight him alone."

"No," said my father. "You'll only get in the way. It's up to Val."

Valentina stood before the nagual, unbowed, a second silver dagger in her hand.

"Come, hell-spawn demon." She beckoned to the monster. "Come against me if you dare."

The nagual lunged for her and she leaped, twisting and turning in mid-air in a desperate bid to reach the creature's heart. But it was too quick, too agile, and threw her aside, raking her right arm with its deadly claws.

Valentina fell to the ground with a sickening thud.

A sudden scream of pain issued from the beast's mouth, and it reached around to withdraw a silver blade from its back.

A small slender figure stepped away from behind the nagual and leapt at it with another silver dagger.

Elliana.

The nagual easily dodged the young warrior's attempt to stab its heart and reached for her, opened wide its huge jaws...

"No!" cried Valentina.

From atop the southern hill came an answering cry, the roar of a cougar queen.

The nagual's eyes blazed a darker shade of red and it bounded down, bellowing in fury and rage.

The cougar stayed still as the nagual charged, then began to back up.

"Cougar doesn't move to meet him, it's dead meat," said Siringo.

The queen backed up another four steps.

On came the nagual. With a final leap it surmounted the southern hill and was upon her, its momentum carrying both of them over the edge.

Only then did my father understand.

"You hear that rushing water?" he asked Siringo. "It's a flash flood that's filled the arroyo, racing up from the Rio Grande. Val told me it's a sheer drop on the other side of the hill."

"Son of a bitch!" exclaimed the detective, as he tore off strips of his shirt to bandage my father. "That cougar suckered him in. At the cost of both their lives, I'm guessing, though I won't rest easy till I find the hellbeast's body and burn it and bury the ashes ten feet deep. I'll be damned, McRae! Never seen anything like that demon wolf—and I never seen a big cat that didn't either fight or run." He looked my father over. "You okay for now?"

"Yes. Go help the others."

My father struggled to his feet. The field of battle was a gruesome scene, strewn with bodies, bone-white in the bleak moonlight and streaked with red. The terrible weight of it pressed down on him, took his breath away.

Valentina was sitting midway down the north hill, letting Siringo tend to her ravaged right arm. Elliana was caring for Louis at the base of the cross. Then his heart leapt; fifty yards away, Henry came limping slowly toward him, a bloody bandanna wrapped around his head.

"Get a move on!" my father called out.

His lover smiled.

Can't even put these useless arms around him. But thank you, Lord, for this blessing, for this mercy. For one more day.

My father's legs gave way and he sat back against the outcrop to regain his strength.

It's really all pretty simple, Charlie, he thought. From the moment she'd appeared, he'd known the cougar was the same creature who had succored him and Henry in the desert four years before, and in the next heartbeat he'd understood who she really was.

Interesting thing about the nagual, Henry had told him all those months before, *legend has it there's good ones as well as bad.*

When the flood waters receded and searchers went out, they found no trace of the monster Siringo described, nor of the cougar who had lured it to its death, only the broken bodies of Sofia Osorio Jones and Harlon Gale.

Part Four

Downdraft

Chapter Thirty-Two

Red Grapefruit

Charlie Siringo had little difficulty convincing Governor Lanham that no charges should be brought against any of the Avengers. The Governor, a great admirer of the Texas Cowboy, had long been fearful of Gale's growing influence and power, and was not sorry to see him gone.

My father felt no sense of triumph, however, only grief, and blamed himself for the lives lost. During my youth, he never once mentioned his time in the Rio Grande Valley. It was something he came to terms with only in his twilight years.

The hardest thing for him was seeing that, after all the bloodshed, not much had really changed. Violence against the Tejano ranchers abated, but only for a while. When rumors spread that Mexican Americans were plotting to rise up in bloody revolt, the Texas Rangers joined local vigilantes in killing sprees throughout the Rio Grande Valley, targeting anyone whose skin was brown.

The Avengers could no more stop sporadic violence born of hatred than they could halt the incoming tide.

"This is the way it's always been, and ever will be, until hearts are changed," Elijah said late one night as he sat in the kitchen with my father and Henry and Valentina, drinking the last of the Tepeztate. "And what are the odds of that?"

"Nil," said Valentina.

"Baltasar believed the Almighty would have his way with every one of us," said my father. "That He'd bring all home to Him, if only in the life to come. God bless our friend for his hopefulness, but I don't believe it. I don't even want to believe it. May the Lake of Fire be Gale's home forevermore."

He had begun to think Sofia might be right about non-violence being the Way of Christ—at least, just maybe!—but if so, the eternal punishment that would be meted out on Judgement Day was the only way to balance the scales of Justice.

"What happens to Harlon Gale matters nothing to me now," said Elijah. "All that sustains me is the hope that Sofia and I will be together soon." The old man poured himself another shot. "Only these days I find it harder to believe in heaven than hell. I've no doubt there are demons, and I've stood close enough to the inferno to feel the blast of its heat, but I can't help fearing Paradise is but an empty myth."

"Ah, come now," said Henry. "You sound like the Old One who claimed the Negro Seminoles were nothing but a crazy dream. Souls like yours and Sofia's can never be extinguished. A better world awaits you both."

"Indeed. To Sofia!" exclaimed my father, and the four clinked glasses and downed their drinks. "She had faith enough for the four of us, Elijah, let the memory of its strength lift you up. But I won't deny I'm troubled as well, for it seems to me we've accomplished next to nothing."

"We did what every man must do," said Henry. "We did our duty, regardless of the outcome. We stood up to evil. Do that often enough and you end up bathed in blood. But we're here and the bad guys ain't."

"Our duty?" said my father. "I'm no longer so sure what that was, nor what it is now. And if a few so-called good guys are left standing, do we call that a victory, no matter how many bodies lie rotting on the ground?"

"I'm with Henry," said Valentina. "Elliana and Louis are alive, and Gale is dead, and that's enough for me."

"Ah, gracias, *mi querida hija,*" said Elijah. "You remind me of the young ones. I would not want them to hear us talk like this."

Under Elliana's care, Louis was slowly recovering from his wounds, and the two had become inseparable.

"We're done for tonight, in any event," said my father, downing the last drops of Tepeztate with his one good hand. "Perhaps in the morning the way forward will be clearer."

It seemed there was little more the Avengers could accomplish in the Rio Grande Valley. The power of the marketplace—that idol men worship, at times not much less cruel than the Knights of the White Camelia—accomplished what guns and demon beasts could not, and soon enough the Valley was in Anglo hands. Cattle ranches were replaced with farms and citrus groves.

A way of life had come to an end.

I was reminded of Harlon Gale's prescience while reading the newspaper one morning shortly after my sixty-fifth birthday, when a headline below the fold caught my eye:

Red Grapefruit Adopted as State Fruit of Texas

My father was long gone by then. For breakfast, he'd have dry toast, black coffee, and a few strips of bacon, which he preferred burnt to a crisp. He never cared for grapefruit; I think its crimson color reminded him of the hellfire that shone in the nagual's eyes.

Chapter Thirty-Three

Thine Own Understanding

"Sofia told me she wanted her ashes scattered to the winds from the top of Black Mesa," Elijah said to my father, Henry, and Valentina over dinner one evening. "How soon can we set out?"

It was the fall of 1905, and the wounds his companions had suffered were pretty well healed.

"That's a thousand-mile journey," said my father, concerned over how frail the old man seemed. "Much of it over rugged terrain."

"It would take two months of travelling, at least," said Henry. "Sofia wouldn't want to put you through such an ordeal. Caleb and I would be more than happy to carry out her wishes."

Elijah looked at the Avengers with eyes at once piteous and baleful. "Will you deny me one last adventure?"

There was nothing for it but to hitch Bonita to a wagon, make it as comfortable as possible for their friend, load it with supplies, and take to the road.

Elliana and Louis went to live with his parents, hoping to marry the following spring.

"I'll be back in time for your wedding," Valentina told her, and rode off with the men.

In addition to Sofia's ashes, they brought along Fr. de Souza's remains in an urn.

"He's an excellent travelling companion," Elijah remarked early on in their journey. "Sofia's heard my stories too many times, but Baltasar never complains."

Henry felt sure their friend would have wanted to be interred at his beloved Mission Nuestra Señora de Guadalupe, so they planned to head north to San Antonio, pick up the road to El Paso, then continue through the New Mexico and Arizona Territories, reaching Black Mesa before year end.

The bigtooth maples were just beginning to turn ruby and gold, the weather held fair, and my father's spirits lifted with every mile they travelled from Brownsville. The trip was a godsend, helping to distract him from the memories that haunted his dreams at night: a field of bodies, bloody and broken, under a ragged sky; the nagual's slavering jaws.

One morning in late November, just after they'd come in sight of El Paso, a lone rider approached them from the west.

"Hold up, McRae," said Jude Bryce. "Heard you and Midnight were headed this way. I'm here to tell you to steer clear of my town."

"*Your town?*" said my father to his erstwhile lieutenant. "You get elected Mayor, Jude?"

"It's Captain Bryce now. You'd best head pronto for the border, you and the outlaw and your nigger and greaser pals."

"Watch your tongue," said Valentina, "or I'll remove it from your mouth."

"Never mind him," said my father, then turned around. Some sort of vehicle was coming toward them, raising a cloud of dust and a considerable racket.

"You're a traitor to your own," Bryce continued. "The Rangers will not forget."

"You've the memories of elephants, I'm sure," said Henry.

A splendid motorcar came to a skidding halt behind them with a stupendous blare from its double-bell bulb horn and a great screeching of brakes. Even covered with grime, it couldn't fail to impress.

The Avengers steadied their steeds and Bonita barely twitched her ears, but Bryce's horse reared up in terror, sending the captain tumbling into a ditch.

A middle-aged fellow wearing an especially fine set of boots stepped out and waved his Stetson in frustration. "Y'all can't just stop and block the damn road!"

My father did a double-take. "Jenks, isn't it?"

"Hmm?" Eustace Jenks squinted at him and frowned. "Do I know—" his eyes widened as he glanced at Henry. "Hell, if it ain't the crew I met on the way to San Antone!"

A loud groan came from the ditch as Bryce tried to stand and then fell back down. "Broke my damn leg, you bastards!"

"Hold on, Jude," called my father, jumping down beside the mortified Ranger. "We'll get you to the sawbones soon enough."

"What brings you to West Texas?" Henry asked Jenks. "Bored already of the big city?"

"Big? *That* cowtown? I'm headin' for Frisco. Met a Chinaman in Dallas knows all the ins 'n outs of import-export. Dragon's blood and rhubarb root, that's what's gonna make me a pretty—"

"Eustace?" A daintily attired young woman emerged from the chariot holding a parasol and looked in dismay at the commotion around her. "This is not at *all* what you promised."

"Just have a seat, Priscilla, honey."

"Our most abject apologies, Mrs. Jenks," said Henry. "You'll be able to pass through in just a moment."

"*Mrs. Jenks?*" Priscilla exclaimed. "You couldn't possibly confuse me with that old bag. Eustace, I insist we leave this minute!"

Jenks flushed and eyed his companion nervously as she climbed back into the motorcar. "Reckon I'll be movin' on, boys, you can see the lady's a bit put out." He began to hand-crank the engine. "Them priests don't understand a man's natural urges," he added peevishly. "Just as well that Padre's not with y'all."

"He is, actually," said Henry. "Only at the moment the Padre is somewhat indisposed."

My father emerged from the ditch carrying Bryce and set him in the wagon next to Elijah. The Ranger, taking note of his travelling companion, grimaced in disgust.

"Pleased to meet you, too, Captain," said the old man. "You lie there and moan and we'll get along just fine."

"Our dear friend's proficiency with firearms, while extraordinary," said Fr. Alejo toward the end of his homily, "was hardly the most remarkable of his attributes."

My father, Henry, Valentina, and Elijah were attending the requiem Mass for Fr. de Souza at the Mission Nuestra Señora de Guadalupe.

"No," Henry whispered. "It was his *appetite*."

He grunted as my father and Valentina elbowed him from both sides.

"Baltasar's understanding of Scripture was unique, to be sure," Fr. Alejo continued. "But he was no individualist, much less an iconoclast. Rather, he put all his trust in the guidance of the Holy Spirit, wherever it might lead him—and in this he followed in the very footsteps of St. Ignatius."

That you love a man *is not the issue...*

Fragments of his last conversation with Fr. de Souza ran through my father's mind. How does one know when it's truly the Holy Spirit leading a man—that he is not fooling himself, pursuing his own willful ways? Wouldn't Satan set just such snares before us?

Lean not on thine own understanding...

My father felt the priest's absence like a deep, bitter ache. All the time they'd spent together, and not until the very end had they discussed what mattered most! What he wouldn't give to have his friend back, to talk things through just one more time. But he'd failed him, led Baltasar to his death.

Dark-robed brothers intoned a *Dies Irae*, the smell of frankincense and myrrh perfumed the chapel, and the rubies in the Mission's monstrance gleamed in the Paschal candle's lambent glow.

Chapter Thirty-Four

Song of Solomon

The foursome woke early, bade farewell to Fr. Alejo, and crossed over into the New Mexico Territory. They reached Tucson, Arizona two weeks later, resupplied, and began heading northwest, up into the high desert, on the final leg of their journey.

They rode through meadows blue-green with bunchgrass and mountain brome, through stark badland wastes, past fortress-like buttes that towered overhead.

Warm days gave way to frigid nights.

"Well glory be," the old man exclaimed one morning. "I do believe the good Lord has provided us with manna!"

"I'm afraid that's only frost on the ground," said Henry.

"Only on account of your lack of faith," muttered Elijah. "You've got to look with *spiritual* eyes. Sofie? Sofia?" He glanced about and frowned. "Where is that woman? She's better at explaining these things."

My father and Henry exchanged worried glances, but they brewed up a pot of especially sludgy joe and Elijah seemed more himself after he'd slurped down a few cups.

"I need time to myself," Valentina told them, and often went off hunting with her Sharps. She'd return with a pronghorn or jackrabbits and once with a bighorn ram that had just lost out in a rut fight. "I heard the crash of their horns half a mile away," she explained. "He has the most remarkable *cojones,* yes? Which his opponent kicked mercilessly, bringing the poor brute to his knees."

"Ah," said Henry, "your mercy droppeth as the gentle rain from heaven."

"Couldn't you have brought us the victor?" asked my father.

"And deprive the ewes of their champion? *Ni hablar!*"

"'Unto everyone that hath shall be given;'" said Elijah, who'd been quiet and withdrawn all day, staring off into the middle distance, "'but from him that hath not, even that which he hath shall be taken from him.'"

"We'll make a fine meal of it, eh?" said Henry, putting his arm around the old man's shoulders.

But the light faded from Elijah's eyes, and he made no response.

The nights grew yet colder as they followed the trail higher, through stands of juniper and pinyon pine. One evening, while the four travelers were drinking coffee and watching their campfire send sparks up toward the stars, a screech owl shattered the silence.

Henry's eyes narrowed and Valentina frowned.

They believe owls are an omen of death, thought my father. *And perhaps this time they're right.*

"An angel from the high heavens," said Elijah, smiling for the first time in a long while. "You know what he's saying, don't you, like all Messengers before him? *Do not be afraid*." He tilted his head toward the treetops. "I assure you, Blessed One, I feel no fear at all. My Sofia and I will be together soon enough."

Two days before Christmas, Black Mesa came in sight, rising a thousand feet above the broad grassland plateau they'd been traversing.

"Elijah, look," said Henry, offering his field glasses.

Elijah waved them off. "She's already told me. That's Walpi, on First Mesa, where Sofia was born."

That night he shivered no matter how many blankets they heaped on him or how hot they stoked the fire. Early the next morning, my father heard Elijah talking in his sleep.

"*Behold, thou art fair, my love; Thou hast doves' eyes.*

"*For, lo, the winter is past, the rain is over and gone.*"

They were the last words he ever spoke.

My father, Henry, and Valentina ascended Black Mesa on the afternoon of Christmas Eve, bearing Elijah's body and Sofia's ashes. First Mesa was a long, narrow finger that looked out over a desolate landscape. Walpi consisted of pale sandstone dwellings that seemed carved out of the crumbling white cliffs.

"Their shaman was already ancient when I lived here eight years ago," said Henry. "I doubt he's still among the living."

It turned out, however, that Qaletaqa the shaman was very much alive, though wizened with age and half blind.

They embraced with great joy and Henry explained why he and his friends had come.

"I share your grief," said Qaletaqa, "I was fond of Soyala—that is what we called her, for the sixth letter of your alphabet is not easy for us to pronounce. Her grandmother Kaiah was dear to me, and Soyala spent much time here as a child. May she and her husband find their way to the Cloud People and return as rain." He grabbed hold of Henry's arm and pulled him forward. "Come! Our water jugs are freshly filled, you must wash and rest. Tonight we feast!"

"Use only the smallest amount," Henry whispered to the others. "On Black Mesa, water is more precious than gold."

That evening they sat on the floor of a large, low-ceilinged room in the shaman's home and dined on prairie dog and spicy hominy stew and all manner of wild greens. Two small twin girls laughed with delight as they ran their fingers through my father's curls and braided Henry's long hair.

"My great-great-granddaughters, Chosovi and Chosposi." Qaletaqa shrugged helplessly. "I have much power, but none over them."

Four candles burning in a corner of the room caught my father's attention. A white one at the center remained unlit.

The shaman followed his gaze. "Yes, those are Advent candles. It was Henry who told us of them."

My father turned to his partner with raised brows.

"Oh well," said Henry, "I told him Buddhist and Hindu and Zoroastrian tales, but it's your Bible that caught his fancy."

"You await the second coming of your Lord," said Qaletaqa. "We too await a savior. He is the *Pahana*, the Lost White Brother, he who left for the east when we entered the Fourth World. Upon his return he will be the joy of the virtuous and the ruin of the wicked and will lead us into an age of peace and perfect gladness."

"Into the Fifth World," Henry added.

"Yes," said the shaman. "What foolish hopes we had when the Spanish came! Still, I think there is much good magic in the Way of Christ. But for us, the very meaning of life is in the Hopi Way."

"I'd like to learn of that way," said my father. "If it's not presumptuous of me to ask."

"No, it is simple enough. Welcome the stranger and feed him. Be kind to one another and do no injury. Care for the old ones when they can no longer fend for themselves. Defend yourselves if need be, but do not seek war. These things are close to the Christian Way—"

"Agreed," said my father.

"—though not to the ways of white men. This matter of burning the body, however, as you have done for Soyala and wish for her husband, it is new to me."

"It was her wish," said Henry. "Can we not free his soul to join Soyala's and let their ashes be borne on the wind?"

"Do you imagine the man's spirit is trapped?" The shaman laughed. "The body dies, a mere husk, but the breath of life goes on. Fear not, my friend, we will create a great pyre and accomplish this thing. Then, when it comes time for the scattering of ashes—" Qaletaqa frowned and furrowed his brow. "It is the duty of Makia, high priest of Second Mesa, to call on Yaapontsa, god of the winds. Makia is not so powerful as I, though he thinks himself my better. Yet in my graciousness I will overlook his arrogance and ask him to intervene on your behalf."

My father was disappointed there was no alcohol to be found on Black Mesa. Soon it would be time for sleep, and then would come the dreams: Josiah, slumped over in the saddle; Baltasar and Marguerite, surrounded by Knights; the sun beating down on an endless field of bones...

But their host led them outside after dinner, and he found himself grateful to God for the sharp, bracing cold of the night air.

"Look!" shouted Chosposi, pointing to a meteor briefly blazing across the heavens. "A *sohuluqu!*"

"A star who has married," explained the shaman, "and thus falls from the sky."

Valentina scowled and shook her head. "A myth of *la emasculación* if ever I heard one."

"Come now," said Henry. "Are men better off whirling about in the dark, empty vastness, rather than nestled in the bosom of Mother Earth?"

"*Ay, ya.* What would *you* choose? I'd opt to soar in the heavens, however cold and lonely. There's star-fire running through my veins."

"You've lived but twenty years," replied Henry, smiling. "The choices you make later in life might surprise you."

"I know myself well enough," said Valentina. "I'm no Earth Mother. I'll never marry or bear a child." She turned and walked away.

"What do you call *that?*" my father asked the twins, pointing to the Big Dipper.

Chosovi and Chosposi giggled at his ignorance. "Sootuvipi, of course!"

"The great star sling," explained Henry.

"I look at those girls," said Qaletaqa, watching as they ran to catch up with Valentina, "and see myself in the life to come."

"How so?" asked my father.

"After death we are reborn in the spirit world. When Coyote visited Maski, land of the dead, he saw only frolicking children. So I study my grandchildren, that I might remember what it is to be young."

'Unless a man turns and becomes as a child," said my father, paraphrasing from Matthew's Gospel, "he will by no means enter the kingdom of heaven."

"Indeed," said Qaletaqa. "Now you are thinking like a Hopi."

My father went to sleep with a light heart, yet that night the dreams came back with more force than ever before.

Chapter Thirty-Five

The Ghosts of Wounded Knee

"Why did you leave Texas?" I asked my father when I was young and he was still my hero.

"Sometimes a man just wants to move on," he said, not looking up from the draft of the sermon he was preparing. "Anyway, I'd hurt my shooting hand and couldn't much Ranger anymore. Still aches when it rains."

"How'd you hurt it?" I asked. He mostly used his left hand, and yet had mentioned to me he'd once been right-handed. Surely there'd be a good story to follow! "In a fight?"

He put down his pencil and glanced at me briefly. "Yes, a fight."

"Who with?"

"With *whom*, son." Picked his pencil back up. "With bad guys, of course."

"What kind of bad guys? Train robbers? Rustlers? Hold-up men?"

"I don't know, Matthew, it was a long time ago." My father crossed out the last few lines he'd written and frowned.

"Oh, come on, dad—you don't remember the guys who ruined your right hand?"

"What sort of fool questions are these?" The tip of the pencil broke off and he brought his great fist down hard on the table. "Damn it, anyway! This hand's still strong enough to give you a whipping, boy. Now leave me in peace."

I learned something that day. More and more, I asked questions not to elicit stories but to get under my father's skin. This became my version of seeking out danger, of poking a very large bear with the sharpest stick I could fashion. I was fleet enough of foot, and his temper sufficiently short-lived, that I could get away with it.

Most of the time.

After Elijah and Sofia's ashes were borne away on the westerly winds, Valentina gave Bonita to the shaman as a parting gift.

"Many thanks," said Qaletaqa, "for she is a stalwart mule with the heart of a lion. And I have a gift for you, young woman." He handed her a rod about ten inches long, carved from cottonwood, wrapped in buckskin, and affixed with feathers. "Henceforth, your Hopi name shall be *Lomaquahu*, which means beautiful eagle. On this prayer stick are the feathers of a golden eagle. I myself have breathed prayers into them, to safeguard you on your way home."

"Ahem," said Henry, when it seemed the old man could not take his rheumy eyes off Valentina. "Caleb and I ask your blessing and offer you this." He handed him a large packet of tobacco. "May its smoke carry your prayers to the gods."

"Most excellent," said Qaletaqa. "And I have prayer sticks for both of you." He handed one to each and then turned to my father. "You, Caleb McRae, will be known as *Sikyahonaw*, which means yellow bear. For the color of your hair and your great height and strength. Henry Midnight of course already has a Hopi name."

"I'm honored," said my father. "But my friend never told me what you named him."

"Oh, you know," said Henry, "some things are only spoken of in whispers among the tribal elders."

"*Istaqa,*" said Qaletaqa. "Which means coyote-man. The cunning trickster."

"How utterly unfair, I'm as guileless as Nathanael! Tell him, Caleb!"

My father only raised his eyebrows.

"Surely, o venerable mentor," said Henry, turning back to the shaman, "you can come up with a moniker more fitting to my present state of blessed innocence."

"Alas," said Qaletaqa, "once a man has accepted his name, it is his for life."

Valentina was intent on returning to Texas for the wedding of Elliana and Louis. My father, for whom every memory of the Lone Star State was tinged with regret, decided he and Henry would journey north to visit Abarran and his family in Nevada's Ruby Valley. They'd figure out their next move from there.

The three descended from the wind-swept mesa early on the last day of 1905 and halted before parting ways.

"Hasta la vista, amigos," said Valentina. "I will never forget our comradeship on the battlefield."

"That's all very well," said Henry, "but keep in mind you've promised me another game of knives. Let's have that before long."

"Give our blessings to your sister and Louis," said my father. "I couldn't be prouder of them, or happier they're together."

Valentina rode over close to my father and grasped his scarred right hand.

"Take care, Caleb." For a moment her stoic warrior's mask vanished, and there was only the warmth of her smile and a glistening in her eyes. "I will not always be there to save you."

Then she wheeled her steed around and took off swiftly, heading south.

Three days west of Black Mesa, Henry insisted my father accompany him on a slight detour to the north.

"We're entering the land of the Havasupai," he explained, "the People of the Blue Green Waters."

"Waters? This land seems dry as bones."

"There's a limestone aquifer that's sustained them for untold generations, hidden from white man's eyes. I'm one of the few who's seen it. But it's the water in their origin myth I want to tell you about. They say at the dawn of time the good god Tochopa battled the evil Hokotama to see who would rule the world. Facing certain defeat, out of sheer spite the evil one unleashed a great flood over all the land. But Tochopa hollowed out the trunk of a great tree, loaded it with provisions, and set his daughter afloat that she might survive to become the mother of all the peoples of the earth. So there, you see, is the story of Noah and the ark and the infant Moses, all rolled into one." Henry flashed a broad grin. "Only I rather prefer the flood being the bad guy's handiwork, don't you?"

My father rolled his eyes. As though the justice meted out by a righteous God would always be gentle!

"Oh, don't get your back up," Henry continued. "Let's just say both myths have their own special charm. We're just now coming to the reason I brought you here. For when the flood waters retreated, *this* is what remained."

They rode up to the rim of the Grand Canyon and looked out on its impossible vastness. My father had heard of the place, but assumed the stories were wild exaggerations. *No,* he thought, *they didn't begin to capture its grandeur.*

The striated cliffsides, bathed in the rays of the rising sun, glowed in bands of carnelian and coral and rose. Nearby, ponderosa pine and cottonwoods were graced with the whiteness of new-fallen snow.

They looked on in silence for a while.

"It's beautiful of course," Henry said softly, "but it's what's *not* there that thrills me most: the magnificent emptiness of this place."

"Yes," my father murmured. He felt a stirring within and willed the feeling to grow, take shape, become a thought.

Emptiness.

The wind moaned and swirled about him and phrases from the letter the Apostle Paul had written to the church at Philippi came to my father as though whispered into his ears.

Have this mind in you, which was also in Christ Jesus.

What would it mean to have the mind of Christ?

Though He was very God, Paul had written, He'd *emptied himself, taking the form of a servant, being made in the likeness of men.*

My father must have read those words more than a hundred times, yet now their import stunned him. Long ago, the Lord, creator and sustainer of the universe, entered his own creation, his fallen kingdom, this ruined land where demons prowl. Came into it as a helpless babe, forsaking all his heavenly powers.

And in so doing, was never more divine.

For a moment, clouds obscured the sun, and the landscape turned slate blue before shafts of light again set fire to the canyon walls.

It's what's not *there that thrills me most.*

The Apostle's words sounded in his ears once more: The Lord had *humbled himself, becoming obedient even unto death, yea, the death of the cross.*

To follow Him in this, my father realized, is to enter into His glory.

He turned to Henry, wanting to tell him everything...

"What is it, Caleb?"

But he shook his head, stayed silent, as though the words were locked inside some secret corner of his heart.

The sun inched higher.

A peregrine falcon rode the wind, then dove down out of sight.

They rode for hours along the canyon's southern rim before encountering two young Havasupai men who'd been out hunting and had bagged a decent-sized deer.

"There were other whites here yesterday to see the visiting medicine man," said one of the men after they'd exchanged greetings. "You're too late if you have come for him. He left this morning."

"Must be someone special," said Henry. "What's this medicine man's name?"

"I don't know, only the old ones were interested. Ask them."

"He's just some Paiute from up north," said the other. "They say he can light his pipe with the sun and cause rain to fall when drought parches the land. But I saw nothing like that, only an ordinary man."

My father and Henry left the canyon perimeter and put in two days of hard riding, eager to take advantage of fair weather and find a town where they could resupply. They passed over a landscape barren but for patches of greasewood growing in the odd desert wash. Just shy of the Nevada border, they came upon three men engaged in an altercation by the side of the trail.

They were all Indians. Two younger ones, their long hair in braids, were taunting an older man dressed in a dark wool suit who stood stock-still, his face impassive, arms hanging limply at his sides. A few drops of blood trickled from his nose.

"They're Paiutes," said Henry. "I understand enough to know they're calling that fellow a fraud. Seems like we've caught up with the medicine man."

One of the young men turned to them with a sneer, then shouted angrily and shoved the bleeding man to the ground.

"That's enough," said my father, and rode over next to the trio.

"Do not harm them," the medicine man said in perfect English. "I will have no violence on my behalf."

"All right," said my father. "I'll honor that." He dismounted and stood in front of the medicine man, facing his attackers.

The fellow struggled to his knees.

Henry spoke a few words in the Indians' language, then came and stood at my father's side.

The two young Paiutes did their best to stare them down. At last one of them spoke, then spat on the ground before he and his partner turned and walked away.

"He said I call myself their savior," said the medicine man, "but it is the white man who must save me."

My father gave him a hand up. "I'm Caleb McRae, and this is Henry Midnight. Are you well enough to ride?"

"I've been through worse. Jack Wilson." He shook hands with both.

"You're Paiute, also, aren't you?" asked Henry.

"Yes, but from the Northern tribe, in the Mason Valley. Those two were Southern Paiutes."

"There some sort of blood feud between your tribes?"

"No." Wilson smiled grimly. "I've enemies in more than a few of the nations."

"We're heading north, too, up toward Elko," said my father. "You want some company, we could ride together a ways."

"I would enjoy that," said Wilson. "This can be a lonely land."

"How far are we from the nearest general store?" asked Henry.

"The Union Pacific Railroad just laid tracks through the Las Vegas Valley, a day's ride north of here. Only place you can find water in these parts. You'll find some stores by the train stop. That's where I'll turn west."

The trio stopped at midday to rest, warm up by a fire, and eat a meal.

"You're welcome to share our grub," said my father. "We've hardtack and jerky, and I've got coffee grounds boiling that haven't been used more than three or four times."

"The coffee will be much appreciated," said Wilson. "But I've got my own eats." He reached into a pouch and withdrew a rawhide bag, then laughed when his companion's eyes widened as he brought forth a feast: pemmican, dried elk meat mixed with melted fat and chokeberries pounded into powder. "Here, partake with me. I am grateful for your help this morning." He handed them two healthy portions, made the sign of the cross, and offered thanks to Jesus. "I'd meet the Lord again sooner than I care to if I ate like you boys."

Henry snapped his fingers. "*Now* I know where I've heard your name before! You're Wovoka, the prophet-dreamer."

"It is Wodziwob who most deserves that title. My father served him, as I now serve Christ Jesus."

"But the Ghost Dance," said Henry. "That was your idea. My God, you're still among the living! I thought you'd perished along with Sitting Bull."

"Sitting Bull had *nothing* to do with the Dance." There was a bitter edge to Wovoka's voice. "That was a lie of the Indian Agent, McLaughlin, may he be forever haunted by the ghosts of Wounded Knee."

"I was a youth back then, and know only enough to want to know more," My father handed two steaming mugs of coffee to his companions, then poured one for himself. "But I do know a great deal about bad memories. If you'd rather not talk, I understand."

"There's no escape from bad memories, Mr. McRae. Or rather, the only end to their pain is in the setting of things right." He chewed some pemmican and washed it down with coffee. "Perhaps you think the dance some sort of pagan ritual. Not so. I became a Christian as a boy, working for a good man named Wilson, and somehow found favor with the Lord, though I deserved it not. On the first of January 1889, during an eclipse of the sun, I was lifted into the Third Heaven. There I saw a vision of things to come: our ancestors rising from the dead, forests filled with wild game, and buffalo once again covering the plains, more numerous than the stars. The white men and all their ugliness—their fences and factories, their telegraph poles extending ten thousand miles, their mines that scar the sacred ground—had vanished, as if they had never been here at all, as though they were only the figments of an evil dream. But much would be required of our people; they must neither lie nor steal, only love one another and forswear war. I was shown the way of the circle dance and told that for five days the peoples of all the nations must dance this dance. And then the Lord might hasten the day when all these things would come to pass."

"Fascinating," said Henry. "I'd heard the Ghost Dance was a prelude to battle, a holy ritual to inspire warriors to rise up against the whites."

"No. I preached the Way of our Elder Brother. We were to turn the other cheek. Our reward would not always be in this life."

He sounds much like Sofia, thought my father, and the stories he'd heard of the slaughter of the Lakota merged in his mind with the bloody battle at the Gutiérrez ranch. "Were you there, at Wounded Knee?"

Wovoka shook his head. "I have seen it through the words of those who were. If you have read the white man's telling, you know only lies."

"Then tell us the truth."

"*Why?* What makes you eager to know of such great evil?"

So intense was Wovoka's gaze that my father wondered if the man could see into his soul. "Many things I once held dear turned out to be lies," he answered. "I'm grateful for truth when I find it."

Wovoka nodded, then rolled a cigarette, filling it with wild tobacco, red willow bark, sweet grass, and sage. He took his time smoking before beginning to speak.

"In the same year I was blessed with my vision, Kicking Bear, a leader of the Lakota Sioux, came to me from the Dakotas and brought the Dance back to his people. Agent McLaughlin's mission was to turn Indians into whites; the Lakota were to farm the arid soil, send their children away to boarding schools, learn

English, and give up all the ancient ways. They were desperate for the Dance, for they were starving, both in their bellies and in their souls. When the soldiers saw the dancing, they became afraid, though the dancers were but skin and bones and freezing in the bitter cold that terrible winter. So great was the legend of the Lakota Sioux!

"Sitting Bull and his people desired only to be left alone. But McLaughlin accused him of using the Dance to work his people into a rage for war and sent men to arrest him while he and his wife still slept in each other's arms. When the people heard what was happening, one foolish man shot at the soldiers. The bullet he fired was Sitting Bull's death warrant, for McLaughlin's men swiftly gunned the great chief down."

Wovoka closed his eyes and bowed his head before continuing to speak.

"Was there a Christmas that dark December? Were those who called themselves Christians celebrating the entrance of the Savior into the world? Were faith, hope, and charity born again in their hearts? If so, the Lakota knew it not. Chief Spotted Elk had set out with his people to seek food and shelter with Red Cloud. They never arrived. The Seventh Cavalry, five hundred strong, tracked them down and told them to make camp by a nearby creek called Wounded Knee. They surrounded the camp and set their big wagon-guns in place, and at daybreak they ordered the Lakota to surrender their weapons.

"The soldiers searched every tepee, taking no heed of the old and the sick, the women and the young. A deaf man who did not understand the soldier's orders clung to his rifle, and in the struggle that followed a shot went off. And then the gates of hell swung wide open.

"I have heard White men speak of the *battle* of Wounded Knee, but there was no battle. It was a massacre. The young Lakota braves ran for their rifles, but in vain, for the cavalry rained death upon them from all sides. No mercy was granted. Those who sought to hide were hunted down and slaughtered. My friend Black Elk told me of seeing butchered women and children lying heaped and scattered all along that crooked gulch. Of three hundred fifty Lakota, less than a hundred survived." Wovoka drank down the last of his coffee and stared into the fire. "Sixteen years have passed since Wounded Knee, but it lives in my mind as the eternal present."

"It's a tale of horror," Henry said softly. "There are no words."

"We think differently," said Wovoka. "There must always be words."

"Henry and I, too, have passed through a time of death and darkness," said my father. "What is Black Elk to do, what are we to do, with the images that linger in our minds, that come back in dreams? You said the pain goes away through the setting of things right. But how can such savagery and madness *ever* be set right?"

"Are you a follower of Lord Jesus?"

"I hope so," said my father, shocked to hear himself say anything other than a simple *Yes*. "I used to think I knew what it meant to follow Him. Now I'm not so sure."

"To lose false confidence is to gain a great deal, however it might make you feel." Wovoka reached out and grasped my father's hand. "Never forget: the spirit world is yet more real than the world around us. You must learn to see with spiritual eyes. The ghosts of the Lakota who perished at Wounded Knee will always be with me. But at the same time as I see their broken bodies, I see their risen selves. I hear the beating of the drum, the dancing of the Great Dance, the laughter of children. For our Heavenly Father *will wipe away all tears from their eyes; and there shall be no more death, neither sorrow, nor crying, neither shall there be any more pain.*"

"The Fifth World," Henry said softly.

"Some call it that. But all that matters is what we do with this knowledge in our lives, this very day." Wovoka turned to my father. "There is something else troubling you. Speak."

"If the Lakota could have defended themselves, if they could have fought back and saved the lives of their women and children, wouldn't that have been right?"

"No."

"Then you believe *all* violence is against the way of Christ?"

"Of course."

"I just don't see how turning the other cheek makes sense when innocent lives are at stake." My father pounded his fist against the ground; in the months since his final battle, he'd been wrestling with Sofia's words, now echoed by the prophet-dreamer. "That can't possibly be what the Lord meant."

"Tell me what He meant, then, my friend. Turn the cheek, love and bless your enemy, but only to a point, only if he is not too bad, if he does no harm? You are wrong. Jesus preached no half measures."

"Are we not to push back against the darkness?" asked Henry. "It seems you would have us surrender to the forces of evil."

"On the contrary, I would have you die into the only victory worthy of the name."

Jesus had humbled himself, thought my father, *becoming obedient unto death.* He'd forsaken even the power of defending the defenseless; for nearly two millennia, untold innocents had been set upon by unspeakably cruel oppressors, and the sovereign Lord of all creation had let them suffer and die. My father reeled, thinking of this. Must he disavow violence at all cost? What role was there, then, for an Avenger, if vengeance were the Lord's alone?

Justice, it seemed, would be found only in the flames of hell.

"I think I understand," he said at last.

Henry raised his eyebrows but stayed silent.

"Do you?" Wovoka brought forth his tobacco pouch, rolled another cigarette, and regarded my father as he took a long first drag. "It is not easy for those who have lived by the sword to grasp the full meaning of my words," said the prophet dreamer. "But you will, in time."

That night the three men took rooms at a roadhouse near the train station in the newly formed town of Las Vegas.

"I'm glad you were able to talk so freely with Wovoka," said Henry, as they lay together, my father's head upon his chest. "To unburden your heart. If only I could inspire such outpourings from your soul!"

"Hmm?" My father looked up at him, genuinely surprised. "All that about non-violence? I struggle to understand what it means to follow Christ, that's hardly news. And you know I suffer from bad dreams."

"Yes, and yet you hardly speak of them to me." Henry played with the ringlets of my father's hair. "But it's all right. You'll open up in your own time."

"I'm sorry," said my father. "You know I couldn't imagine life without you."

"Well of course not," said his lover. "I'm the sun and the moon and the stars. Without me you'd be a lost and lonely man."

"I would, wouldn't I," said my father.

That night there were no dreams.

Early the next morning, Wovoka left for his home in western Nevada, while my father and Henry resupplied before continuing on north to Elko. Most days the weather held, and they rode hard and covered the four hundred miles to the Zabala ranch in just two weeks.

They were greeted warmly by Abarran and Arrosa, whom they'd last seen in Austin two years before, but soon found that all was not well between husband and wife.

Chapter Thirty-Six

The White Stallion

"You know where the kitchen is, Abarran," said Arrosa, after inquiring into the men's health and assuring them their horses would be well looked after. "There is more than enough dinner on the stove for the three of you. As for me, I am retiring for the night."

"So soon?" asked her husband, frowning.

Arrosa walked off without making any reply.

"Ah well, gentlemen, tonight we men shall dine like kings!" he exclaimed, clapping his hands in what seemed a forced display of gaiety. "Come!" Abarran led my father and Henry into the kitchen, handed them bowls, then paused by a large black pot for dramatic effect before lifting the lid with a flourish. "Behold paradise," he said reverently.

They breathed in the enticing aroma.

"Ah! Every mile we've travelled since leaving Brownsville last November makes sense at last," said Henry. "Or at least so my stomach tells me. What, pray tell, hath Arrosa wrought?"

"*Piperrada*. Onion, bell peppers, tomatoes—look, they are the very colors of the Basque flag!" Abarran pointed to a red, white, and green pennant hanging on the wall. "Flavored with much Espelette pepper, which is made from red chilis, but have no fear, they are not too terribly hot."

"I fear only the Lord," professed my father, and his host ladled the piperrada and chunks of lamb into their bowls.

At table Abarran broke bread, recited a brief Basque prayer, and filled his guests' goblets from a large decanter. "*Sagardo*, made from the apples of our own orchard. Do you know how long we Basques have been drinking Sagardo? This is liquid history, my friends! There is a diary that survives to this day, written by a pilgrim who walked the Camino de Santiago in the year of our Lord 1134, who remarked on our passion for this divine distillation. Ah, it is a pity your Jesuit friend is not here! How is the good Father?"

"He has gone to his eternal reward, Abarran," said my father. "We laid him to rest not two months ago."

My father and Henry told the story of all that had transpired since their time together in Austin, and many toasts were drunk in memory of the departed.

"How fare Zorion and Joska and the other little Zabalas, more numerous than the stars?" asked Henry.

"My first-born does me proud, he has learned to manage cattle almost as well as he shepherds our sheep. And Joska! More than ever she is the apple of her father's eye. But of late, Arrosa and I—" Abarran pulled at his beard and scowled —we do not see eye to eye on how to raise her."

"I'm sorry to hear that," said my father. "She's an extraordinary young woman."

"Yes, exactly!" Abarran smacked the table. "And such talents as hers must be developed, such rich soil cultivated, not left to lie fallow. At the age of seventeen, Joska knows more than any of the teachers in this little town of perhaps a thousand souls. We could send her away to university, in some far-off city, yes, but who would look after her there, who would guard her virtue?"

"I see your dilemma," said Henry.

"*Dilemma?*" exclaimed the Basque, and brought his fist down hard enough that his guests had to take hold of their bowls. "The answer has been handed to us, thanks be to God, only my wife does not understand a miracle when it is right before her eyes. What are the chances that a learned man, a man of letters, of the *world*, would be found in this wind-swept wilderness, I ask you? And that he would take on my Joska as his pupil, agree to be her mentor, her guiding light?"

"Long odds you'd find such a fellow," said Henry, "though once found, it's a certainty he'd take your daughter on. Who is this remarkable man?"

"A graduate of the great Princeton University, gentlemen—a scholar, and an author of no little renown: Cornelius Griffin."

"I know that name," said my father. "As a youth, I lived for the next installment of *Johnny Dallas, Texas Ranger*, desperate to find out how Johnny would defeat his nemesis, stagecoach robber Raswell Gore. 'Curse you, Johnny Dallas!' were always Raswell's last words as he was being led off to prison. Griffin was king of the dime novels back then. Still is, I imagine."

"Those dimes bought Mr. Griffin five hundred of the most beautiful acres in the Ruby Valley." There was no jealousy in Abarran's voice, only awe. "He moved here from New York last year. One of Joska's schoolteachers introduced them, for which I am eternally grateful."

"No doubt," said Henry. "Is there a Mrs. Griffin and any little Griffins in the picture?"

Abarran's face fell.

"You have hit precisely on the matter which has so upset my wife. Mr. Griffin is a single man, but one of lofty thoughts and the highest virtue, of this I am quite sure. She is a fine woman, my Arrosa, and I love her with all my heart, but the demons of suspicion hold her in their thrall."

"He and Joska are together a great deal, I take it?" asked my father.

"Yes, Mr. Griffin has been most generous with his time, and my daughter is blossoming under his tutelage. Only yesterday she recited lines from a poet of ancient Rome, telling of a Queen who was off hunting with some Trojan fellow—and in Latin, my friends, Latin!"

"Ah, the story of Dido and Aeneas," said Henry. "Interesting choice. Where do they study together, pray tell?"

"In this very home!" Abarran replied. "For the most part. Mr. Griffin insists that the finest education cannot be obtained merely from books; one learns by being out in nature, observing the miracle of animal and vegetable life, as he puts it, seeing and touching and tasting the things of this world. In this I support him one hundred—"

"Your Mr. Griffin can do his seeing and touching and tasting well away from my Joska!" Arrosa came storming into the dining room. "*Ergelak!* You would welcome a thief into your house and hand him the gold in your safe."

"This is not right, my dear," Abarran protested, his face growing red, "to carry on in front of our guests."

"Someone under this roof must speak sense, guests or no guests."

"My daughter will continue her studies under Mr. Griffin—the wisdom he imparts is more precious than gold." Abarran drew himself up to his full height and pounded the table. "I have spoken!"

"I will hold you responsible, husband." Arrosa turned to my father and Henry. "The great seer will be here bright and early tomorrow, judge him for yourselves. I came to say your rooms are made up, if there is anything you lack, please let me know."

"Thank you ma'am," said my father, standing up from the table. "It's been a long journey, and the night's rest will do us good."

"The *piperrrada* was exquisite, Mrs. Zabala, we couldn't be more grateful for the hospitality." Henry turned to Abarran and embraced him warmly. "Until tomorrow, my friend," he said, and left with my father.

The muffled sounds of their hosts' heated conversation carried into their bedroom well into the night.

Joska had not yet come downstairs for breakfast when the dime novelist arrived the next morning.

"She's primping in the mirror," said Arrosa, *sotto voce*.

"Gentlemen, my daughter's tutor, Mr. Cornelius Griffin," said Abarran, pretending he hadn't heard his wife's comment.

"Just think of us as Joska's doting uncles," said Henry, after they'd introduced themselves. "We look out for the lass."

"I'm even more delighted to meet you then," said Griffin. "She's one in a million."

He was a handsome specimen, tall and well built, with a strong jaw, a cleft chin, and an impressive head of dark wavy hair slicked back with some sort of lustrous pomade.

"Good-looking hair," said Henry. "I've been wondering whether to use something on my own." He wrapped a few of his long strands around one finger and regarded them with a frown. "They say mutton oil lends a distinctive gleam. What do *you* use?"

"Brilliantine," said Griffin. "Promotes the health of the scalp."

"Knew a man who swore by bear grease," said my father. "Claimed it cured baldness and the nastiest-looking sores. Stunk something awful, but he'd sweeten it with lavender and thyme and vanilla and the like so you'd hardly know. You might give it a try."

Griffin narrowed his eyes, then laughed, showing my father the whitest teeth he'd ever seen. "It's an honor," he said to Abarran, "being joshed by such celebrities as these." He turned back to my father and Henry. "I was in El Paso not long ago, they still speak of you there, or rather, *sing*."

"Yes, 'The Ballad of Midnight and McRae,'" Abarran said proudly. "Come, we'll talk over breakfast."

"And to think the Great Chase ended up here!" Griffin laughed again as they sat down at table. "The balladeer would be chagrined, I think, to see Midnight and McRae sitting down together to eggs and bacon. But I well understand; there's still something of the Old West in these parts, the smell of it, if the wind's blowing the right way. That's why I'm here, you know. The frontier's little more than a memory most places, unless you're up at the Klondike. Which would make for a decent adventure, eh? Might just head there myself one of these days." He squinted at my father and Henry as though taking their measure. "You know, I really ought to feature the two of you in one of my novels."

"Just make sure it's my *left* profile that's featured on the cover," said Henry. "I'm terribly vain that way."

"I shelled out more than a few dimes for your stories in the early 90s," said my father. "You're younger than I thought you'd be."

"Published my first novel in '87 at the tender age of eighteen and paid for a Princeton education with the royalties. I'd read one of Ned Buntline's stories about Buffalo Bill a couple years before, and it set my imagination on fire."

"Read that one, too," said my father.

"Buntline wasn't his real name, of course, it was Ed Judson." Griffin leaned back in his chair and took a moment to light up a large cigar, oblivious to Arrosa's glowering gaze. "He met Cody after the Civil War, made the man's legend bigger than it ever would have been. Judson was quite the character himself, married half a dozen times, romanced the young wife of a fellow in Nashville, then killed her husband in a duel. Lynch mob strung him up, but somehow the rascal got away, ended up in New York City. Not a few scribblers hailed from there, you know—Whitman, Melville, James, and yours truly. But the Ruby Valley, that's the place for me now."

"I grew up not far from New York myself," said my father. "Wanted to be Johnny Dallas so badly I joined the Texas Rangers."

"I'm afraid I was rather a poor stand-in for Raswell Gore," said Henry.

Griffin grinned and slathered his toast with butter and jam.

"The thing is, though," said my father, "as I look back on your tales, there's not much *truth* in them."

Griffin raised his eyebrows. "If you can find a flaw, I'll be impressed. I researched every detail that went into those books, down to the barrel markings on the outlaws' guns."

"That's not the sort of truth I'm talking about," said my father. "Those are mere facts."

"Ah. Well, then. What *is* truth?" The author took a contemplative puff from his cigar. "That's a perfectly fair question old Pilate asked. I don't recall he received an answer."

"The Truth was standing right before him. But let's turn to facts. You write of noble Rangers, savage Indians, incorrigible villains. Real life is rarely so simple."

"'Real life,' my friend, is exactly what my readers are trying to escape. Weren't you? Real life, the *truth*—" Griffin waved his cigar dismissively—"these things only depress the common man, disgust him, or, worst sin of all, bore him to tears. Whereas I captivate the multitudes, enchant them, *thrill* them. Come to think of it, though, I think my stories succeed even on your lofty terms. After all, Caleb—" He blew out a cloud of smoke and tapped an inch of ash onto an empty plate. "When I thrilled *you*, did I not hit on some truth deep inside your soul?"

"Yes, you did; as a youth I wanted to believe in something bigger and better than my own flawed self. In a world where Goodness defeats Evil. But how is that done, exactly, and what does it mean in these lives we lead?" My father smiled at

Griffin. "I'm just giving you a hard time again, Cornelius. All that's more than can reasonably be expected from a dime novel."

"Joska!" called out Arrosa. "Enough of your primping!"

Abarran, who'd been following the conversation with a puzzled expression, glowered at her, then turned to the writer. "You must tell them about your latest project. About the uncatchable horse."

"Mmm-hmm." Griffin shoveled down a forkful of eggs, then picked up his cigar. "I'm glad you mentioned that, Zabala. How would you boys like to join me on an extraordinary adventure?"

"Chasing after uncatchable horses?" said Henry. "Why that's Caleb's specialty! Wherever will we find this creature?"

"Nowhere and everywhere," said Griffin. "Have you heard of the White Stallion?"

"If it's the Ghost Horse you mean," said my father, "yes, many times."

"The White Steed of the Prairies," added Henry. "The Indians tell of him, too. I knew a man who swore he'd trailed him for three days through the Panhandle, clear up into the Oklahoma Territory. O'Brien was his name, claimed he'd seen the Little People as well."

"You can't be serious about this," said my father.

"On the contrary! *The Saturday Evening Post* will pay a pretty penny for our story. I'll pitch it like this—" Griffin leaned forward and spoke with dramatic intensity. "*Your intrepid correspondent, Cornelius Griffin, chronicler of the Wild West, has joined forces with two legends of the American frontier, Captain Caleb McRae, lately of the Texas Rangers, and Henry Midnight, Bandit of the Brazos, son of a British Lord and his Apache bride.*" Griffin winked at Henry, who'd arched his eyebrows. "One embroiders the facts ever so slightly in this sort of thing, you understand. *Our objective: nothing less than to capture the White Stallion, whatever it takes, whatever the cost. He's a mustang like no other, a kingly creature who stands at least eighteen hands and races over the open range fast as the wind. P.T. Barnum once offered five thousand dollars to anyone who could bring him the beast. Riders in relays with packs of hounds did their best to run him down; a team of cowboys chased him into a blind box canyon, yet somehow, against all odds, the White Stallion escaped. But never have two such as Midnight and McRae joined in the hunt, and we've every hope of success where all others have failed."* Griffin leaned back and flourished his cigar. "Do you see the brilliance of playing off the legend of your own great chase? Not the real chase, of course, but the myth enshrined in song."

"I take it the adventure you'd have us join you in," said my father, "is one that will take place solely in your mind."

"And afterwards in the imaginations of half a million readers. Which will whet their appetite for the White Stallion novels to come. I'll cut the two of you in, of course, for, say, a third of what the Post pays, merely for lending me your names. Really, when you consider the value of the publicity, you ought to be paying *me*—but that's not my style. So—" he took a last puff of his cigar and ground it out in the plate he'd been using as an ashtray. "What do you think?"

"Well, do we catch the creature in the end?" asked Henry. "I've my reputation to consider, you know."

"No, of course not." Griffin scowled. "That would ruin everything. It's the stallion who's the star of the show, don't you see? He's the one the reader's rooting for. Look, you're not literary men, but I can assure you, never will failure have been more romantic. Here's the way my piece will end—"

"Joska!" exclaimed Abarran as his daughter entered the room. "It's about time."

"I'm sorry to be late, father." Her face lit up at the sight of my father and Henry. "Mr. Midnight, Mr. McRae, what a delightful surprise! How long will we have the pleasure of your company?"

"Only until we wear out our welcome," said my father.

"Then you will be here for ages and ages. But please, Cornelius—"

"*Mr. Griffin*," Arrosa said sternly.

"—do continue, I'm dying to hear how you'll end the story."

"Yes, well, picture this: These fine men and I, we've been chasing the mustang for months only to be foiled by him time and again until we finally call it quits. We're riding for home in the twilight when I hear a distant neighing and turn to see the White Steed rearing back on his hind legs, silhouetted against the rising moon, before he gallops away, wild and free, and vanishes into the night."

"Bravo!" cried Joska. "How thrilling!"

"That it may be," said Henry, "but I'm quite sure there are others Mr. Griffin could bring along on this adventure whose fame far outstrips our own."

"Oh, very well, then." The author-cum-tutor furrowed his brow and buttered another roll. "I'll see old Earp about it. Wyatt and his bride were up in Nome, Alaska fleecing the miners, now he's here in Nevada staking claims this side of Death Valley. I'm sure my story will tickle his fancy." Griffin lit up another cigar and turned to my father. "But at least, you, Caleb, truth-seeker that you are, ought to appreciate how my tale reveals just what we Americans hold most dear. Why is the white stallion the hero of the story? Because he's the very epitome of freedom, pure and, shall we say, unbridled. Like him, we'd rather die than submit to a master. Parsons can prattle on about this or that on Sunday mornings, and their congregations might give lip service to what they say, but what we *really* worship—more even than silver and gold—is the right to do what we damn well please."

"You *are* quite the romantic!" said Henry.

My father made no comment. There was some truth in Griffin's words, cynical though they were, and they pricked at his conscience. What most called freedom was nothing more than slavery to sin.

Was he any different from them?

If the Son therefore shall make you free, Jesus had said, *ye shall be free indeed.*

What *is* freedom? he thought late that night, wide awake and staring at the ceiling while Henry slept blissfully by his side. Now there's a decent question. And how could he deny the answer to it, the answer he'd sensed looking out over the rim of the Grand Canyon: obedience, even unto death. The only freedom lay in abject surrender, in becoming a slave of Christ.

It was a paradox, it followed no worldly logic, and yet it was true.

Was he truly a free man, he wondered, as Fr. de Souza had tried to persuade him, or merely another self-justifying prisoner of sin?

Chapter Thirty-Seven

Mustangers

"You've got to put us to work, Abarran," my father said for at least the tenth time, after they'd been at the ranch for several days. "We're not used to lives of leisure."

"All right, all right, my friends, if you insist, there is perhaps something you could do. We have a problem here with wild horses."

"Ah yes," said Henry. "The heroes of the western range."

Abarran laughed, though without much humor. "Mr. Griffin, he writes wonderful stories. But real life is something else again. These mustangs, they eat the grass that should be for our sheep and cattle, knock down fences, make off with our mares. To us ranchers, they are just varmints by another name, worse than prairie dogs or coyotes. Here in Nevada we are allowed to shoot them on sight."

"I've heard of that," said my father. "Only, much as I want to be of help, Abarran, I couldn't bring myself to kill horses."

"I'm sure there's another way," said Henry. "Aren't they also rounded up to be sold?"

"Yes," said Abarran, "but that is more complicated by far. I tell you what, we will go into town and I will buy us a meal at Shorty's. There we will find a man who knows all there is to know about this matter of mustangs."

The man in question, Roscoe Greer, turned out to be a rough-hewn fellow in his fifties who was playing poker at the back of Shorty's Eats and Drinks.

"Hell, there's only regulars in this game," said Greer, when Aberran asked him if he'd mind talking to some friends, "and they're all tighter than a gnat's chuff. Not a sucker in sight, goldarn it. You spring for a rib-eye and a pitcher of beer, Abe, I'll talk your ears off."

The deal being struck, the foursome found a table in one of the quieter corners, ordered steaks all around and ample libations, and Aberran laid out their dilemma.

"You don't have the stomach for killing, huh," Greer said to my father. "Well, I didn't much either, at first. I'd been a wolfer for years, killin' wolves and mountain lions, mostly. But you got to attract the predators with somethin' tasty, and it was easy pickins to drop a few mustangs, then wait for wolves and big cats to come feed on the carcasses. Them mustangs made themselves such a nuisance, though, pretty soon ranchers were payin' bounties for 'em. I'd get four dollars for a pair of wolf ears, but five, six times that much for the scalp of a wild stallion.

"So pretty soon I was a mustanger, plain and simple. This ain't exactly a new problem; back when I was workin' out California way, old-timers told me stories of how the Spaniards would drive hundreds of wild horses off the sea cliffs of San Jose. These days, though, right here's the place to be. Stockmen strung a hundred thousand miles of barbed wire through Texas and Oklahoma and the Great Plains. Nevada's the last of the open range, ain't nobody layin' claim to this godforsaken land. But mustangs, they're so ornery they thrive in it."

"There's trade in these creatures, though," said Henry. "Used to be, anyway. Or are you telling us they're worth more dead than alive?"

"No, but it takes some work and you need a pardner or two. Me, I'm a one-man show. Back just a few years when we was fightin' the Spanish, and the Brits had something goin' on over in Africa—"

"With the Boers," said Henry.

"There you go. Well, there was more 'n half a million horses sold off during those two dust-ups, most of 'em wild. You couldn't round up mustangs fast enough to fill the orders. U.S. Cavalry's a pretty steady customer, though right now mustangers ain't exactly gettin' rich. There's peace these days, but sit tight, there'll be fightin' again somewhere before long."

"Looks like we might just turn your problem into profit," my father said to Abarran, before turning back to Greer. "Any part of Nevada better than another if a man was going to make his living that way?"

"Oh, wild horses are everywhere in this state. But you'll always find the serious mustangers near the railway line. That's what I like about Elko. It was the transcontinental railroad made this town."

The men talked about methods of capture while they polished off their steaks, then Greer went back to playing poker and Abarran and his guests returned to the ranch.

"You've got it in your mind to make us mustangers, don't you?" said Henry, as he and my father strolled over to the stables to check on their steeds. "Serious ones, I gather."

"We can catch horses as well as any," said my father, "and break them better than most. I've seen what you learned from the Apache."

"That's true enough, but..."

"Come on, do you have a better idea? Anyway, I like it out here," said my father, with an air of finality.

His lover sighed. "What is it, exactly, about the desolation that appeals to you? Aside from its not being Texas."

"Hard to say, really."

"*Try,*" said Henry, with infinite patience.

"Well..." My father paused at the stable doors and looked off into the distance. "There's something about the great lonely vastness out here...it's got that same beautiful emptiness as the Grand Canyon, just spread out in a different way."

"Ah!" Henry laughed and embraced him. "How can I say no to that, Caleb? You endlessly charm me."

They joined forces with Roscoe Greer, who knew an East Coast dealer always in the market for horses to pull carriages and trams. There was a water seep near the Zabala ranch where the mustangs liked to drink, so they built a corral around it, shut the gate at just the right moment, and shipped off more than two dozen horses from the Elko Depot. My father and Henry split their share of the proceeds with Abarran and began making plans to set themselves up in the business of catching wild horses, breaking them, and selling them off.

Most of the mustangers worked northern Nevada, where the rail service had been in place for years; my father suggested moving down to Las Vegas, where the railroad had just been established, and Henry readily agreed.

They were back in the stables, grooming their horses, when Cornelius Griffin came in, having just finished the day's lessons with Joska.

"Hold on a moment, Cornelius, old boy," said Henry. "We'd like a word with you."

"All right, but make it quick, I've things to do."

"This won't take long," said my father, walking over close to the author. "I'm sure, as Joska's tutor, you're as concerned for her as we are. So rest assured, if anyone were ever to take advantage of the girl, or mistreat her in any way, we'll see to it he regrets he'd ever been born."

"Oh, you needn't worry about *that,*" said Griffin. "I'd take the blackguard apart myself." He swung up onto his steed and looked down, his expression somewhere between a sneer and a smile. "Even if there were two of the bastards."

Chapter Thirty-Eight

Phaethon

"Tell me again about the wild horses," I'd beg my father when I was still young enough to enjoy his stories, before his harshness and dark moods took their toll. "You know, when you and Henry hung out your shingle as Midnight & McRae."

I loved seeing the light come into his eyes, hearing the joy in his voice when he told stories of those days.

"You remember when I took you to Vegas?" he'd ask me, and I'd nod, and he'd say, "Well, this was back when it wasn't hardly a town at all..."

My father and Henry reckoned they wouldn't need much land, most of Nevada being open range, so they bought a modest parcel some fifteen miles west of the Las Vegas train depot, not far from the Spring Mountains, where wild horses were known to roam. They put up a small cabin, then got to work on a corral and a smaller pen where they'd gentle the beasts. To keep the mustangs from leaping over or crashing through the fencing, they built them six feet tall, using two-by-sixes lag-bolted into sections of old telegraph poles. The corral was set close to the end of a narrow trail, and they connected the two with fencing made from ponderosa pine that Henry said smelled like the butterscotch he loved as a child.

"What's captured your curiosity?" my father asked after his partner had stopped and dismounted during their first foray to scout the herds.

Henry was down on his knees, carefully pulling up some flowers. "Wild roses." He came over and showed them to my father. "A tonic for the liver and heart, and effective for moving the bowels. Why I stopped, though, is the Paiutes and Nez

Perce swear they keep ghosts at bay. So I'm going to grow them in our garden and make a tea from the petals, and see if that won't put an end to your bad dreams."

It was all nonsense and superstition, of course, but still! My father leaned over and kissed Henry's upturned face, his heart full. Gone were the days when lust would come upon him like a sudden summer squall; was this not love, pure and simple? Love which bears all things, believes all things, hopes all things, endures all things.

Which never fails.

And if so, how could it be anything but a gift of the Spirit?

Many years later, when I knew many of my father's secrets and guessed at others, I thought surely these were the memories playing through his mind when he would pause in his storytelling and smile. These were the stories he wanted to linger over, hold on to, keep alive.

As a child, of course, all I thought of was action and adventure.

"The buckskin stallion," I'd say, if I saw him lost in thought. *"He was your first capture, right?"*

"That he was, Matt. It was our third day in search of wild horses..."

"Finally," my father whispered, handing his field glasses to Henry. "This is just what we've been waiting for."

They staked out a hidden watering hole in Red Rock Canyon, a place of tall, sheer sandstone cliffs that glowed at sunset like the dying embers of a fire. The mustangs were upwind, some hundred yards away, their leader a golden buckskin, the lead mare a chestnut roan with a yearling colt close by her side. The other mares were grooming, nibbling each other's necks and back.

For the first time in years, my father felt a deep sense of peace.

It was more than just a good-looking drove he'd been waiting for. *This* was contentment, searching out these magnificent creatures amid the beauty of God's creation, with Henry by his side.

Most mustangers tried to capture as many as they could, but my father had decided Midnight & McRae would become known as providers of a limited number of fine, well-trained horses that could command top dollar. Some captures they'd handle themselves, but often they'd go into town and hire on cowboys whom they could trust to follow their lead, do things their way.

The watering hole didn't lend itself to the same sort of trap they'd used in Elko, so my father and Henry planned to run the mustangs till they were tired enough to be led to the narrow path and into the corral. They came back with the hired men and spent the next few days shadowing the horses at a distance and discovering the trails they preferred.

"That way we could anticipate which way they'd go, Matt, get there first and cut 'em off."

"But this wasn't just any stallion, dad, it was Phaethon, and he didn't make it easy for you—it was a hell of a chase, right?"

"You watch your language, boy." My father gave me his angry, squint-eyed stare. How I could have made such a stupid mistake? These were good memories, though, and his gaze soon softened. "Yes, he gave us a run for our money..."

The hired men would dog the mares; my father and Henry wanted to bring in the stallion themselves. They'd anticipated the stud would split off, try to lead them on, lose them, and let the mares escape. What they didn't expect was that he'd charge them, causing Arion, my father's steed, to rear back and send him tumbling to the ground.

"A most ignoble debut, Caleb!" cried Henry, who found more than a few chances to remind my father of his fall in the months that followed.

Henry set off in pursuit and my father quickly closed the gap, Arion being no less swift than Boaz or Achilles. The stallion led them through side canyons, past Joshua trees and Mojave yucca and over endless fields of blackbrush scrub. Day became night; my father praised God for the moonlight as the buckskin led them up into the mountains, where they nearly lost him amid the juniper and scrub oak. And still he raced on.

Had it only been five years since my father had pursued Henry over the salt flats and through the Chihuahuan desert and up into higher ground?

No, surely a lifetime had passed, and he'd been reborn, a new man.

The mustang circled back with the break of day, and that's when my father knew they had him. He was slowing down, no longer fleet as the wind, and within the hour Henry, the more skilled of the two at roping, had lassoed him with a wide loop that settled behind the stallion's shoulders. My father's rope was tied with a figure-eight knot that would close around the horse's neck but not let him choke.

Together they worked the buckskin back to the narrow trail, steered clear of the corral which now held the drove of mares, and brought him to the holding pen.

"We're not selling him," said my father as they swung the gate shut.

Henry laughed. "I'm hardly shocked to hear you say that. Look, let's get some eggs and bacon in our bellies. After that, do as I say, Caleb, and you'll be riding that stud before dinner."

"He needs a name. Have you any more Greek ones for me?"

"Hmm." They watched the buckskin stamp and snort and pace the perimeter of the pen, his coat shining with sweat. "Well, we captured him not long after sunrise. Let's call him *Phaethon*, then, the steed who drew the chariot of rosy-fingered Eos, goddess of the dawn."

"Perfect. Phaethon it is."

"You'd never seen anything like how Henry gentled Phaethon—he knew all the Indian ways, huh, dad!"

My father seemed to be daydreaming, his eyes staring into the middle distance.

"Dad?"

"Hmm? The Indian ways? Well, he knew a few of them, anyway. And the Indians weren't so special, often enough they'd break mustangs like most white men do, beat them into docility if they had to. But it was amazing what Henry did after an hour or so of getting the beast used to his presence. Got close enough he could put his hand over Phaethon's nose and eyes, and then breathed into his nostrils. Had me do it, too. I was riding him before dinner."

"I wish I *could have ridden him, it would have been so—"*

"Don't waste my time wishing for something impossible." My father stood up abruptly, all the gentleness gone from his voice. "Now go find something that needs doing around here and do it. You hear me, boy?"

"Yes, sir."

Anything could trigger my father's darkness, perhaps even a memory that Phaethon had died in 1928, the same year I was born.

At first, my father was relieved and gladdened when Henry took an increasing interest in the flora of the Nevada landscape, its shrubs and bushes and flowers and trees. Both men had a love for the desert's stark, subtle beauty and for the mountains and canyons where the wild horses roamed. They sought out the flickerings of color amid sagebrush and sand: the yellow petals of a greasewood bush, a beavertail cactus just starting to show its bright pink blooms. Henry taught him to distinguish between a bewildering variety of cacti: buckhorn cholla, hedgehog and beehive and barrel cactus, and half a dozen different kinds of prickly pear.

"Cactus juice," he informed my father, who became adept at removing the plants' spines from Henry's hands and arms, "eases joint pains, calms inflammations of the gut, and—blessings to the Deity, whoever he or she may be!—does wonders for one's hangover."

When my father delighted in the musky aroma emitted by the greasewood chaparral on those rare days when the land was blessed by rain, Henry explained how its leaves could be used for snake bites, and to lessen a woman's menstrual cramps, and cure the clap.

My father was fascinated by the evening primrose's nocturnal blooms, its petals golden in the moonlight, and smiled indulgently as Henry told of how it clears the skin of eczema and could be used as a poultice for wounds.

And what of pennyroyal, whose leaves my father loved to gather and crush so he could breathe in its spearmint scent? "Ah, Caleb!" exclaimed his lover. "The oil from those leaves can dry watery eyes, settle a queasy stomach, even cure gall ailments and gout."

My father found Henry's obsession with folk remedies amusing, but only for so long. He didn't mind being awakened at night by urgent knockings at the door from folks desperate to avail themselves of Henry's skill with herbs and ointments—a husband concerned about his wife's difficult pregnancy, a wife distraught over her husband's terrible pains—but as the years went by, Henry was hardly involved with their horse business at all.

"We're supposed to be partners," said my father, as they sat out on their front porch at sunset, passing a bottle of mezcal back and forth. "Midnight & McRae. But there's days I barely see you."

"You've good men working for you now, Caleb. Wild horses, that was your idea, and I was glad to help you with it. But I've got my own interests, my own passions."

"You really fancy yourself a medical man?"

Henry took a large swig and set the bottle down hard. "'Fancy myself'? Who healed you when you threw your back out and could barely stand up straight?"

"You did, and I'm grateful for it. I only meant—"

"I know what you meant, damn it, and let me tell you something. Most who call themselves 'doctor' are naught but crooks and quacks. If they're not hawking elixirs from the back of a medicine wagon, they're bleeding some poor bastard with leeches. They concoct medicines thinking the viler the taste, the quicker the cure. Sulphur, that's what they'll have you drink for anything that ails you. And chloride of mercury, a splendid purgative indeed if you don't mind your teeth falling out one by one. People come to me because I do them good, Caleb. You're a fine one for saying we shouldn't kill—well here I am giving folks *life.* Would your Jesus have me stop?"

"*Henry.*" My father kneeled before his lover, grasped his hand and placed it against his heart. "I'm sorry. I'm in awe of what you do, it's been like that from the beginning, when you healed our burns, when you cured the governor's daughter. It's only that I miss you. Really, that's all it is."

For a long while Henry ran his fingers through my father's hair, the only sounds the chirping of crickets and the wind, incessantly rearranging the desert dust.

"I never could resist your curls, Caleb." Henry reached for the mezcal, took a sip and handed it to my father. "And I'm hardly a wonder-worker, Mrs. Smither's dropsy has eluded all my treatments, defeated every unguent and potion and salve."

"Oh, you'll cure her yet, Henry." My father stood up, leaned against a porch post, and gazed at the fading light on the western horizon. "It'll all work out. I'll be happy as long as we end up in bed together at the end of each day."

"That we always shall."

They clung to each other that night, but long after Henry had fallen asleep my father lay awake, haunted by the sense that they were growing apart.

And then came the Great War.

Chapter Thirty-Nine

The Silver Ghost

"We give a quarter of everything we make to the poor," said my father. It was the spring of 1915, and he and Henry were having it out at their kitchen table. "We're of one mind on that, you and I. But to up our numbers and deliver horses to fuel the engines of war, that I won't stand for, no matter the good we could do with the proceeds. It's blood money."

"Let's put aside the madness of doing nothing while Europe is ravaged by Teutonic hordes—and please, I can't take another lecture about pacifism and the Way of Christ. I'm asking you to think logically about this."

"Don't patronize me, Henry."

"Look, you don't have to be Nostradamus to see there won't be much need for horses in a few years, there's likely already more motorcars than equines in the land."

"So? What will be will be, I'll not worry about the morrow."

"A most pious sentiment, I'm sure. Be reasonable, Caleb. Every cowboy and his idiot cousin is going to be out catching horses and delivering them to the armies of the world, and if we're the ones, at least the money will be put to good use." Henry reached for his lover's hand, but my father drew back and crossed his arms. "Look, this may be our last chance to raise a considerable sum to help those in need. The British and French are paying more than one-fifty a head these days, but the war won't last for—"

"Stop, Henry, just stop. If you were talking about the price of petunias, I'd give you some credence. Since when are you up on the value of horses?"

Henry winced, realizing he'd said too much.

"Remember Floyd Bard, the bronc buster we met up in Sheridan back when we were first getting started? You liked the man, we had lunch with him at the Bucket of Blood Saloon. Well, he's a buyer now for the brave boys standing up to the Huns. He's the one got word to me how much the Brits and Frogs are paying."

"*Got word to you?* You don't ride with me anymore, but you trade messages with Bard behind my back?" My father stood up, his face red. "Fine, Midnight, you go on out there and catch all you can and ship them off as cannon fodder, and good luck to you. I'll have none of it."

He rode off on Phaethon, was gone all night and came back the next day, soaked through and shivering with fever after having been caught in one of that summer's monsoon rains. Henry stripped my father, dried him off, wrapped him in blankets, and brought him mugs of olive-leaf tea sweetened with spoonfuls of honey.

"We won't sell horses for the war, Caleb," he said late that night, holding my father as tightly as he could. "I'm sorry for having made you so angry."

"It's all right, Henry. We'll put this behind us. There's just some things I can't abide."

"Yes, I've noticed that."

My father lay listening to the deep-pitched hooting of a great horned owl who lived in their cottonwood tree, and struggled to understand his own anger. *It's something I ought to talk through with a pastor,* he thought. But he hadn't been to church in ages...

"I love you," Henry whispered. "It's been fifteen years since we met, you know. Do you still love me, after all this time?"

"Ah, Henry," said my father. "You know I do. I couldn't live without you."

It troubled him, though, that as he'd been drifting into sleep, wrapped in his lover's arms, he'd imagined the Lord asking him much the same question.

"Are you two aware we live in a 'World of Wonders?'" asked my father, looking up from the newspaper he'd been perusing.

It was the fall of 1920, and he and Henry were sitting on their front porch with Wovoka, drinking coffee.

"Of course," said the prophet dreamer, who often came by when he passed through Las Vegas. "I have marveled at the Lord's Creation since I left my mother's womb."

"I suspect you're thinking far too poetically," said Henry. "What is it you're reading, Caleb?"

"The San Francisco paper." My father handed it over. "It seems we are becoming like gods."

"'Astonishing Innovations and Inventions 1910-1920,'" Henry read, while Wovoka looked over his shoulder. They scanned the article in silence for a few minutes.

"What are 'escalators'?" asked Wovoka.

"Stairs that do the walking for you, evidently," said my father.

"Now here's something that's got my attention," said Henry. "'Electric washing machines.' We do tend to stink rather badly, Caleb, I can't remember the last time we scrubbed our shirts and trousers. Have we any electricity?"

"I'm afraid not."

"Drat. Well, what do you think, Wovoka, is any of this sufficiently wondrous in your eyes?"

"'Instant coffee,'" said the holy man. "I could make good use of that. But what is *this?*"

"Hmm?" Henry squinted intently at the small print below a picture of a metallic cube with two slits on top. "Ah, it seems some fine fellow's just invented a rather clever contraption. He's placed a heating mechanism and a set of springs inside a metal box, and one's toast just pops right up when it's ready."

"Is it so difficult for white men to make toast?"

"It's a challenge for some of us, anyway. Caleb tends to char the bread rather badly."

"I see no mention of Oreo biscuits," said Wovoka. "Such sweets did not exist in my youth, and I have grown fond of them."

"We'll stock up for your next visit," said Henry. "Now, look here, the transatlantic telephone line, that *was* a rather impressive achievement, laying all that cable across the ocean floor. Astonishing to think we could sit at our kitchen table and talk to some chap in London or Paris."

"Who is it you'd want to talk to?" asked my father. "Certainly not your parents."

"True, that. I'll admit it chills me, thinking of my words passing through those vast, cold, dark depths. You know, I've read of folk who put the listening end to their ear and hear the voices of the dead."

"No telephone is needed for that," said Wovoka. "But hush now—" He shaded his eyes and peered into the distance. "Two riders approach. Women. One with a great sadness."

"It spooks me how you do that," said Henry, looking through the field glasses. "I can barely make out anything at all, other than the dust they're kicking up on the trail."

"Two women?" My father stood and took the field glasses from Henry. "Val wrote last year that she hoped to come with Elli and Louis one day. I've a grim feeling about what's brought them without him."

"You have visitors, and I have many miles to travel." Wovoka rose and embraced both men. "I will give your friends my blessings as I pass them on the road."

"There's no need to exchange pleasantries," said my father, after Valentina and her sister had washed the dust from their faces and joined the men at their kitchen table. "I can see something's wrong."

"Yes," said Elliana. Though shy of her thirtieth birthday, she looked older than Valentina, her face haggard and drawn. "It's Louis. He's gone missing."

"You'd best start from the beginning," said her sister.

"I'll make us some lunch while you're talking," said Henry.

"No," said Valentina, "I'm in no mood for man-food, I'll search the cupboards and make us something worth eating."

"I wrote you he'd been wounded in France," said Elliana, "but not too badly, and that was true, at least physically. But Lou wasn't the same when he came back. Something had happened and he—he couldn't—"

"Just say it, Elli," said Valentina.

"He couldn't perform as a man. He'd so wanted to have children, from the earliest days of our marriage, and we'd tried—my God how we tried!—for twelve years. I said it was likely *my* fault, but Lou blamed himself, and that was already weighing on him when he went off to war. Then, when he returned, he was ashamed to lie with me in bed. I told him I loved him no matter what and always would, told him to be patient, but it was as though he *wanted* to be miserable. He started sleeping in another room, then staying out to all hours, drinking—and worse."

"What kind of worse?" asked Henry.

"Morphia. Laudanum."

"He's led her to the edge of disaster," said Valentina, who'd been busying herself peeling potatoes.

"Don't blame him, Val."

"I'm just telling our friends the truth. She tracked him to an opium den in Corpus Christi last winter and nearly killed two Chinamen who tried to stop her while she was dragging Lou away. If they'd been white, the law would have been after her for sure."

"It was all a waste, in the end," said Elliana, her voice thick with weariness and sorrow. "He took off a week later. We've been searching for him ever since, but the trail's gone cold. I've my doubts whether he's even still alive."

"Henry and I could join you in the search," said my father. "We've some skill in that line of work."

"There's no point in searching for a man who doesn't want to be found," said Valentina.

"There are times when I think she's right," said Elliana. "When I imagine the pain of finding Lou only to lose him again. And yet I hate myself for thinking that way. I won't ever give up on him, Val, I won't! I just need time to think."

"Will you return home, then?" asked Henry.

"I can't bear returning to an empty house," said Elliana. "Not yet, anyway. I'm thinking we'll stay put for a while somewhere. That'll make it easier to keep in touch with Lou's parents if he should show up at home."

"'Somewhere' shall be here, of course," said Henry.

"Really?" asked Elliana, her eyes glistening.

"Really," said my father. "For as long as you like. Henry and I would be glad for the company."

"Well," said Valentina, who was pouring oil into a hot pan, causing a mouth-watering sizzle. "For a while. On one condition: Elli and I do the cooking."

My father and Henry looked at each other with raised eyebrows.

"You drive a hard bargain," said Henry. "But I suppose, if you insist..."

Later that day the four friends gathered in a small room Henry had added on to the cabin, looking at an array of herbs organized in boxes, jars, and tins, and various tinctures, distillations, and decoctions in bottles and phials.

"Amazing!" said Elliana. "What is this?"

"My laboratory," said Henry. "Where I practice the healing arts."

"We'll put out word about Louis to everyone we know between here and Texas," said my father. "And some in San Francisco as well. He'll turn up one of these days, and when he does, Henry will cure him."

"His addictions, that's the main thing. Look, Val, how beautiful." Elliana pointed to some delicate white blooms and turned to Henry. "What are these?"

"Hummingbird blossom. Makes a soothing tea, I might well have your husband drink some to lessen his craving for morphia or the opium poppy. But first, Elli, we'll surround him with the fragrance of burning sage, for its smoke will draw out all his demons. I'll improvise from there—it will all depend on the nature and degree of his afflictions—but I can well imagine rosemary and wild ginger and oil extract of yarrow—" Henry pointed to a spray of scarlet and sunshine-yellow flowers—"which relieves a mind beset by worries, and was used by brave Achilles to heal his wounds."

"You once taught me the art of escape," said Elliana. "How to free myself from any bonds. Now I'd give the world to free Louis from the evils that hold him in their power. I want to learn these healing arts. Will you teach me?"

"With pleasure," said Henry. "Consider yourself my apprentice."

"The Barnum and Bailey people made me a standing offer to toss knives in their circus," said Valentina. "But it's a few short steps from that to the freak show. I wouldn't mind chasing after mustangs for a while, seeing if I could earn my keep as a wrangler."

"Well that's just fine," said my father. "I can use the help."

Not long after, the men invited Elliana and Valentina to join them on a trip to the Zabala ranch.

"They're fine people, Abarran and Arrosa," said my father. "And it's beautiful country, up against the Ruby Mountains. I've another motive, however. We've known their daughter, Joska, since '04. She's a wonderful young woman, about your age, Elli. Only now she's Joska Griffin, and her husband's a blackguard, full of himself and too slick by half. He treats her and their children shabbily, but she's begged us not to have words with him. He hasn't laid a hand on her, or so she says, so for now we're respecting her wishes."

"She doesn't have much to do with her family anymore," said Henry. "Joska could use a friend of her own sex. Perhaps you could learn more about what her life's like, how she feels."

Elliana vowed to do her best. The foursome rode north together, passed by the occasional Model T, though when the drivers agreed to a race, it was never a contest, their horses easily defeating every automobile.

"What do you think?" asked Henry. "Should we surrender to the twentieth century one of these days?"

"You mean purchase a motorcar?" asked my father. "I can't imagine why. I'd sooner acquire a toaster."

"I might buy one, sometime," said Elliana. "An auto, I mean. If it made it easier to search for Louis."

Over the years the ranch had been transformed into a compound, for Zorion and several of his siblings had built homes there as well.

"I've lost track of the number of grandchildren I have," crowed Abarran, "and can hardly remember all their names!"

"I would not boast of your dotage," said Arrosa, but she put her arm around her husband, whom she had at long last forgiven for having brought Cornelius Griffin into their lives.

Joska's absence was an ever-present shadow in the Zabala home, and their hearts were gladdened to learn that Elliana and Joska had indeed become fast friends. There was nothing she could tell Abarran and Arrosa, however, to give them hope that their relationship with Joska would be restored anytime soon.

"She loves him despite everything," said Elliana, talking to Valentina and Henry and my father as they rode back home, "much as I still love my husband. Louis would never harm me, but I don't trust Cornelius. Still, I know well enough you can't talk a woman out of love. I did find one occasion, when Joska was occupied with her youngest, to show the man the flash of my blade. I told him if anything ever happened to her, he needn't worry about Abarran and the two of you, I'd feed him his own entrails."

"She would, too," said Valentina. "You don't want to get Elli riled up."

On the outskirts of Las Vegas the *a-ROOOO-gah!* of a klaxon horn startled their steeds, and they turned to see a Rolls Royce Silver Ghost eager to pass them on the road.

"I heard some fellow owns half of Block 16 drives that machine," said my father.

"What's Block 16?" asked Valentina.

"Stretch of town where a fellow can gamble, drink bootleg liquor, and dally with ladies of the night," Henry explained.

"Hey, mister big shot," Elliana called out. "Let's race!"

An elegantly dressed fellow with a neatly trimmed mustache rolled down the backseat window and peered out.

"I am a sporting man, *mio amica*," he said, with a marked Italian accent. "Though I do not make a habit of racing young women. You're on, though—but what shall we wager?"

"I've got a five-dollar gold piece that says the lady beats you to the city limits." My father pointed to a sign just over a mile down the road, welcoming visitors to Las Vegas.

"You do, eh? *Bene*. Give us a count, then, cowboy, and I will wish my young friend *buona fortuna*."

"If that means good luck," said Elliana, "I won't be needing any."

"We'll head down there first to call the finish," said Henry, and he and Valentina sped away.

My father waited for a bit, then counted down and fired his pistol into the air.

"HEE-YA!" cried Elliana as she spurred her horse on. She was ahead by a good margin after a quarter mile and still in the lead at the half, but the Rolls was gaining on her steadily and at the signpost had her by a nose.

The window was rolled down once again. "We'll call it a draw, yes?" asked the gentleman.

"Valentina?" asked my father.

She nodded her head toward the Rolls.

"No, you won fair and square." My father tossed over the gold coin.

"The name's Guerriero, Salvatore Guerriero." He turned to Elliana and smiled. "But call me Sal, Miss—".

"Cooper." She looked at him, steely-eyed. "And it's Mrs."

"Ah. Your mister, he is a lucky man. Here—" he tossed the coin over to her. "Buy yourself something pretty. And if you are ever in want of work, you have only to ask for me at the Arizona Club downtown."

The window went back up and the Silver Ghost took off in a cloud of dust.

"Arrogant ass," she muttered, and handed the coin over to Caleb.

"Quite a chariot, regardless," said Henry.

"I suppose." My father looked at the five-dollar piece, turning it over in his hand a few times before returning it to his pocket. "If I believed in bad luck, I'd say that man brings it." He squinted into the distance, where the Rolls was rapidly disappearing from view.

"Yes," said Valentina, and she spat on the ground. "He has an aura of evil."

Chapter Forty

The Jenny

"The detective who fought with us so bravely against Gale—have you kept in touch with him?" asked Elliana.

The four friends were enjoying Valentina's huevos rancheros on their front porch one morning in the spring of 1921.

"Charley Siringo," said my father. "We saw him just a couple years ago. Spends a fair bit of time in Los Angeles these days, playing pinochle with Wyatt Earp. What made you think of him?"

"I'm ready to resume looking for Louis. But it's going to take a professional to find him."

"Siringo's long retired, though I'm sure he could find you a good man. Investigators aren't cheap, though. It'd be better if Henry and I took over the hunt."

"No," said Elliana. "Thank you, Caleb, but Lou might be anywhere, and I won't have the two of you off on what might well be a wild-goose chase."

"We have a way to pay for it," said Valentina. "I've been back in touch with the circus, asked them what they thought of getting both of us, and they couldn't say yes fast enough. We'll be the Juarez Sisters and their Blades of Death, each of us making a hundred a week, maybe more if the act draws enough of a crowd."

"I noticed you two had put in more than a few hours practicing your craft," said Henry. "Though I flattered myself it was to prepare for the rematch you promised me back in '04."

Valentina unsheathed one of her knives and hurled it into the inner circle of a target nailed to the cottonwood tree over ten yards away. "Anytime, *amigo.*"

"Ah well," said Henry, "it wouldn't be the same, what with hooch being hard to come by these days. And I don't fancy paying the likes of Salvatore Guerriero for bootleg mezcal."

"We'll contact Charley," said my father, "and see if there's a detective he especially recommends. It will be lonely here without you, but it's a good plan you've hatched. When will you be leaving, and where will you go?"

"It's best to leave right away, or I'll lose my nerve," said Elliana. "I want to see Joska again, first, though. Then we'll meet up with the circus in Cincinnati."

"You can pass through Chicago on your way, that's Pinkerton's home turf. Speaking of wild geese, however—" he looked over at Henry. "Do you remember when we used to talk of flying?"

"I do. Have you begun to sprout wings?"

"No, but I've stumbled onto the next best thing. The Army's got more aircraft than they know what to do with now that the war's over, Curtis JN-4s in particular—Jennys, they call them. They were used to train pilots, supposed to be easy to fly. A fellow in town has one he's willing to sell for three hundred dollars. I'm thinking we'll bargain him down some and ask for flying lessons as well."

"How extraordinary!" said Henry. "We could use it to follow up on leads when their detective gets word of Louis."

"My thought exactly. Might come in handy for spotting horses, too."

"And I could fly to San Francisco and bring back herbs of the Orient one simply can't find here. Some have marvelous properties, Elli, and might be just what we need for Louis: Chinese skullcap and ginseng and leaves of the Ginkgo tree, which calm a disordered mind."

"Wonderful!" exclaimed Elliana. "Ah, this lifts my spirits. And you must promise to take me flying one day!"

"We will," said my father. "You and Louis both."

"Elli and I will leave for Elko in the morning," said Valentina. "I shudder to think how you'll feed yourselves once we're gone. But cheer up, gentlemen, for this evening I will make you a *mole poblano* to remember me by."

The four friends feasted late into the night before retiring to bed.

"I know we've been at odds more often than not these past few years," said Henry, as he and my father lay together. "But you still surprise and delight me,

Caleb, you do! Flying machines! I'd nearly forgotten our discussion, a thousand years ago, on the beach by Corpus Christi Bay. Can you imagine us, swooping down from the sky to rescue poor Louis and bring him home?"

For a long while the two talked about the journeys and adventures that might lie in store, before falling at last into a blissful sleep.

The biplane had seen better days, its owner admitted, but my father and Henry could learn its workings by helping him restore the Jenny to its former glory. He took a swig or two of whiskey in between every instruction he shouted from the comfort of a garden chair, but it seemed the man knew his plane down to the smallest nuts and bolts. So they patched it up, took apart and rebuilt its V-8 engine, painted it a vibrant blue and gold, and within a month were winging their way through the desert sky.

My father sat in front and worked the controls while his partner climbed out onto a wing, grasping the struts with one hand and waving to crowds who looked up, gaping in wonder. They buzzed Las Vegas a time or two, Henry dashing in his leather helmet and goggles and silk scarf, and the girls of Block 16 who were relaxing on rooftops laughed and waved back. Then they climbed, flying as high as the Jenny would allow them, passing not far below Mt. Charleston's snow-covered peak. It awed my father, seeing God's glory all around him to the far horizons, the desert and mountains and flawless sky, and the beauty of it made his heart ache with joy.

The following year, they heard the Greatest Show on Earth was heading west and flew to Sacramento, California to meet their friends.

"I can barely stand to watch this," said my father, while in the center ring Valentina flung daggers at a spinning wheel to which her sister had been strapped.

Over dinner that evening Elliana showed them a letter from the Pinkerton detective who'd been looking for Louis. *I've travelled over five thousand miles these past twelve months,* he'd written, *talked to four hundred twenty-three men and women, followed up on every lead, and nothing's panned out. I'm happy to keep cashing your checks, Mrs. Cooper, but it's my best guess your husband is deceased.*

"I just don't believe that's true," said Elliana. "I met his parents when we were in Dallas a few months ago, and they haven't lost hope either. With the bonuses we've been receiving, our pay covers the Pinkerton bills with enough left over to get by. I just know he's alive."

"Then he is, I'm sure," said Henry. "There's a connection forged in love that science can't explain. Trust your feelings."

"Perhaps it's Louis who will have to find *you,*" said Valentina to her sister. "But it's all right, we're in this together. We'll get a new man on the search and keep it going another year."

On their way home my father and Henry landed in a field in the Sierras and hiked to Lake Tahoe, picnicking beside chill, depthless waters by turns emerald, turquoise, and the darkest of blues. In the far distance children chased each other over the beach, shouting with delight. My father lay shirtless in the warm sun, feeling at one with the world. The war was over, as were all his quarrels and quibbles with Henry, and before long Louis would surely be found. What's more, when they returned to Las Vegas, he'd start going to church! Perhaps Henry would even come with him—why, it might have been for that very purpose the Lord had brought them together! *I'm forty-six,* he thought; *midway through life's journey I've at last found my way.*

Not long after their return from California my father and Henry began exploring the southern end of the Spring Mountains, one looking for new herds of mustangs, the other for medicinal herbs.

"The front seat's not your exclusive property, you know," said Henry, as the men prepared to board the Jenny one day in the spring of 1923. "It's been ages since I had a turn at the controls."

"They're all yours," said my father, and they took off into a cloudless sky.

The plane had climbed only a thousand feet when a sudden downdraft sent them plunging toward the ground. My father could never remember exactly what happened, for it was all over in a matter of seconds, but Henry must have regained control at the last moment, averting total disaster. Still, it was a hard landing, the wheels coming off as the Jenny skidded through a field of ragweed, and both men were thrown from the craft.

"Caleb!" Henry was bruised and shaken, though not badly injured. He could see my father was in pain, his left shoulder dislocated and his right arm dangling uselessly at his side. "I'm going to sit you up, then I want you to arch your back. Now!"

The shoulder popped back into place.

My father stifled a groan. "Arm's broken for sure. And it feels like I got kicked in the head by a mule." He looked around, collecting his thoughts. "You're alright, at least. Don't feel bad, Henry, this wasn't your fault."

"I'm feeling pretty *good,* actually, for having saved both our lives. But no need to thank me." Henry kneeled down, kissed my father on the forehead and stroked his hair. "Rest for a bit, I'll rig a splint for your arm and get us home. You'll be fine, Caleb—as soon as we're back I'll make a salve of turmeric and peppermint oil that will ease your pain." He glanced over at the plane. "Jenny doesn't look in too bad a shape, I'll get her fixed easily enough. We'll let those bones of yours heal and be back in the sky before you know it."

"It's not the pain I'm worried about," said my father, "it's how I'm going to wrangle horses."

He slept fitfully that night, and many others, for despite all Henry's efforts, pain radiated from his neck up to the top of his skull and back down his spine. He began to wonder, as the weeks and then months went by, whether what had happened was a sign of heaven's displeasure, a warning that he'd been living in a fool's paradise. And often he found himself thinking, *if only I'd been at the controls, this wouldn't have happened, I'd have brought us down safe and sound.*

"You've always been one to get back on the horse that threw you," Henry said to my father that summer. "You're riding again, and sold more than a few ponies this past month. What do you say we celebrate at six thousand feet?"

"I've learned to make do without much use of my right hand all these years," said my father. "But another accident like the last one and I'd be useless in the saddle. I won't fly again, it's not worth the risk."

"Well, all right." His partner sighed and sat down beside my father on their front porch steps. "I understand. But here's some good news for you. There's a fellow in San Francisco, a Chinaman who deals in herbs and has just what you need: corydalis, brought here from the high Himalayas. Its lavender flowers are a superb analgesic, and a soporific as well. I'll take off in the morning. With any luck, by next week your pain will be but a memory and it'll be me kept awake at night by your snores."

"You're flying off again?" My father stood up and looked out into the distance. "Fine, enjoy yourself, but don't say you're going on my account."

"That's not fair, Caleb, I—"

"Oh, stop. You can't blame me for losing faith in your ointments and potions."

"It's not me doing the blaming in this house. I'm going tomorrow because I love you and won't rest till you're fully healed. Though it's your dour disposition that needs healing most." Henry pursed his lips thoughtfully. "Valerian and lemon balm perhaps..."

My father was still in bed when he heard the Jenny's engine starting up early the next morning. He walked out in his underwear and stood on the porch, waving, as Henry taxied down the field they used as a runway.

"I love you," he called out, though it seemed doubtful Henry could hear him. "You know that, don't you? You know it's true."

He watched the plane take off, followed it with his eyes until it dwindled down to the tiniest speck and vanished into the vastness of the summer sky.

The corydalis did little to ease my father's pain. That fall he joined the Free Will Baptist Church of Las Vegas and began attending Sunday services, and Saturday breakfasts, and prayer meetings on Wednesday nights. Sometimes he'd stay over at the Gold Strike Inn when prayers lasted until the early hours, then return to the church in the morning to see if there were some way he could help out. How good it felt to be worshipping with fellow believers and once again feel himself part of the Body of Christ!

"Why don't you start coming with me to church," he said to Henry as they sat in the kitchen on a brisk winter evening in 1924, the room dark but for a single flickering candle. "You'll turn fifty this year, it's well past time to put away childish things and declare yourself for Christ. Even an Indian holy man like Wovoka has done that much."

"Yes, and bless his soul he's never once tried to convert me. Tell you what, partner, first you come with me to a sacred pipe ceremony at the Paiute sweat lodge a half-day's ride north of here."

My father felt a rage rising in him and thought, *Control yourself, it's only Henry's usual nonsense.* "Why in the world would I go to a pagan ritual?" he asked as calmly as he could, but his fuse had been lit, and the flame was travelling up from the base of his spine.

"Because it's a sublime experience, a rite of purification and the bringing together of souls—and isn't that just what we need, to be cleansed of our demons and united anew? Face facts, man, we're outlaws in the eyes of your church. Ah, Caleb. Do you remember that blowhard we met outside Corpus Christi and then again near El Paso? When he asked if we were married I made a joke of it, but only to keep from shedding tears. If there is indeed a Creator, a Great Spirit, a God of Love on the throne of heaven, then surely in His eyes we are as married as two people ever were."

"There's a *King* on that throne, Henry." My father winced as pain ripped through his neck and back. "And His name is Christ Jesus."

The room was silent but for the ticking of a timepiece on the mantle.

"So you've told me." Henry stood up and pushed in his chair. "I'm flying to Phoenix in the morning, be back in a couple of days."

My father could barely understand his own anger, much less control it. It seemed everything fed his fury: his physical torments, which never ceased; Henry's obstinate refusal to bow down before the Lord; the church, which would surely spit him out if ever it knew who he really was.

His own sorry self, so unworthy of love.

He continued to sit at that kitchen table long after the candle had guttered and failed.

Chapter Forty-One

Stealing Fire from the Sun

The lovers found themselves quarreling more and more, not least over how to give to those in need.

"When you were the 'Midnight Bandito,' you handed all your loot over to the Jesuits to do with as they saw fit," said my father. "So I don't understand why you won't support me in tithing to my church."

"I had faith in Baltasar back then, Caleb, because we were of one mind." Henry looked off into the distance. "How long ago and far away that was! The century was freshly born and anything seemed possible..."

For a moment, remembering their early days, my father's heart was moved. How had they come to this sad point?

"...but I'm not at all eager to swell your plump pastor's coffers."

"You seem to forget it's the money from my mustangs we're talking about," said my father, his good feelings vanishing like the morning mist.

"So it's *your* money, now, is it? Which you condescend to let me live on?"

"Don't twist my words, Henry. Go ahead, do what you want with your half, give it to whomever you please."

Henry's reputation as a healer spread throughout the west, leaving my father to wonder if he were the only patient his partner couldn't cure. Where once he'd only be gone a day or two, Henry's trips to San Francisco and Denver and Salt Lake City began keeping him away for a week at a time.

One day, while my father was having breakfast at the Gold Strike Inn and perusing the out-of-town papers, a headline in the San Francisco Examiner caught his eye:

Jewel Theft Shocks Nob Hill

Wall Street tycoon Wentworth Sullivan robbed of small fortune in precious gems

Work of a "master burglar," say police

Henry had been in San Francisco when the robbery took place.

My father tore out the article and put it in his pocket. Others soon joined it in a scrapbook: a daring bank heist in Denver, investigators at a loss how the thief could possibly have got in and out; an exhibit of rare coins at a Salt Lake City museum, snatched from under a guard's nose.

Each crime corresponded to one of Henry's trips.

"If you and your Baptist brothers were praying for rain Wednesday night," said Henry, one overcast summer morning in 1925, "looks like you might just get your wish."

My father grunted in response.

"You ought to talk to them about providing aid to the tribes in these parts," Henry continued. "The Washoe and the Paiute and the Western Shoshone. This country's never been more prosperous, but the Indians are still getting the raw end of the deal."

"You'd love to get more money to those tribes, wouldn't you," said my father. "In fact, I reckon there's little you wouldn't do to help them out."

"Well of course." Henry regarded him warily. "What are you getting at, Caleb?"

"*This.*" My father handed him the scrapbook and watched, hands folded across his chest, as Henry leafed through the pages. "Have you gone mad? Are you trying to ruin our lives, taking these risks?"

"It's not me who's gone mad," said Henry. "Do you actually think—"

"Are you telling me these crimes, each unsolved, committed in the very towns to which you travelled, on the dates you were there—that it's all mere coincidence?"

"That's exactly what it is!"

"Don't lie to me, damn it!" My father stood, his hands balled into fists.

Henry rose and faced him, the two men nose to nose. "I'm telling you the truth!"

"*Bull.* All your trips, the weeks you've spent away—I want you to swear on whatever you hold holy that they've only been for buying herbs and healing the sick. Go ahead, swear to me. I'd bring over a Bible but that wouldn't mean anything to you."

Henry backed away a few paces, his face white, and was silent for a while. "I haven't been stealing. It's not that."

My father felt a churning in his stomach. "What, then?"

No answer.

The timepiece ticked on, impossibly loud, until my father smashed it to pieces against the wall.

"Speak to me!"

"It's been women," said Henry, his voice hardly more than a whisper.

"What?"

"I've slept with a few women. It's been a terrible mistake, but I—"

"I don't believe you."

"You've been so distant, Caleb, so uncaring. But I swear to you, none of them have meant anything to me. I swear it on my very life."

"This can't be true," said my father, and he sat down and held his head in his hands. "You're just making it up."

"I only wish I were." Henry came and kneeled by my father. "You've got to forgive me. I won't go any more, I'll stay right here from now on. Forgive me, I'm begging you."

"The things you expect me to believe, Henry," said my father, his voice halting and broken. "Spider grandmother and guardian spirits and foxes stealing fire from the sun. This is just more of the same." He rose and walked to the door before turning to look back. "It's good you'll be staying, though. We'll talk no more about this."

My father walked out into the pasture till he found Phaethon nibbling a sparse patch of grass. He fed the old horse carrots and rubbed its shoulders and withers and ears until it finally began to rain.

"Whatever happened to your friend Henry?" I asked my father on more than one occasion when I was young. "All those years together, and now you don't ever see him, don't even know if he's still alive?"

"Sometimes people go in different directions in life," he'd tell me. "We just drifted apart. Especially after your mother came into my life."

I could never get him to open up about my mother, though I tried whenever he seemed in a decent mood.

"Tell me about her, dad. Tell me again how you met."

"She was a beautiful woman, Matt, sweet and kind. We met at church, and I guess it was love at first sight, for just a few months later we were married. Soon after we found out you were coming to join us, and that was wonderful news. And then she was gone."

"Was it my fault she died?"

"No, son, not at all. Childbirth can be dangerous, and there weren't hospitals nearby like here in L.A. It can be terribly hard to understand the Lord's will at times. But we trust in Him."

Back in my room I took out the shoebox I kept hidden under my bed and removed a single faded photograph. Cameras weren't as common as they became after I was born, he'd explained. So that one snapshot was all that remained of my mother, Tina McRae.

Was she beautiful? I wanted to think so, though she looked somber in the picture, with worry lines and shadows beneath her eyes. Her parents had been Mexican, my father had told me, and I'd inherited her slender physique and dark looks. I'd stare at that picture, trying to puzzle out the mystery of who she was. My father had called her sweet and kind, but the woman looking back at me seemed tough, determined, and strong.

You'll meet her one day in heaven, Matthew, he'd said, and I'd daydream of that and try to imagine the serious face in the photograph breaking into a smile as she wrapped me in her arms.

There was one odd thing about the picture: the belt my mother was wearing was slightly out of focus, but it seemed bulky and decorated in a curious say. When I'd asked my father about it, he'd shrugged and told me men could never hope to understand women's fashion.

There were nights when I'd study that photo for hours, give my imagination free rein, and sometimes the dark shapes circling my mother's waist seemed very much like the handles of knives.

Chapter Forty-Two

The Morning Star

"Valentina!" Henry exclaimed one day in the summer of 1927. "Come in. What an unexpected pleasure!"

My father emerged from his study, as relieved as his partner to have a distraction from the tension that had been steadily building between them for the past few years.

"Thank you," she replied. "I've just come from Elko."

"We've yet a bottle of Tepeztate," said my father. "I'll bring it out with some bread and sausage and we'll talk."

"Elko, eh? We heard Elli's up there," said Henry, after they'd settled at the kitchen table—as in days gone by!—and drunk toasts to the quick and the dead. "I wish she'd come by as well."

"I've lost my patience with both of them," said Valentina. "Joska for putting up with that brute of a husband, and Elli for wasting her life, despairing over a man who's likely no longer in this world."

"I'm guessing you're not going back to the circus, now that she's quit," said my father.

"Good guess. I'm done tossing knives for a living."

"Then I wish you'd stay here and help me chase mustangs. We were a pretty decent team back in '20 and '21. Not to mention I miss your huevos rancheros."

"I do want to stay, *mis amigos*. But for another reason." She reached for the bottle and refilled her glass.

"Any reason will do," said Henry. "Or none at all."

"The truth is, I've nothing much to show for my forty-three years in this world. *Ay, por Dios,* I couldn't even help my sister, and now we've grown apart. So I've done a lot of thinking, riding all this way once again from Texas. About what to do with the rest of my life, you know? And here it is: I want to have a baby. To raise a child."

"My word," said Henry, glancing at my father for a moment. "That *is* a change in direction. You'd be a most excellent mum, Val. I wouldn't bet against anything you set your mind to."

"We'd be proud uncles, of course," said my father. "But you've never mentioned a man in your life. Do you have someone in mind?"

Valentina was silent, her gaze shifting between the two men.

"Ah," said Henry. "The plot thickens."

"Look," she said. "You're the two finest men I know. And we wouldn't be a burden to you—after I was up and about, I'd take the little one with me, back to Texas, and raise her myself. Or him, of course, though I'm sure it will be a *bebita*."

"You do realize," said Henry, "there can actually only be one father?"

"Yes, of course, but how to choose? You're both precious to me—"

My father was moved; how rare it was for Valentina to reveal the depth of her feelings!

"—and each of you is admirable in different ways. So, I thought perhaps a game of chance."

"Let the heavens decide, in other words," said Henry. "Well, that suits me just fine."

"You're sure about this?" asked my father, who was not at all convinced any of it made sense.

"I am." Valentina topped off their glasses. "Drink to me, *mis queridos amigos,* and to the child I will bring into this world, and I will drink to you, brave and stalwart men that you are."

Had twenty-three years really passed since the night they'd played at knives and drained every drop of Tepeztate from four bottles? Yes, indeed, thought my father. All that was a lifetime ago, in an age of innocence and hope.

"No reason to drag this out," said Henry, after they'd finished their toasts. "We've a deck here somewhere. I'll shuffle, Caleb will cut, and we'll draw for high card."

It turned out Henry had been using the cards as bookmarks for his many volumes, manuals, and notebooks on herbology, plant-spirit shamanism, and other, yet more arcane, healing arts. When all fifty-two were finally accounted for, the two men faced off.

My father turned over the king of diamonds, his partner the ace of hearts.

Twenty-five years would pass before I learned Henry Midnight was my birth father.

"Listen Val," said Henry, as the three sat down to breakfast. "I've been hashing things through in my mind these past weeks. It's all well and good to talk of raising a baby on your own, but that hardly seems fair to the child, to be deprived of a father. And I'll speak openly, Caleb, for our friend's not blind to the stink of unhappiness in this house. It's clear I can't provide what you need in life; you're yearning to devote yourself to the church, you live for the Sundays when they let you preach. The truth is, you're embarrassed to be seen as an old bachelor, sharing a house with an odd duck like me. You could never be a pastor the way things are now, a wife and young one is precisely what you need to be accepted by that crowd. Am I right?"

Valentina chewed her lip and gazed at Henry in silence.

My father looked down at his plate.

"Val, you and Caleb are the best of friends," Henry continued, "which is more than most husbands and wives can boast. Surely you can see it would be best to give a child some stability in her life, and a mother and father, at least at the start. From the very first I knew him, I thought Caleb would make a good papa. What little girl wouldn't be thrilled to be hoisted up on those broad shoulders for piggyback rides? Even if the arrangement couldn't last forever, there'd be the most special of bonds between the three of you. And your Baptist brethren would forgive a failed marriage far more easily than they'd overlook rumors that you're swish."

"But Henry," said my father, "the child is *yours*."

"Oh, come now, I told you long ago I'm not father material. No one need know the baby's not yours, Caleb. And if she looks like me, well, that's simply Val's blood coming to the fore."

Henry refilled their three coffee mugs.

The clock on the kitchen wall tick-tick-ticked for a good thirty seconds.

"I'll say this much," Valentina said at last, "It's not been easy being constantly on the move all these years. I'll be in no rush to leave after giving birth. We could play it by ear, Caleb, yes?"

My father nodded, looked down into his flapjacks, and flushed, thinking, *Yes, Henry's right, I could lead the life God has always meant for me to have...*

He felt a strange mixture of excitement and shame—but surely the latter was of the Enemy and could rightly be ignored!

"Still," Valentina continued, "it grieves me, thinking of the two of you splitting up. Surely, Henry, you would not disappear from our lives?"

"Well..." Henry drank his coffee, ran his hands through his long hair, the black now tinged with gray. "As you said, Tina, perhaps that's something we could play by ear."

Henry offered to stay until after the baby was born, but Valentina could see he grew more uncomfortable with every passing day.

"We won't be needing your ointments and herbs, if that's all that's keeping you here," she told him. "My mother was only in labor for three or four hours with each of us. And Juarez girls are born healthy and strong."

"You should begin the right way," said Henry. "As a family, just the three of you. Don't you think so, Caleb?"

"I reckon so," said my father, but he couldn't meet his lover's eyes.

"Well, all right, then," said Henry. "I'll pack my things."

By morning he was gone.

"How perfect," Valentina said happily, "that the wildflowers are beginning to bloom." Her water had broken early that morning, and they were sitting on the porch, enjoying the silverleaf sunrays, desert marigolds, and globemallows flashing orange and yellow in the slanting light of dawn. "Is this not the most beautiful spring day? I could have asked for none better to bring my *bebita* into the world." She'd decided not to name the child until she could look into her eyes and catch a glimpse of her infant soul.

My father's mind was elsewhere. *How Henry would have loved to see nature's glory unfurling*, he'd found himself thinking, then pushed the thought away. He was on the threshold of a new and better life; time to leave the old one behind.

"*Oye! Qué te pasa?*" she said, seeing my father staring off into the distance. "You're nervous, aren't you, cowboy."

"Hmm? No, I'm fine. Maria will be here soon, I'm sure."

Maria Navarro was a midwife and one of Valentina's best friends, a woman who shared her penchant for straight talk.

"Battle doesn't faze you, Caleb, but a woman giving birth, that's another story. Well, saddle up one of your mustangs and go for a long ride. Perhaps when you come back it will be to take *nuestra dulce hijita* up into your arms."

"A ride?" he said. "I might just do that."

After Maria arrived, he chose Alastor, a newly-gentled stallion, and rode the ranch perimeter looking for sections of fence that might need repair. No, it was all in good shape, he'd checked it out only a few weeks before. *I'll head up the trail for an hour or so*, he thought, *then return in plenty of time for the little one's entry into the world.*

About ten miles on, just past a thick stand of Joshua trees, Alastor raised his head and flared his nostrils.

Something's spooking him. "Easy, boy," said my father, stroking his steed's neck.

A wolf's howl rent the air and the horse reared back, sending my father tumbling to the ground.

Impossible, wolves in these parts are unheard of.

He rose, drew his revolver, and looked about. Was that a flash of gray among the Joshuas, or only his imagination?

No eyes looked back at him, nothing moved among the trees.

"Alastor!"

His voice echoed back from the nearby canyon walls.

No use. The stallion had bolted to the north, the howling having come from behind them. There was no choice but to head home on foot. *Alastor will find his way back, or I'll search for him on horseback after the baby's delivered.*

He began walking briskly and tried to think things through. *There are no wolves in the desert*—and yet its howl had been unmistakable.

A thought came to him like an icy blast of winter wind: *The nagual is still alive, stalking me, looking to settle the score...*

It could be heading for the ranch right now.

My father began running through the rough terrain, stumbled, and sprawled on the hard ground. His right knee was bloodied and his ankle throbbed.

This is absurd, I've worked myself up over wild imaginings and panicked like a fear-stricken fool. Now Lord only knows how long it'll take to hobble home.

It took him the better part of five hours, and storm clouds had darkened the sky by the time the ranch came in sight. The downpour lasted for only a few minutes, but that was long enough to drench him before he limped through the front door.

"*Dios mío!*" exclaimed Maria. "*Estás bien*, Señor McRae?"

"Never mind me. How are Tina and the baby?"

"*La bebe*, she is not yet ready to leave the comfort of the womb."

"It's been all day—how much longer?"

"Babies do not always come so fast, especially a woman's first. You must have patience."

He dried off and changed before knocking on Valentina's door and entering into the dim, candle-lit room.

"How are you?" he asked.

"*Pésimo,*" she said. *Lousy.* "Maria's been having me drink tea made from papoose-root until it's coming out of every pore of my body. It's to strengthen the contractions, but they're only strong enough to wake me whenever I fall asleep. *Ay ya!*" She shook her head in disgust. "How I hate the sound of my own whining."

"I'm sorry it's taking so long, Tina." My father kneeled down and bent his head close to her belly. "Come out into the world, little girl, we can't wait to meet you."

"She'll come when she's ready," said Valentina. "Have no fear."

"Señor!"

My father woke with a start. He'd fallen asleep on the living room couch sometime after midnight; the clock now showed a quarter to four.

"Is it time, Maria?" He followed her to Valentina's room.

"The baby, she wants to be born," said the midwife. "Only, the contractions are not strong enough—"

"I'm failing her," Valentina said through gritted teeth. "I'm too weak."

Her eyes were pools of darkness, her face bathed in sweat.

"I'm going to call Doc Murtaugh," said my father. "Or we drive to the hospital in Vegas."

"*No,*" said Valentina. "I trust none of them. Maria—" she paused as a spasm of pain passed through her. "You have a way, yes?"

"*Sí,* Tina. I can use forceps and guide the little one out."

"Aren't there risks?" asked my father. "Might it be better to let nature take its course?"

"Tina and the baby are already at risk," said Maria. "Nature's course may well be to take the life of mother and child."

"Come, Caleb," said Valentina. "Hold my hand."

"You must still push with every contraction," said Maria.

"*Ay,* I fear I've no strength left."

"Find some," said her friend. "Summon it from the depths of your being."

Dear God, give her mine, my father prayed, remembering that long-gone, savage day when he'd lain on his back, helpless, black clouds boiling in a storm-haunted sky. There was the jangling of silver spurs, Garrison's shotgun aimed at his chest, and then the flashing of Valentina's blade, saving his life....

"You're stronger than you think," he told her. "I've seen you triumph, time and again, against all odds."

"I was fighting others then. This time the enemy is me."

"Push!" Maria called out.

Valentina groaned, squeezed my father's hand.

"Again, harder!" the midwife implored her.

"Madre de Dios," Valentina said through gritted teeth, her face a mask of agony.

"*Hostia!*" Maria exclaimed. "You must push harder!"

"*Ay, Ay, Ay Dios!*"

Sweat poured from Valentina's brow, and my father thought of Jesus in the garden of Gethsemane, sweating blood.

Each time she squeezed his hand he could feel her grip grow weaker.

My God, he thought, struggling to keep a growing sense of horror from showing on his face. *I'm going to lose them both.*

No, that must not be.

"The strength is there, deep within you," he told my mother, willing his own to pass through to her, "claim it, fight for it, as never before!"

She held his gaze, and it seemed to him a spark, a fierceness, had come back into her eyes.

"Now, Tina," Maria called out, beyond exhaustion yet resolute, "with everything you have, girl, *push!*"

Valentina howled, an animal cry of anguish.

Her nails dug into my father's hand, then it felt to him as though she'd gone limp, all her energy draining away...

"Ay caramba," the midwife murmured.

"What is it, Maria?" he said, unable to keep the panic from his voice.

"*Un bebito*," she replied, smiling for the first time in hours. "*Gracias a Dios!*"

She held me up and smacked my butt.

I gulped in air and wailed.

My father reeled, hardly able to believe his eyes. If St. Peter himself had descended to pluck him from the gates of hell, he could feel no greater elation. The nightmare was behind them, it was all going to be okay.

"A *boy*..." Valentina barely had the strength to lift her head. "How strange. A gift from God, nonetheless."

"Yes," said my father, feeling his heartrate beginning to slow. "Then *Matthew* should be his name."

"Here, *señor,*" said Maria, handing him a knife, "the honor will be yours."

After he cut the umbilical cord, she wrapped me tightly in a blanket and placed me by my mother's side.

"Look at you," my mother said to me, "wrinkled like a little old man. And those dents on the side of your head! I'm sorry, dear one, that I was not stronger."

"They will not last long," said Maria. "Soon enough he'll be as handsome as his mother is beautiful."

Valentina flinched, closed her eyes, tried to stifle a gasp of pain.

"What's the matter?" My father kneeled down next to my mother and me.

"Something's wrong, it's like one of my own blades is stabbing me from the inside."

"You are bleeding," said Maria. "I am going to apply pressure to stop the flow. Go quickly," she said to my father, "and bring me ice and any clean sheets and towels you have left."

He hurried to the ice chest, broke off some chunks and wrapped them in his remaining clean shirts.

"What can I do to help?" he asked, stunned to see how much blood Valentina had already lost.

She took the ice from him. "Press here, firmly, like so. I am going to massage your belly, Tina, to help the uterus contract."

There was no stopping the blood, it soaked through everything and dripped onto the floor, an unceasing crimson flow.

Christ Jesus, as long as I live, I'll ask nothing else, my father prayed, *only work one more miracle in this world and save Valentina's life.*

"Call the doctor," said Maria. "We have no choice."

"No point," murmured my mother.

My father rushed to the phone in the kitchen, roused Murtaugh from his slumber, and returned with the news that he'd arrive within thirty minutes.

"Raise the boy to my lips, Caleb." My mother kissed me for the first and only time. "Grow to be a knight, *mijo*, like your papa."

"Don't quit on me, Valentina," he said. "I need you."

"Remember, on Black Mesa, how we bade farewell to Elijah and Sofia?" Her voice was a hoarse whisper. "Take my ashes to Red Rock Canyon, where we chased after mustangs, and send me off on the morning wind."

"Tina—"

"Hush, Caleb, please." She paused, took in some ragged breaths. "Be a good father, *mi querido amigo,* that's all that matters now."

"As God is my witness, I will," he said, but his mind was racing. *There must be a way, there's always a way.*

He cast a desperate glance at Maria, but found no hope in her eyes.

It seemed everything in the room was stained with my mother's blood. He lifted me up, pressed me against his great, broad chest, cradled me in his arms.

"Stay with us, Tina," he said, thinking Murtaugh might somehow get there in time, with some miraculous apparatus in his medicine bag.

She gazed vacantly at the ceiling, her breath a shallow rasp.

Words the dark-robed monks intoned at the Mission Nuestra Señora de Guadalupe, their pleadings to Christ, came back to him: *Agnus Dei, miserere.*

Lamb of God, have mercy.

With a sickening sense of defeat, my father watched the rich caramel brown of her skin turn deathly pale.

Maria came over, sobbing, closed my mother's eyes and reached out her arms to take me.

He shook his head, held me tighter yet, did not release me to her until, a long time later, I began to cry.

From somewhere in the far distance, faint but clear, came the howling of a wolf, though he found no trace of it in the days that followed.

My father hired Maria's daughter, Flora, who moved in to serve as housekeeper and nanny. The day after receiving Valentina's ashes he rose before dawn, saddled

Alastor, and set out to fulfill my mother's dying wish. It was a fine morning, still cool, with sweet zephyrs blowing gently from the west. Venus blazed in the sky above the Rainbow Mountains. *The morning star—that was a name Jesus called Himself in Revelations. A good omen, perhaps.* He took a winding trail to a clifftop and looked out over the Las Vegas valley. The sky was beginning to lighten, the clouds on the eastern horizon glowing in shades of coral and gold.

She did this for me, he realized. *Probably figured it would bring me peace.* My father dismounted, secured Alastor, and scattered my mother's ashes. He closed his eyes, prayed that the wings of the morning would take my mother to a better place, a brighter world.

But this is nonsense! A sense of doom overcame him, buckling his legs and sending him to his knees. *What sort of fantasy am I entertaining?*

Valentina had died in her sin, an unbeliever.

He'd long ago memorized the words of Jonathan Edwards, preacher of the Great Awakening, describing the racking torments of the damned: *How dismal will it be to know assuredly that you never, never shall be delivered from them. When you shall wish that you might be turned into nothing, but have no hope of it. Still there will be the same groans, the same shrieks, the same doleful cries, and the smoke of your torment shall ascend up forever and ever...*

The saints in heaven, Edwards had claimed, would delight to hear those anguished wails.

Impossible, unthinkable! She'd fought for righteousness by my side, fearless and true, and been the best and most loyal of friends.

Venus burned overhead, looking down on him like a pitiless eye. *The morning star*—hadn't that been used to signify Satan as well as Christ? He wept, beat his fists bloody on the dry, hard ground.

No, this way madness lies. Divine justice was inexorable, unyielding, and perfect. It didn't matter if he understood it; God's ways are as far above ours as the heavens are above the earth.

My father gave a last great cry, trying to empty himself of despair, and listened to its echoes fade away. The sky lightened as the world turned another fraction of a degree. A sagebrush lizard skittered by, while far above a Cooper's hawk soared in a widening gyre.

He rose, weary and bitter, found a carrot in his saddlebag for Alastor, and set off for home.

Sometimes, returning from the church in Las Vegas, he'd ask Flora to bring me to him while he sat on the front porch. He'd hold me in the crook of his left arm, set a bottle of mezcal to his right, and scan the far horizon, looking for—he knew not what.

You shall wish that you might be turned into nothing, but have no hope of it…the racking torments never cease…

But this is the perfection of divine justice, he told himself, that though each of us deserves hell, the Lord in His mercy spares those who repent and follow Him. Valentina had withdrawn into silence every time conversation touched on religion. There was only herself to blame, she'd had every opportunity to turn to Christ.

And yet, was that really true? Had he done everything in his power, given his all, to bring her to the Lord?

The answer sickened him: *No, I failed her.*

Well, he wouldn't fail others, he'd gain a pulpit and preach hellfire every chance he got, sound a clarion call for salvation…

And so the nights passed, my father holding me in one arm, and drinking with the other, and sometimes, in the small hours, searching the hidden places of his heart to find his love for God.

Chapter Forty-Three

Flight

When I turned seventeen in 1945 and my father refused to give me permission to enlist, I decided, *to hell with his rules.*

My girlfriend, Anne Marie, was a year older than me and had graduated from our high school that spring. It was thrilling and utterly illicit to be dating a girl who was waitressing at a diner on Wilshire Boulevard and shared a room in an apartment downtown. We'd sit on her bed and neck for hours, though it was clear anything more than that would have to wait till we'd tied the knot.

Mostly, though, we danced.

"Matthew McRae," she whispered to me one night amid the tumult of a club on Central Avenue, "there is no one in this city who can move like you."

I loved the scent of her at the end of an evening, when she smelled of sweat and Chesterfield cigarettes and peppermint gum. Saturday night didn't end until sunrise the next morning, and I'd be exhausted, yet joyful and dizzy with desire when we'd part. But the joy drained away with every step toward home.

Once my father was just leaving for church when I arrived.

"Change your clothes," he said. "You're coming with me."

"Forget that," I replied. "I'm going to bed."

I was shocked to hear my own words, yet too tired to care. I walked past him, expecting him to reach out and stop me, but he only stood there, staring. I had just gotten out of the shower when I heard my father start our Ford pickup and motor off to deliver his sermon at the Free Will Baptist Church.

"Come meet my parents next weekend," Anne Marie said the next time we met. "They'll like you, I know they will. And I want to meet your dad."

"*That* will never happen," I replied, and steeled my heart against the hurt look in her eyes. "I mean, your folks, sure, maybe, sometime, just keep my father out of it. Anyway, I've been thinking, we could elope, get married in Vegas after I turn eighteen. Before I enlist. That'd be romantic, right?"

Anne Marie wasn't happy, but what broke us up was something entirely different.

She wouldn't fly.

I first saw an airplane up close when I was eight years old, when my father took me on a trip to where he used to live in Nevada. It was the Jenny my father had kept all those years under a tarp, tucked away in a small airfield not far from Las Vegas.

"You flew this?" I asked him, awestruck. The blue and gold biplane was the most beautiful thing I'd ever seen.

"Yes, a lifetime ago. It was army surplus, left over from the Great War."

"Can we go for a ride? Please?"

"No, this thing's a bucket of bolts, a museum piece now."

"You flew it with your friend Henry, didn't you? Henry Midnight."

"Yes, that's right. And often enough he flew it alone." He frowned and set the tarp back over the Jenny. "I don't know why I came out here, Matt. Just taking inventory, I guess."

A bright yellow Curtis Robin taxied for takeoff and I watched, enthralled, as it raced down the runway and took to the air. We left the field shortly thereafter, but something had changed inside of me, something had come alive in my mind.

From the time I was nine I worked weekends and summers and saved every dime. I hung around the Metropolitan Airport, did chores in return for flying lessons, soloed at sixteen and bought a second-hand Piper Cub the same year.

Flying gave me a sense of freedom from my father, and yet at times a strange sense of connection to him as well, moments when I could almost believe in a grand and good Creator of the heavens and earth.

But that part I kept to myself.

"You can't imagine what it's like, flying over the San Gabriels," I told Anne Marie. "I've looked down on the Bridge to Nowhere, buzzed big-horn sheep on the flanks of Dawson Peak. You've got to come with me."

"Why can't we just *drive* into those mountains like everyone else?"

I stared at her, aghast that she could ask such a question. "You don't understand. I've seen the sun melt into the Pacific from ten thousand feet—" I faltered, at a loss for words.

"But Matt," she said. "I'm too afraid."

From that moment I knew our days were numbered. It never occurred to me to help Anne Marie overcome her fear; I wanted a girl who'd be thrilled by the very idea of flight. Such was my selfishness at seventeen.

I had mixed feelings on V-J Day—proud of my country for its triumph, but disappointed that I hadn't had a chance to get in on the fight. Still, I'd read enough history to know peace never lasted for long. I marveled at newsreels that showed the Army's new propellerless planes, sleek, brutal flying machines that soared like eagles. My destiny was clear: I'd be a jet fighter pilot, ace of aces, hero of the next great war.

My father had found glory on horseback, I'd find mine in the air.

Part Five

Blood Ties

Chapter Forty-Four

The Atomic Man

I returned from Korea in the summer of 1953 and, after a short stay in Camp Pendleton, was discharged from the Marines. My first day as a civilian, I hitched a ride to Santa Monica, bought a used Indian Chief motorcycle, and took off at sunset, heading northeast on Route 66. I had a decision to make and figured the answer would come to me as I rode.

Halfway to my destination, I stopped at a roadhouse in Barstow to cool down and quench my thirst. There were long-haul truckers gathered off by themselves, locals playing cards toward the back of the room, and a scattering of others listening to an old-timer singing country songs. I washed my face with cold water in the men's room, then sat down, ordered a Schlitz, and read the material on a paper placemat the Chamber of Commerce must have provided. Evidently, Steinbeck had mentioned their town in *The Grapes of Wrath*: "They drove away into the darkness and the little hills near Barstow were behind them." They'd be behind me soon enough.

Gradually it sunk in that the old-timer was singing "The Ballad of Midnight and McRae." In his song, the outlaw raced over the West Texas badlands with Captain McRae of the Texas Rangers in endless pursuit. Not for the first time, I wondered about tracking down Henry Midnight to find out if he'd ever met my mother and if he could untangle the stories my father had told that never made much sense.

When the balladeer put down his guitar and ambled over to the bar, I asked if I could buy him a drink.

"Ain't gonna stop ya," he said, and motioned to the bartender for a shot of Jack Daniels.

I put a five-spot on the counter, ordered another Schlitz, and sat down.

"That song about Midnight and McRae, is it yours?"

"As much as it can belong to any man. Been singing it for near fifty years."

"Nice tune. The way it ends, though, with the chase still going on, left me wondering what happens next."

"Yes sir, that's the way I planned it." The balladeer tapped a cigarette out of a pack of Camels and lit up. "I want to get folks thinking, set their brains on fire. Maybe they'll imagine something wonderful, something no one else's ever thought of. Make the song their own."

"Huh. I heard it's a real story, that chase through the desert. Do you know whatever happened to those two?"

"You're not the sort wants to do his own thinking, are ya."

He downed his whiskey and I ordered him another.

"All right, son," he said, "I did learn a bit during my days in Texas, a thousand years ago. Midnight gave up his outlaw ways, then he and the captain joined up and fought bad guys for a spell. But I never cared to end their story that way—it just wraps things up too neat. Like a happy ending you'd see at the Saturday matinee."

What a joke that is, I thought. "The bandito must be an old man by now. Think he's still around?"

"Beats me. Funny thing, gal asked me about him last month, when I was working L.A. It's always the outlaw that gets the attention, ain't it."

"Well, I guess any of us who've had the law breathing down our neck feel kindlier toward the desperado." I was thinking of my father, of course, not the cops.

"Ain't that the truth," he said.

Just as well he had nothing new to tell me, I thought. *I'm done with the past.* I collected my change, wished the balladeer well, and hit the road.

I settled into a booth at the Starlight Diner on the outskirts of Las Vegas just after midnight. Saddle-sore and weary, I drank coffee and flipped through the pages of a magazine someone had left behind. Then stopped, transfixed by photographs of waterfalls tumbling through forests of spruce and fir, and of a mountain, violet in the light of dawn, reflected in the still, clear waters of a lake. I studied them for a while, then read the accompanying text.

"You okay, mister?"

"Hmm?" I looked up blearily at the waitress, whose nametag read Betty Lou. I'd dozed off and been dreaming of Korea, the Naktong River running red with blood. I'd been flying a few hundred feet above the ground, searching for a railway tunnel where KPA troops had taken cover...

"Sorry, hope I wasn't snoring."

"Don't worry, it's just the two of us, and Eduardo in the kitchen's half deaf. Say, where's that?" She pointed to the photographs.

"Two Medicine Valley in Glacier National Park. About a thousand miles north of here."

"How beautiful!" She sat down across from me. "Mind if I look?"

"Not at all. I'm Matt, by the way."

"Mildred. Millie to you. I only wear this tag 'cause it's been good luck for tips."

She gazed at the pictures, then lit a cigarette, leaned her head back, and blew a cloud of smoke toward the ceiling. "Montana. What I wouldn't give to dive right into that lake. I'd leave for there in a heartbeat, it's hotter than Hades in this town. Bet you it's still over a hundred out there."

She was an attractive woman, maybe a few years younger than me. For a few moments I thought of suggesting we take off that very night, leave everything else behind. Dive together into those glacier-fed waters, warm up on the beach in the sun...

Stop. I let the moment pass and took out an article I'd clipped from the *Los Angeles Examiner* that morning.

Las Vegas Atomic Man: Healer, Horror, or Hoax?

Military Refuses to Rule Out Possibility of Commie Plot

"Did you see this, Millie? What do you think? There really some radioactive fellow wandering the desert, leaving glowing footprints only some people can see?"

"Oh geez, that. Don't tell me you're one of those tourists who comes to Vegas to see the mushroom clouds."

I shook my head. "Not hardly. I've been offered a job here, but I haven't made up my mind."

"Yeah? I had any other option, I'd make tracks, I were you."

"Thanks for the advice—but you haven't answered my question."

"The atomic man, you mean?" She took another drag and exhaled through her nostrils. "Sounds crazy. But the beggar who says he was cured last week—Old Blind Bart? I used to drop spare change into his hat when I passed him on Fremont. His eyes were messed up, scary to look at. No way he could see. If Bart really was healed by the touch of a man who lit up the night with his glow—" She shrugged. "I don't know. Maybe those nukes the Army's setting off in the desert are good for something other than killing folks."

The decision I needed to make suddenly seemed obvious. I thanked Millie, asked her where I could find a pay phone, and fished a scrap of paper from my pocket. On it was a phone number and one word: *Dan*.

I was sure he was still up, awaiting my call.

My first run-in with Daniel de Carrion had been in a bar in Okinawa.

A recruiter talked me into enlisting in the Marines the day I turned eighteen. It hadn't taken much persuading. Images of leathernecks raising the flag on Iwo Jima and Marine pilots dueling with Zeros were fresh in my mind. They paid for me to attend two years of college—that way I'd start out as an officer—put me through training in Pensacola and Corpus Christi, and in January of 1950 I joined VMFA 323 in El Toro, California.

Marine Attack Squadron 323! Everything about them stoked my imagination. They were known as the *Death Rattlers*—three of their pilots had once killed a six-foot rattlesnake and hung its skin in the squadron's briefing room—and were featured in a John Wayne film that had come out that Christmas. They flew F4U Corsair fighter-bombers, prop planes, hardly the jets I'd envisioned, but that no longer mattered. I was flying with legends.

All that was lacking was a war.

We were assigned to the U.S.S. Badoeng Strait—a carrier known as the Bing-Ding—and that March set out on maneuvers that took us to Okinawa, scene of one of the Marines' bloodiest victories six years before. When we were granted some rare R&R, I went to meet my comrades in a bar in Naha and wound up in the wrong watering hole.

I was nursing a beer, wondering when the others would show, when trouble broke out.

An Army sergeant and several of his buddies had been hassling their server, a comely young local, their banter growing increasingly lewd until one grabbed her and pulled her onto his lap. Her cry of dismay brought the bartender, a skinny gray-haired Okinawan, over to their table, wielding a short staff.

"Sirs, you will let her go and leave now please, yes?"

"You're scarin' us, gramps. Come on, we're big tippers, let the good times roll." The sergeant tossed a few bills at him and laughed drunkenly as they fell to the floor.

I walked over to their table. "Let the girl go, guys."

"Buzz off, flyboy," said the sergeant. There were smirks all around. "This is Army business."

"I'm not going anywhere, pal."

The sergeant set the girl aside and rose from his chair, his beery breath hot in my face. He had at least three inches and fifty pounds on me. *Swell,* I thought. I kept my eyes locked on his while I tried to think what John Wayne would do. Probably lay him out with an uppercut to the point of his jaw, then turn to the others and ask, "Who's next?"

Before I'd figured out my move, the old bartender rammed the butt end of his staff into the sergeant's solar plexus, sending the big man down. In the next instant the rest of the U.S. Army swarmed the two of us and I found myself pinned to the floor.

There was the sound of shattering glass and a booming voice said, "*You will fucking well cease and desist right now.*"

The room fell silent. I turned my head enough to see a man of average height and build, chewing on an unlit stogie and wearing green-tinted aviator glasses. What captured my attention, though, was the broken beer bottle he gripped by the neck, gesturing with its jagged edge.

John Wayne could have done no better.

"Holy crap," someone whispered. "That's de Carrion."

It was a name known throughout the Pacific Theater. Lt. Col. de Carrion had scored nineteen kills over the Solomon Islands as a Marine pilot, some of them against seemingly impossible odds. He'd been shot down, taken prisoner and escaped—an infamous brawler who knew no fear.

"Are you all right, Tamaki-san?" De Carrion helped the old man to his feet, then turned to the young woman. "And you, Kanami-san?"

"We are fine, Colonel," said the bartender. "Do not be concerned."

"What do these pukes owe you?"

"Fourteen dollar."

The sergeant tried to rise to his knees, then collapsed with a groan.

De Carrion regarded him with disgust, then addressed the others. "Leave two sawbucks on the table, then haul Sarge and your own sorry selves out of here. *On the double.*"

They were gone in a matter of minutes.

"You," he said, turning to me. "If you hadn't gotten in Mr. Tamaki's way, he'd have sent them packing."

I felt my face turn red.

"But I like your style," he continued, and took off his shades. "Come on, I was just starting to work on a good drunk. Care to join me?"

"*Oorah,* Sir!" I said, and followed him to a table in the back.

Chapter Forty-Five

Two Kinds of Men

I knew de Carrion had flown with the Marines' Black Sheep squadron during the war, and now discovered he'd transferred to Air Force Intelligence in '48. When I asked why'd he made the move, however, he shook his head. Not something he was going to talk about.

He had stopped in Okinawa on his way to Japan after spending a week on the island of Formosa. It was common knowledge that Chiang Kai-shek had fled there with his troops a few months before and was scheming to take back mainland China from the Reds, so I couldn't resist asking what was in the works. All de Carrion would tell me is how much he enjoyed eating fried oysters at the night market in Taipei.

It didn't take long to answer his questions about my first few months with squadron 323. "I'm still with the squadron in my dreams," he said. "I've been toasting fallen comrades, those who spiraled down into the briny deep. So this is serious and solemn business we're engaging in, McRae. That piss-water you're imbibing will never do."

I set down my beer bottle.

"Let's drink something you can tell your fellow Death Rattlers about." He stood up and waved. "Tamaki-san! *Habushu!*"

Kanami brought a hefty bottle over to our table. A snake lay coiled in the bottom half, its mouth frozen open in death to reveal the long, hinged fangs of a viper.

"*Arigatou,*" said de Carrion as she filled two glasses with the amber-hued *habushu*. "That's a *habu,*" he said with a nod to the snake. "They're common around here. Venomous as hell, but the alcohol neutralizes the poison, and honey and herbs mask the stink of snake." He handed me a glass and lifted the other to his lips. "Cheers."

Short of scoring my first kill, this was about as good as my twenty-two-year-old self could imagine life in the Marines. We clinked glasses and drank to the Black Sheep pilots who never made it home.

"It was poetic license when I said they *spiral* down," de Carrion said many toasts later, after he'd named the last of his friends. "No, they plummet, they plunge, in pieces, in flames. But there's something so friggin' beautiful, so eternal, in the geometry of these things—" he drew a spiral on a cocktail napkin "—that I transform their descent in my mind's eye. *Spira mirabilis,* "he murmured, staring at what he'd just sketched.

"I'm with you, Colonel," I said, the *habushu* having loosened me up more than a bit. "That was Bernoulli's pet name for the logarithmic spiral. *Mirabilis* meaning wondrous, much to your point."

"Well I'll be damned." He looked at me with new interest. "Yes, Bernoulli wanted one etched on his tombstone, but the bastards gave him an Archimedean spiral instead. 18th century SNAFU. Studied math, I take it?"

"Yeah. Well, two years at San Diego State, anyway. I like the black-and-white-ness of it. No matters of opinion or conjecture. And nailing a difficult proof feels almost as good as dancing swing on a Saturday night."

De Carrion smiled for the first time. "It was physics for me—Berkeley, class of '41. I'd just started grad school at Cal Tech when the Japs hit Pearl. Suddenly the halls of academia lost their appeal. Ain't it funny where life can lead."

"You must have been pretty damn good at physics. Ever regret not sticking with it? Once you heard about the A-bomb, I mean."

"I could give a rat's ass about the bomb," he snapped.

I felt my face flush.

"Oh, relax." He topped off our glasses and proceeded to down half of his. "I'd have been a decent physicist, but I'm a natural-born gladiator. A samurai. Tamaki, he understands." De Carrion caught the old man's eye, raised his glass, and Tamaki acknowledged him with a modest bow. "Those trophies behind the bar? He was a kobudō champion in his younger days. Still has the moves. Anyway, McRae, thing about war is, you find out who you really are."

Our conversation grew more personal the more we drank, and by the time the *habushu* dropped below the viper's fangs, we were talking about our fathers.

"Enlisting in the Marines, that was the last straw," I told him. It was taking some effort to avoid slurring my words.

"How so? Most dads'd be proud." De Carrion's eyes were bloodshot and had lost focus, though he was clearly a practiced drinker.

"He's a pacifist. Even preaches that way in church."

"Well, I credit him for swimming against the tide. Probably be a pacifist myself if I wasn't such a bloodthirsty bastard."

I couldn't quite process that comment, so I just blinked a few times and let it go.

"What most pissed off *your* old man?" I asked him.

"I became a Jew. He was as Catholic as the Pope."

"Huh." It took a moment for that to sink in. "Wait—seriously, you converted?"

"It was no picnic, let me tell you."

I'm thoroughly sauced, I thought, *but this is no time to fade out.* "Can I ask how you came to the decision? Couldn't have been just to get under your father's skin."

He grinned. "Ever wonder about my last name?"

"Well sure, it's one of a kind. Makes it sound like you've got ice water in your veins. Your own invention?"

"Nah, it's for real. De Carrions have been Catholic for hundreds of years, but according to family lore, I'm descended from a fourteenth century Castilian Jew, Shem Tov of Carrión. A poet and holy man. Then came the Spanish Inquisition, and legions of my forbears forswore their faith. Rank cowardice! I'm redeeming the honor of the family name."

"Whoa." This was not a part of the de Carrion legend I'd ever heard. "But do you actually worship as a Jew—go to synagogue and all that?"

"On the high holy days, if I can find one. Which ain't often in this part of the world. Not even on the Solomon Islands."

I smiled at that, then gripped the table tightly to stop the room from spinning.

"I'm gonna escort you back to the Bing-Ding, McRae, make sure you get there in one piece." He poured the last of the *habushu* into his glass, tossed it back, and we made our way out onto the street.

I have no memory of the cab ride back to the carrier, but the next morning I found a cocktail napkin in my breast pocket, on which de Carrion had written in remarkably neat block letters:

From my ancestor's book of moral proverbs:

"I find in this world two kinds of men and no more, and I can never find the third:
A seeker who seeks and never finds, and another who is never content with whatever he finds.
One who finds and is satisfied I cannot find..."

So, Matt, which one are you?

My night drinking *habushu* with de Carrion made for a predictably entertaining tale at breakfast, though I left out our personal conversation. Once I was alone, I unfolded his message and read it again.

Two kinds of men...

Could humanity really be divided in that way? Were all men seekers? Was I?

And if so, what did I seek?

That last one was easy enough to answer: *glory*, bigger and better than anything my father had achieved. In my dreams I imagined the experience of glory as a feeling like no other—as though I were dancing but never growing tired, flying without ever having to come down. Oh, I'd be content, all right.

I wondered in which camp de Carrion belonged, or if he believed himself the exception to his ancestor's rule, but heard nothing from him before we left Okinawa. Early that May a postcard he'd mailed from Tokyo caught up with me at El Toro, showing young women in kimonos standing under blossoming cherry trees, with Mt. Fuji in the distance. On the back, in neat block letters, he'd written

Attended Passover seder with fellow sons of Abraham. Finding gefilte fish and tzimmes in Tokyo was a challenge fit for a Marine. Semper Fi!

–Dan

What was I to make of the man? And were we now on a first-name basis, or did he just want to avoid drawing attention to himself? Regardless, I had no way to get in touch with him, and life settled back into the routine of training and maneuvers and drills. De Carrion and his progenitor gradually faded from my mind.

Then, in late June, the North Korean army swept down across the 38th parallel, routing the South Koreans and swiftly seizing Seoul. Within weeks we received orders and departed on the Bing-Ding, bound for Korea.

President Truman's insistence that this was a mere "police action" the U.S. would lead on behalf of the United Nations elicited much derisive laughter from the Marines of Attack Squadron 323. Truman could call it what he liked; the war I'd been waiting for had finally arrived.

Chapter Forty-Six

Whatever it Takes

"I know some of you don't have much notion of just where the hell Korea is. Well, take a good look." Our commanding officer rapped on a map of Asia with his pointer. "Right here, five hundred miles west of Japan, hanging off northeast China like a limp dick. It's a godforsaken little country, so why do we even give a crap what happens there? I'll tell you why: last year the Russkies got the A-bomb and the Reds took control of China. Someone's gotta stop these bastards, and as usual it's gonna be up to the U.S. Marines. We fight the Commies here—" he gave the Korean peninsula another whack—"or we'll be fighting them back home soon enough."

That made sense to me. Hitler and Hirohito had been bent on global dominion, and Stalin and his minions seemed like more of the same. So this was big! My father had been a sort of cowboy policeman, but I was fighting for the freedom of the world.

Grim reports from the front came to us en route. The South Korean army was close to worthless and the first divisions the U.S. and U.N. assembled were poorly equipped and vastly outnumbered. Following a series of defeats, our forces had retreated to defensive positions in the country's southeast, near the port of Pusan. That city was essential to bringing in more men and supplies, and General Walker of the U.S. Eighth Army had ordered his men to stand to the death on the east bank of the Naktong River, the last natural line of defense.

His men put up a heroic effort, but the North Koreans were relentless and breached the Naktong in early August. We arrived just as the Marine infantry was attempting to push them back across.

To do that meant retaking an ugly piece of real estate known as No-Name Ridge.

The soldiers of the North Korean People's Army—the KPA—were well protected, having dug in on the ridge's eastern and western sides. They'd take up positions in deep trenches on the far slope when artillery or air fire threated them, then come forward when the Marines advanced. The hillside was steep and stark, and the KPA poured down machine-gun and mortar fire and grenades. Every inch of ground our riflemen gained came at a terrible cost.

The enemy was shielded from everything but direct strikes from above. Dive-bombing was the only effective option, and our squadron joined the battle with a simple directive: "blow the bastards to hell." Well, I'd gone through the same basic training as the infantry, crawled through the mud with them. I'd do whatever it took to be their hero.

I watched the first Corsair's run, saw its bomb miss the gun emplacement we were aiming for, and knew why: its dive had been just a bit too shallow. Steeper descent, more accurate bomb placement. My turn came soon enough.

Whatever it takes...

I rolled my plane over on its back and came down as close to vertical as I dared, let its five-hundred pound bomb go at the last moment, then pulled up, the G-forces slamming me back into my seat, my cheeks feeling like they were being stretched down to my shoulders, and I didn't need forward air control to tell me I'd obliterated the target, I knew it, knew there'd be nothing but smoke and dust where those guns had been, and all I could think was, the life I've always dreamed of is beginning at last.

A few weeks later I was on break, drinking a beer and leafing through an ancient copy of Life magazine, when a shadow fell across the page.

"Well if it ain't Matt McRae," said de Carrion.

"Colonel!" I stood and clasped his outstretched hand.

"Been hearing tales of your derring-do. I expected no less, of course."

I did my best to seem nonchalant, but was thrilled he'd heard of my success. No-Name Ridge had been only the first of a string of missions where I could do no wrong. "I'd ask what you're up to," I said, "but you'd never tell me. In Korea for long?"

For the duration of the war, he guessed, and at least for a while the Bing-Ding would be his home. We soon settled into the same easy rapport we'd had in Okinawa.

"So, what sort of man are you finding yourself to be over here, Matt?" he asked me, not long into our first conversation. "With respect to Shem Tov's proverb, I mean."

"You were right that war would show me who I really am," I replied. "But I don't find myself fitting into your ancestor's paradigm."

"How so?"

"I'm a seeker who has found what he's looking for. Or nearly enough, anyway, to feel satisfied."

De Carrion raised his eyebrows. "Well, hot damn. Maybe you'll be the one to beat the odds."

I beamed, oblivious to his irony. "How about you?" I asked.

"Oh, I'm a seeker who is never satisfied." He paused to light up a stogie. "Becoming a Jew, for example. It wasn't just contrariness that led me to convert. I loved the Old Testament, the wildness of it, the red meat of it. The bloody god of it, Jehovah, mightiest of the desert deities. Taking on Ashtoreth and Moloch and dozens more and just *smoking* them, each and every one. And all the lonely prophets, pissing into the wind, railing against their adulterous, stiff-necked people, the chosen of God. But it ain't enough. The first passion of faith falls away, like love. Can't remember the last time I honored the Sabbath."

I understood well what had gripped him about the Old Testament tales. Bible stories my father had told me came to mind, Elijah facing off alone against the four hundred fifty priests of Ba'al. Heaven's fire consuming only Elijah's offering, leaving the followers of the false god writhing in rage. "When I was young," I said,

"I used to wonder whether the idols were real, and simply lesser deities, or merely figments of the heathen imagination."

We were leaning our forearms against the rail, gazing out in the twilight across the still waters of the Korea Strait, a handful of stars visible in the evening sky.

"They're real all right," he said. "All the demons, all the dark gods men have worshipped since the dawn of time. Soldier on long enough and you'll know just how real they are."

"You asked me once why I left the Black Sheep and joined Air Intel," de Carrion said one night when he'd managed to score a bottle of Johnny Walker Black. "My sense of balance went to hell, that's why. Inner ear's messed up. Doesn't affect me much on the ground anymore, but there's no way I can pilot a fighter."

"Shit," I said, wondering how I'd deal with not being able to fly. *Better to go down in flames.*

"There is one thing about this affliction I appreciate," he continued. "It's called labyrinthitis."

"Labyrinthitis? As in, the legend of the labyrinth?"

"That's the one. Be worth it if my life could be transported into the realm of myth."

"Wait, remind me—is that Greek or Norse mythology? I can't recall the story."

"Well, I'll school you, no extra charge. Daedalus—a clever SOB if ever there was one—built the labyrinth as a prison for the minotaur, a creature with a bull's head and human body, who feasted on the flesh of maidens and young men. It was an underground maze so impossibly complex the monster could never escape—nor could any poor bastard who entered find his way out. But Theseus took on the challenge, solved the mystery of the maze, and slew the beast. An honorary leatherneck in my book." He topped off our glasses and we drank a toast to the mythical Greek. "I keep asking for more dangerous assignments, but it seems there're no minotaurs to be found."

We talked for a while of the war and the technical aspects of flying a fighter-bomber, the little details that made the difference between life and death.

Talked of the battles I'd been in so far, of the things I'd learned in my first few weeks.

"I'm envious of you, I'll admit," he said, after we'd downed a considerable portion of the Johnny Walker. "Though only up to a point. I used to like marking my kill count in red rising suns on the side of my plane. But those were Zeros I'd shot down; these days it'd be villages I'd napalmed and peasants I'd strafed. Not sure how I'd mark those."

"Come on, you're in Intel," I responded, "you know what's going on out there. The Reds run tanks through farmhouses and hide them in the rubble. Disguise themselves among the refugees. It's the KPA setting the rules, not us. They could care less about the people they claim to be fighting for. What the hell choice do we have?"

He'd touched a nerve. What I didn't mention were the thoughts I'd tried to banish from my mind after the North Koreans were finally driven off No-Name Ridge, the excitement and horror I'd felt when they abandoned their weapons and fled and we pursued them, our Corsairs gunning them down by the hundreds, the Naktong River filling with the bodies of the dead. I said nothing of what it was like to bomb pack horses and oxen and handcarts and hospitals turned into Red barracks. And yes, to strafe caravans of peasants who'd been pressed into service to carry the weaponry used to kill our men, or who might have been KPA soldiers in disguise. Or maybe they were just the unlucky ones, poor doomed souls who'd picked the wrong damn day to flee south toward the American lines.

I thought the churning in my guts flying back afterward was a sign of weakness. That I'd toughen up soon enough.

"I get all that," he said after I'd finished defending our tactics. "You do what you have to do. I wasn't trying to kill your buzz. I hate war, I suppose. It's the duel, the clash of warriors I used to live for. Maybe I should take on the KPA armed only with the jawbone of an ass."

I laughed—it wasn't hard to imagine de Carrion doing just that. "When you joined Air Intel, you must have thought of yourself as Joshua, signing up for spy duty and sent into Canaan to size up the enemy and report back to Moses."

"Well, yeah, pretty much. Of the two great Yehoshuas, he's the one I identify with, that's for sure."

Yehoshua was the Hebrew name for both "Joshua" and "Jesus", as I'd learned from my father. Something bothered me about what de Carrion had just said, and I had enough liquor in me to tell him what it was.

"I don't know. If it's the challenge of taking on a powerful enemy all alone, seems to me no one did that better than Jesus."

He gave me one of his appraising looks. "The temptation in the desert, you mean."

"Sure, going *mano-a-mano* with Satan, and that was just for starters. Facing down legions of demons, and Pontius Pilate, who had all the might of Rome."

"Huh." He poured us each another shot. "Not my style of combat, exactly, but I get your point."

"Hey, you know the rule of war." I clinked my glass to his. *"Whatever it takes."*

Chapter Forty-Seven

In Flanders Fields

I was ninety-two years old, hunkered down at home in 2020 while a virus raged in the great wide world, when I first began writing about my father and Henry and myself. Three years have passed since then, and this morning, prompted by a keen sense of my own mortality, I finally had the strength of will to type "napalm" into my laptop's search bar and scan through the results.

It was created—though *conjured* might be a better word—on Valentine's Day, 1942, at one of Harvard University's secret labs. A love offering from the Prince of the Power of the Air. For use in fire-bombing campaigns, napalm had no peer. Drop enough of it from a fleet of B-29s and you create your own weather—self-perpetuating windstorms clocked at seventy miles per hour!—and whomever you don't incinerate suffocates as flames exhaust every bit of oxygen in the atmosphere.

The lethality of the stuff, the scorching heat of it, was hardly news to me. A napalm bombing run didn't have to be all that accurate; even a near miss could ignite the fuel inside a T-34 tank and blow it to kingdom come.

The first time I saw napalm in action up close was not long after the Inchon landing, when I spent a few days on the ground with forward air control. Our squadron provided close support for the infantry, sometimes attacking enemy positions less than a hundred yards from our own men—so close that empty shell casings from our M2 cannons would shower down on the troops watching below—so it helped to have pilots on the front lines, radioing detailed information to those in the skies above.

One fine day in early October, we attacked a KPA redoubt in a village just north of Seoul. The North Koreans were putting up a fierce fight, though the Marines had laid waste to much of the battlefield with artillery strikes. Then our Corsairs let loose with a wave of napalm drops. I can close my eyes now, seventy-odd years later, and still see and feel and taste what those were like: the bursts of orange, so intense they were painful to the eyes, the thick, oily smell, the air almost too hot to breathe. The sound of the napalm going off was like the tearing of silk, dialed up to a roar. I had the strange thought that it was the same sound heard when Jesus delivered his soul into His Father's hands and the veil of the temple was torn.

Shimmering rivers of napalm found their way into foxholes and bunkers. In my dreams they pursue men like fiery, glowing snakes.

The hills of Korea were honeycombed with railway tunnels, and there was one nearby where KPA troops had taken shelter and likely stored arms and munitions as well. I radioed the location; an experienced pilot could lob a few napalm tanks into those tunnels with skill and a little luck. I was watching through field glasses, saw the initial burst and the secondary explosions, and a great cheering went up from our side.

Then suddenly it seemed as if the world had gone silent.

I stood, transfixed, looking through those glasses at a woman running from the tunnel, her clothes and hair and hands on fire, running as though directly at me. I had the illusion she was looking into my eyes, and then she fell and I could see a baby strapped to her back, and it too was burning, and then they were only twisted, blackened forms on the ground.

Gradually, I again became aware of the urgent shouting of soldiers, the angry rattle of machine guns, the scream of a Corsair's dive. The static from my headset resolved itself into a pilot's repeated question, and I collected myself, answered, returned my focus to the job at hand. I did my best to push the burning woman and her child from my mind, never mentioned them when I returned to the carrier. *Look,* I told myself, *napalm wins battles.* It would end the war sooner, get the job done. *The math of it, that's the key.* Net lives lost from those saved, horror inflicted from that averted, and come down to a bottom line. There was an equation I could solve, that could yield the answer and show this all made sense, if only I could exorcise the memories, bury them in some deep dark place, and think it through.

That fall we routed the KPA, pushed across the 38th parallel and on up toward the Yalu, the river that separates North Korea from China, and MacArthur crowed that we'd be home by Christmas. Then three hundred thousand Chinese troops poured across the border, attacking at night, always under cover of night, when our Corsairs were useless. Word spread of the disaster that befell our infantry on those terrible nights, how the enemy emerged from the darkness in wave after wave, heralded by a great pounding of drums and crash of cymbals and ringing of gongs, by the harsh shriek of whistles, by strange-sounding flutes and stranger chants and fierce, wild songs. It fell to twenty-five below every evening after sunset and when Marines found they couldn't dig foxholes in the frozen ground, they stacked up the stiff bodies of the dead like sandbags instead. Men could be riddled with bullets in that frigid cold and not bleed out until they made it to the seeming safety of a heated tent.

We provided air cover for the agonizing retreat from the Chosin reservoir that dark December, and the fighting settled into a bloody stalemate, with never more than a few miles of ground changing hands. Still, there was always some general keen to execute his bold, brilliant plan to turn the tide of war.

And so I soldiered on.

I was promoted to captain in 1952, not long after I turned twenty-four, the same age as my father when he gained that rank. And did I attain glory before an armistice was agreed to the following year? Glory yet greater than my father had achieved?

Yes, indeed, if only by the standards of the world.

The Distinguished Flying Cross, our nation's highest award for aerial heroics, is a handsome medal, a bronze cross pattée suspended from a rectangular bar which in turn hangs from a ribbon dyed red, white, and blue. The cross pattée—whose arms narrow towards the center, then widen into broad, flat ends—was emblazoned in red on the white shields of the Knights Templar during the Crusades. No doubt they, too, imagined themselves bound for glory, defending the Holy Land against the enemies of Christ.

Two hundred eighty-seven DFCs were awarded during the Korean War. There are brief citations that memorialize each one.

This is mine:

The President of the United States takes great pleasure in presenting the Distinguished Flying Cross to Captain Matthew McRae (USMC) for heroism and extraordinary achievement in aerial flight of a plane during operations against enemy aggressor forces in Korea on 17 August 1952. (It was, however, a mere colonel who awarded me the medal in a blessedly short ceremony on the tarmac of a windswept airfield south of Seoul.)

Participating in an aerial strike against a group of cleverly camouflaged enemy supply caves and personnel shelters, Captain McRae, who was first to locate the concealed objective, initiated a daring dive-bombing assault, scoring direct hits that closed two of the enemy caves and clearly marked the obscure target for the other members of the flight. Seeing additional targets of opportunity, Captain McRae pressed his attack to treetop level to achieve maximum effect. Despite intense small-arms fire which hit and damaged his aircraft, Captain McRae made repeated bombing and strafing attacks against the enemy until his ammunition was expended. His persistent attacks in the face of great personal danger were largely responsible for the success of a mission that closed eight enemy caves, destroyed three personnel shelters, and inflicted numerous casualties upon the enemy, thereby upholding the highest traditions of the United States Naval Services.

This Captain McRae sounds like a hell of a guy, doesn't he? But here's the truth: I wasn't brave. I had simply lost all regard for my own life, so intent was I on wreaking havoc, on delivering death and destruction, driven to near madness by the demon of rage.

The previous day we'd helped ground troops take a village—a key objective, of course, which the generals of both sides had deemed worth however many lives to seize or to defend. It was a nightmare mission. Anti-aircraft weapons the KPA had positioned in a schoolyard sent two of our Corsairs down in flames. The rest of us circled and dove and bombed the AA emplacement into oblivion, and then nearby munitions blew and took the school out as well. Of course, the enemy had made sure there were children inside; what better propaganda to display to the world than pictures of the charred, broken bodies of innocent youth?

That night I dreamed of the woman with the baby on her back, the one who'd run toward me, in flames, awoke with blood in my mouth and fury in my heart, determined to take revenge. There were no women and children on that North Korean hillside on the seventeenth of August, 1952, only enemy troops, and I exhausted every bomb, every rocket, every round of ammo my Corsair held, killed until I could kill no more and had no choice but to head back to base, void of feeling and soaked in sweat.

I'd lost touch with de Carrion the previous year after squadron 323 moved off the carrier, but he found me one night early that fall at Pyeongtaek airfield. He'd brought along a bottle of Jim Beam, and sometime in the small hours, sitting together in the privacy of a small supply shed, I opened up about everything I'd been keeping inside for the past two years.

"I hate the goddamn KPA," I said when I'd finished describing the horrors that were haunting my dreams. "For the nightmare they've brought down on all of us, on their own people most of all."

We lowered the level of the bourbon more than a little before de Carrion broke the silence.

"'*The heart of the sons of men is full of evil, and madness is in their heart while they live, and after that they go to the dead.*' It's my favorite part of the Bible, Ecclesiastes, because the Preacher is such a clear-eyed bastard, and about as burned out as you and me. So, yeah, Matt, welcome to the world as it really is. The Sabre jockeys dueling MiGs over the Yalu, they're the ones getting their pictures in *Life* magazine, but the real war—the one *we're* fighting—no one wants to read about that."

"*We?* What is it you're doing, anyway?" I asked him. "If it's not too fucking secret to share."

"All right." He took out one of his stogies and lit up. "I run herd on a team of Koreans—some from the south, some we've recruited from the north—who find targets worth bombing. Incendiary raids, for the most part. Only, the work's a lot easier now—everything north of the 38th is a target. The press is told it's all 'precision bombing,' which would be funny if it wasn't such a sad, sick joke. We send reports to Washington estimating how many have bit the dust since this farce began, and it's north of four million, over half of them civilians. What are we accomplishing? There isn't a city in the north or south that's not in ruins. It ain't just the KPA, pal, there's more than enough madness and evil to go around."

"Is there? I'm putting my life on the line for *liberty*. At least when this is over the Koreans will be able to rebuild in freedom." I felt a growing sense of anger at de Carrion's words; I didn't need to feel yet worse about the war.

"I doubt that. Syngman Rhee's a sewer rat," he said, referring to the president of South Korea. "We only prop him up because he's not a Commie. But even if you were right, scant comfort that would be to the dead. I've wondered what the shades of those who've fallen would have to say. What do you think, Matt? Would they cry out, like those in Flanders Fields, 'take up our quarrel with the foe?'" He paused and looked at me.

I met his eyes in stone-faced silence.

"Perhaps they would," he continued. "Maybe we're in thrall to a madness that ends only with the Bomb, locked on this bloody trajectory, a logarithmic spiral into the abyss."

"You're a friggin' hypocrite if that's how you think." Any constraints I'd ever felt in talking to the man had vanished. "Perpetuating a war you think a waste."

"Guilty as charged," said de Carrion. He lifted his glass. "Meet my wingman, Mr. Beam. Look, I'm a warrior, this is what I do, I know no other life."

"No, you're a coward is what you are, like those ancestors of yours you so despise." I stood up and pushed back my chair. "If you had the courage of your convictions, you'd quit. You just can't handle what people would think, can't live with the shame."

"Maybe so. I won't defend myself." He regarded me calmly, took a last puff on his stogie and stubbed it out on the floor. "But somehow I think you're talking to yourself as much as to me."

I walked out into the cold night air, kept going until I'd walked off the anger and was tired enough to sleep. De Carrion's last remark had hit home; I loathed the thought of getting into my Corsair, dreaded each mission, no longer had any sense of what *glory* even meant. But I was a Death Rattler, a hero, a man other pilots looked up to. Besides, we were fighting to defend against an evil aggressor, and if some of our tactics were wrong-headed, well, the North Koreans had brought this on themselves. Anyway, my five-year commitment to the Marines would be up in nine months. I'd bought into the game with all my psychic capital; to cash out now was unthinkable.

What choice was there but to play out each remaining hand?

Chapter Forty-Eight

Into the Labyrinth

The following May I received word from de Carrion that he'd be in Tokyo that summer, and asking if I had any R&R saved up to join him there. We met a few weeks later at an Air Force base just outside the Japanese capital.

I was escorted to a stark meeting room lit by fluorescent lights. When de Carrion entered, the silver eagles on each shoulder of his jacket caught my eye.

"Didn't know I'd be meeting a full bird colonel, or I'd have done a better job shining my shoes." I shook his outstretched hand. "Congratulations. Your intel must be wowing the brass."

"It wasn't the Air Force that got me this promotion," he said. "Come on, I've got a place we can talk."

We walked down a series of hallways to a small office, and after I sat down he locked the door. I looked around; there were pictures taped on the wall and stacks of papers piled on a desktop, but not a bottle of whiskey or bourbon in sight.

"I took a new position stateside last December," he told me, "working out of the old Las Vegas Bombing and Gunnery Range. Seven hundred square miles of the most desolate wasteland you've ever seen. Makes Korea look like the Garden of Eden. It's been renamed the Nevada Proving Ground."

"What is it you're proving?"

"Atom bombs." De Carrion regarded me steadily, impassively. He'd aged since I'd last seen him, with deep lines in his forehead and dark circles under his eyes.

"What the hell," I said, and moved some papers off a chair so I could sit down. "I thought you wanted no part of that crap."

"Just listen to me, Matt. I didn't ask you to meet me on a lark." He spoke with a quiet intensity that stilled any impulse I had to give him a hard time. "We try out new A-bomb designs there, airdrop 'em from B-50 bombers, fire 'em from cannons, send 'em up in balloons or set 'em up on towers and light the fuse. Assess what kind of damage they do, physical and mental both. Two months ago we had a Marine battalion dig in four thousand yards from ground zero, then proceed toward the fireball and execute a mock assault, see if they could keep their wits about them as they charged the gates of hell. I was one of a dozen officers positioned *two* thousand yards from the blast—the closest humans have ever been to a nuclear detonation, other than the citizens of Hiroshima and Nagasaki we torched eight years ago. At zero three thirty we were crouched in a trench six feet deep, field jackets over our heads, arms crossed over our knees, face buried in our arms, eyes tightly closed." He turned and shook his head, reliving the moment. "Matt, through my jacket, through my arms, through my fucking *eyelids* came a whiteness so bright I saw every one of the bones in my hands. That's just the show of it, though, the spectacle, the kind of thing my superiors don't mind seeing in the papers. What really counts isn't making it into the news. There's a dark fucking evil at work, and *that's* why I'm there. The only chance to fight it is from the inside."

None of this was remotely what I'd been expecting. "You recruiting me, Dan, to join this rogue mission you're on?"

He took a deep breath. "There's no one else I think more highly of, no one else I trust, however much I may have pissed you off. I know you're sick to the depths of your soul with what you've had to do these past three years. We're warriors, Matt. We've just been fighting the wrong war."

"And just what exactly is the *right* war?"

He took a few moments to think that over. "Ever read anything about atomic fallout, or nuclear radiation?"

"Not much. Nothing, really. I assume it's nasty stuff."

"You don't know the half of it. There's not many who do, among the public, anyway. But I've gone to school on these things. Talked early this year to Dr. Hermann Muller—sounds like a Kraut but he was born in New York, turns out he and I are both descended from Spanish Jews. Won the Nobel Prize in medicine in '46. His research proves radiation can cause lethal *mutations*. Meaning changes in our genes, which are the building blocks of life. Muller's been warning about the dangers of radiation for decades, only that ain't exactly convenient news right now, and he's a socialist to boot, so no one in Washington's overly fond of the man."

De Carrion stood up, walked over and tapped on a picture that I assumed was the mushroom cloud from an atomic explosion.

"Trinity bomb test in Alamogordo, New Mexico, July, 1945. Top secret at the time. Not long after, business clients of the Eastman Kodak company started pitching a fit. The x-ray film they'd purchased had all been ruined, and they wanted their money back. Well, Kodak has a physicist on staff—guy named Julian Webb—who figured out the film's protective packaging was radioactive. What's more, whatever was emitting that radiation was beyond strange—it had never been seen on planet earth, wasn't supposed to exist. So Webb travelled to the plants in Indiana and Iowa where the packaging was manufactured and figured out the radioactive contamination had come into the local water supply through *precipitation*. It had just fallen from the sky.

"From the Trinity test, obviously," I said. "New Mexico to Indiana—whatever that stuff was, it travelled well over a thousand miles."

"Turned out to be Cesium-141, which is created only in the maelstrom of a nuclear blast. But that thousand-mile journey was nothing. The next atomic detonation on U.S. soil was at the proving grounds in the winter of '51. A few days later, a Geiger counter started going nuts at Kodak's headquarters in upstate New York, twenty-three hundred miles away. They were having a winter storm and the town was blanketed in radioactive snow."

"Was it known this stuff—this fallout—could travel so far?"

"Oh, hell yes. That's why scientists originally proposed locating the test site on the East Coast, so the westerlies would blow the shit out to sea. But it would have taken years longer to acquire the land. Vegas was easy, it was a quick fix. Now I'm gonna lay one more story on you."

He went over to the wall and tapped on a picture of a monster fireball lighting up the desert sky. "A couple weeks ago we did a test, code-named Harry. Dirty Harry, we call it now. Surprised everyone with a thirty-two kiloton yield—that's twice the force released at Hiroshima, and twenty kilotons above the acceptable level to limit radiation exposure. Then the winds shifted north right after the blast, spreading fallout from Mesquite to St. George. If the docs had anything to say about it, the public would have been warned, told to stay indoors, avoid local produce and milk for a time. But, see, that might trigger a panic. Nothing can get in the way of atomic testing. So the brass told people there was nothing to worry about, they could get on with their lives." He closed his eyes, shook his head. "I lay awake thinking about those school kids in southern Utah, playing outside at recess while fucking radioactive dust settled all around them."

He opened his eyes, straightened and rolled his shoulders as he moved to the chair behind his desk. "I'm here, ostensibly, to find out how the U.S. military's been stifling reports of the effects of atomic fallout on the Japanese. It ain't pretty, what radiation poisoning will do."

I found myself wishing we were sharing a bottle of Scotch. "I don't know, Dan. Isn't this the kind of thing you leak to an enterprising reporter, someone at *Time* magazine?"

"Planting stories in the press won't be enough. The evil runs deep, pal, but you're not ready to hear more just yet."

De Carrion's eyes had a light in them I hadn't seen before. "How'd you get this gig, anyway?" I asked, stalling for time as I tried to come to terms with all he'd said. "Guess your physics degree came in handy after all."

That elicited a sad smile. "My degree didn't count for a hill of beans. They came after me because I'm a gung-ho sonofabitch who can take care of problems, who does what has to be done. Who can operate in secrecy and kill if need be. Are you getting it, Matt? I was hired to make sure truth never sees the light of day."

He paused, looked down, rubbed his temples wearily and returned his gaze to my eyes. "The war's winding down, it'll be over soon. You planning to re-up?"

"No," I said. "I've had enough."

"Good. I'm supposed to find a private contractor with a military background. Some cold-blooded bastard like me." He leaned forward. "I need you, Matt. Let's take this on together."

"I don't know." I stood and walked over to the wall and spent a moment looking over the pictures. "This is a lot to take in."

He handed me a folded piece of paper. "My home phone number in Nevada, call me when you're back and out of the Corps and we'll talk. Just know this: I've found my way into the maze, and I'm damn well going after the minotaur."

Three months later I stepped into a phone booth at the Starlight Diner in Las Vegas.

Chapter Forty-Nine

Man and Superman

"These bomb-test bastards don't need to know who you are," said de Carrion. "They don't really *want* to know—all my CO cares about is keeping the dirty work at arm's length."

It was our first meeting since I'd arrived in Las Vegas. We were having lunch in a seedy neighborhood across the railroad tracks from downtown. Aside from a boarded-up church across the street, it was all liquor stores, bail bondsmen, and bars.

"Still," he continued, "when I finally make my move all hell's going to break loose. I don't know if I can keep you out of the line of fire, let alone make it out of this alive myself. I pushed you hard to join me, but this is my fight, it doesn't have to be yours. You can walk away any time."

"Like hell, Dan. I've never backed out of a mission."

I'd felt dead inside for a very long time; now the risk of death in the quest to do something decent was stirring me back to life. As if on cue, someone slipped a dime in the juke box and LaVerne Baker started singing "Soul on Fire."

"Okay." He paused when a tired-looking waitress dropped off two beers, then he filled me in on the latest bomb-test mishaps. "Sounds bad, right? But radiation burns on sheep and cattle, radioactive iodine in children's milk—none of that's enough. The ranchers get bought off, government lab boys assure the public there's nothing to worry about, and the health effects and genetic mutations may not show up for years. Something else has come up, though, that might just allow us to turn the tables on these sons of bitches. Heard of the atomic man?"

I pulled the *Examiner* article from my back pocket and showed it to him. "Anything about this for real?"

De Carrion took a quick look at the story and handed it back to me.

"General Carlton—my CO—received a communication marked top secret from a unit of the Atomic Energy Commission, the Department of Operations Management. They believe a Communist agent may have been exposed to radioactive fallout while prowling the Proving Grounds—"

"And this Commie spy's now performing miracle healings?"

"Who knows if those have anything to do with him, or if they're even true at all? But here's the main thing: the DOM's not on any org charts. It doesn't officially exist. That tells me it's deep inside the labyrinth. My orders are to bring them the atomic man, alive if possible, dead if need be."

"Holy shit." I sat back in my chair and chewed over what de Carrion had just said. "I don't see how their interest in a Commie spy does us any good, though. You must be thinking there's something else going on."

"Bingo. I don't trust anything these people say, Matt. All I know is, they want the atomic man out of the way. If he spells trouble for them, he could play into our hand, whoever—or whatever—he turns out to be."

"Makes sense." *In a Salvadore Dali-esque way,* I thought. Though all this was no more surreal than the war I'd fought in for the past three years. "Might be worthwhile to talk to the two beggars he's rumored to have cured, on the off-chance they really did meet him."

"Right—a broad, goes by Ashcan Annie, and an old wino known as Blind Bart. Your job's to find them. Trouble is, they both seem to have vanished."

"Think your mystery Ops folks might already have them?"

"That's possible, but it seems at this point they're relying on me. So here's the plan." De Carrion took a moment to light up a stogie. "That story you read is a knock-off of what's been printed in one of the local papers, the *Morning Sun*, by a reporter who claims to have interviewed both Annie and Bart. Far as I can tell, he's the last one to have seen them. You can read these to catch up —" he handed me some clippings—"then find out what else he knows."

I glanced at the byline. "You kidding me?"

The reporter's name was Clark Kent.

De Carrion shrugged. "It figures, right?"

Another dime, another song, this time Bill Haley and the Comets singing "Crazy, Man, Crazy."

"Let's talk about money. I can pay you two-fifty a month, cash." He handed me an envelope, which I slipped into my pocket. "There's the first month in advance. Copacetic?"

"Sure, that's swell." And better than I'd been expecting. Hell, a burger and fries was two bits, a decent room five bucks a night, less if I paid by the week.

"In all our conversations," said de Carrion, "it's never been clear to me whether you believe in God. What's your gut tell you?"

I raised my eyebrows at the sudden change in conversation. "I don't know. Sometimes I want to believe and other times the very idea of God fills me with rage. Why'd you ask?"

"I've got my own doubts. But the world seems a friggin' horror if He doesn't exist."

"Yeah? Better to have no God than the one my father preaches. Who resurrects the heathen dead—the Koreans we napalmed into oblivion—only to subject them to infinitely worse torment in Hell. And your Old Testament Ancient of Days, Dan, your fierce desert deity, what comfort can he possibly bring you?"

"Maybe not much." He took a swig of beer. "I woke this morning from a dream I've had a few times before. I'm watching a bomb test, off by myself, a couple miles from ground zero. After the shock wave passes and the wind stops howling, I hear the thundering of a herd of mustangs spooked by the blast, racing down an arroyo, eyes wide, nostrils flaring. And all around me the Joshua trees are burning, their fiery arms raised in prayer." De Carrion stubbed out his cigar. "Let's pray, Matt. Pray there's a God in Heaven, a God of infinite goodness, one who sets things right. Pray when all around us is in flames."

I hesitated for a moment, then nodded. What could it hurt?

We bowed our heads in silence.

All right, I thought, old Bible stories coming back to me. *Let there be the Father of Lights who sent ravens to feed Elijah as he hid in the desert, and bade him drink of the brook Cherith...*

Back in my motel room later that day, I read through the articles de Carrion had given me. Unlike *The Examiner* article's wild speculations, Kent's reporting was straightforward to the point of dryness. The earliest reports that had attracted attention were from a handful of Christians who worshipped at the Las Vegas Wash, an arroyo that feeds into Lake Meade, and claimed to have seen luminous, golden footprints in the sand. Once word of the healings came out, they declared those footprints the tracks of an angel, or a sign of the second coming of the Lord Himself.

De Carrion had underlined the reporter's interviews with Miss Arnold—Ashcan Annie—and Mr. Trunnell—Blind Bart.

This reporter asked each of the two what they could tell me about the man who healed them.

"He was gentle," replied Mr. Trunnell. "His fingers, when he touched my eyes? So damn gentle. Ain't nobody touched me in years, neither. Only him."

Unfortunately, Kent explained, it seemed Bart was overwhelmed by the novelty of sight, his mind suddenly flooded by the brilliance of light, and he could provide no further description. Annie, who claimed to have been freed from the demons of madness, was similarly vague:

"I don't know, mister," said Miss Arnold. "Couldn't even tell you if he was young or old, strange as that might sound. All I can say is, he was kind. I used to wander the streets, howlin' like a madwoman. Now look at me, sane as the next gal."

That's just swell, I thought. We're looking for someone gentle and kind, who's young or old or in-between and may or may not leave glowing footprints to mark his path...

While considerable anecdotal evidence suggests Mr. Trunnell and Miss Arnold were previously afflicted, Kent wrote at the end of his most recent article, *this reporter has found no way to medically verify their claims. To date, only known con men have come forward to take credit for their alleged healings, as previously documented in this publication.*

If Kent had any theories about the atomic man, he was keeping them to himself. I leafed through back issues of the *Las Vegas Morning Sun* at the municipal library. Several of Kent's articles over the past few years were exposés of phony faith healers and smooth-talking preachers who'd bilked the faithful for all they had. I wagered he'd have a theory about what was really going on.

"I'm busy, Mr. McRae," he said, when I finally got through to him on the phone. "Tell me what you want, and keep it short."

When in doubt, de Carrion had advised, *stay as close to the truth as you can.*

"I'm a Marine vet writing an article on spec about the Proving Grounds, and I've gained access to confidential information about the atomic man. You've reported on the two street folk who say they were healed. Nothing I've heard or read about all this adds up—the puzzle pieces don't fit. I'm thinking if we talk, share information, we can do each other some good."

"Huh." For a while all I heard through the receiver was the clacking of typewriters and a hubbub of voices in the background. "Okay," he said at last. "Meet me at eight this evening at the Long Shot Saloon. I'll be the guy in a tan suit and turquoise tie."

"See you then," I said, and made a mental note to find something more presentable to wear than my t-shirt and jeans.

The reporter turned out to be a short, slightly-built man about my age with dark, slicked-back hair and a rakish mustache—a diminutive Rhett Butler, more Gable than Kent. He was seated in a booth, drinking whiskey, neat. I ordered one, too.

"You know who *I* am, Mr. McRae," he said. "But I know next to nothing about you. You said you were in the Marines—what unit?"

"I flew Corsairs for attack squadron 323."

He whistled. "The bent-wing bird? I'm impressed. Not that it means you can write worth a damn. This story you're working on—what's your motivation, and what are you trying to prove?"

Connect with this guy, I told myself. *Get him to trust me. And when in doubt...*

"I want to make amends for my part in turning Korea into a wasteland. You unmask religious fakes and frauds—I'm seeking to do the same when it comes to nuclear fallout. More than that I'm not at liberty to say."

"Let's cut to the chase: what can you tell me about the atomic man?"

I looked at the light refracted in the amber liquid in my glass. "There's a handful of theories making the rounds, one of them the notion he's part of a Communist plot. Of course, there's folks who see Commies under every rock. But suppose I told you there are people whose job it is to know these things, who believe the atomic man really *is* a Red agent—one who's infiltrated the Proving Grounds?"

"Okay," said Kent, poker-faced. "What if you did?"

"One theory rules out the others. I mean, what are the odds there's both a spy on the loose *and* a benevolent healer haunting Las Vegas? If the Red agent's for real, doesn't that tell you Annie and Bart's healings are a fraud? Not to mention both of them turning publicity shy seems a curious coincidence."

I paused, giving him a chance to speak.

He looked at me in silence.

"Trouble is," I continued, "the folks who say the atomic man's a Communist spy are holding their proof close to the vest. The only tangible evidence he exists are the testimonies of Ashcan Annie and Blind Bart. You're an expert on faith-healing fakery. What's your gut? Do you believe they met someone who miraculously healed them?"

He looked down, took a sip of his whiskey, then returned his gaze to my eyes. "Yes, I do."

"And yet the only ones who've tried to take credit for the healings are con men. How does that figure?"

"Think about it: the real healer has not come forward. That's a clue, right?"

"Well...there're those who claim the atomic man's some sort of radioactive freak who's able to cure with the touch of his hands. A benign monster, fearful of the limelight. But that's cheap science fiction, B-movie stuff."

"I'm with you there. Tell me something—" Kent leaned forward. "Do you believe in God?"

I settled back, drummed my fingers on the table, and sighed. "That's the second time in the last twenty-four hours I've been asked. I should have a better answer by now. But I just don't know."

"It's a question whose answer changes everything."

"I don't see how—" The implication of his question was suddenly obvious. "Unless you mean—"

"There's only ever been one worker of miraculous healings who tried not to call attention to himself, at least at first."

"So the true believers who say they saw Jesus' footprints, you agree with them? Somehow a Communist agent sounds more plausible."

"Why do you assume it must be one or the other?" Kent's smile was as roguish as any of Clark Gable's.

I stared at him blankly.

"You've shared a tidbit of moderately interesting, if predictably vague, information," he continued. "But I like where you're coming from and what you're trying to do. So—" he lifted his empty glass—"buy me another and I'll give you my two cents."

I caught the cocktail waitress's eye and motioned for two more drinks.

"Do you know the New Testament?" Kent asked.

"More than a little. My father was a preacher." *Was?* Why had I used the past tense? I felt a stab of guilt, not even knowing if he was still among the living.

"All right, then. Ever wonder what would happen if Jesus returned in our own times? He'd go to the down-and-out, the Barts and Annies, that's easy enough to surmise. But how would he be received by those in power?"

"If I'm to believe what I read in *Life*, with open arms, a marching band, and the keys to City Hall. Though I have my doubts."

"Me, too. I've lost track of how many times people talked of 'government under God' at Ike's inaugural, and his cabinet meetings all start with prayer. America, I keep hearing, is a 'Christian nation.' But if so, it's a strange Christ we worship—one wrapped in the Stars and Stripes and preaching our God-given freedom to make a buck. Well, the Jesus I know warned time and again against the worship of Mammon. He said we'll be judged by what we do for the naked and hungry, for the 'least of these.' Yet these days the New Deal is branded communism by the pols and corporate bigwigs and by the ever more popular preachers like Billy Graham. The minimum wage, social security, unemployment insurance, veteran's benefits? All a Marxist ruse, as un-American as they are un-Christian. Love our enemies, the Russkies and the Red Chinese? Turn them the other cheek? That'll get you called up before the House Un-American Activities Committee faster than you can say 'Joe McCarthy.'"

He paused as our waitress delivered the next round, watched her walk away, then launched back in.

"The Son of Man was the greatest possible threat to the powerful nineteen hundred years ago, and He's no less of a menace today. I'll tell you how the Lord would be received: He'd be crucified again, sure as we're sitting here drinking Old Fitzgerald. And what better cover than to brand him a Communist spy?"

"None I can think of," I said, without much enthusiasm. On the one hand, painting the Atomic Energy Commission as Christ-killers would make for a hell of a headline; on the other, we'd be promptly packed off to the loony bin.

"You were hoping for a more prosaic hypothesis? Sure, the atomic man might very well be something else again. But for those of us who believe in the Gospel, we live in imminent expectation of an event the world dismisses as wildest fantasy: the Return of the King. So ask yourself, if the dark forces that rule this planet suspected He had at last arrived among us, how would they respond?"

Perhaps through something more terrible than a Department of Ops Management, I thought, but a chill ran down my spine nonetheless. What if there *were* an atomic man out there, a gentle soul of infinite kindness? *Bring him to us,* they'd told de Carrion, *alive if possible, dead if need be...*

"Can you tell me," Clark asked, "off the record and in strictest confidence, which authority has named the atomic man a Communist agent?"

"When I can, I will. Look, I'd love to talk to Bart and Annie myself. Any clue where I might find them?"

"No." He shrugged. "Would it shock you if they've taken off? Not everyone likes the glare of the spotlight."

"Hey Kent!" shouted the bartender. "Call for you."

"My office away from the office." He flashed me another Clark Gable grin. "Back in a bit."

I was dubious he was telling the truth about Bart and Annie. *What would Sam Spade do? Put a tail on him, no doubt, on the chance the reporter still sees them.* I'd talk to de Carrion.

Kent returned in less than a minute and didn't bother to sit down. "There's word of a third healing, out at the Wash. The lame can walk! I'm heading there now."

I left a few bills and followed him out the door.

Chapter Fifty

The Woman in the Torchlight

Word spread fast.

A crowd had already assembled at the Wash, and more were arriving every minute. I parked the Indian Chief behind Kent's Buick about a mile from the river, and we started walking.

"I had no idea this was here," I said to him. Even in the twilight, the vastness of the wetlands was startling.

"The Wash looks more grandly mysterious this time of night," he replied. "By day it's just great swaths of quailbush and scrubby stands of mesquite. Sunset it becomes a gathering place for the curious and the desperate. Some come every evening, hoping to see the Lord, or the atomic man, take your pick. Praying that He'll bless them, return lost lovers, cure their afflictions, heal their wounds."

We passed old couples clinging to one another as they plodded along, passed the crippled and the maimed. How could we stop and help any one of them, I wondered, and not another?

"Whoever is doing this, isn't it cruel to raise so many hopes while working wonders for a lucky few?"

Kent shrugged. "Not if the purpose is to point us to something even more miraculous than the healing of our flesh."

I know what you mean, I thought cynically, and my mind flashed to images of Jesus on the Cross, eyes upturned, dying to satisfy the wrath of God. "My father would say the greatest wonder is that the Almighty doesn't send all of us to the eternal torment we so richly deserve. That's the party line, right? It seems to me sadistic nonsense. Hence my own lack of faith."

"Ah. I wouldn't believe in the sort of God your father preaches, either, Matt. To doubt *his* existence is the first step on the road to faith."

"Well, the next step eludes me, much as I'd like to take it. I'm not going to believe in Father, Son, and Holy Spirit because of a miracle I read about in the news any more than I believe in the Norsemen's Thor because I've heard the rumble of thunder. There's always some other explanation—you, the great debunker, would surely agree with that."

"I'll tell you what leads to faith, Matt." He slowed down and turned toward me. "It's seeing lives transformed by the miracle of His loving kindness. Perhaps even one's own."

The warmth in Kent's smile made me flinch with guilt. *If he knows where Bart and Annie are, maybe he'll open up on his own, maybe we don't need to have him tailed...*

"Clark!" A man in a battered fedora waved from the edge of the gathering crowd.

"Showtime," said Kent, breaking into a jog. "That's Arnie, my assistant. Let's continue this later."

Even from twenty yards away I could tell Arnie did not have good news.

"It's a washout at the Wash, boss," he said. "The man's nowhere to be found."

"Shit." Kent took out a pack of Lucky Strikes and lit up. "Tell me what you know."

"Fellow in question is Gaylord the Gimp, supposed to have been born with a withered leg. Hangs out at Fremont and Fourth—or used to, anyway. I've put a few dimes in his cup myself." Arnie tapped his notepad. "Got some decent quotes from two of the regulars, they're over by the water, where folks are getting baptised. Told me they saw Gaylord here early this evening, 'running and dancing and leaping like a gazelle.' Nice line, huh?"

"I doubt they've seen a gazelle in their lives," said Kent. "But they do read their Old Testaments. What else?"

"They saw glowing footprints, too. Which've vanished, of course, along with whoever left them. And Gaylord's MIA. I'll look for him on the streets, but I ain't holding my breath."

"All right, go back downtown and put out word there's a ten-spot for whoever helps us find him. Then meet me in the office in two hours and we'll write up the story, thin as it may be."

"You got it."

Kent took a last drag, field stripped his cigarette, and turned to me. "Well, crap. Figures, though. Give a man back his power of locomotion, he's likely to vamoose."

"So you think this one's for real?" I asked.

"Most likely. I'm going to talk to those old boys who say they saw Gaylord—but I need to do it alone."

The baptisms were taking place in a torchlit area not far away, where a man in priestly garb was immersing one pilgrim after another in the Wash. The crowd was growing ever larger and rowdier. A fellow dressed in a bee-keeper's outfit came up to me, carrying an impressive piece of electronic equipment.

"What's that you've got there?" I asked him.

"Geiger counter." He waved it over me. "You're clean. But if the atomic man arrives, head for the hills or the radiation'll fry ya."

I thanked him and wandered about, observing the scene and listening to snatches of conversation.

"Save us, Lord!" someone shouted.

From what? I thought, instinctively recoiling from this most basic of Christian pleas. *From God Himself?*

A chorus of voices chimed in, as if in answer to my silent question.

"From the Reds!"

"From the Feds!"

"From Satan's snares!"

"No," said a woman standing in the torchlight. "From ourselves."

She was young, no older than me, slender and tall, with long, raven hair and skin a pale shade of brown. I gasped with the shock of recognition.

A wailing of police sirens grew steadily louder and the mood of the crowd began to change.

"Coppers got a bead on the A-man and they're closing in!"

"Not before he cures my lumbago they ain't!"

"Nah, betcha anything those're vice cops, gonna roust the queers who hide back of the tall reeds and do their filthy deeds."

I fought my way through the throng toward the woman to get a closer look.

She turned in my direction and, for just a moment, our eyes met.

"Watch where you're going, you young whippersnapper!"

In my haste I'd jostled an elderly man, who tumbled to the ground. I helped him to his feet, dusted him off and made sure he wasn't hurt, then looked around.

Where was she?

"*Attention!*" came a voice from a bullhorn. A dozen or more police cars had pulled up, lights flashing. *"This area must be vacated immediately, by order of the Sheriff of Clark County!"*

Some fled further into the wetlands, but most of the crowd surged toward the roadway and I was carried along by the human tide.

A spotlight played over us, blinding with its glare.

"Exit this way, or be subject to arrest!"

Could the police be taking orders from de Carrion ? No, this wasn't his style.

"Sergeant!" Kent was up ahead, flashing his press pass, Arnie a step behind. "What can the *Morning Sun* tell its readers about why the police showed up in force tonight?"

"Move along, newshound. We got nothing to say."

When I caught up with the two men, the reporter took me aside.

"Are the mystery folks you were telling me about behind this?"

I admitted to having no idea.

"Well, let's get the hell out of here, Arnie and I have a front-page story to write. This raid might just get it above the fold."

"I'm going to hang around awhile, Clark." I was already scanning the faces of folk leaving the Wash, searching for the woman I'd glimpsed. "Thanks, I owe you."

Kent raised his eyebrows. "Take care, then. And stay in touch, okay?"

We shook hands and he and Arnie set off down the road.

"If you weren't a fellow Marine, pal," said the hulking police officer who'd warned me more than once over the past hour not to loiter near the Wash, "I'd have you in cuffs. Clear out *now*, you got that?"

"Yes sir." It was hopeless, anyway. The flow of refugees had slowed to a trickle; the woman I'd seen had vanished into the night.

I headed back toward my bike, took out my wallet, removed a faded photograph, and studied my mother's picture in the moonlight.

It had been her I'd seen at the Wash, her face and figure.

Shards of memories came back to me from long ago: waking in the predawn darkness, seeing a woman much like my mother standing over my bed. She had put a finger to her lips, whispered, *Shhh, dear one, go back to sleep.* And another time, playing in the park and seeing my mother peering at me from a stand of birch. I ran toward her, calling out to her, but only finding the trees' dappled shadows.

Were these real things, or the workings of a boy's overactive imagination, fragments of dreams? I studied the picture in my hand; a thousand women might look like her, and already my memory of the woman at the Wash was blurring. Anyway, my mother would be twice her age! And I had been her only child. Ridiculous to give it another moment's thought.

I reached the Indian Chief, put the photograph back in my wallet, and took a long last look around.

Bats flitted overhead, and from somewhere in the darkness came a loon's haunting wail.

Weary to the bone, I kickstarted the engine and set off for my room at the Last Chance Motel.

Chapter Fifty-One

Quid Pro Quo

I dreamed that night of the atomic man, a golden figure striding through the desert leaving luminous footprints in his wake. De Carrion and I had arranged to meet that morning, but he called before dawn to let me know he couldn't get away until the next day. So I went out in search of breakfast and the *Morning Sun.*

Kent had made it above the fold, all right.

THIRD MIRACLE AT THE WASH?

Bystanders Claim Lame Man Healed

Police Disperse Crowd after Hundreds Gather

He'd milked the story for all it was worth, made me feel I was there along with Sonny Sierra and Blackjack Pete, the two old-timers gaping at Gaylord as he gamboled through the wilds of the Wash. Still, it was thin stuff indeed. No comment from the Sheriff's Office, no trace of the erstwhile cripple. Nothing I didn't already know.

I ordered steak and eggs at a nearby diner and thought things over. Kent, a revealer of religious frauds, believed these spontaneous healings to be legitimate; a federal agency had ordered the capture of the healer, dead or alive, while covering up brutal consequences of nuclear fallout. It was beginning to hit home that we might not have much time. The sheriff's deputies' arrival at the Wash was like the first chill wind heralding the coming of winter—and they were small potatoes compared to the powers that might soon be arrayed against us. The long odds stirred something deep within me: we were underdogs in a righteous cause!

Feeling a surge of energy, I paid my bill and went outside. It was hot already, the harsh light bouncing off the sidewalk and stinging my eyes. A bleary-eyed gambler walked by, muttering curses; a drunk retched in a trashcan; and, incongruously, a young mother pushed a baby carriage down the street, her gaze fixed straight ahead. Swell, just swell. It takes some fortitude to keep one's spirits up in Las Vegas in the morning. Who doesn't need healing in this world?

A marquee a few blocks away caught my attention:

Vegas Dance-o-Rama!

Dance till you drop at our Swing-a-thon Saturday night!

I hadn't danced in the longest time...

It was Thursday. *If I'm not engaged in pitched combat with the minotaur by then,* I thought, *I'll check it out, shake a leg for a change.*

And then a thought came to me from out of the blue: *Call your father.*

Just like that, as if someone else was speaking, or one part of me was talking to the other.

It was, of course, the last thing I wanted to do. Dancing, like flying, meant freedom, while my father had always chained me to the earth, made prayer a tedious exercise, stripped the joy from church. Embarrassed and enraged me with his stance against the war.

So why this feeling of guilt?

His letters, that's why. The first I'd received after leaving home was one long expression of disappointment, so I'd burned it and marked the rest *return to sender*. We were oil and water, and I was relieved when he finally stopped writing.

But that was six years ago, before Korea, in what might as well have been another lifetime. The sharp edge of my anger had dulled. I'd seen my dreams come unraveled, knew there was no one to blame for that but myself. After what I'd been through overseas, his aversion to violence no longer seemed disgraceful. Standing up before his congregation and declaring himself a pacifist must have taken a good bit of courage.

Maybe he'd even have some thoughts about what de Carrion and I were facing. After all, once upon a time, he'd been a hero.

"Your call please," said the long-distance operator.

I was ensconced in a phone booth with two rolls of quarters and an assortment of nickels and dimes. A small boy in a sailor suit pressed his nose against the glass, looking in at me, making faces.

"Hello? Are you there?"

"Yes, operator, just a moment." I took a deep breath, exhaled slowly. "Los Angeles, California. Osborne six, oh-eight-two-eight."

"All right, sir, hold on."

This is madness, I thought. *I should hang up right now.*

But the receiver stayed pressed to my ear.

"I'm sorry, but that number has been disconnected."

"You're kidding." We'd lived in that home for as long as I could remember. Had my father moved? Passed away? For all that I'd kept him at a distance, I was stunned, realizing for the first time that he could just vanish from my life.

"No, sir. Is there anything else I can help you with?"

"Wait. Give me another second."

The little sailor walked away, bored.

"Sir?"

"Listen operator, can you connect me with the Los Angeles Free Will Baptist Church? It's on La Cienega Boulevard."

"Hold on."

I listened to telephone line static for a minute or so before she came back on the line.

"Please deposit two dollars and thirty-five cents for the first three minutes."

I opened a roll of quarters, which proceeded to spill out onto the floor. *"Crap!"*

"Sir?"

"Sorry, ma'am." I gathered up nine quarters and a dime, dropped them into the emotional slot machine known as a payphone, and the call went through. After a couple of rings, a woman picked up at the other end and informed me her name was Gladys.

I asked if Pastor McRae was available.

"McRae? Oh my word, he hasn't preached here since '47. He's retired, I believe."

"Really?" Impossible to imagine my father playing shuffleboard in some old folks home! "Do you know where's he gone, or have any way to get in touch?"

"I'm afraid I don't. To tell you the truth, he didn't leave on the best of terms. But if you haven't been here since his day," she said, her voice brightening, "you owe it to yourself to come by! Pastor Noel Holstein is simply remarkable, the congregation must have tripled over the past five years. Can I ask your name?"

I bid Gladys good day, hung up the phone, and gathered the rest of the change from the floor.

Once de Carrion and I made it out of the labyrinth, my next mission would be to find my father.

Late the next morning I rode the Indian Chief northwest along a bleak stretch of Route 95, the landscape little more than cactus, salt brush, and sand. In the far distance, blunt, barren mountains rose up from the desert floor. Twenty miles south of the Proving Grounds I turned off onto a dirt road called Dead Man's Cutoff that ended in an outcropping of rock.

De Carrion was waiting for me in the shade of an overhang, where I briefed him on my time with Kent.

"A lot's changed in the last forty-eight hours," he said. "This third healing's brought the head of Ops Management out from the shadows. Name's Marlon Storm, made his fortune as an armaments dealer in the two world wars. We talked yesterday, just the two of us, for close to an hour. I played gung-ho, as always, but couldn't shake the thought he was trying to see into my soul, find out who I really am."

"Think he's our minotaur?" I asked him.

"He's one stone-cold sonofabitch, that's for sure. Wants Annie, Bart, and Gaylord rounded up and sent to D.C. for 'testing and observation.' Like you, Storm thinks Kent might just know where to find them, so he wants him apprehended and compelled to spill the beans."

"Who'd do the compelling, us or them?"

"Neither. Here's where things get interesting. Ever hear of Salvatore Guerriero?"

"Mafia biggie, right?" I'd seen his picture while leafing through an issue of *Life* in between bombing runs in Korea: an older man posed in front of an antique Rolls Royce, his fedora at a jaunty angle, grinning sardonically at the camera.

"The biggest. Got started here before anyone had ever heard of Las Vegas, now he's boss of bosses. Storm's pissed the atomic man's still at large and wants Guerriero and his minions to capture him and take care of Kent and the three who were healed at the same time. Told me he's 'done business' with the Don over the years, but of course the federal government can't get its hands dirty making deals with La Cosa Nostra." He opened a cooler in his pickup, cracked open two Ballantine Ales, and handed one over. "So that's where you come in."

It was oppressively hot, even in the shade, and I rolled the cold bottle slowly across my forehead before taking a swig. "I'm your man, Dan. What is it you need me to do?"

"Meet with Salvatore Guerriero at sixteen hundred hours at the Roma, he'll be expecting you. He and Storm agreed to a quid pro quo: his boys will do Storms's dirty work, but the Don wants an outsider to silence a local pastor who's been causing him trouble, name of Amos. Your job is to play the tough guy, tell him you'll handle it. String him along. That's our best bet for keeping Amos alive."

"Since when does the mob need help pulling off hit jobs?"

De Carrion shrugged. "Guerriero thinks it's bad luck to kill a man of the cloth, though communist miracle workers and their beneficiaries seem to be fair game. It's a sweet set-up: no money changes hands, and the only other people who know about the arrangement—that's you and me, pal—can soon enough be sent to the silence of the grave."

I'd heard about bodies being weighted down with bricks and dumped into Lake Meade, and felt a keen longing for the M1911 pistol I'd carried in Korea, if not a Corsair with a full load of five-hundred-pound bombs. "We're about as far into the labyrinth as it gets, I take it. Any bright ideas how we slay the beast and get out alive?"

"This deal with the Don is the tipping point, Matt, if it can't win us allies, nothing will. Tonight I'm taking off for Camp Pendleton to see the one man I can trust with both our lives: General James T. Grant, Ulysses's great-grandson. Jimmy and I fought together in the South Pacific, he's a blood brother. Three hundred fifty miles, I'll be there by dinnertime."

"Well, that's encouraging news for a change. So then, exposing this scandal gives us the credibility to blow the lid off the fallout coverup, that what you're thinking?"

"Bullseye, McRae."

I could feel my spirits lifting. We had a plan!

"Something I've been meaning to give you." De Carrion handed me a small envelope. "Microfilm. It has all the evidence I've collected, everything that's been concealed about the dangers of atomic fallout. I'll be giving one to Grant, too, but it's best you have a copy, just in case. Speaking of which—" He rummaged through an impressive supply of weaponry in the backseat of his Ford F-1 and handed me a Browning Hi-Power and a box of ammo. "It'll be the Alamo all over again if we actually have to use any of this, and I don't relish the thought of ending up like Davey Crockett. So let's bow our heads, ask for blessings from the Ancient of Days."

I closed my eyes, then opened them, something inside me rebelling. "Hedge our bets with prayer, you mean? No, fuck that, if the Lord's our shepherd, why do we need these?" I set the pistol and ammo back in his truck. "You with me on this?"

De Carrion raised his eyebrows. "I thought you weren't even sure you believed."

"I'm not. But so what? We're in Vegas, Dan, let's bet big. Gamble that there really is a Father of Lights, and take him up on his offer."

He stood there, stock still and silent, then smiled for the first time that morning. "All right, I'm in. *You* do the praying, then. Show me what you got, preacher's boy."

"I never cared for the formulas—the *dear heavenly Father* at the start and *in Jesus' name* at the end. But when I was a kid my father made me memorize a dozen verses from one of Paul's epistles, always thought they were the best lines in all of Scripture. They'll be my prayer."

I got down on my knees, and he joined me.

The desert landscape shimmered in the distance, looking, I imagined, much like the wilderness of Judea.

"*Put on the whole armor of God, that ye may be able to stand against the wiles of the devil.*" The Apostle's words came back to me effortlessly, though I hadn't recited them in years. "*For we wrestle not against flesh and blood, but against principalities, against powers, against the rulers of the darkness of this world...*"

Chapter Fifty-Two

An Adversary There Shall Be

It wasn't hard to find the Roma Hotel and Casino, an impressive edifice surrounded by a tall palisade fence topped by spikes of silver and gold. After handing the Indian Chief off to a valet, I spent an hour cooling my heels before a young woman in a revealing tunic, her hair garlanded in roses, ushered me into the Don's office. His lair was a vast expanse on the top floor, replete with Grecian urns, leather-bound volumes on bookcases of dark burnished wood, and oriental rugs adrift on a sea of Italian marble. Floor-to-ceiling windows on three sides displayed the sun setting behind Mt. Charleston and the Strip extending north to the glitter of downtown Las Vegas. And there, sitting behind a massive mahogany desk, a bright yellow handkerchief tucked into the breast pocket of his white linen suit, was the boss of bosses himself, Salvatore Guerriero.

"Nice set-up you got here," I said, trying out my tough-guy persona. "I take it the customers don't win all that often."

He smiled, but his eyes were arctic cold. Reptilian. Hence the nickname I'd seen in *Life Magazine*: Sal the Snake.

"Please, Mr. McRae, have a seat." He gestured toward a Chesterfield sofa whose burgundy leather proved soft as butter. "Your reputation as a war hero precedes you. Most impressive. I understand you dropped bombs from planes?"

"Sure, when I wasn't firing M3 cannons and five-inch rockets."

"Hmm. Ever kill a man at close range?"

"Close enough to see the fear in their eyes."

"*Bene*. To dispose of a pastor, would that bother you? Offend your sensitivities, perhaps?"

"I don't *have* sensitivities, Mr. Guerriero."

"Well, well. Did you hear that, Bobby?" The Don turned to his left, and for the first time I noticed a figure sitting off to the side in the shadows. "A man after your own heart. If you had one, I mean."

Bobby grunted.

"Be civil." Guerriero gave him the evil eye for just a moment. "Matthew McRae, meet Robert Schultz, on loan to me from my friend Mr. Lansky. He will be helping to fulfill my end of the bargain."

The same issue of *Life* which had profiled Guerriero had featured other mob worthies, including a sadistic enforcer known as Blowtorch Bobby. He was a lean, hatchet-faced man with a twitch in his right eye.

Bobby and I nodded in each other's direction.

"I'm not seein' why you need Audie Murphy here, Sal," said Schultz. "I can take care of that *shtik drek* of a pastor along with the other five, no problem. I don't work for you any more'n McRae does, so you wouldn't have to worry about no jinx."

"True, Bobby, and in the unlikely event Mr. McRae lets us down, you'd get your chance. But it pleases me to think an operative of the federal government will remove this irritant from the face of the earth. *Capiche?*"

"Tell me about Amos," I said. "Wouldn't hurt to know his full name."

Guerriero leaned back in his chair and regarded me for a moment before speaking. "You're not a churchgoing man?"

"Got dragged along on Sundays like most kids. It didn't take."

"Hmm. For my part, I've learned much from studying the church and the ways of its pastors and priests. You're familiar with tithing? The collection plate being passed around?"

"Of course," I replied, starting to see where this was leading. "I learned to palm the dime my dad gave me to drop in each week."

The Don flashed me one of his mirthless smiles. "The Good Book calls on Christians to hand over ten percent of their income to their church, yes?"

"That pre or post tax?" asked Schultz.

"All the best scholars say pre," said Guerriero. "A position I strongly affirm. And Jews, Bobby? Do your fellow Hebrews tithe?"

"Hell no, not anymore. That *shmegegge's* strictly for *goys*."

"*Ho capito.* Consider this: what induces the voluntary payment of such a sizable tax? It's an easy choice: swear allegiance to the Lord, join His church and tithe, or roast for all eternity in the flames of hell. That convenient arrangement inspired me to craft a proposition of my own, *una variazione su un tema*. I offer each church in Las Vegas salvation, not from some distant day of judgment, but from their own imminent fiery demise. And all I ask in return is a mere ten percent of the ten percent they collect each week! Entirely reasonable, yes?"

Bobby nodded his head. "I keep sayin', you're too easy on 'em, Sal."

"Indeed. And yet, believe it or not, Mr. McRae, my associates met with some resistance from the first house of worship they approached. Of course, after my friend Bobby reduced it to a pile of ashes, the others quickly fell into line."

"Sweet," I said. "Only I take it a certain Pastor Amos has thrown a monkey wrench in the works."

"*Precisamente.* He has been stiffening the spines of the local clergy, encouraging them to take defensive measures and coordinate with the police. The man operates in a cleverly clandestine fashion. All we know is, he goes by Amos, and is rumored to have formed a church that meets under cover of darkness. Now, that shiny medal you earned in Korea will get you a warm reception in any church in this town. You've heard of the brutish threats they've received and are eager to put your skills at their disposal. A meeting with the good pastor should follow in short order." Guerriero leaned forward and fixed me with his saurian stare. "I see no reason why my problem should not be resolved within one week. Are we agreed?"

"We are," I replied. "And when is Mr. Schultz expected to complete *his* assignment? The people I work for are eager to know."

"What do you say, Bobby?" said the don. "Can you round up that reporter tonight?"

"It's Friday, Sal. Look out the window, that's called a sunset. You know I don't work on the Sabbath."

"*Ma dai,*" Guerriero muttered, rolling his eyes. "Very well, Sunday, then. Tell your people, Mr. McRae, that though our task is by far the more challenging, we will have matters in hand soon enough."

"They'll be glad to hear that," I said, and our meeting swiftly drew to a close.

Fifteen minutes later I was in my room at the Last Chance Motel, leaving messages for Kent at both the *Morning Sun* and the Long Shot Saloon: *Urgent you call me ASAP*. Then I reached over to the side table by my bed, opened up the Gideon Bible, and turned to the Book of Amos.

The prophet had preached justice and the judgment of God to the Kingdom of Israel. I read every line, stopping at times to read aloud.

For they know not to do right, saith Jehovah, who store up violence and robbery in their palaces. Therefore thus saith the Lord Jehovah: An adversary there shall be, even round about the land; and he shall bring down thy strength from thee, and thy palaces shall be plundered.

An adversary.

One who would stand up for those who could not defend themselves, who would take on the rich and powerful, lay low their fortresses, against all odds.

My heart beat faster, remembering stories from my youth, stories of a lawman driven by a passion for setting things right...

And then, in the twenty fourth verse of the fifth chapter, there it was, the line I remembered hearing at the close of so many sermons I'd been forced to attend:

Let judgment run down as waters, and righteousness as a mighty stream.

There was no doubt in my mind: Caleb McRae was the pastor standing against the mob.

Guerriero wanted me to kill my father.

Chapter Fifty-Three

A Lion in Winter

De Carrion called from Camp Pendleton not long after I'd finished reading the Book of Amos. I gave him a quick summary of the meeting with Guerriero and Schultz.

"Good work. Just tell Superman to lay low until we bust this thing open—he should clear out of town for a while. The General and I are about to sit down to dinner, he's eager to hear all the details. I'll be back up tomorrow night unless we decide to fly to D.C. and bring this thing to a head. You take care, Matt, okay?"

I wished him good luck and went back to waiting for Kent to call.

A long hour passed before the phone rang again.

"Clark here. I'm at the Long Shot, what's up?"

"We need to talk in private," I said. "I'll meet you wherever you like, but this is too important to take any chances."

"Huh." I listened to the clinking of glasses and hubbub of voices in the background while he thought. "All right, I'll be home in twenty minutes."

He gave me an address and I fired up the Indian Chief.

"Matthew McRae, man of mystery," he said, welcoming me into his apartment on Bonanza Road. "Somehow I have the feeling this is not good news. Something to drink? I'd been intending to swill down Sazeraks at the Long Shot, but now I'm thinking straight cognac."

"Sure, why not." I took a seat in his living room and looked around. Half a dozen framed movie posters were hanging on the walls: Clark Gable and Claudette Colbert in *It Happened One Night*, an especially garish one of Gable, Ava Gardner, and Grace Kelly in *Mojambo*, Vivien Leigh staring up at the rakish hero in *Gone with the Wind*. Gable in every one.

"Cheers," he said, coming back in with two snifters. "Now tell me what's going on."

"I wasn't completely honest with you the other day. So I'm going to tell you everything, because it's life and death that you believe me now." I began with what de Carrion revealed to me in Japan and brought the story forward to my meeting with Guerriero and Schultz, leaving out only any mention of my father. I felt a churning in my guts as I talked; it had been pure folly to turn down de Carrion's Browning!

Kent stared down into his drink. "Those bastards can't be allowed to harm Amos."

"They've given me a week, Clark. Col. de Carrion and General Grant will blow this thing wide open well before—" I did a double take as Kent's words caught up with me. "Wait a minute. Do you know Amos?"

"Yes." Somewhere in the apartment, the second hand of a clock ticked forward three times. "He's my pastor."

Stay focused, I told myself. *Think clearly.* "Look, you're in immediate danger. Can you take a leave from the paper, get out of Vegas before sundown tomorrow? And if you know where Annie and the others are, we need to get them to safety, too."

"I wish I did know, Matt. But you don't have to worry about me. I can stay in town and still vanish into thin air."

"Come on, these are vicious thugs, psychopaths who'll comb every square block to track you down. This is no time to prove how clever you are, let alone try and play the hero. Unless you really *are* Superman, in which case, this would be a good time to let me know."

"No, I'm no Superman, that's for damn sure." He sighed deeply. "Ah, what the hell. You're going to meet Pastor Amos, you may as well know my secret." Kent carefully peeled off his mustache, then walked into his bedroom and returned carrying a tube of lipstick and a shoulder-length wig. "I should really use liner first, but fuck it." He applied the lipstick, set the wig in place. "This, plus the right outfit, is how I disappear."

"That's amazing." He actually looked kind of cute. "I'm glad you can disguise yourself, Clark. Must come in handy for your investigative reporting, dressing up like a broad."

"It does, but that's not what I'm trying to tell you. Matt, I *am* a broad. Physically, that is. My parents named me Claire Kent, dressed me in frilly clothes, bought me dolls. But I wasn't a girl then, not on the inside, and I'm not a woman now. I'm a man trapped in a female body, a nightmare impossible for others to imagine. Only now maybe it'll save my life, for whatever that's worth."

I gaped at him, speechless.

"Come on," he said, "after all you must have seen in Korea, and what you're dealing with now, is what I've told you really so shocking?"

"No, of course I've heard of men *dressing* as women, but not—I mean—how can you be sure—"

"That I'm a man? I'm as sure as you are about yourself, have been for as long as I can remember."

"My God."

"Yes, my God indeed. My God, why have you done this to me, my God, when will you lift this from me, let me I live as I really am. When a child is born with a cleft palate or a twisted spine, we don't say it's God's will, we do everything to heal them, make them as He surely intended them to be. But not with this."

"I can't imagine what you've had to endure. It isn't fair." I felt useless, a man without a weapon to defend the defenseless, without the words that could make a difference to a man in pain.

"Yeah, well, there's a lot of shit in this world that isn't fair." He removed his wig and tossed it aside, wiped off the lipstick with a wet napkin, put his mustache back in place. "Anyway, there's a ray of hope on the horizon. Ever hear of Christine Jorgensen?"

"Yes, I saw the headlines when I was still in Korea. Had surgery overseas that changed her from a man into a woman."

"The process of transformation's a little more complicated than that, but yes, her body and soul were brought into harmony thanks to a doctor in Denmark. I'm saving my money." Kent drained the last drops from his glass. "I could use another, how about you?"

"Oh yeah." I was relieved that Kent looked like a man again, and felt ashamed of my squeamishness.

"I'll tell you why I care so much for Amos." He retrieved a bottle of Hennessy VSOP from his liquor cabinet and refilled our snifters. "He's a shepherd to outcasts. To losers. To the spat on and shit upon, to misfits and freaks like me. He's our comfort, our light in the darkness when we're too sick at heart to pray and Jesus seems like a distant dream."

Could that possibly be my father he's talking about? I wondered, feeling alternating waves of skepticism and pride, but reluctant to reveal any of that to Kent. "Could you take me to Amos? I'd like to warn him of the danger myself."

"Our next service is Sunday evening, I'll call you a few hours in advance. We change location frequently, so I don't yet know where we'll be meeting. Arnie can be our point of contact if you need to reach me before then. I'll find somewhere else to stay."

We talked of the mystery and wonder of the healings, of how de Carrion's gambit might play out, of the implacable evil that stalks the earth.

"I'm surprised you've held on to your faith," I said. "If I were in your place, I doubt I'd believe until I saw the Almighty appearing from out of the whirlwind."

"That'd be a mixed blessing—I'm not sure I could handle getting my ass chewed out quite as well as Job did. It's the Gospel stories that have kept me going, Matt. The kindness and compassion of Christ."

We drank in companionable silence for a while

"How'd you end up as a reporter?" I asked. "I'd been thinking the name Clark Kent decided your destiny, but seeing these posters makes me wonder."

He flashed me the trademark smile. "I've been a fan of Gable's ever since I saw *San Francisco* when I was ten years old. I wanted to *be* him, wanted his manliness and suave, roguish charm. But I wanted something else, too—the reporter's power to shine a light into the darkness, to separate truth from lies. What I owe to Jesus gives me a passion for exposing the hypocrites and hucksters who prey on folks in His name."

"I get it. Clark Kent is perfect."

"Irony of it is, a colleague who covers the Hollywood stars told me Gable was mistakenly listed as female on his birth certificate, and as a young actor he had a disconcertingly feminine voice. So, who knows, right?"

I laughed; who knows, indeed, about so many things. How to reconcile the compassionate pastor with the hellfire preacher? Perhaps I was reading too much into those lines of Scripture, perhaps this was all just coincidence...

Go ahead, I told myself. It shouldn't take much probing to determine whether Amos and my father were one and the same. "Hell of a challenge your pastor's taken on—he's a younger man, I imagine?"

"Actually, he's got to be pushing eighty," said Kent. "But I don't doubt Amos could make mincemeat of most younger men, the man's a veritable Samson. Has this magnificent head of hair, if I have half as much at his age, I'll give thanks. Distracting at times, that mane of his. Wasn't until I met him that I really understood what people mean by *a lion in winter*."

Ah. All doubts were laid to rest; by Sunday evening, after seven years, I'd be reunited with my father.

For better or for worse.

Chapter Fifty-Four

The Bloody Men

A great golden moon was setting behind the Spring Mountains when I returned to the Last Chance Motel and stopped at the office to check for messages. No one there, just Patti Page on the radio, singing "How Much is That Doggie in the Window?"

I read in the papers there are robbers

With flashlights that shine in the dark

I rang the bell until a bleary-eyed night clerk came in from the back room.

"Any messages for McRae, room twenty-four?"

"Sure don't think so."

"Well, check, will you?"

"Okay, okay, hold your horses."

My love needs a doggie to protect him

And scare them away with one bark

"No, sir, there ain't nothin'. That it?"

"Yeah, that's it. Thanks." I handed him a dime, which went swiftly into his pocket.

Well, what was I expecting, anyway, it could easily take all night for de Carrion to brief Grant and then agree on a plan. I was just glad the cognac would make it easier for me to fall asleep.

That night I dreamed a Doberman lay at the foot of my bed, his ears pricking up at the slightest sound from outside. He was a slavering beast, fiercely loyal to me, the name Cerberus inscribed on his spiked collar. But then, what was this? Blowtorch Bobby, coming in through a window I'd carelessly left open, and instead of being greeted by my Doberman's bared teeth and guttural growling, there were only a lap-dog's high-pitched yips...

I woke with a start, drenched in sweat. It was after eight, sunlight filtering in through the threadbare curtains. Surely de Carrion would call soon, let me know how things were going. I sat up in bed, tried to distract myself by opening the Gideon Bible at random and reading the verses at the top of the left-hand page.

And they slew the sons of Zedekiah before his eyes, and put out the eyes of Zedekiah, and bound him with fetters of brass, and carried him to Babylon...

Swell, I thought. Let's try that again.

The men that were at peace with thee have deceived thee, and prevailed against thee; they that eat thy bread have laid a wound under thee...

All right, then. Time to put the Good Book aside.

I showered and shaved, listening for the phone.

The noon hour approached, and still nothing from de Carrion.

He'd said Marlon Storm had been trying to see into his soul, find out who he really is. What if he'd slipped up somehow, and they'd intercepted him on a lonely stretch of Route 91...

Come on, McRae, I told myself. What was the point of worrying? De Carrion and the General might well be on a plane to Washington at that very minute. And I'd been the one to suggest we abandon arms for prayer.

So, pray then, fool!

King David had gotten in deep more than a few times. I opened the Gideon to the Psalms, then dropped down onto my knees.

Deliver me from mine enemies, O my God: defend me from them that rise up against me.

Deliver me from the workers of iniquity, and save me from bloody men.

For, lo, they lie in wait...

Time to leave my prison cell of a room, take a walk in the fresh air and burn off some of this nervous energy. I put a handful of dimes in my pocket so I could call in for messages, and hit the streets.

The shadows lengthened steadily, and still from de Carrion there was only silence.

Finally, as the neon lights of Las Vegas began flickering on, I found a payphone and called Camp Pendleton.

"Connect me with General Grant's office, please," I told the Marine who answered the phone.

"Neither he nor his staff are available, sir. How can I help you?"

"Is the general still on site? It's important."

"Tell me what you need, sir, and I'll see who can help you."

"Is Col. de Carrion on the premises?"

"If you're with the press, we're not making any further comments."

What the hell—could he have broken the story already, and not told me? "No, I'm just a friend of the Colonel's, one of his comrades-in-arms. What's going on?"

A moment passed, then I heard a whispering of voices.

"Who is this?" said the Marine, and something in his tone sent a chill down my spine.

I hung up the phone.

The competitor to Kent's paper, the *Review Journal*, came out in the early evening. I jogged over to a newsstand a few blocks away and forked over a nickel.

The headline was right at the top of page three:

Proving Grounds Security Chief Killed in Car Accident Near San Diego

WWII ace Col. Daniel de Carrion escaped death in the air countless times but lost his life early this afternoon in a fiery crash on California's Highway 101.

"It's a real shame," said Marine General James T. Grant. "Dan de Carrion was a good friend and a great American. Had a pleasant dinner with him just last night, but I could see the man had a drinking problem. Wouldn't doubt that's why he lost control of his car..."

Waves of shock and anger and grief ran through me. *Grant, you Judas motherfucker, there is no hole you can hide in, no corner of hell where I cannot hunt you down...*

I took a deep breath, exhaled slowly, got myself under control.

Revenge would have to wait.

Back in the phonebooth I dialed the number Kent had given me for Arnie, let it ring a dozen times before calling the *Morning Sun*.

"Is Arnie Flynn on shift tonight?" I asked.

"He was supposed to be," said the receptionist. "Hours ago. Can I take a message?"

I struck my fist against the glass wall of the booth in impotent fury; if they had Arnie, they might well find their way to Kent. "I'll call back."

Storm and Guerriero knew I was working with de Carrion, so their underlings were no doubt searching for me. Not to mention the police, and perhaps even the Marines. That I was still alive, though, meant de Carrion hadn't broken. No matter what they'd done to him, he'd toughed it out to the end.

It was up to me, then, to slay the minotaur, with whatever help the heavens cared to offer.

A fragment from the Psalms came into my mind: *Plead my cause, O Lord, fight against them that fight against me, let them be as chaff before the wind...*

Some say the age of miracles is over, my father had once said, but he didn't agree, for he'd seen them with his own eyes.

The Long Shot was only a few blocks away, but there was no point in going back there. I had the microfilm, most of the two hundred fifty bucks de Carrion had given me, and it seemed best to stay on foot, much as it pained me to abandon the Indian Chief.

Wait a minute.

I reached into the left front pocket of my Levi's. *Empty.* After my shower, distracted by my concern over de Carrion's silence, I'd put on the wrong jeans.

The microfilm was in my other pair.

All right, nothing to do but retrieve it. I backtracked to an F.W. Woolworth, bought a cheap fedora, pulled it down low to shadow my eyes, and walked with shoulders slumped, bent over like a thousand other losers on the streets of Las Vegas.

I walked slowly past my motel room. The curtains were still drawn, just as I'd left them, and the couple in twenty-five were arguing loudly. *Okay, let's get this done.* I circled back, slipped my key in the lock, turned the handle, and stepped inside the darkened room.

Then froze at the sight of a man's body on the floor, lying in a pool of blood.

"Don't move," someone whispered behind me, and, swift as a shadow, held a six-inch blade to my throat. "Matthew McRae?"

A woman's voice.

"What the hell's going on?" I asked. "Who *are* you?"

"What's your mother's name, McRae?"

The steel on my neck stole my breath.

"Answer me."

I could hear the faint sound of a police siren in the distance.

"Valentina," I said, and the knife was withdrawn.

I turned to see the slender young woman from the Wash.

Chapter Fifty-Five

Tom Collins, Extra Cherries

"I'm your cousin Valerie," she said. "Elliana's daughter."

I stared at her blankly, in a state of shock. "My father never told me I had any relatives at all." *Much less a knife-wielding cousin.* I knelt down to get a closer look at the corpse on the floor, a Smith & Wesson .357 still clutched in his hand. *One of Guerriero's goons, no doubt, shame it's not Blowtorch Bobby. The sun's only just set,* he'll *probably be coming after me next.* I considered taking the revolver, then thought better of it. I'd stick with the plan, it was working well enough so far.

"You owe me one," she continued. "He was bad news."

The police siren was growing steadily louder.

"There's one thing I need to do, then we gotta get out of here." I retrieved the microfilm, feeling as though I were waking from a dream. There were a thousand questions I wanted to ask, but no time...

"Relax, it was self-defense." She slipped her blade back into a hidden holster.

I thought once again of the photo in my wallet, now certain my mother's waist had been encircled by a belt of knives.

"This guy's got mob written all over him," Valerie continued. "What'd you do, borrow from a Shylock?"

"It's a long story, but trust me, we don't want anything to do with the cops."

A shadow crossed her face. "*Fuck.* I just killed a man. Running away is only going to make me look guilty. If those cops are heading this way, great, why wouldn't I clear things with them right now?"

"Because they're on the take," I said, figuring I'd keep it simple for the moment. "Look, I'm one of the good guys, Valerie, you've got to believe me. I'll explain as soon as I can."

Her eyes bore into mine for an agonizing few seconds.

"Okay. You're lucky I need you. So what now?"

"Did you drive here?"

"No, I rode the Dog from LA. I've been hitching or hoofing it since."

"Good, we're better off on foot." And they'd trace a car to her for sure. "Come on, there's a place nearby where we can lay low."

Valerie followed me out the door.

"They won't be looking for a couple." I put my arm around her. "If you don't mind."

She rolled her eyes but leaned in close to me.

We were walking briskly, passing others on the sidewalk. *Not a good idea.* "Much as I'd like to hightail it, let's slow down, blend in with the crowd. And call me Matt, cousin."

"All right. It's Val for me. I was named after your mom."

"I'd likely have been a dead duck if you hadn't shown up, Val. But how in the name of God—" The sound of the siren peaked, then cut out, not far away. *Just another block to go.* "Of course, you must have recognized me at the Wash. Only we've never met, I never even knew you existed."

"I found your old high school and sweet-talked my way into looking through its yearbooks. Would have found you sooner, but I fell ill that night at the Wash and spent yesterday sleeping it off. This morning, after I tried all the Matthew McRaes in the phonebook, I began calling every hotel and motel in Las Vegas. Started with the Acme Inn; good thing you weren't staying at the Zanzibar Lodge. I'd torn out your picture, showed it to Eddie at the front desk, so I knew it was the right McRae at the Last Chance. Then when I saw Bluto breaking into your room, it pissed me off. You can figure out the rest."

"So you came here from L.A. How'd you know I was in Vegas?"

"I didn't. I was looking for your father, and when I couldn't find him in L.A., I came here, where you were born and Aunt Tina died."

"Ah. So that's why you need me."

"Actually, it's my own dad I'm looking for, I was hoping yours could help me find him. I only just found out who my father is."

"I'm not sure which of our stories will end up being stranger. Your dad anyone I might know?"

She looked up at me.

"Henry Midnight."

Inside the Dance-O-Rama, the Swing-a-thon was just shifting into high gear. We made our way to the farthest, darkest corner which still afforded a line of sight to the front entrance. Concern over my decision not to take the Smith & Wesson gnawed at me; what good would Val's blade be against Blowtorch Bobby and the muscle he'd no doubt bring with him? What if I'd used up my quota of miracles?

O ye of little faith!

Worst case, there was an emergency exit not ten yards away.

"I've more than half a mind to cut out now and take my chances finding Henry Midnight on my own," Val said after we'd sat down. "But I'm going to hear you out. What's going on here, Matt? Just what sort of trouble am I mixed up in?"

Where to begin? "I flew fighter-bombers for the Marines in Korea," I told her, and described how the nightmare I experienced in the war had made me eager to join forces with de Carrion. I spoke of the evil that was being worked at the Proving Grounds; of the unholy alliance between the feds and the mob; of my meeting with Guerriero and Schultz at the Roma, how they had their sights set on the Atomic Man and those he'd healed, and on Kent and the pastor I was sure was my father.

I told her Dan had been killed that morning, betrayed by a man he'd trusted like a brother.

That it was up to me to carry on and slay the minotaur.

Val was silent for a while. "That's a hell of a story," she said at last. "Inspiring, actually. Damn shame I just quit smoking, though. But I haven't given up liquor." She waved to a cocktail waitress. "Hey, over here!"

"Maybe that's not such a good—"

"Order yourself a glass of milk if you want, flyboy," said my cousin. "I need a drink."

"What'll you love birds be having?" asked the waitress, whose nametag read Betty Jo.

"Tom Collins," said Val. "Heavy on the cherries."

"Same for me." I raised my eyebrows at her as Betty Jo walked away.

"We're blending in, right? And I've got a soft spot for maraschinos."

Could I laugh in the midst of such a dire situation? Apparently so.

"So do you have a plan?" she continued. "For going after the minotaur, I mean. Not to mention escaping from the Marines, mobsters, and crooked cops. Or are you just winging it at this point?"

"Do you believe in God?" I asked her. "Because at this point, I'm just trusting in Him to guide me."

"Oh, swell. So you figure *He* sent me to the Last Chance motel to save your ass?"

I shrugged. "Who knows? I'm grateful to you, Val, either way. And don't feel bad about cutting out, this isn't your fight."

"Ah, jeez, relax. Shouldn't have given you a hard time, I've been trying to cling to faith myself. We can help each other, Matt. You need a wingman, right? Or better yet, a wingwoman who's handy with knives. Truth is, I've dreamed of fighting in an epic battle, one like my mom fought in long ago—and what better than side by side with my long-lost cousin? So here's how I see it: we wend our way through the labyrinth, deep-six any bastards who get in our way, make mincemeat of the minotaur, and find both our fathers. What d'you say?"

An electric thrill ran through me. As bad as things seemed, this was a gift I wouldn't trade for anything, this sudden sense of connection between Val and me, coming out of nowhere, and I found it astonishing and wonderful. We were blood, we were a team.

That she didn't share my jaded view of combat was another matter...

"I've fought enough battles to pray I never need fight another, epic or otherwise. But you're on. I'm glad not to be in this alone."

"You said your dad never mentioned my mom, Elliana? She and Tina fought alongside him in Texas—they were friends for over twenty years!"

I felt a surge of anger. How much of what he'd told me had been a lie? "Son of a bitch, Val. The story was, he'd met Tina Juarez for the first time at his church in '27, the year before I was born. He told me it was love at first sight, and they were married a few months later."

"Oh wow. That's—" She stopped abruptly.

"What? Don't you hold out on me, too."

"All I know is what mom told me: that her sister went to the ranch because she wanted a child by either Caleb or Henry. Obviously, Tina chose your dad, but she was going to go raise the kid by herself. She just never planned on dying in childbirth."

"Swell, I'm a bastard. Well, that figures." A thought occurred to me, and I took out my wallet and showed Val the picture. How could I trust *anything* my father had said? "This is her, right? It's the only one I've got."

She studied the photograph for a while and smiled. "Oh yeah. That's from back in the days when she and my mom were The Juarez Sisters and their Blades of Death. They were one of Barnum & Bailey's star attractions."

"She taught you well, huh. And told you the truth, which is more than I can say for dear old dad."

"You two look entirely too serious," said Betty Jo, as she set down our Tom Collinses. "Now drink up, join the party, and shake a leg."

"Hey, the night is young," I told her. "Give us time."

"I can see he's the shy type," she said to Val. "You just pick your moment and drag him out there." Betty Jo winked at me and moved on as the Dance-o-Rama band struck up "Keep Cool, Fool," their singer doing a fair impression of Ella Fitzgerald.

"I know what it's like for the world to get turned on its head, Matt," said Val. "I didn't meet my mom until I was six years old, and only just learned Henry's my real dad."

"You may have me beat after all. Tell me more, especially about Midnight. I never met the man."

"Okay. But maybe we ought to lower the level of these drinks a bit—just for appearances, of course."

We clinked glasses.

"Back in the aughts," she continued, "when my mom was in the Rio Grande Valley, fighting bad guys with your dad and Henry and Tina, she met a young man, Lou Cooper, who joined their cause. The four of them were among a handful who survived a big, bloody battle. Not long after that, Lou and my mom were married, though they weren't but sixteen or seventeen years old."

I listened as she told me the sad story of what had happened to Lou in the Great War and after his return. Out on the dance floor couples were jitterbugging and jiving, whirling and diving, doing the Boogie Woogie and the Balboa and the Carolina Shag. *That was me, a million years ago, in another life, dancing away Saturday nights without a care in the world. But that's a lie, isn't it, there was always my father in the back of my mind.*

Why had he hidden so much from me? What else didn't I know?

"My mom searched for Lou," Val was saying, "even hired a detective, and came up empty year after year. She and Tina travelled to Nevada on one of those expeditions and stayed with your dad and Henry. That's when she met the Zabalas, a Basque family who ranched up in Elko, where I spent the first ten years of my life. Mom became best friends with their daughter, Joska Griffin. She'd married a man you might have heard of, Cornelius Griffin."

It only took me a moment to place the name. "Sure, the guy who wrote all those western novels and then met some sort of untimely end."

"Oh, it was plenty timely, Matt. Griffin was a despicable bastard. The longer he and Joska were married, the more abusive he became. Not that he ever touched her, but words can do more damage than fists. My mother told me his were sharper than any blade."

"It was his wife who killed him, then?" I asked Val when she paused.

"Other way round. He drove Joska into the depths of depression until one night she ended her life. Mom had sworn to him she'd exact revenge if he ever harmed her friend, and she was true to her word. I don't think she went there intending to kill the man, but mom herself was in a dark, despairing mood and the confrontation got out of hand. She was convicted of manslaughter and sentenced to ten years in the State Penn in Carson City. And that's where I was born, in 1929."

"My God, Val. So then, how in the world—"

"Did Henry Midnight become my father? I'm getting there, cuz." Our drinks had quickly become more than props, and she motioned to Betty Jo for two more.

Was that wise? Well, neither Blowtorch Bobby nor the Marines had yet come storming in. I resigned myself to the protection of our guardian angels and sent up a silent prayer for a few hours of peace.

"Back in '28 mom had just about given up hope of ever finding her husband. She and Tina had left the circus and gone their separate ways, mom to Elko so she could be close to her best friend. Not long after she received the news of Tina's death, Henry showed up, morose, unsure of what he'd do with his life now that he and Caleb were no longer together. He and Mom had always been close friends, Matt. The two of them got to drinking and comforting one another and ended up sleeping together that night.

"The next morning they both awoke feeling guilty as sin. Henry swore he was going to make amends, move heaven and earth to find Lou Cooper and bring him back to her. Well, those were just empty words as far as mom was concerned, she grew more despondent than ever even before word came just weeks later that Joska had done herself in. So it was little short of a miracle she didn't follow in her friend's footsteps when a doc at the State Penn told her she was two months pregnant."

"Honestly," said Betty Jo, setting down our drinks, "you two are going to have to lighten up before the night's done."

We made a pretty good dent in those Tom Collinses before Val resumed her story.

"After I was born, Joska's brother Zorion and his wife took me in, just as they had done for Joska's children, and loved me like I was one of their own. But I don't think mom would have survived behind bars, Matt, if Henry Midnight hadn't been true to his word and tracked down her husband not two years later. Henry could work wonders with herbs and ointments and the healing wisdom he'd learned from the Indians, and he brought all that to bear on Lou Cooper, got the man back on his feet, restored him to his right mind. By '33 Lou was living in Carson City and visiting mom as often as they'd let him. He drove to Elko once a month to see me, too. Uncle Lou, that's how I knew him. Then in '35 mom was released on parole. We all lived together in the Zabala compound for the next few years, she and Lou worked on the ranch, and I came to know them as mom and dad.

"Best part of the story, though, is what happened next. She and Lou couldn't have kids, so they started taking in strays, children who'd been abandoned, or whose folks were in jail, or had passed away without a relative to claim them. By the time the war broke out, they had five or six, and then Grandpa Abarran—Zorion's dad—put up the money for them to start a little orphanage, help as many youngsters as they could. Named it *Children of God*. They moved to Reno five years ago, now they care for more than fifty kids. Then this spring, mom started wasting away from a cancer that just ate up her insides, took her down faster than I could ever have imagined. Before she went, she and Lou told me the truth about Henry. Told me he was a fine man, someone I could be proud of, that he'd stayed away because he didn't ever want to come between me and Lou. I don't even know if he's still alive. Been twenty years since my folks last saw him, so I was hoping you or your dad knew something, or at least had a lead I could follow."

"I don't, but we'll get the truth out of my old man, whatever it takes, once we track him down. So—" I lifted my glass. "Here's to finding lost fathers, wherever they may be."

"Now you're talking," she said, and her smile warmed my heart.

"Tell me something," I ventured, half thinking about asking Betty Jo to bring us two whiskeys. "I can see why Henry chose to give you guys space, but it's never made sense to me Henry and my father would just vanish from each other's lives. I mean, after two decades of friendship, and God knows how many adventures."

"Friendship?" Val looked at me with raised brows. "I guess that's one way to put it."

"Well, business partners, too, but my father never came clean with what went wrong. So he chose to raise me after my mother died—wasn't that simply the right thing to do?"

"Oh shit, Matt. You don't know, do you."

"Know what?" I asked, but there was no need for her to answer, for the clues Kent had given me had just fallen into place. "Oh, of course. They were lovers."

I spoke without expression, though inside I was reeling. *My father's decision to raise me, that must have broken them up.*

"Look, if finding this out about your dad upsets you, get over it. Mom looked up to your dad and Henry, thought they were two of the finest men she'd ever known."

He's a shepherd to outcasts, Kent had told me, *to misfits and freaks.* And he hadn't wanted his son to think of him that way, so he'd buried the truth under layers of lies...

"What must it have been like for him, all those years, as a Baptist pastor?" I mused out loud. "Maybe now he's finally got a pulpit he can preach from without feeling like a fraud. You know what? Strange as all this is to me, for the first time in my life, I'm starting to understand him."

"I know a man working up his courage when I see one," said our waitress, who had an unnerving ability to catch us unawares. "Refill might just do the trick, what do you say?"

"I'm game," said Val.

"Hold on, Betty Jo," I said. "How's the Dance-o-Rama fixed for mezcal?"

Chapter Fifty-Six

Our Lady of Lourdes

Up on stage, the band had a railway theme going, with "Take the 'A' Train" followed by "Chattanooga Choo Choo." Val and I drank toasts to the departed, to Elli and Joska and Dan, to the nameless Korean woman and her baby, whose fiery deaths still haunted my dreams. We even drank to the memory of Cornelius Griffin, that his soul might find redemption in the afterlife, if such a thing were possible.

"I think mom wanted that for him, too," Val said. "In her better moments, at least. And oh! She'd gone to see you a couple times. Secretly, like a shadow, without letting you or your dad know. Henry had told her to stay away, that Caleb wanted to start over, start fresh, but it was killing her not to at least get a glimpse of her nephew now that her sister was gone."

"I'm glad you told me. I've wondered whether the woman I saw was just pure imagination, a phantom born of longing for the mother I'd never known. Another mystery solved."

We drank and talked, shared the triumphs and disasters of our young lives. I told her stories from my childhood, tales of the tumultuous relationship I'd had with my father—my hero and my tormentor!—and how I'd found relief in dance and flight.

Just then the band broke into "Lady, be Good," my foot started tapping, and I thought, *Sweet Jesus, it's been forever since I've had a chance to swing.* "Hey Val, what do you say we make Betty Jo's night and cut a rug out there?"

She looked at me blankly.

"For just a few tunes, anyway," I continued. "I mean, it being Swing-a-thon Saturday Night and all. Just for the sake of appearances."

A few moments passed before she spoke.

"I'm a strange girl, Matt. I can hurl blades with the best of them, make your jaw drop with the Wheel of Death and the Devil's Door and the William Tell. But I'm a zero when it comes to dancing, I'd only trip over my own feet."

"*That's* what your worried about?" I refilled Val's glass from the bottle of mezcal Betty Jo had brought us. "Look, you don't know who you're dealing with here. I'm the best lead there ever was, cuz. In no time I'll have you thinking you were born to dance. We'll wait till they slow down the tempo, then I'm going to take you for a whirl."

"Ah jeez. Okay, but don't say I didn't warn you."

When the band struck up "Easy Does It," I took Val's hand firmly in mine and led her out onto the floor. Had I lost a step or two in the years since I'd last danced? No, I'd been blessed with a body that didn't so much move as *flow*, the music running through me, filling my lungs and coursing through my veins, tingling in my fingers, passing through to my partner as a current of joy.

She was fine, of course, shedding her awkwardness in the first few minutes, gaining confidence through "Ain't Misbehavin'" and "Sunrise Serenade" and "String of Pearls."

What a splendid time! It was almost as though we were in another world, an alternate universe where there were no malevolent forces seeking me out...

Almost.

Out of the corner of my eye, I saw what I'd been foolish enough to think might never happen: two policemen entering the Dance-o-Rama and scanning the crowd.

"Don't look," I said, "but we've got company."

"Give me the word," she whispered, "and I can have a blade in each hand."

"*No,*" I whispered back. "Ixnay on the knives. Fighting with cops is a bad—"

"We gonna slow things down now," said the band leader. "Give y'all a chance to get close, startin' with one of my favorites, 'Come Rain or Come Shine.'"

We drew together and stayed toward the middle of the dance floor, sheltered from view, for several numbers. Eventually, I worked up my courage, maneuvered us through the crowd to the strains of "It's Only a Paper Moon," and took a look around.

"They're gone," I told her, and we headed back to our table.

"Well I'll be damned," she said. "Maybe there *is* someone up there looking out for you."

Had the police even been there at all, or had I only imagined them? Regardless, I felt jolted back into reality. We couldn't stay at the Dance-o-Rama forever.

"What we need is rest," I said. "Look at things fresh in the morning. When we were walking I noticed a place a block from here, the All-In Motel." I handed her some of the cash from my billfold. "Safest bet is for you to go there and get us a room; I'll watch from a distance and knock when the coast is clear."

I left a dollar tip for Betty Jo, then we lingered near the entrance until a large group left the Dance-o-Rama and we followed them out into the night.

"You know what's the most amazing thing about this whole damn day?" I said after settling in on the motel room couch, Val having taken the bed at my insistence.

"Tell me."

"You coming into my life, when all these years I thought my father was the only family I had."

"I wish my folks had told me about you years ago, Matt. Can you imagine if I'd sought you out in L.A., when we were both in our teens?"

I smiled into the darkness, thinking of us double-teaming my father. "We'd have been serious trouble, that's for sure."

"Shitty that we're only meeting now," she murmured. "When there's so little time."

She's finally letting down the façade of bravado, I thought. "It really isn't fair to you, Val, getting sucked into this mess. This is my fight. I should have set you straight on that from the start."

"The hell with that, we're in this together. What I said about time, it came out wrong, I'm just too tired to make sense right now. Got to sleep."

I left it there, closed my eyes, and soon fell asleep myself.

She's hiding something from me, I thought, finding myself awake in the hour before dawn, musing over the words Val had spoken: *So little time.*

"You up?" I whispered.

"Oh yeah."

"There's something that's been prowling in the back of my mind ever since I first saw you. A question."

"Well, out with it. I don't bite."

"What brought you to the Wash, Val?"

"Oh, that. And I thought you were going to ask my astrological sign. Which is Scorpio, by the way, if you hadn't already guessed." She turned on the light by the side of her bed and looked over at me. "Okay, here it is: There's a tumor growing somewhere deep in my brain. Like mother, like daughter, right? The damn thing's only recently started to affect me, and most days I can almost pretend it's not there."

"There's a cure, isn't there? There must be," I said stupidly. The thought of losing my new-found cousin was a punch in the guts. "How do they treat tumors in the brain?"

"Zorion arranged for me to see a big-shot doc in L.A., who told me surgery's not possible. There's a new approach, though, using atomic radiation, he thinks might have a chance of working. But honest to God, Matt, the treatment sounds worse than death, and I can tell from his voice it's a long-shot bet. So, yeah, having the Atomic Man work one of his miracles seemed a damn sight better to me. Just the sort of thing a flighty girl would do, right? But what the fuck."

"What's the doc say the outlook is if you do nothing?"

"Maybe a year, if I'm lucky."

"If there's any chance atomic radiation can heal you, Val, you've got to do it, no matter how bad it sounds. Look, we're blood, right? So let's make a deal. We get through the labyrinth together, then I'll be by your side while you go through that treatment, every step of the way."

She studied me for a few moments.

"That's gallant of you, Matt, but I'm not yet ready for an atomic head massage. Let's exhaust all supernatural options first. How're you at prayer?"

"I've spent more time on my knees than I care to remember, though admittedly much of that was under duress. I gave it up for years after leaving home. Of late I've taken to it with a new enthusiasm."

"Born of desperation. I know the feeling."

"As did King David, so we're in good company. Got a Gideon's over there?"

Val opened the end-table drawer and handed me a well-worn Bible. "The Zabalas were church-going Catholics. I was baptized as an infant, attended mass once or twice a week. So I prayed for my mom when she got sick. Priests say God always answers prayers, but in His own way and in His own sweet time, though that's not quite how they put it. That's the part that's hard to swallow."

"Toughest thing for me is when I finish praying and all that follows is a mocking silence. I feel I'm sending my prayers up into the void, the great emptiness. Truth is, I have a pretty meager faith."

"I don't know, Matt. That was one mammoth leap of faith when you and Dan left your weapons behind." She sat up and wrapped the covers around herself. "I'll show you something, if you promise not to laugh. Bring me my bag, will ya?"

She rummaged through her shoulder bag, bringing out a small bottle about a quarter filled with clear liquid.

"Lourdes water," she told me. "From France. Zorion brought it to my mom; Lord only knows what it took for him to get it. Pilgrims drink it, bathe in it, seeking miracles. There are prayers you're supposed to say, of course. At first mom spoke them just to make Zorion happy, but by the end she clung to the hope of those words. I told her to go ahead and down the whole bottle, but she insisted on saving some in case I was ever in need. Think it'd be batshit crazy for me to try it?"

"Hell no, if this isn't the time to pull out all the stops, when would be? Bottoms up, I say. Do you know any of the prayers?"

"Well, the gist of them, anyway." She pulled out the cork and bowed her head. "*Blessed Virgin Mary, Our Lady of Lourdes, pray for me, have mercy on me, heal me for the greater glory of Our Lord Jesus Christ.*"

"Amen," I said as she downed the sacred water. "Now let's have David pray for us." I flipped through the Bible till I found the Psalm I was looking for. "Here we go, this one works for the both of us:

Bless the Lord, O my soul, and forget not all his benefits:

Who forgiveth all thine iniquities; who healeth all thy diseases;

Who redeemeth thy life from destruction; who crowneth thee with lovingkindness and tender mercies..."

"Tender mercies, I like that." She lay back down and switched off the light. "Keep reading, Matt, it's soothing as shit to just lie here and listen."

I read half a dozen Psalms before the soft sounds of Val's breathing told me she'd fallen asleep. My mind soon filled with the threats we faced: how to evade the enemy and warn my father now that there seemed no way to contact Kent? And how could I bring down Marlon Storm, if indeed he was the minotaur at the heart of this darkness?

Come on, I told myself. *Think like a Marine. What would I have done back in Kor—*

No. That's exactly how I don't *want to think.*

So, then, what?

Pray, fool, I told myself, and got down on my knees.

There followed, of course, only that same yawning chasm of silence. Apparently, the Lord doesn't bark out orders like a CO in the Marines. Fine, I'd settle for a still small voice, anything.

But maybe this is about patience.

All right, so be it.

I lay back down and soon dozed off.

"Matt!"

I was doing my stint with forward air control, just north of Seoul, the air crisp and cool on a fine October day, watching the bursts of orange fire as the incendiaries found their targets, the sound of napalm like the veil of the temple being torn, and then the woman came running from the railway tunnel, her baby strapped to her back, both of them engulfed in flames; but how was it possible that she was calling my name?

There's no one else to blame, not the KPA, not the generals who believe each battle is the one that will turn the tide of war, not the madmen in Harvard's secret labs, not Satan himself; there's only my sin, only me...

"Matt, wake up!"

I fought my way free of the dream like Houdini escaping from his manacles and chains after being tossed into the depths of the sea, swam up to the surface of consciousness and opened my eyes.

"Come quick." Val was standing by the window, peeking through the curtains.

I joined her and looked where she was pointing.

"What?"

"Don't you see them?" she asked me, incredulous.

"See what?"

"Damn! Close your eyes for a moment, then look again."

I did as she said.

There in the parking lot of the All-In Motel, luminous in the early light of dawn, was a trail of golden footprints, extending out into the street beyond.

Part Six

The Burning

Chapter Fifty-Seven

The Church on Misfit Row

"Part of me says this is only a damn dream," said Val. "Or a hallucination born of desperation and desire. But you see them too, I can tell, and you're right here in the flesh."

I stared out the window in awe and amazement. There were more than a few people up and about, and it was clear no one but us could see the miracle that to my eyes was now plain as day. "I admit, when I read about the footprints in the paper, I didn't believe they were for real. But there they are. And why not? There'd not be much point in praying if prayers were never answered."

A lone tear trickled down the side of her face.

"I'm not even going to shower, let's just get out of here." She gathered up her handbag and tossed me my fedora. "I don't think I could stand it if we let those footprints disappear."

"Val, with the cops and mobsters and Marines that are sure to be out on the streets, you'd be safer walking that golden path without me. This is about *you* getting healed. I'll wait for you here and figure out what we do next."

She came over and put her hands on my shoulders, a fierce look in her eyes. "Fuck that. I don't know if it's our prayers for healing that've been granted, or for your quest to slay the minotaur, but I'm willing to bet on both."

Ah! We were fellow warriors, we were blood.

"You're right," I said. "We'll follow those footprints together, wherever they lead."

No one paid us any attention as we walked briskly along the golden trail. It led across the railway tracks, through the seedy quarter where only days earlier I'd met Dan, then skirted a junkyard where small children scoured the trash for treasure and played in the rusting shells of abandoned cars. Eventually we came to the outskirts of a settlement of sorts, separated from us by a deep ditch. Whoever left the glowing footsteps had crossed a rickety wooden bridge with not a few large gaps between its rotting boards.

"Well ain't you two just as cute as a basket o' kittens," said a voice drenched in scorn. A man stepped from the shadows, dressed in ragged clothes. He had a hunchback and a scraggly beard and an evil glint in his eye.

"What's goin' on up there, Homer?" called a querulous female voice from down in the ditch.

"Just some fools followin' the gold, Hazel darlin'."

"Well, slit they's throats pronto, hon, and I'll fix us a fine stew for dinner."

Val took a step forward and unsheathed her blade.

I motioned for her to put it away.

"I'm Matthew, and this is Valerie," I said. "We've got no quarrel with you, Homer. Nor with you, ma'am," I added in a louder voice. "All we want to do is cross this bridge."

"Oh! Is that all?" asked the hunchback, more sardonic than ever. "Hear that, Hazel? All they wants is to come across!"

A double-headed battle axe appeared in his hand.

"That'll be an icy day in the bowels of hell, husband."

Hazel rose up from the ditch bearing a pitchfork, the irises of her eyes crimson red.

"I can take them both," Val whispered. "Just say the word."

"No," I said, for the first time in a long while confident I knew exactly what had to be done. "Follow me."

I walked forward, took the first step onto the bridge, Val right behind me, and as we passed them, Hazel's and Homer's forms shimmered, became translucent, then dissolved into smoke and blew away.

"Holy shit, McRae!" Val let loose with an appreciative whistle once we'd reached the other side. "Now *that's* what I call trusting in the Lord."

We followed the glowing footprints along a dirt road and into a ragged little town, a place of ramshackle homes built of wood scraps, tar paper, and tin. We'd been walking for the better part of three hours; the sun was nearly to the zenith and our throats were parched, so we paused by a handpump in the shade of a sweet acacia, home to a mischief of magpies who filled the air with their raspy chatter. We drank our fill and washed our faces with cold water.

"Matt!" Val grasped my arm. "Is it just me, or have the footprints ended?"

I looked around. There were none to be seen ahead of us, and already the ones behind were fading.

"*Dante!*" called an unseen girl. "Come here, you naughty boy!"

A small, brown-skinned child toddled into view, naked but for his poopy diapers. He looked up at us, wide-eyed, and sucked his thumb.

"There you are!" A young girl joined us under the acacia and took hold of Dante's free hand. "Oh, hello!" She favored us with an ingratiating smile. "Sorry for the stink! I'm this little one's sister, Miranda."

"Where are we?" I asked her after we'd introduced ourselves. "Is this still Las Vegas?"

"I'm not rightly sure," she said. "We just call it *home.*"

"We're home, then," said Val. "I like that."

"There's that there, though," said Miranda. "If you want something official."

She was pointing to a street sign, no different from the ones downtown, that seemed out of place next to the tumbledown hovels lining the dusty road.

"'Empyrean Way,'" I read aloud. Some city planner had either named it in a moment of manic optimism or with cruelly dark humor.

"Most folks call this Misfit Row. Come on, Dante," she said to her brother, "let's get you outta those so I can wash your little butt."

"We'll give you some privacy," I said. "But did you happen to notice any, uhm, golden footprints? Maybe you get those here from time to time?"

"Yup," she said. "We were playing in them before they disappeared."

"Do you know where they led to?"

She favored us again with the sunniest of smiles. "To the church, of course! It's just down the street."

And so off we went.

A man with stumps for legs waved to us from his doorstep, and we greeted him in return. Occasionally, faces peered out at us, one of them with only a cavity where his nose should have been.

A leper, perhaps.

Fifty yards or so farther on, a somewhat taller building came into view, though it was no more impressive than any of its neighbors. Its paint was peeling, its windows cracked or boarded up. I could just make out faded letters above the weather-beaten front door, that read:

House of Glory

I turned the handle, and we entered.

"Hello?" I called out. "Anyone here?"

No answer.

Though the plank flooring seemed ancient, it had been swept clean, and the air smelled of sandalwood and amber. Dust motes sparkled in the sunlight filtering in through the higher windows.

All I could hear were our own footsteps.

We walked through an entryway that led to a worship room and stood there for a moment, looking at the empty pews.

"Listen," Val whispered.

From somewhere in the distance came the muffled sound of a man praying. Or was he chanting?

We traversed a hallway that led past a warren of small rooms, ending in a chapel at the back of the church. Inside, kneeling at the altar, was a Native American man, his hair in two braids that hung down nearly to the middle of his back.

"Excuse me, sir," I said, once he'd risen from his knees. "I'm Matthew, and this is my cousin Valerie. We've been following the trail of golden footprints, and it's led us here. Are you the one who can help us?"

He was a middle-aged man with a long, thin, face, his skin a dark, rich, reddish-brown, and he studied us before talking. "Always the Healer has been the one to seek out those who need him. This is the first time any have found their way here—it's wonderfully strange. You met Homer and Hazel, then? And were you frightened?"

"No," said Val.

"I was," I admitted. "But only for a moment. If you're not the Healer, sir, can you tell us where we can find him?"

"All in good time. I'm Benjamin Black Elk, my young friends, though just Ben will do. Perhaps *I* can help you. What is it you need?"

"Miracles, I'm afraid. Valerie has a tumor growing deep in her brain, where the doctors can't get to, and time's running out. And I'm fighting a powerful evil that's bent on destroying the Healer and those he's healed, and also—" I stopped, suddenly aware I'd missed the obvious.

He's a shepherd to outcasts, Kent had told me. *To misfits and freaks.*

Of course. This is the church on Misfit Row...

"Pastor Amos preaches here, doesn't he," I said.

A faint smile played on Ben's lips as his gaze shifted to something over my shoulder.

"Yes, Matthew," said a familiar voice. "He does."

I turned and found myself engulfed in my father's mighty arms.

How many times I'd thought back on the grievances I nursed against him, imagined what I might say, confronting him as a grown man and putting him in his place!

"I'm so sorry," I said, my face wet with both our tears. "For returning your letters unopened, cutting you out of my life."

He hugged me yet closer. "*Provoke not your children to wrath, ye fathers*. Forgive *me,* Matt; it was my failure when you left."

"I know the truth now," I whispered, overwhelmed by the emotions coursing through me. "Or at least more of it. About you and Henry, I mean. And when you met my mother."

If his embrace had been any tighter, it would have been impossible to breathe.

"Father!" I exclaimed, realizing with a start how awkward Val must feel. "This is cousin Valerie, Elliana's daughter."

"I've been looking for you, Uncle, because I'm trying to find *my* father, Henry Midnight."

"She's gravely ill," I said. "We came here following the Healer's footsteps."

"I'm sorry for your suffering, Valerie." He reached out and took her hands in his. "But you've come to the right place. For the two men you seek are one and the same."

"*Henry Midnight?* My father is the one who guided us here?"

"That you followed in his footsteps I have no doubt. But Henry will be as shocked as you are to hear of it. Early this morning he left to help a man afflicted by the most terrible pain. This time he was not successful; still, he returned spent and exhausted, as he always does, and must sleep, or I would take you to him right away."

"I can't imagine better news than learning your own father is the one who's been working miracles," I said to Val, and then turned to my father. "We met only yesterday, and yet it's like she and I have known each other all our lives."

"That's not surprising," he replied.

"It is to me," said Val. "Usually takes me ages to warm up to my fellow humans, though I bond well enough with cats."

"Tell them, Caleb," said Ben.

"All right, I'll keep secrets no longer. You're not cousins, dear ones. You are brother and sister."

Chapter Fifty-Eight

Of Darkness and Light

"Henry Midnight is my father?" For a moment I felt like I was back in my Corsair, pulling out of a steep dive, slammed back into my seat, the blood draining from my head.

"Biologically, yes, but to me—"

"What *didn't* you lie about?" I exclaimed, a wave of rage crashing over me.

"—you could not be any more my son."

"This fucking well explains a lot. All your petty cruelties, all your—"

"Matt, take a deep—" Val started to say, but I was in no mood to slow down.

"All those years, pretending to be the perfect preacher man, you were nothing but a fraud. Well, all I care about now is my *sister* getting healed. When can Midnight work his magic?"

"It takes Henry at least a week to recover his strength." He looked at me, his blue eyes full of sorrow. "You're right, Matt. I *was* a fraud. Everything I hid from you, from the world—it was pure cowardice on my part. I don't blame you for being angry with me."

My fury drained away, leaving only a weary sense of shame at my self-righteous indignation. Would I have done any better if I'd been in my father's place? I looked back at the great lion of a man who stood before me. "You know, as a kid, it about killed me at times, thinking I couldn't measure up to you. To the legend of Caleb McRae. But the way things were between us wasn't all your fault. I went out of my way to get your goat, more often than I care to admit. It was—what do they call it? A vicious circle."

"You've turned terribly pale, Valerie," said Ben, who'd been sitting quietly nearby. "Do you need to rest?"

"I'm famished, actually," she replied. "Been a while since we last ate."

"There's makings for lunch in the kitchen. Why don't you and Matt whip something up, Caleb, while I walk the perimeter and make sure Homer and Hazel are in place."

"They're on *your* team?" I asked.

"I've got myself in a dust-up with the Mob," replied my father, "and they're a sort of defensive measure. Henry's idea, actually. He's—well, you'll see. In a league of his own. Come, we'll break bread together, and I'll tell you the story of our lives, as close to the truth as I know it. Then it's my fondest hope you'll tell me yours."

My father began with Valentina's arrival at the ranch in 1927, and the harrowing story of birth and death that followed. Then he moved on to the tale of what transpired after I left to join the Marines.

The exodus of his flock at the Los Angeles Free Will Baptist Church accelerated after the end of the war. Americans were triumphant, feeling their oats, in a mood to celebrate, not bemoan the heroic role they'd played. No one wanted to hear pacifism preached from the pulpit, even if my father justified it by reminding them of God's terrible justice, of the vengeance He would wreak upon the workers of iniquity, painting gruesome pictures of the torments of hell.

One Sunday morning, when there was only a scattering of congregants in the pews and my father was so weary and dispirited he could hardly bear to deliver his sermon, two newcomers sat down in the very last row. *Indians,* my father noted. One yet older than he was, the other middle-aged and, judging from appearance, almost certainly the man's son. After the service concluded, he walked up the aisle and greeted them warmly.

"I'm Benjamin Black Elk," said the younger man, "and this is my father, Nicholas. May we invite you to lunch, so we can talk? We've travelled far to see you."

Black Elk. He'd heard the name before, but the memory was just out of reach. "Yes, of course," he replied, his spirits rising. How long had it been since anyone had sought him out? "Only it will be my treat."

"Dad speaks only Lakota, Pastor McRae, I'm here as translator. Please bear with us." Words were exchanged between Black Elk senior and his son, then Benjamin turned back to my father. "We are staying just a few blocks from here, at the City of Angels Hotel. It would be best to meet in private. We can have lunch brought to our room."

My father agreed, and after excusing himself to make sure the church was properly locked up, off they went.

Benjamin talked at first of their journey from the Lakota reservation at Pine Ridge, South Dakota, while the elder Black Elk leaned back in his chair, eyes closed. My father wondered if he was sleeping, but during one of Benjamin's pauses the old man cleared his throat and began to talk.

"We had a friend in common," he said, speaking through his son. "Wovoka. Though he was more than friend—he was my *c'iyé*, my elder brother."

Memories flooded back into my father's mind of the Paiute holy man, whom he had last seen in 1928, shortly after I was born. Bitter memories, for they hadn't parted on the best of terms, Wovoka having fiercely criticized my father's decision to move away and raise me on his own after Valentina died. *For once, turn from your pride*, he'd told him. *Give it up as an offering to the Lord. Then go, find Henry, and raise the boy together.*

"He called me to his deathbed, McRae. We shared every hour of his last days, before flights of angels sang him to his rest. How many years Wovoka and I had been brothers! I'd revered him since first we met, in the days when the Ghost Dance was still spreading among the Nations." He paused to drink some water, his hand trembling slightly as he raised the glass to his lips. "Wovoka told me of his friendship with you and your partner, Midnight. He cared much for you, Caleb McRae, and asked me to give you guidance in life, for he feared you had lost your way. Now I, too, am not far from crossing over into the next world, and it is my deepest shame to have failed in my obligation to you both. I have prayed for his forgiveness, and ask yours as—"

A knock came at the hotel room door, and an attendant entered with a cart laden with food and drink. After my father said grace, Nicholas Black Elk kept his head bowed and began to chant.

"Oh Father and Grandfather *Wakan-Tanka*, You are the source and end of everything, the One who watches over and sustains all life. Oh my Grandmother, You are the earthly source of all existence! Give to us strength which comes from an understanding of Your powers. Because You have made Your will known to us, we will walk the path of life in holiness, bearing the love and knowledge of You in our hearts. For this and for everything we give thanks."

"Amen," said my father. "That was a prayer to your God?"

"To *our* God," said Benjamin. "Dad was baptized over forty years ago and has brought many hundreds in the Nations to Christ. We find the faith of the Lakota and that of the Christian in all essential matters to be the same."

Well, thought my father, *I wonder just what you consider essential,* but he held his peace.

The three men broke bread together, and for a while there were only the sounds of munching and the clicking of soup spoons against the sides of bowls.

At last my father removed the napkin from his lap, folded it neatly, and looked across at the old man. "You were asking for forgiveness a while ago, Nicholas, but really, there's nothing to forgive you for. I've always been hard-headed, and now, at seventy-one—" He shrugged dismissively. "It's a bit late for me to change my ways."

"Nonsense." Black Elk spoke calmly, his face impassive, all the power in the import of his words. "Life changes in an instant once the eyes of the heart are opened. And only *Wakan-Tanka* knows how many winters await you, how many summer suns." He filled their coffee cups from the pot with his trembling hands without spilling a drop. "You talked much of Hell in your sermon, Pastor. Is it so important for your flock to feel fear?"

"Fear of the Lord is the beginning of wisdom," returned my father.

"Yes, but I suspect with you it may also be wisdom's end. Tell me, what is God?"

My father smiled wryly. "You mean to remind me that God is Love? I know it well. But He is also perfectly just. For our sinfulness, we deserve the flames of Hell; yet the Son willingly took the Father's wrath upon Himself instead. His sacrifice satisfied the demands of Justice, and there will be no condemnation for those who are in Christ Jesus! That is the Gospel, the Good News, the very foundation of our faith."

"Your Good News sounds exceedingly grim. Explain to me this justice you believe in, the inflicting of a punishment infinitely worse than any devised by mortal man: *eternal torment,* agony unending, for those consigned to the Pit."

It was only with some effort that my father stopped himself from rolling his eyes. "You fail to grasp the enormity of sin, Nicholas. God is utterly, infinitely holy; to Him, even the smallest offense is a horror, an intolerable affront to His righteous name."

"Your logic eludes me, my friend. The holier a *man,* the more forgiving and inclined to mercy, even to the most miserable of sinners. Am I then to believe when holiness ascends to the highest level, grace falls away?"

"Not at all!" exclaimed my father, his temperature rising. "Salvation is ours simply by repenting and trusting in Jesus. Are you demanding the Lord save even those who will not accept Him into their hearts? Who will not repent?"

"I make no such demands. I ask you, Caleb, those who have not sought refuge in the Son before the moment of their passing, once in the fires of Hell, *will* they repent?"

My father crossed his arms and scowled. "There is no repentance after death."

"Oh? Was this by decree of the God who is Love, the One who died that Death itself might be defeated?"

"The words of Scripture suffice; in the face of mystery, I'm content to stay silent." It was absurd, debating matters of theology with Nicholas Black Elk! An estimable man, yes, but surely self-taught. And yet, something was bothering my father, something he couldn't quite name. He felt it like a stone in the pit of his stomach, growing heavier by the minute...

"Consider, Caleb: If the damned *refuse* to repent, then their sinful rebellion persists into the Ages, and they are eternally triumphant over God. But if they regret their unbelief and turn to the Lord, can you imagine Him refusing them?

He who is the Good Shepherd, who spares no effort to bring the last lost sheep back into the fold?"

Images from twenty years before, scenes my father had tried to banish from his thoughts, now filled his mind. What sins had Valentina ever committed that God could not forgive? "You speculate on matters that are beyond mortal understanding," he said, but without the passion he'd given voice to just moments before. "This is idle talk."

"Yes, it would be, if it had no bearing on the lives we lead. But we are talking about the very nature of the God we worship, what sort of Father He is—hence, what sort of fathers, what sort of men, *we* ought to be." Black Elk leaned forward, his voice calm yet intense, and he held my father transfixed by his gaze, by the light in his eyes. "Caleb, friend of my brother and thus brother to me, I speak to you as Wovoka himself would do, for our only hope lies in the truth, however painful. You drove away the love of your youth—of your life—and it has left in you a terrible emptiness, a wound you try to hide but that never heals. The boy you raised as your own son—does he love you, or only fear you? Can you say that, as the Lord is to you, so you have been to him?"

My father sat in stunned silence.

"I will show you what is at the heart of the matter," Black Elk continued. "Tell me, which is the greatest of the Commandments?"

"Thou shalt love the Lord thy God with all thy heart, and with all thy soul, and with all thy mind," my father said softly.

"Do you, my brother?"

How dare he! thought my father, and the words, *Of course, no less than you, sir,* formed in his mind, to be said in the most withering tone, but he found he could not speak.

"Caleb," said Black Elk. "You hide behind lies, thinking they keep you safe, but they have become your prison walls. Let go of your pride and speak the truth, and He who is Truth itself shall make you free."

He took my father's hands in his, and oh, what warmth and strength were in the old Lakota's hands! They had trembled only a short time before, but now seemed to possess a power that flowed through to my father like an electric current.

"The God you preach," Black Elk continued, "do you love Him with all your heart and soul and mind?"

My father looked down, overcome by despair. If only one of those hundred-pound hailstones could strike him now, if the heavens could blot out his existence, make it as though he'd never been born!

"No," he whispered, returning his gaze to Black Elk's eyes.

And with that confession, he felt the darkness lifting from his soul.

"Be of good cheer, my brother," said Black Elk. "The Gospel brings news unspeakably good: *God is light, and in Him is no darkness at all.* I am saved from sin and death through Christ Jesus, saved into eternal life! Never did I need saving from the vengeance of an angry Father."

A flood of memories swept over my father; the dreams he'd dreamed in his youth, his triumphs and then disillusionment with the Rangers, the thanks he'd given to God for the love of Henry Midnight, the battles he'd fought at his partner's side, the blessing and terror and joy he'd felt, cradling an infant boy in his arms...

The torrent of memory slowed, then ceased, and he came to himself, on his knees, his face wet with tears. Benjamin and Nicholas had both laid their hands on him and were chanting prayers in their strange and beautiful language.

Were they praying to *Wakan-Tanka*, or to the Triune God of Grace?

Interesting, thought my father. *I no longer think it makes a difference.* And at that moment a flame of love for the Creator, for Love Itself, was kindled in his heart.

Chapter Fifty-Nine

The Night of Falling Stars

The elders of the Los Angeles Free Will Baptist Church gladly accepted my father's resignation and encouraged him to move on as quickly as he could, for they'd been talking to Noel Holstein for some time behind his back. He'd sat at his kitchen table, opening up his soul in letters he sent to me that I never read, and tacked a large map of the Southwest on the wall. Dear God, let Henry still be among the living, he prayed, and tried to imagine where his lover might have gone.

Not that he had much doubt where to begin his search.

For a while he entertained the notion of saddling up and seeking out Henry on horseback, but his bones ached at the very thought, and besides, the world had changed, the roads resounded with the angry whoosh and whine of speeding steel. The days of the cowboy were truly gone. So one fine fall day my father put on his jeans and a worn flannel shirt—a bright red Scotch plaid, one Henry had given him for Christmas a lifetime ago—packed a bedroll and a change of underwear into his old Chevy pickup, and headed east on Route 66.

He stopped for dinner at the Lone Spur Café in Flagstaff, Arizona. Then walked and walked, looking for some lonely place where he could kneel down amid the glory of God's creation and pray.

Let Henry Midnight still be among the living, dear Lord, I beseech you.

Above him, the Milky Way blazed so brightly he felt he could reach up and touch the stars.

He was dressed and filling his thermos with coffee as rosy fingers spread across the eastern horizon. It's a hundred thirty miles from Flagstaff to Black Mesa, and for a while he had the radio turned up full blast, Eddy Arnold and the Tennessee Plowboys crooning "I'll Hold You in My Heart (Till I Can Hold You in My Arms)" and Tex Williams belting out "That's What I Like About the West." Then shut it off and relished the silence. He sped past fields of pale green cholla cactus, watched a Peregrine falcon swoop down on a startled starling, gazed out at fortress-like rock formations glowing in the warm light of dawn.

He parked at the base of First Mesa and walked up the steep path that led to the village of Walpi, a thousand feet overhead. What was the name of Henry's friend, the shaman? Ah, yes, unusual enough that it had stuck in his memory: Qaletaqa. But more than forty years had passed, and he'd been an old man even then.

Those young girls, though, who'd so charmed him, the shaman's great-great-granddaughters, they might still be around. Surely Midnight visited from time to time, they might well know where he lives.

When he reached the summit, my father sat down on a large rock to catch his breath.

"You are tired, sir," said a woman passing by, a large basket balanced on her head. "May I be of any help?"

"Thank you, m'am," he said, grateful for Hopi hospitality. "I'm looking for two woman I met here when they were children, who'd now be about fifty years old. They're descendants of a holy man from long ago, named Qaletaqa."

She looked at him blankly.

"They were twins," he added.

"Ah!" Her face brightened. "You mean Chosovi and Chosposi! There are some who say they turn themselves into *tu'alangwmongwu*—ghost owls, in your tongue—to take revenge on those who bring them displeasure, but they have never done me any harm. I'll take you to them."

The twins were delighted when they heard my father's tale of meeting them when their great-great-grandfather still held sway on First Mesa, and nearly crushed him with their embraces, for they had grown into women of substantial girth.

"Do you know of a man named Henry Midnight?" my father asked. "He lived here in his younger days and learned much from Qaletaqa."

Chosovi and Chosposi looked at each other and furrowed their brows.

"His accent and manner of speaking are very different from mine," my father added, "though he's about my age, and wears his hair quite long, or he used to, any—"

"*Istaqa!*" they exclaimed at the same time, reminding my father of the Hopi name Henry had been given. Coyote man, the cunning trickster.

"Where can I find him?" asked my father, his heart racing.

"Come," said Chosovi.

"Follow," said Chosposi, "and you shall see your friend shortly. He has long lived on First Mesa, in Sitsomovi. It is not far."

The threesome walked along the narrow finger that is First Mesa, a bleakness of rock high above the grasslands below, toward a cluster of stone structures several hundred yards in the distance. My father resisted the temptation to break into a run, instead matching the sisters' slow and stately pace.

After a while, Chosovi pointed to one of the humbler dwellings, about a rock's throw away. "That one. We will leave you, yes?"

My father hugged her and Chosposi, who wished him well and turned back toward home.

He jogged the rest of the way, then stopped outside the open doorway, sent a silent prayer toward the heavens, and entered into what seemed more a cave than a home.

An old man was sitting at a small table, reading a book by the flickering light of a candle. The top of his head was shaved smooth as a billiard ball, his face framed by a neatly trimmed white beard.

"Henry?" said my father, his voice a hoarse croak.

The old man turned, put down his book, and raised one eyebrow.

"Is that you, Caleb?" asked Henry Midnight. "Used to be I could count the needles on a piñon pine at a hundred paces with my naked eyes. But the flesh fails, doesn't it. Though I must say, *you* look remarkably hale."

In his imagination, my father must have rehearsed their meeting a hundred times, yet he found himself unable to utter a word.

"Oh, come, speak to me, Caleb, reassure me you're no phantom and this is not a dream."

"Henry, I—I've been the worst sort of bastard and fool. I drove you from me, and now we've wasted all this time, all these years, and I don't know if you—if you—can ever forgive—" His voice broke and he dropped to his knees.

"Ah, Caleb, I well remember how it was when I was your age." Henry moved his chair closer so my father could rest his head in his lap. "At seventy-one, things all seem a muddle, don't they, but buck up, at seventy-four enlightenment breaks upon you like glorious dawn." He ran his hands through my father's hair and sighed. "I never could resist these curly locks."

"How can you be so kind, Henry?" My father looked up at him in wonder, tears spilling from his eyes. "How is it you don't hate me?"

"Well, I *have* read that Bible of yours." Henry pulled his shirt tail out from his pants and used it to dry my father's face. "The prodigal comes stumbling back, blubbering, mouthing all manner of nonsense, but his lover—well, all right, *father*, the way Jesus tells it—pays no attention, just wraps him in his arms and kisses him and then it's fatted calf and mezcal all around, and plenty of it. But I dare not compare myself to the father in that story, Caleb, for I'm a dreadful sinner myself, as you well know. I was unfaithful to you and then went and fathered a son and daughter I've never seen, never been of use to at all." A wave of emotion passed over his face. "How *is* your boy?" he whispered.

My father rose and drew Henry to him. "Matthew's turned out much like you. He goes his own way, got your outlaw spirit, I suppose. I tried to break him like the worst sort of horseman, Henry, and now he won't have anything to do with me and has gone and joined the Marines. I've written to him, though, and tried to make amends. But wait—you said you've a daughter, too?"

"A shameful story, Caleb, though at least there's a twist to it that will warm your soul. But first, heart of my heart, do you know how I've longed for you, dreamed of you, prayed you would come and find me? Tell me, what led to this magnificent transformation?"

And so my father told Henry his tale, and once again they found joy and peace in each other's arms.

"Do you know the legend of Daedalus?" Henry asked as they lay together, side by side.

"A bit. Isn't he the one who built a labyrinth to contain some sort of fearsome beast?"

"Yes, the minotaur, half man, half bull. The evil King Minos imprisoned him and his son Icarus within the maze. But Daedalus built them wings, so they could fly away."

"Then his boy flew too near the sun, which melted his wings, and Icarus tumbled down into the sea."

"Just so. I had a dream not long ago, that you and I were the ones with those wings, soaring and swooping, and then I watched you spiraling higher and higher, and called out, Caleb, come down, you're too close to the sun. And sure enough, your wings melted."

"That figures. Leave it to me to mess things up."

"Only it turned out you needed no wings to swoop and soar," said Henry. "You could fly perfectly well all on your own. And so you can, and so you did. Straight into my arms." The candle had guttered and failed, and the sky outside his small bedroom window was dark violet. "It's the twelfth of August, by the way. Do you know what we were doing, round about forty-three years ago?"

My father laughed. "Eating roast rabbit in the desert, I imagine?"

"Well, yes, most likely, but I'm thinking of something less prosaic. We're right in the midst of the Perseids. The meteor shower we watched together, not long after we first met."

"Oh? Let's have a look, then, for old time's sake."

The two men pulled on their clothes, clambered up onto the roof of Henry's stone dwelling, leaned against each other, and gazed up at the glory of lights God had set in the great vault of the sky.

Stars tumbled from the heavens until the early hours of the morning, graced the earth with their brightness, then vanished into the velvet darkness of the night.

Chapter Sixty

Days of Rain

We talked for the next few hours, my father's face darkening as I related the grim events that had led us to the House of Glory.

"How foolish of me to think I'd have more time," he said. "One can only skirmish with evil for so long before the conflict must come to a head. Like the battle I told you about that Henry and I and both your mothers fought against Harlon Gale."

"Matt—" Val turned to me with furrowed brow. "That bastard at the AEC, what did you say his name was?"

"Marlon Storm." I did a sort of mental double-take. "*Oh*. Harlon and Marlon, Gale and Storm. What do you think?" I asked my father. "Coincidence?"

"The longer I live," he replied, "the less I believe there are any coincidences at all."

"I've had a bad feeling these past two days," said Benjamin. "Something wicked this way comes."

"If the same demon's loose in the world," said my father, "then Matt and Valerie's presence here puts them at far greater risk. Once Henry is strong enough and works his healing, you must both get as far away as you can. General Grant betrayed you, but surely not everyone's in thrall to Storm. The microfilm and your witness to the collusion between him and Guerriero, that's what counts. Even if the Enemy were to do me in, the outrage of it would only lend credence to your claims."

"You're my father," I said, looking him in the eye. "I'm not going anywhere."

"Nor I, Uncle Caleb." Val unsheathed her blade. "I'm my mother's daughter."

I'll tell you more of what I learned from my father that day, dear reader, while Henry slept. A shaman—*povosqa* in the Hopi tongue—is one who *sees,* truly and clearly and to the heart of things. He is, in short, a seer. And for a *povosqa* to see a brother or sister who suffers is to understand the cause of their suffering, and thus to be able to heal.

After Henry had reunited Louis and Elliana, he made his way to Black Mesa and offered his labor if only they would let him live out his days on the high plateau. And so he helped with the daily bringing of water, and hunting of game, and growing of corn, beans, melons, and squash on terraces along the mesa walls. Soon enough he was studying with the *povosqa* who had taken Qualetaqa's place, adding to his knowledge of the healing arts, of plants and potions and deep secrets of the spiritual realm.

There are times during *yooyangw*—the days of rain—when fierce storms are unleashed from the heavens, with great crashings of thunder and rivers of fire that rend the sky. And it's said that if a man should be struck by lightning at such times, and survive, then the cloud deities impart to him the power to heal.

One day, dark clouds gathered over Black Mesa, Yaapontsa let loose his howling winds, and Henry ventured out, walked along the edge of the crumbling sandstone cliff so he could feel the tempest and delight in its fury. He was lashed by rain, blinded by bursts of light, deafened by the storm's rumble and roar.

It's doubtful he would have survived had Chosposi and Chosovi not seen the streak of lighting that struck the mesa, shattering rocks and sending Henry flying through the air. When they reached him, his clothes were in shreds, his arms and legs broken, and the hair had been burned from his head. For days he hovered in the shadowland between life and death. For another week he lay unconscious, and more than a year passed before he finally found relief from the pain that coursed through every pathway in his body.

While Henry had long been known as a medicine man, after the lightning strike his reputation spread to the nearby Navajo and Zuni nations, and north to the Havasupai and Hualapai tribes. If his eyesight was no longer what it once was, still, some heightened spiritual sense led him to just the medicinal flowers and herbs he needed to bring each of his petitioners relief.

All who followed the Hopi Way had only to feel Henry Midnight's warm, strong hands upon them, and they would know peace. But for those who were two-faced, grasping, selfish, or cruel, the fire of the cloud gods would pass through his fingers and burn them.

And so might they be led from darkness to light.

"None of this is my own doing," Henry would say, when people marveled at his healings. "For every good thing, every blessing, comes from the Creator, who is Goodness itself."

My father loved the stark beauty of Black Mesa, which reminded him of what he'd experienced on the rim of the Grand Canyon. Looking out at the great, sacred emptiness of the landscape, he'd remember the words of the Apostle Paul.

Jesus had emptied Himself, becoming a servant...

He would humble himself, then, and place Henry's needs and desires above his own.

For three years they lived there together, until word came in the summer of 1950 that Nicholas Black Elk lay dying in the Badlands of South Dakota, on the Pine Ridge Reservation where he'd spent so many years. My father and Henry drove north through Nevada and Utah, east through Wyoming and Nebraska, then north again across the border to the land the Oglala Lakota still called their own. But at the end of their twelve-hundred-mile journey, they found they were too late, for Black Elk had passed away the night before. He'd fought at Little Big Horn, survived the massacre at Wounded Knee, and grown into a holy man who knew and loved the Creator both as Wakan-Tanka and the Triune God revealed in Christ.

"Your dad was the Lord's own messenger," my father said to Benjamin. "I owe him my very life."

"Make of it a sweet-smelling sacrifice," Benjamin replied.

The three men talked through the night and into the dawn, and over breakfast he persuaded Henry and my father to stay on for at least a few more days.

Those days turned into weeks, then months, and it was January of 1951 before they set off for home. The road back to Black Mesa passed through Las Vegas, where they stopped to refuel and fill their bellies.

"You might want to take a gander at the headlines," said my father, who had asked for a copy of the Review-Journal along with his steak and eggs. The paper's headline banner took up all the space above the fold:

Army to Test A-Bombs at Indian Springs
Secret Project Unveiled

"Feds took over three, four million acres of land north of there just before the war," my father continued. "Made it into a gunnery range. God-forsaken land, but I remember there were mustangs up in the higher elevations."

"More than mustangs," said Henry. "Mountain lions, antelope, and big-horn sheep." He reached for the paper and began perusing the front-page story. "Not to worry, though—it says here 'government scientists have stated the good citizens of Las Vegas have nothing to fear.' Comforting, that. Let's see...seems radioactive raindrops had been a problem after they tested the first of these nasty devices in New Mexico, but Southern Nevada is a far dryer clime."

"Well there you go," said my father.

Outside their diner window, a steady drizzle was coming down.

"A herd or two of those New Mexican cattle had become a bit mottled, evidently—I rustled my share of those beeves back in the old days, if you remember, Caleb."

"How could I forget?"

"No cause for panic over that mottling, however. The Review-Journal reports those formerly mottled cattle have become 'fat and sleek' over the past five years."

"Do they say just *how* fat?" asked my father. "Atomic radiation can do strange things."

The two men continued the conversation as they set out on the road, but twenty miles south of Las Vegas swung around and headed back.

The newspaper article was a sign from on high, Henry said, and his days as the Hermit of Black Mesa had come to an end. There was work to be done, the afflicted to comfort, lost souls to find, wrongs to set right!

Steadily the erstwhile outlaw's powers of healing increased. And then came a day in the spring of 1953, when he awoke from a dream into that mystical life which is yet more dreamlike than dreams. *Henry,* my father whispered. *Look in the mirror.* A golden glow shone all about him; but whether it was the shimmering of the Shekinah, or some lambent radiance imparted by Spider Grandmother, who could say?

Chapter Sixty-One

The Life of Things

We decided some rest would do us good, so my father cleared space in a storage alcove in the modest living quarters attached to the church. Val curled up on an army surplus cot while I sacked out in a sleeping bag and soon drifted off. Only to be awakened not long after by my sister's moans.

Her tumor was working its evil, unfurling tendrils of pain.

It had started with cascades of colors in shades she'd never seen before, Val told me, and the faintest sounds of music, a melody from childhood she was aching to remember. A blissful peace was waiting for her, nearby, in the comforting darkness, tempting her to give in, give up, submit...

I put a cold compress on her forehead, applied pressure between her eyes, and eventually Val's agonies subsided.

We talked for a while, the conversation soon coming around to the man whose blood we shared.

"The revelations have come at you thick and fast this past twenty-four hours, brother of mine," she said. "How're you dealing with this latest one, anyway?"

"About Midnight?" I shrugged. "In a way it's made me feel closer to my father. I mean, he didn't *have* to raise me. Whatever his shortcomings, he chose to be my father, made me feel I was his very own. However often I wished I weren't."

"I don't know what to think of this birth father of ours," Val said. "Sure, he wanted me to think of Louis as my real dad, wanted you to feel that way about Caleb—still, there's something cold-blooded about staying away so completely."

I nodded. "Totally cut off, knowing nothing of our lives."

"Mom honored his request to leave you and Caleb alone, but she couldn't resist catching at least a glimpse of her nephew on the sly. I'm sure your dad would have said something if Henry Midnight had ever done the same."

I thought about that for a bit and was starting to reply when my father's bedroom door swung open. A pale, gaunt figure emerged and began making his way slowly down the hallway toward us, supporting himself with one hand against the wall.

"Henry," my father said unhappily, trailing closely behind him. "You've no business being out of bed. Matthew and Valerie will still be here in the morning, they're not going anywhere. Tell him, you two."

"Back off, I go where the Spirit sends me." Henry stopped a few yards away and stared at us in wonder. "My God," he said. "There you are."

In that candle-lit room he looked more wraith than man.

"My father's right, sir," I said. "We can wait until you're feeling better."

"That wouldn't be wise, Matthew. And please, both of you, call me Henry, or a dim-witted dotard, anything but *sir*." He sank down on a chair my father had placed behind him. "Even before I woke, Valerie, I felt the darkness that's taken root in you, entering into my dreams. I wept bitter tears when Caleb told me of your mother's passing, I won't stand by when her daughter's at risk. Come closer, dear girl, that through me the Light Eternal might rid you of your demon."

"*Henry,*" said my father. "You've hardly the strength to stand. Fortify yourself with some dinner, then sleep, and work your healing in the morning."

"Yes," said Val. "You don't need to do this now, really."

"*No*. This is the moment. The Enemy prowls like a roaring lion, there's no telling when our defenses will be breached and battle joined. Time's not on our side."

"All right," said my father, nodding to Val. "May God be with you."

She came over, put her arms around Henry, and kissed his cheek.

"My mom thought the world of you," she said softly. "Thank you for what you did for her and Louis. And for today, whatever comes to pass."

"Sit close by me, Valerie, and close your eyes. Let the tension go from every muscle in your body. Concentrate on each breath you take." He placed the palms of his hands on either side of her head, closed his own eyes, and remained like that for some time before beginning to speak. “Grandfather, Great Spirit, once more behold me and lean to hear my feeble voice. You are older than all need, older than all prayer. All belong to You—the two-legged, the four-legged, the wings of the air, and all green things that live. You have made me cross the good road and the road of difficulties, and where they cross, that place is holy. Day in, day out, forevermore, You are the life of things. Grandfather, Creator of the Cosmos, Lord and Savior, grant me the strength to defeat this death-force that grows within my daughter, I beseech you. And yet, in this as in all things, Your will be done.”

A great silence filled the room.

I was hoping to see something that marked a miracle—a glow, a scintillation in the air, if not the full-throated singing of a choir of angels; but there was only the play of shadows on the wall as the candle flames danced. After a while I noticed a trembling in Henry’s hands; was it only an old man’s palsy, or a sign of the struggle between light and darkness, of spiritual strength passing through to my sister? His face glistened with sweat. The more I watched, the surer I became that a mighty contest was taking place. I knew a fellow warrior when I saw one; who was I to judge him, to second-guess the decisions he’d made in life?

My father knelt nearby, deep in prayer.

I realized at that moment this was merely one battle in a war he and Henry had been fighting for years, the only war that could ever be called righteous, one no less real than what I’d faced in Korea. And I knew I was in the presence of heroes.

Slowly, slowly, the minutes ticked by, until I realized Henry had lifted his hands and was gently stroking Val’s hair.

“It’s done,” he whispered. “The demon has fled.”

She gaped up at him in wonder. “I don’t know how to thank—“

Henry’s face turned ashen and he slumped forward, the slight rise and fall of his chest the only sign he was still among the living.

My father gathered him up into his arms.

“Damn my selfishness!” Val exclaimed. “I shouldn’t have allowed this to happen.”

“Hush,” said my father. “I couldn’t be happier for you. Don’t fear for Henry, he took a risk, but he’s through the worst of it. Pray for him, though, that he regains his strength before we face our next test. It will be long before he wakes.”

And so we prayed for Henry Midnight, and talked of what had come to pass, and marveled at how the suffering and sacrifice of another can draw us close to the healing heart of God.

Chapter Sixty-Two

Koyaanisqatsi

"You've a grim look about you, Ben," said my father in the kitchen the next morning.

I brought over the pot of coffee I'd been brewing and filled mugs for the four of us.

"Dad talked of the deep ache he felt in the days before Wounded Knee," Benjamin replied. "How fingers of ice gripped him, and not a dozen buffalo hides could warm his bones. These things I now feel, too."

"I've gotten word out to my flock it's not safe to meet," said my father, "and asked those on Empyrean Way to stay home. But they haven't, of course; the worship hall's been packed since the early hours. I'll spend most of the day up there, singing hymns and offering up prayers. I'll tell you where the Spirit is leading me. The Enemy would like nothing more than to destroy the microfilm Matt's friend gave his life for. We need to get it into the right hands, right away. There's an obvious party that comes to mind—"

"Clark Kent," I interjected.

"Exactly. Only, how to reach him now that he's in hiding?"

"Arnie was going to be the middleman, but he's almost certainly in the Enemy's hands. The thing is, though—" I snapped my fingers, stunned to see how obvious the answer was. "Clark's Claire now, hiding in plain sight. So he'd be waiting at the Long Shot Saloon, hoping someone would have the brains to look for him there."

"Excellent," said my father. "Now listen to me. There's little chance Matt could return to Las Vegas without being spotted, but they're not looking for you, Valerie. You've got the best chance of delivering the microfilm to Clark."

He leaned forward and grasped Val's hand. "I would send Ben with you, but his spiritual powers may be sorely needed to protect the innocents of Empyrean Way."

"I'll fend for myself, Uncle. Let's do what has to be done."

I shook off my fears for Val—she could defend herself as well as any man!—then reached into my pocket for the microfilm and handed it to her. "You'll be looking for a woman in her late twenties, about your height, slight of build, with shoulder-length black hair. Wearing lipstick, most likely."

"I'll find her," she said. "Or him, I should say."

"One more thing," said my father. "Senator Kefauver from Tennessee had the courage to lead an investigation into the mob not long ago. There's at least a chance we can trust him, and if not, we've little to lose. I'm going to try to get through to him, and Lord willing, Val, he'll be expecting your call when you're in Vegas. It may make all the difference to have an ally on the outside once the Enemy closes in."

"How can I be of help?" I asked.

"Keep vigil with Ben," he replied. "You'll learn much from his prayers."

"The sands of time are running out," the Lakota said softly. "Valerie should leave *now.*"

Ben and I accompanied Val across the bridge that had brought us to Misfit Row. Homer and Hazel rose up alongside us as two pale specters, the former winking lewdly and the latter blowing us a kiss before descending back into the ditch.

We wished my sister Godspeed, and Val set off at a brisk pace, waving back at us just before a turn in the trail hid her from view.

What were the chances we'd see each other again? A sudden sense of despair, of the long odds against us, overwhelmed me.

Ben must have seen the stricken look on my face as we walked back across the bridge, for he stopped and gripped my shoulders tightly with both hands. "What you are feeling," he said, "the loss of hope and faith, is the Enemy's doing. Much as I would like to fight forever by your side, I don't know if I will survive the coming storm. So listen to me and listen well, for I know the Way of Christ no less than that of Wakan Tanka, and I will tell you all that matters. There will come a time when your strength has left you, and you're broken, and all of Scripture seems only empty words. *Remember then what I am telling you now*: you press on. You leave the past, with all its shame and false glories, all its triumphs and regrets, you leave it far behind you, and with your eyes fixed on the goal He has set before us, *you press on.*"

Warmth radiated from his fingers and spread throughout my body.

I nodded, at a loss for words.

I joined in the singing and prayers of those gathered in the worship hall, did my best to center myself in a place of calm. Still, as the hours passed without word from my sister, anxious thoughts wormed their way into my mind. The Senator from Tennessee had betrayed her; Arnie had revealed Clark's secret, and the Enemy had been watching the Longshot, waiting for whoever would seek him out, and had already seized them both. I imagined Blowtorch Bobby demanding she reveal our location or suffer his merciless flame.

Late that afternoon, the phone rang when it was my turn on duty in my father's office. "Jonah speaking," I said, using the code words that would let Val know it was safe for her to talk. But all I heard were whistlings and rustlings, like the wind blowing paper bags down empty streets.

Enough. I steeled myself, imagined I was in my Corsair, flying low over the frozen Korean landscape, searching for the mission target that lay somewhere ahead, just over the horizon...

Press on.

Henry awakened that evening and I talked with him for a long while, especially of my time in Korea and everything that had transpired since my return.

"What madness Matthew has been through," he said when my father and Ben rejoined us. "We live in an age of *koyaanisqatsi.* Of chaos and corruption. It brings to my mind the Hopi tale of judgment by fire."

"I am eager to hear it," said Ben.

"Not as eager as he is to tell it," said my father.

"There was once a *kikmongwi*—a village chief—whose people had once been virtuous but gradually gave themselves over to temptation and abandoned the Hopi Way. They used the sacred *kivas* for games of chance rather than to worship the Creator, treated elders with disrespect, engaged in brawling and lewd behavior in the village square in the plain light of day.

"So distraught was the *kikmongwi* that he journeyed to the land of the *Yayaponcha*, who were *powakas*, mighty sorcerers who could make the storm gods do their bidding and call forth all their fury. After he told them of the shameful state of his village, and asked for a judgment on his people, the *Yayaponcha* asked him what manner of judgment he preferred: water, storm, lightning, wind, or fire?

"The *kikmongwi* chose fire and then returned home to await the judgement with his people.

"Soon enough red clouds gathered, but the people were too busy satisfying their lusts to pay them any heed. Then a great smoke covered the sky and hid the sun, and the people cried out in fear and fled, but it was too late, for they were surrounded by flames on all sides and none escaped. Neither did the *kikmongwi* leave his home, but rather perished with his people, and of his village no trace remains today."

"Not one of your cheerier stories," said my father.

"Aren't you the one who calls himself *Amos*?" Henry exclaimed. "Your namesake prophesized that Jehovah would send down fire upon the wicked of the nations, did he not? Though at this point any sort of *deus ex machina* would do. What do you think, Ben? Do you have any sway with the storm gods?"

"I'm no *powaka*, sad to say."

"Well, you're a Black Elk after all, sorcery might be a latent talent. One never knows unless one tries."

Ben offered up a strained smile. "Dad once had a vision of a storm approaching from the west, roaring with thunder like the sending of great voices, and the night was black about him and terrible with swift fire. But our prayers were of a very different nature."

"Give us one, if you will," said my father. "We could use it."

"Yes," said Henry, serious for a change. "Please do."

"In the days when my dad and Wovoka were still young, John Yellow Lark was chief of the Lakota Sioux." Ben turned to me. "These are his words, Matt, inscribe them on your heart." He closed his eyes and a calmness came over his features.

"Earth teach me stillness
as the grasses are stilled with light.
Earth teach me to forget myself
as melted snow forgets its life.
Earth teach me to remember kindness
as dry fields weep with rain."

We sat in deep silence for some time.

"How different God's fire is from the earthly sort," mused my father. "For it's the refiner's fire, purifying, not destroying, and leading us to kindness, to the stillness of the grasses, the forgetting of self."

"The hellfire you always preached," I said. "Is that how you think of it now?"

"Yes, though I imagine to the wicked, God's very kindness might be a sort of torment at first. His desire that *all* be saved will not be thwarted, Matt. Christ has defeated Death and shattered the gates of Hell. He will never stop knocking at the door, never cease pursuing his prodigal sons and daughters until the last one has returned to His loving heart."

To that I could only say, Amen and Amen. How could the Good News be anything less?

Later that night my father took Ben and me aside and told us the phone lines were no longer working. "They've been cut, most likely," he said. "And so the endgame is upon us. Ben, I will address the faithful who have gathered here, then you must take them, and the three who Henry healed, and any others in the village, and lead them to safety. There are donkeys and carts to carry those who can't walk, and the strong must help the weak. After that, return but stay hidden in the shadows, and petition the heavens with all your powers of prayer."

"This I will do," Ben replied.

"Henry's fallen back asleep," my father continued. "I fear for him, for he's never attempted two healings in a *week*, let alone in a matter of days. I would send him with you, only there's no reasoning with the man, he's stubborn as a mule. Now, you, Matt," he said, stepping closer to me. "You're young and have everything to live for. Henry and I, we've had full lives. Go with Ben, then rejoin your sister and do your best to bring the truth to light." His face took on a hard look. "And that's an order."

"With all due respect," I said, going eye-to-eye with him as best I could, "what son would desert both his fathers in time of need? I'll not leave your side, or Henry's, come what may."

He sighed, put his arms around me, and hugged me close.

"I'd set Homer and Hazel loose to chase you off," he said, "only you've already called their bluff. And Ben seems to have no other sorcery to bring to bear."

"Nor would I, even if I did," said the Lakota. "For I'd stay, too, were I in Matt's place."

"All right, then," he replied. "Let's get to work."

"I'm taking first watch," said my father, after Ben led the exodus from the House of Glory. "Try and get some shuteye."

That seemed an impossibility, but eventually I drifted into a sleep beset by dreams...

Once again I was in Korea, working forward air control. The hills were honeycombed with railway tunnels, there was one nearby where KPA troops had taken shelter and likely stored arms and munitions as well. I radioed the location and called in a napalm strike, and then a chill ran through me, for there were not only soldiers in that tunnel, but women and children as well.

"Echo Cobra," I barked into my headset, "This is Romeo Viper. Abort. Do you copy? I repeat, ab—"

Too late. The hills were covered with bursts of orange so bright they seared my eyes, and the air grew thick and oily and almost too hot to breathe—

"Matthew!" cried my father.

The House of Glory's front door exploded into splinters, its windows disintegrated into shards, and the air rang with the harsh shouting of many voices as the Enemy swarmed in.

Chapter Sixty-Three

And the Blind Shall See

"There was no need for drama," said my father as the smoke cleared and a dozen of Guerriero's soldiers stormed through. "That door is never locked."

"I seen some piece 'a crap churches before," said Robert Schultz, "but this one takes the cake." He looked around, sneering. "You're Amos, huh?"

"I am."

Schultz was holding something more like a flamethrower than a blowtorch and directed a streak of fire toward the rugged wooden cross behind the pulpit.

It blackened under the onslaught but did not burn.

"And you—" The mobster turned to me. "McRae. You lyin' sack 'a shit."

"That the *sporco bastardo* who gutted Enzo?" exclaimed the largest of his minions. "*Ti prego*, Bobby, allow me to feed him his own entrails right now."

"Hold that thought, Rocco," said Schultz. "The boss says not just yet. Now, tie these scumbags' hands behind their backs, blindfold 'em and gag 'em, and let's scram."

As they led us to the cars I felt the heat of the flames behind me, heard their whoosh and crackle and roar.

Soon Empyrean Way would be reduced to ashes.

"Where's the Atomic Man?" asked Schultz, not for the first time since we'd been taken prisoner.

I guessed we were being held below the Roma, or at least not far from Guerriero's lair. My fathers and I had been stripped, thrown into a sort of prison cell, maybe ten feet by eight, complete with iron bars, and left to sit and sleep on the concrete floor. They'd taken off our blindfolds to make sure we were properly humiliated, but not the gags. Our hands were still tied behind us, and the pain radiating from my shoulders and down my arms grew worse with each passing hour.

I could only imagine how my father and Henry felt.

A latrine in one corner stunk to high heaven, and there was no respite from the harsh light of a dozen bare bulbs just a few feet above our heads.

Whether a day had gone by, or more, I couldn't tell.

"Is it you, Amos? You the Atomic Man? Take off his gag, Rocco. Now, answer me, you old fool. Just how fuckin' stupid you think we are? You were shelterin' the losers he worked his miracles on, means you know the man. So where is he?"

"I don't know." My father's voice was hoarse but strong. "Though I wouldn't tell you if I did."

Schultz slammed the butt of his revolver into the side of my father's face, sending him to his knees.

Rage coursed through me, burning like fire. *Stop,* I told myself. That's the Enemy, too, working from the inside...

"*You* wanna talk, McRae?"

Rocco lifted my gag and I sucked in the fetid air and coughed before responding, "Not a clue."

The metal tip of his boot smashed into my ribs, and I sprawled on the floor.

"I could get 'em talking, Bobby, no problem. So why we bein' nice guys?"

"We do things Sal's way, that's why."

"Well, old baldie here, looks like that Atomic Man didn't do him much good. Got one foot in the grave, y'ask me."

"Ain't our problem, Rocco. Come on, let's head upstairs. I can't take the stink."

Several days passed with only a few crusts of bread and sips of water. My father and I kept close to Henry to keep him warm, but he shivered uncontrollably, though his skin was hot, his face flushed.

"Listen up, boys and girls," said Schultz, bursting in on us just as I'd begun to doze off. "Your ship's come in. Don Guerriero, the boss himself, desires—fuck, how'd he put it—"

"The pleasure of their comp'ny," said Rocco.

Half a dozen mob soldiers stood behind him.

"Yeah, right. So you scumbuckets need ta get cleaned up and dressed." Schultz snapped his fingers. "Untie 'em, get 'em hosed off, and into their clothes. *Now.*"

They led us to what turned out to be a decent shower room, complete with cakes of soap and towels. Afterward, my father and I helped Henry dress and supported him between the two of us on the elevator ride up to the imperial splendor of the Roma's top floor, the throne room of Salvatore Guerriero.

The *soldatos* ushered us in, then left and shut the door.

"*Benvenuti*, gentlemen!" The Don sat behind his massive mahogany desk, filing his nails. "How glad I am to see you. You are hungry, perhaps? Thirsty? Look, I've arranged for a fine repast."

A table had been set and covered with platters of smoked salmon, roast beef, bunches of ripe purple grapes, elegant decanters filled with red and white wine, and what smelled like focaccia, freshly baked.

"Not bad, eh? My friend the good pastor could favor us by saying grace, and then you could all partake, yes?" He grinned, then leaned forward and looked each of us in the eye, one by one. "Only of course, as they say, there is no free lunch."

He stared at us, the silence building like a physical presence in the room.

One of the phones on Guerriero's desk buzzed. He raised an eyebrow, frowned, and picked it up. "Under no circumstances am I to be interrupted, is that clear?"

He hung up, then turned back to us. "The Atomic Man. Deliver him up, and feast, or—well, *miei amici*, let's just say, I will enjoy a different sort of feast. For I am a *buongustaio*, a man of infinite appetite, when it comes to witnessing the sweet agonies of those who defy me. *Capiche*?"

"There is no Atomic Man," said my father. "Only a God who works wonders, only a Lord of Light who will come in power and glory to judge the quick and the dead."

"Of which you'll join the latter," said Guerriero, "though not as *quickly* as you may hope." He looked away. "Mr. Storm? We may proceed?"

In an unlit corner, perhaps two hundred feet away across the vast room, were two figures, one small, one very large.

"By all means," intoned Marlon Storm, his voice a deep, rich baritone.

I glanced at my father and saw his eyes narrow, his face grow yet more pale.

"Bobby!" Guerriero called out. "Bring in our latest guest."

A panel in the wall behind us slid open to reveal Robert Schultz and a middle-aged woman, hands bound behind her back, a gag over her mouth.

A blowtorch in Schultz's right hand projected a blue tongue of flame.

"You know Ashcan Annie, I believe?" said Guerriero, with the grin of a man laying down the winning cards. "We caught her attempting to rejoin you. Such loyalty should be rewarded, yes?"

In Annie's face were both fear and defiance.

"She would not tell us anything. Admirable, yes? But *you* will, gentlemen. Or her life, her torment, will be on your head."

"Don't do this," said my father. "We can work something out, help you find him."

"Mere stalling," said Guerriero. "That won't do."

Schultz grasped Annie with his left hand, dragged her over toward the Don, brought the flame closer and closer to her face...

Henry's lips moved, but his voice was too soft to be heard.

"What's that, old man?" asked Guerriero.

An urgent knocking came from the door.

"*Basta!* Bobby, see what they want and get rid of them."

My father nudged me, motioning with his head toward the tall windows surrounding Guerriero's office.

It was early evening, the sky seething with dark, angry clouds.

Approaching the Roma from all sides were globes of fire.

Schultz opened the door.

"There's some crazy injun outside, bangin' a drum and singin'." Rocco was breathless, his forehead glistening with sweat. "He's been callin' up to them fireballs, pointin' our way, and the casino's already burning. Son of a bitch somehow keeps dodgin' our bullets. Customers are all runnin' for their lives. You and the boss ought'a go, too."

"Get your ass back down there," Schultz shouted, "and blow that injun's fuckin' head off, ya worthless *shlemiel!*"

He slammed the door in Rocco's face and joined Guerriero, who was standing at one of the windows, mesmerized by three luminous orbs hovering on the other side of the glass.

"Had these designed to be bulletproof," the Don muttered. "They're an inch thick. Nothing's getting in."

"Rocco might have a point, Sal," said Schultz. "If the main floor's on fire, maybe we better go."

Guerriero turned to him slowly and sneered.

"Are you scared, Jew boy? You who so love to play with fire? See how Mr. Storm sits there calmly—"

"He's fuckin' *blind*, Sal! Me, I'm outta here."

As the enforcer turned to go, the burning globes moved closer and the window blurred, melted, vanished, and fierce winds howled into the room, and then the fireballs were upon Guerriero and Schultz, swallowing them up in their terrible brightness.

The last I saw of them were their eyes, filled with horror and something else I could not quite name...

"*Enough!*" thundered the voice of Marlon Storm. "In the name of the Prince of Darkness, I command you, be gone!"

The blazing orbs were no more.

Storm emerged from the shadows, wearing dark glasses, one hand on the shoulder of a diminutive man wearing a pork pie hat and carrying a Thompson submachine gun.

"Caleb McRae," said Storm as the winds abated.

My father stared at him, steely-eyed and silent.

"The powers you brought to bear are no match for me," Storm continued. "If you want to save your friends some considerable unpleasantness, reveal the Atomic Man."

"*I'm* the one you want," said Henry, softly but clearly. "I am the Atomic Man."

The dwarf cackled. "This one's so old and feeble he can barely stand."

Henry stood straighter and stepped forward.

Storm came closer, felt Henry's face with his fingers.

"You can tell, can't you," said Henry.

"Maybe. And maybe not. If you are the Healer, then prove it. Heal my blindness."

One heartbeat.

Two.

Three.

"Gladly," said Henry Midnight.

"No!" my father cried, but his lover never flinched.

"One false move," Storm warned, "and my companion will mow all of you down like winter wheat."

"As God is my witness," said Henry, "I will do my best to restore your sight."

He reached up, placed his hands on Storm's head, and began to murmur prayers of healing.

Time passed with excruciating slowness—one minute, five minutes, ten—and still Henry prayed.

"I smell smoke," said the dwarf. "Hurry it up, miracle man."

"It is done," said Henry, and he took a step back and fell into my father's arms.

Storm ripped off his dark glasses and rubbed his eyes.

"Nothing!" he shouted in rage. "Only the same unending night, the same—" He broke off suddenly. "Wait. I see—something, a glimmering, yes—a man—but who—" He fell to his knees. "It's me," he moaned, "I'm seeing myself. *Myself!*" then lowered his head and began to wail.

The man I had thought of as the monster in the labyrinth seemed no more than a pitiful child.

"Treachery!" cried the dwarf, and swung the Tommy gun around toward us.

Annie sprang forward, head-butting the little man in the small of his back and sending him tumbling onto the floor. His weapon landed at my feet.

I picked it up, kept him covered while my father freed Annie's hands and removed her gag.

Storm clawed at his eyes, howling, then stood, wheeled about, ran toward the gaping hole where the window once had been, and leapt.

Seconds later his diminutive companion began to shimmer, became transparent, and disappeared.

The four of us looked at each other in stunned silence.

"Bless you, Annie," said my father. "We'd have been dead men without you."

"What just happened?" asked Annie, embracing my father and Henry.

"Marlon Storm was granted true sight," Henry whispered. "Saw himself as he is seen by his Creator. No punishment is more severe, no gift more precious."

"Don't talk," said my father. "We're getting you to a hospital, and I'll stay every minute by your side, if only to prevent you working more healings until you're well."

"Oh, come now, Caleb, my love. If Shakespeare were writing this scene, he'd have the good sense to end it right here." He tried to laugh, but all that came out were bubbles of blood.

Even in his weakened state my father was powerful enough to hoist Henry over his shoulder. We dunked dinner napkins into the water pitcher on the table and breathed through them while making our way down the smoke-filled stairway.

When we were clear of the burning building, my father laid Henry down, pinched his nose closed, breathed into his mouth, and compressed his chest ten, twenty, a hundred times.

"Don't do this to me, Midnight," he cried.

I had seen enough dead men to know he was gone.

Anger and anguish rose up inside me; I'd been robbed of the chance to know the man who'd given me life, who'd sacrificed himself to save my father, Annie, and me. And perhaps, in some fantastic way, saved even Storm himself.

A cacophony of sirens grew steadily louder. I turned and saw not only the fire engines that were already at work, but a phalanx of soldiers dressed for battle, two Sherman tanks, and a detachment of police.

Another round of adrenaline began pumping through my body. We were fools to think ourselves out of danger. Daedalus had flown to escape from the labyrinth, but where were our wings?

In the next moment, a searchlight beam found us, shouting broke out, and people began running our way.

Chapter Sixty-Four

The One Who Glows

Despite the firemen's best efforts, the Roma was a roaring inferno. I stood there watching the blaze, resigned to whatever might happen next. *Into your hands, Lord*, I prayed. *Your will be done.*

"Matt!" called a voice behind me.

Val.

I turned in disbelief.

My sister and I ran to each other and we hugged, too joyful for words.

A tall man in a three-piece suit was approaching, his security detail close behind.

"Matt, meet Senator Kefauver. He flew in this morning from Tennessee. Senator, this is my brother, Matthew McRae."

"Estes Kefauver, Captain McRae. I had the chance to look up your record. It's an honor to meet you."

The Senator was a man of noble mien, with warmth and wisdom in his eyes. I shook his hand, still too dumbfounded to speak.

"Looks like I could have saved quite a few taxpayer dollars, Captain; I wouldn't have called out the militia if I'd known you already had matters under control. My committee on organized crime uncovered rumors about Storm and Guerriero, but had nothing we could nail them with. Thank you, on behalf of the American people."

"I appreciate that, sir," I said, finally finding my voice. "But it's my father, Caleb, you should be thanking." *And Benjamin Black Elk,* I thought to myself, but figured it best to say nothing of him for now. "Only it's not the right time, he's just lost his—his best friend."

"I'm sorry to hear that," the Senator said softly. "I look forward to meeting him."

"Oh my God," said Val, noticing my father and Annie for the first time, and she knelt down alongside them and kissed Henry Midnight's cold, white brow.

"Did you have a chance to view the microfilm?" I asked Kefauver. "Will you be able to do something about the atomic coverup my friend Colonel de Carrion gave his life to reveal?"

The Senator frowned and put his hand on my shoulder.

"We'll have to see about that, son, that's a whole other matter. First things first. Let me give my condolences to your father, then you and I are heading to police HQ along with General Andrews of the Marines to hear the full story. There'll be time enough to get statements from the others later on."

Andrews, it turned out, was a four-star general who'd put Grant in the Camp Pendleton brig pending a full investigation.

I knelt next to Val. "Does Kent have the microfilm?"

"Yes, Kefauver made us a copy. Now go, I'll stay with Uncle Caleb. We'll meet you at the police station."

I put my arms around my father and told him I loved him, told him how sorry I was, then followed the Senator and his aides into a waiting limousine.

Before the night was over, I heard that Storm had been found, impaled on one of the silver spikes surrounding the Roma Hotel. It had seemed an impregnable fortress, but its very defenses were the demon's demise.

"I thought sorcery was not among your many talents," I said to Ben.

"One never knows until one tries," he replied, straight-faced as always. "Though I suspect Wakan-Tanka had considerably more to do with that heavenly fire than I."

It was a week after Henry's passing, and we were sitting around a campfire drinking coffee, taking a break from the rebuilding of Empyrean Way. Ben had been held in the county jail on suspicion of arson until that afternoon, when we'd finally managed to get him released.

All around us men and women were hammering and digging and removing great piles of debris. My father had insisted on working alongside his flock for long hours each day, to distract himself from grief.

"I've been meaning to ask you to teach me more of your Lakotan prayers," said my father. "They help to lift the sorrow from my heart."

"Gladly. And trust me, Caleb, praying the Rosary would do you good as well."

"*That* I'm not quite ready for," my father replied, and for the first time since Henry's passing I saw something like a smile on his face.

"If you've prayers or sorcerer's spells to spare, I could use them" said Clark, who'd joined us a few hours before. "Whomever Kefauver shared the microfilm with must have leaked it to the military or the AEC, because they beat us to the punch."

"How so?" I asked.

"The feds put out a press release about the studies they've done on A-bomb fallout, revealed how the westerly winds brought radioactive snow to the east coast, and just about everything else we had. But of course, they had quotes from a cabal of experts explaining how it all amounted to a hill of beans, the public was never in any greater danger than from a trip to the dentist."

"Bastards," I muttered, wishing de Carrion were there to help us carry on.

"That microfilm was never going to be a magic bullet," said my father. "Think of it as one battle in a very long war. I only hope I live to see the first glimmerings of our eventual triumph."

"Rest easy, my friend," said Ben. "You'll live to see more than that."

"*Powaka,*" I whispered to Val, alluding to the sorcerers in Henry's tale of judgment by fire, which I'd related to her the night before.

I believe the Lakota winked at us, though it may have been just a twitch in his eye.

At daybreak the next morning my father, Val, Ben, and I left for Arizona with Henry's ashes and arrived at the base of Black Mesa early that afternoon. My father started on the steep trail at a brisk pace but stopped often along the way.

"Just so Henry can admire the view," he explained, leaning on his great prophet's staff.

We weren't in Walpi long before word spread that *Istaqa* and *Sikyahonaw* had returned.

"*Aiee!* Say it is not so!" cried Chosovi and Chosposi, when it had sunk in that *Istaqa* was no more.

"He knew we only called him that in love," sobbed Chosovi. "For never did we think of him as the coyote-man, the trickster."

"Rather was he *Kootálá*," said Chosposi. "One who glows. Evermore shall he be known by that name."

Qaletaqa's great-great-grandson, Tangakwunu, the shaman of First Mesa, made arrangements for a feast to be held in Henry's honor.

"I have already begun negotiations with Kolichiyaw, high-priest of Second Mesa, concerning the calling of Yaaponsta," he confided to us. "Kolichiyaw thinks he has the better of me, but I have outwitted him once again. The wind god will not disappoint us; he will blow mighty gusts from the southwest, from the San Francisco peaks, and speed your friend on his journey to Maski, Land of the Dead."

Before the meal, the twins made off with Val and arranged her hair in the traditional Hopi style, with large buns by her ears that looked like nothing so much as butterfly wings. Her Hopi name would henceforth be *Hehewuti*, they told me, "mother-spirit of the warrior." That evening we dined on cactus fruits, wild potatoes, Piki bread, and roast quail, while the stars wheeled overhead and we listened to many tales of Henry Midnight, of *Kootálá*, the one who glows.

I smiled as we scattered his ashes to the winds at dawn the next morning, imagining him entering into the Kingdom of Heaven with all the joy of a new-born child.

I was taking my turn at the wheel on our drive back to Las Vegas when I felt Val's hand on my shoulder.

"Pull over, Matt, as soon as you can," she said softly.

She was sitting beside me in front, while my father and Ben slept in the back seat, slack-jawed and snoring.

I slowed to a stop and Val jumped out, kneeled down by a patch of greasewood chapparal and vomited up everything she'd eaten the night before.

I walked over by her. "You okay?"

"He tried his best," she whispered. "But it wasn't enough."

"What are you saying?" I asked, though even as I spoke those words, I knew. The colors, like light streaming through a stained glass window, and the haunting music, had returned.

"Please, Matt," she whispered. "It's too soon after losing Henry. Let's just tell your father and Ben something I ate disagreed with me. There's no need for them to know the tumor's still there."

Chapter Sixty-Five

Tongues of Fire

"It's called cobalt therapy," Dr. Epstein told me as he and I sat in his office. "We're one of a few places in the world who perform it."

It had taken the better part of a week to persuade my sister to come with me to the Los Angeles Center for Advanced Oncology. Zorion insisted on footing the bill, telling me his Basque honor and pride were at stake, and Val had finally agreed.

You talk to the doctors, she'd told me. *I'll go through whatever hell you insist on, just don't make me listen to the gory details. I'd rather spend the time in prayer.*

"I'd like to understand how it works," I replied to the doctor, "before we agree to the treatment."

"Of course." He didn't look all that much older than me, but his thick glasses and wooly, unkempt hair surely implied medical genius. "What we do here is use gamma rays to reach deep-seated tumors without damaging healthy tissue. Used to be we'd use radium, which is vanishingly rare and obscenely expensive. But then the A-bomb was developed, and along with it, nuclear reactors, and shazam! Now there's an efficient way to create artificial radioisotopes for therapy, like the Cobalt-60 we use here."

"Okay," I said. "So what are the odds you can heal her?"

He took off his glasses, breathed on them, and wiped them with his lab coat before setting them back on his nose.

"I'll be honest, Mr. McRae, with the type of tumor Valerie has, the survival rate is only about twenty percent. But I'll tell you this, sir, you entrust her to me, and I'll fight for her life with everything I've got."

I felt a surge of love for Dr. Epstein, much as I'd had for the men with whom I'd gone into battle. "I believe you will," I told him, and we shook hands before I returned to the apartment that Val and I would share for much of the next nine months.

I'd studied some introductory physics along with the math courses I'd taken at San Diego State, and during the long hours when Val was undergoing treatment, I read through my old college textbook.

Forty-eight years before, Einstein had changed the course of history with the equation $E=MC^2$, and I looked at it now with fresh eyes. *Energy equals mass times the speed of light squared.* With what breathtaking simplicity and power had God designed the cosmos! The Light of the World had put light itself at the center of the mystery of creation, at the heart of the engine which powers the stars and allows the miracle of life.

Some had taken the gifts of God and used them in unfathomably monstrous ways. Why in the name of all that is holy should men such as Storm ever escape the flames of Hell?

Because my father was right; the Light shines in the darkness, and the Light shall overcome it, even in the depths of the human heart.

"Until this moment, Senator, I think I have never really gauged your cruelty or your recklessness," said Joseph Welch, Chief Counsel for the United States Army. "At long last, have you left no sense of decency?"

It was June 9th, 1954, and Welch's impassioned outcry on national television marked the moment when the demon within Joe McCarthy was revealed for all to see.

One small victory for the Kingdom of Heaven.

Val and I watched it together in a bar on Wilshire Boulevard while drinking Tom Collinses, heavy on the cherries. Just an hour before, we'd received word from Dr. Epstein that no trace of her tumor remained.

It was a very good day.

"When you asked if there was anything I wanted for my eightieth birthday," said my father in the spring of 1956, "I said no. But actually, there is something."

We were having a beer together while I took a break from helping his parishioners build a new home on Empyrean Way. "And what would that be?" I asked, intrigued by the uncharacteristic hesitance in his voice.

"Take me up in the air," he said. "It's been forever since Henry and I used to do that, and I'd like to soar the skies again, only this time with my son."

"Oh man." I felt a twisting in my guts, the bitter memories of Korea having stripped flying of its joy. "It's been over three years since I've flown. It's just not something I do anymore."

"It would mean a lot to me."

"I don't know." I looked down, rubbed my temples. "That's a big request."

"I wish I hadn't lost my nerve all those years ago, when Henry wanted us to take the Jenny back up. I was just an amateur, but you were extraordinary." He reached out and grasped my hand. "You *are* extraordinary. Do this for both of us, Matt."

I didn't promise him anything, but there was little else I thought about for the next few days. There'd be practical advantages to having wings; Val had taken over from Louis, running the Children of God, and I'd been driving up there regularly to help out. It was eight hours each way, and flying would cut the time in half. So I bought a 1950 Piper Super Cub, got my license in order, and spent a few days getting used to the plane.

What the hell, I'd give the old man a thrill.

My father and I took off on a cloudless June morning, heading west across the Mojave Desert toward the San Gabriels. We circled the peak of Mt. Baldy, then flew over Los Angeles and out above the vastness of the Pacific.

"Ah, Matt!" he exclaimed as I turned the plane around so we could land and refuel before heading home. "I can't thank you enough for this. The beauty of this world God's given us—how I've longed to see it again, spread out before me, like a vision of glory itself. You've made me a happy man."

But I was more grateful yet, for my father's delight in our journey had brought back my own sense of joyous abandon, my own love for flight. And so it was with a light heart that I crawled into bed back home, sometime in the small hours, and drifted off to sleep.

Only then came the darkness of my dreams.

"Echo Cobra, come in Echo Cobra," I said into my headset. *"This is Romeo Viper."*

Echo Cobra was flying low over the hills of Korea, searching for targets of opportunity, while I was doing a stint with forward air control.

"I read you, Romeo Viper. What've you got for me?"

The hills were honeycombed with railway tunnels, and we'd seen a detachment of KPA troops taking shelter in one nearby. Echo Cobra was a skilled pilot; he needed just a modicum of luck to lob a few napalm tanks inside. I radioed the location, peered through my field glasses, waited for the fireworks to begin. After an initial burst of orange flame came a series of secondary explosions—it seemed we'd taken out a munitions dump, too!—and a great cheering went up from our side.

Then suddenly the world went silent.

I've been here before, I thought, *in this same moment, and the gates of hell are about to open and swallow me up...*

I stood, transfixed, looking through those glasses at a woman running from the tunnel, her clothes and hair and hands burning, running directly at me, a baby strapped to her back. Then the world shifted, tilted, transformed, and there she was, only a few yards away, surrounded by a halo of fire. She looked at me, and there was no accusation in her eyes, only forgiveness, only love, and the child on her back was laughing, the tongues of fire all about them dancing in celebration, in adoration.

I lay on the ground before them and wept, for I was an undeserving man, and all the tears I shed could not wash the blood from my hands.

Chapter Sixty-Six

Homeward Bound

I believe dreams are rich with meaning. The Bible is filled with the nighttime visions of prophets and kings and ordinary men like me. They're messages from the spirit world, as Ben would put it, a realm yet more real than our own. So I came to accept the forgiveness I was granted in my dream as a gift of grace.

Still, forgiveness doesn't heal the maimed, raise the dead, restore ruined lives. The horror, the savagery, the violence I wreaked in Korea haunted me still. My father understood this; Wovoka had told him there's no escape from bad memories, the only end to their pain is in the setting of things right.

What did that mean, then, for me? Perhaps I should have gone back and helped the Koreans to rebuild, but in the end, I decided that whatever good thing was set before me to advance the Kingdom of Heaven, inch by inch, that was what I would do. I helped my sister expand the Children of God and worked with my father and Kent to fight to end the testing of atomic and hydrogen bombs. We travelled to Tularosa, the small town just north of Alamogordo that had been covered with radioactive ash after the Trinity blast. It seemed no one cared about the families who'd lived there for generations, so we resolved to tell their story to the world. And we scraped together the money to make half a dozen trips to Japan over the years and became close friends with several of the *hibakusha*, the survivors of Hiroshima and Nagasaki.

My father argued for total disarmament, unilateral if need be. I wasn't convinced, despite having persuaded de Carrion that we should face the Enemy unarmed. The fate of the world was at stake; without the deterrent of mutual assured destruction, how could there ever be peace? That's a fool's argument, my father would respond, for we'd have only the illusion of safety, while perched on a precipice of doom. Better for a people to put their time and treasure into feeding the hungry, sheltering the homeless, providing sanctuary for the oppressed. Better to stake everything on the transformative power of love.

I've come to believe he was right.

In the summer of 1963, just after his eighty-seventh birthday, the United States, Russia, and the United Kingdom signed a treaty that effectively ended above-ground testing of nuclear weapons.

Caleb McRae passed away in his sleep three days later.

Not long after his funeral I awoke in the silent stillness of the early morning hours, remembering the dream of mother and child surrounded by tongues of flame. Ben was staying with me, having driven out to pay his last respects. I woke him and put on a pot of coffee and we talked in my kitchen for long hours.

The dream, I realized, was not only about forgiveness.

I was being called.

Nicholas Black Elk had brought hundreds into the Catholic Church; that night his son brought one more.

I'd always found the Jesuit, Fr. de Souza, one of the most intriguing figures from my father's past, and even more so when my father revealed the stories he'd kept from me in my youth. In the weeks that followed I read everything I could find about the Society of Jesus, traveled to their Dolores Mission in East Los Angeles and talked to any of the brothers and priests who had time for a man with an endless thirst to know more. One theme stood out clearly from all my conversations.

Justice was their passion.

Like both my fathers, they fought for the poor, the dispossessed, for outcasts and misfits and refugees. That fall I entered the Jesuit's West Coast seminary, set on a narrow ridge in the Santa Cruz mountains amid groves of madrone and redwood trees.

In 1974, at the age of forty-six, I was ordained as a priest.

I am now in my ninety-fifth year, dear reader. One by one, those I've known and loved have left this world for the life to come. Val joined her mother and Henry six months ago, and this is the first time since then that I've picked up pen and paper to add to this tale.

How I miss our conversations, our shared memories!

Sometimes the echoing emptiness of my home is more than I can bear.

Listen to you, Matt, my sister would surely tell me; *what an ingrate you are!* For some of the children and grandchildren of my parishioners, and of those I helped raise at the Children of God, come to see me. And they are a comfort, yes.

But still...

What roused me from bed this morning is a visit from a priest from South Dakota, who sits before me at my kitchen table.

"I read about you at seminary," Fr. Reynolds tells me. "There's a scrapbook in the library filled with clippings about the Jitterbugging Jesuit, the dancing priest!"

It's true, I'd often expressed my joy in the Lord through dance, like King David in his wild whirlings. But all that's ancient history now, and I simply smile and nod.

"Your rather unconventional views made headlines, too," he adds. "Denying the eternality of hell and blessing same-sex unions! Not to mention speaking out on the abuse of children in the Church. It must have taken some fancy footwork to avoid losing your collar."

I shrugged. "Well, I was never going to be made a Provincial Superior, that's for sure."

Oh yes, I'd been admonished more than a few times for celebrating the relentless love of a God who pursues us beyond the grave and judges us not on whom we love, but how well we love them. Standing up against monsters within the priesthood, though, that had been a darker, more dangerous battle. A time when my faith nearly failed and all of Scripture seemed only empty words.

But the Lord lent me His strength when mine was gone, and I pressed on.

"Speak your heart's truths, Fr. Reynolds," I tell him, "and let the chips fall where they may. Now, I don't have the strength for long conversations these days, remind me what brings you here."

"Of course, forgive me. As I wrote to you, the Church began a Cause for Canonization for Nicholas Black Elk a few years ago. It's our hope and prayer that he'll become one in the communion of saints for his life of heroic virtue, holiness, and intercession."

"Wonderful," I reply. "But what do you want of me?"

"Stories about him. Especially any miracles he may have worked, which we'll need for the Vatican to declare him a saint. Your father met him during a momentous time in his life, so I hear."

"Ah. I see." I think for a while, then relate the story of how Nicholas restored my father's love for God and inspired him to leave his life of lies, reach out to me—his prodigal son! —and reunite with Henry Midnight.

"This Midnight fellow; your father and he were, uhm, intimate friends?"

I can see he's disappointed.

"What you really ought to do," I tell him, "is talk with Black Elk's son, Ben. He's got all the good stuff, I'm sure."

Fr. Reynolds raises his eyebrows.

"Fr. McRae, Benjamin Black Elk passed away in 1973."

Hmm? Well, yes, he did, didn't he. And yet, there Ben is, standing a few feet behind Fr. Reynolds, brewing a pot of coffee on my range. Hearing my guest's words, my old friend turns to me with just a trace of a smile, and winks.

Though I suppose that may have been just a twitch in his eye.

"You got any more of that Tepeztate?" asks the balladeer.

It's a bit annoying how he comes and goes without warning, though on balance I'm glad for his company.

"In the cabinet next to the fridge," I reply. "If you didn't already drink the last of it, that is."

"Yep, here we go, still some left." He pours a finger's worth into each of our glasses and we drink to each other's health. Amazing how he hardly looks a day older than when I first met him in—what was it? 1953. Vitamin supplements, no doubt, ought to be taking them myself.

"Did you finish reading what I gave you?" I ask him.

He's always pestering me for new material so he can add a few more stanzas to "The Ballad of Midnight and McRae," and I finally broke down and showed him the story you've been reading.

"Yeah, 'bout burned out my eyeballs reading it. You do go on!"

"So, what d'you think?"

"Well...it's good stuff, sure. But here's the problem: we need to work on the ending, you 'n me. I mean, a tale like this, you can't just repeat the chorus and fade out."

"Okay." I reach for the bottle and pour us each another finger. "Any ideas?"

"Tell you what, old-timer." He takes his guitar out of its case, adjusts the tuning, and strums a few chords. "Let's just take it from the top and see where it leads us."

"All right," I say. "I'm game."

It's August 1901, and once again I'm racing over the salt flats in the cool of the morning, then through pale green fields of bristlegrass and on into the high desert, thick with agave and Spanish dagger. Day turns into night, and javelinas snuffle up out of the wash, and kangaroo rats, their huge eyes luminous in the light of the moon. The heavens unleash a fierce summer storm that sends flash floods coursing through the arroyos, but the dampness and danger only revive me, sharpen my senses, and I breathe in the sweet musky smell of the chaparral.

On and on goes the chase, for days—or is it weeks, or months, or years?

There comes a moment, though, when I realize my thinking's all wrong. I've got things backwards, it seems, for it's not me chasing Midnight.

I'm the one being pursued.

"Woah, Boaz," I say, pulling in the reins to turn him around.

Sure enough, there's someone coming after me.

I dismount, shield my eyes from the sun's glare, and try to make out who it is.

"Henry?" I call out, and then it comes to me: *I'm not Captain Caleb McRae.*

"Matt! Hold up, son. The chase is over, it's done."

"Dad?" I say. "Is that really you?"

For he looks just as he did in my youth, tall and strong, his hair like a lion's mane.

"Come on," he says. "They're all waiting for us—your mother and sister and Elli and Henry and Nick, Ben and Dan and so many more."

"But how?" I ask. "I'm old and weak, and the desert is wide."

"We'll fly, of course. Look—right over there, don't you see?"

I turn my head to where he's pointing, and there it is, the Jenny I'd seen under the tarp at an airfield in Las Vegas all those years ago, gleaming as though brand new.

"You took me on a flight once," he tells me. "Now I'm going to return the favor."

I follow my father, each step I take feeling easier than the last, then climb into the seat behind him. And ah!—how wonderful to rise into an azure sky and see the Chihuahuan desert far below, to soar high over the Sangre de Cristo mountains, over the San Gabriels, and farther on, to see the sun melting into the Pacific, the far horizon fretted with golden fire, and to know soon, so very soon, we will be home.

Love (II)

Immortal Heat, O let Thy greater flame
Attract the lesser to it; let those fires
Which shall consume the world first make it tame,
And kindle in our hearts such true desires.
As may consume our lusts, and make Thee way:
Then shall our hearts pant Thee, then shall our brain
All her invention on Thine altar lay,
And there in hymns send back Thy fire again.
Our eyes shall see Thee, which before saw dust,
Dust blown by wit, till that they both were blind:
Thou shalt recover all Thy goods in kind,
Who wert disseized by usurping lust:
All knees shall bow to Thee; all wits shall rise,
And praise Him Who did make and mend our eyes.
— George Herbert

"Our life is no dream, but it should and will perhaps become one."
— Novalis

Historical Notes

The Ballad of Midnight and McRae incorporates fictional representations of a number of historical characters, and deals with some tumultuous times in our nation's history. Readers seeking to learn more can avail themselves of the texts cited below.

Charlie Siringo: To get a feel for his voice, I immersed myself in Siringo's autobiographies, *A Texas Cowboy: Or, Fifteen Years on the Hurricane Deck of a Spanish Pony*, and *A Cowboy Detective: A True Story of Twenty-Two Years with a World-Famous Detective Agency*. Are there some self-aggrandizing tall tales in those? Well, sure, but they're delightful! For a more objective look at Siringo, refer to *Charlie Siringo's West: An Interpretive Biography*, by Howard R. Lamar.

John Horse and the Black Seminoles: There are several excellent books on the great man and his community: *Freedom on the Border: The Seminole Maroons in Florida, the Indian Territory, Coahuila, and Texas*, by Kevin Mulroy; *The Black Seminoles: History of a Freedom-Seeking People*, by Kenneth W. Porter; and younger readers will enjoy *A Man Called Horse: John Horse and the Black Seminole Underground Railroad*, by Glennette Tilley Turner.

Frederick Douglass: At 912 pages, *Frederick Douglass: Prophet of Freedom*, by David W. Blight is an authoritative portrait of Douglass's life and influence. Douglass wrote three fascinating autobiographies, *Narrative of the Life of Frederick Douglass, an American Slave; My Bondage and My Freedom;* and *Life and Times of Frederick Douglass*.

The Transformation of the Rio Grande Valley: For those interested in learning more about how agriculture controlled by Anglos drove out the Tejano cattle ranchers, I recommend "The Making of the Magic Valley," by Neveena Sadasivam, published in the Texas Observer in 2018: https://www.texasobserver.org/the-making-of-the-magic-valley/

Hopi Culture and Mythology: *The Fourth World of the Hopi: The Epic Story of the Hopi Indians as Preserved in Their Legends and Traditions,* by Harold Courlander, and *Hopi Stories of Witchcraft, Shamanism, and Magic,* by Elkehart Malotki and Ken Gary.

Nicholas Black Elk: *Black Elk Speaks,* by John G. Neihardt is a wonderful, though controversial, work. Neihardt, an eminent poet, conducted extensive interviews with Black Elk, and while the book is presented as though it were Black Elk's own voice, translated into English, some scholars argue it reflects more of Neihardt than of Black Elk. Raymond J. DeMallie's *The Sixth Grandfather: Black Elk's Teachings Given to John G. Neihardt* presents the complete transcripts of Neihhardt's interviews, translated as literally as possible, and explores the cultural and spiritual significance of Black Elk's visions and experiences. Certainly Neihardt's priority was presenting Black Elk as a holy man following the traditional religion of the Oglala Sioux. What Neihardt leaves out is well covered in Jon M. Sweeney's *Nicholas Black Elk: Medicine Man, Catechist, Saint*, which focuses on Black Elk's Catholic faith and his potential canonization within the Roman Catholic Church. While some believe Black Elk's conversion was merely a pragmatic concession to living in the white man's world, Sweeney and others argue that he in fact integrated his Lakota spirituality with his Christian beliefs. That's the perspective I brought to bear in my story.

Wovoka: *Wovoka and the Ghost Dance* by Michael Hittman is the definitive biography of the visionary prophet who sparked the Ghost Dance revival, and explores how his message was adapted and transformed by other Nations, especially the Lakota.

The Korean War: I'm especially indebted to James Salter's 1956 novel, *The Hunters*. Salters used his experience as an F-86 Sabre pilot during the Korean War to portray the psychological and physical challenges of aerial combat. I borrowed his description of exploding napalm bombs as sounding like silk tearing, vastly amplified. Readers interested in overall studies of the Korean War can turn to *The Coldest Winter: America and the Korean War,* by David Halberstam, and *This Kind of War: The Classic Korean War History,* by T.R. Fehrenbach.

Above-Ground Testing and Nuclear Fallout: The following books discuss the consequences of nuclear testing and the U.S. government's failure to protect public health: *Fallout: An American Nuclear Tragedy*, by Philip Fradkin, and *Downwind of the Atomic State,* by James C. Rice. The story of the survivors of Hiroshima and Nagasaki is related in wrenching and unforgettable prose in John Hersey's *Hiroshima* and Takashi Hagai's *The Bells of Nagaskai.*

LGBTQ Christians and Transsexuality: *God and the Gay Christian*, by Matthew Vines, is a superb book for anyone looking to better understand the struggles of those like Caleb McRae. Readers intrigued by investigative reporter Clark Kent can turn to *How Sex Changed: A History of Transsexuality in the United States*, by Joanne Meyerowitz. It's a highly-regarded academic history that includes the story of Christine Jorgensen, whom Clark mentions in Chapter 53.

Acknowledgements

First and foremost, thanks to my editor, Ami McConnell, for her literary wisdom, keen insights, and artful suggestions. Ami was a constant source of encouragement and inspiration during the more than two years I spent writing this novel. A big thank-you also to my friend, author Randy (R.S.) Ingermanson, a master of historical fiction about first-century Israel, and to all the members of his Columbia River Christian Writers critique group. I was not plugged in at all to the larger literary world when I was writing my first novel, and it made all the difference being able to share chapters with other authors each month and learn from their feedback. I'm grateful as well to another of the Pacific Northwest's roster of great writers, Jim Rubart, author of mind-bending best-sellers like *Rooms*, whose advice and support has been wonderfully helpful. Credit also to the University of New Mexico Press for allowing me to use the epigraph to *The Fourth World of the Hopis,* by Harold Courlander, which is the basis for Qaleteca the Shaman's summary of the Hopi Way in Chapter 34.

About the Author

Jess Lederman writes historical literary fiction. His first novel, *Hearts Set Free*, was an award-winning Amazon best seller that Kirkus Reviews called "a tapestry of faith, yearning, and wonder at the majesty of the universe." Both that story and *The Ballad of Midnight and McRae* are primarily set in the deserts of the American West. Jess is currently at work on his third novel, *Miracle Man,* which takes place in the melting pot of lower Manhattan in 1904 and is expected to be released in 2026.

Jess writes, "People who know that *Hearts Set Free* contains autobiographical elements (and several historical characters) sometimes ask me, 'How much of the story is true?' And I answer, 'Perhaps twenty percent—and the rest is even more true!' What drives my writing is the desire to convey truths that transform lives. Truths of the heart."

When Jess isn't writing or chasing his young son around, he can usually be found at the piano, playing Chopin and Brahms for his wife. For more information about Jess and his work, visit jesslederman.com.

If you've enjoyed *The Ballad of Midnight and McRae,* please leave a 5-star review on Amazon— they make a big difference!

Hearts Set Free

An excerpt from Jess Lederman's award-winning, Amazon best-selling novel

"Readers of inspirational fiction will love this moving story."
—*Publisher's Weekly*

Chapter One
The Alaska Territory, 1925

My father deserted my mother and me when I was thirteen years old. He had become famous that winter on the Great Race of Mercy, one of the Athabascan mushers who brought diphtheria serum to Nome and saved ten thousand lives. He'd done the impossible, a blind run in the howling darkness, crossing the open ice of the Norton Sound, the temperature falling to sixty below, the sun a distant dream. He was our hero, our North Star.

And then he was gone.

He left us, of course, for a woman. A blizzard had hit him at Unalakleet, a storm so powerful that it travelled four thousand miles, till at last it reached New York and froze the Hudson River. The woman lived in just that far-away land, on the wild island of Manhattan, and her name was Kathleen Byrne. The Hearst papers had been giving the Great Race front-page headlines; Kathleen was a reporter, lean and hungry, she'd go to the ends of the earth for a good story, and one day she got her chance. No one in my home town of Nenana had seen anything like her, a slender redhead with emerald eyes, smoking Lucky Strikes and exhaling expertly through her nostrils, this coolly confident young woman with fiery hair.

She wanted details that would bring the story to life, so father brought her to our home to show off his sled dogs. At least, the ones who'd survived; for three he had raised since they were pups had died on the trail. Somewhere in the madness of that journey he'd forgotten to cover their groins with rabbit skins, and they'd perished of frost bite in the unfathomable cold.

I gaped at her stupidly.

"Excuse my son," said my mother. "He has no manners."

Eighty-six years have passed since that time, but from old photographs I understand just what my father must have felt. She seemed audacious and yet fragile, and she had the sort of smile that made men who'd known her barely fifteen minutes want to say, if you smile that way at any other man I'll lose my mind. I'm not talking about lust, you understand; rather, a sort of greed combined with something barely distinguishable from rage.

And what did Miss Byrne want with my father? Ah, but what an outrageous trophy to bring back from the Arctic frontier! His native name was Taliriktug, strong arm, but he went by his English name, Victor. He was sinewy, powerful, and, for an Athabascan, unusually tall. His maternal grandfather had been an Orthodox priest, a Russian who came to Alaska as a missionary and proceeded to lose his faith in this strange new world. He joined some fur traders, then married a native woman, my great grandmother. All local legend, all stories overheard when my father and his friends had been drinking, for the Russian and his wife both died years before I was born.

When Kathleen left, my father went with her. He said there'd be interviews with The Saturday Evening Post, and on something called radio that could send his voice into a hundred thousand homes, maybe more. He said Miss Byrne had reason to think the Lambert Pharmaceutical Company might pay him a lifetime's wages for endorsing a product called Listerine. He said he'd write letters and be back in just a few months.

But I was the only one he fooled.

"When will father come home?" I asked incessantly. At first my mother said, "Soon;" and later she said, "When the winds that took him blow him home;" and finally she answered me only with silence. So I stopped asking, I never spoke of him, though a great grief lay on my heart.

I heard mutterings around the village, but no one dared to say anything against father, for my mother was fiercely loyal to him, and loved him with a warrior's heart. The months passed, winter came again and turned into spring. One day, the Angakkuq paid a visit, and in the low murmuring of voices I heard my father's name. I saw mother turn from the old man, her eyes bright with anger. The Angakkuq could commune with spirits, with the elements and animals; had one such spirit snatched away my father's soul?

That evening at dinner I found the courage to speak.

"Why doesn't he love us anymore?" I asked.

Her eyes met mine. We looked at each other for a long while, and, though she said nothing, we wordlessly shared our pain. That night, I watched as my mother packed our clothes and valuables, and the last thing she packed was her ulu knife, a knife she'd received from her father, its handle of musk ox horn.

"Are you going to kill father?" I asked her.

"Don't be stupid," she said. "I'll bring him back with us in one piece. Everything will be just as it used to be, the two of you will be off hunting caribou when the leaves turn, and of what has happened we shall never speak. But the white woman must die."

Have I told you my mother's name? It was Yura, which means beautiful. As for me, I was born Uukkarnit Noongwook, though I have lived here in the Nevada desert for lo these many years, and men have always called me Luke.

Available from Amazon in print, Kindle, and Audible editions

www.ingramcontent.com/pod-product-compliance
Lightning Source LLC
LaVergne TN
LVHW041058080826
845145LV00007B/1626

* 9 7 8 0 9 9 8 6 0 3 0 8 7 *